Praise for
The Game

"Wood's third novel to feature this fascinating antihero demonstrates once again the author's keen talent for balancing great character development with fast-paced action. It's difficult to root for someone who does not personify the typical hero, but Wood makes the reader care about a cold-blooded and ruthless killer. Definitely give this thriller a shot." —*Library Journal*

"Compelling . . . the tension builds to a gorgeous crescendo." —*Mystery Scene*

"If there's anything . . . Tom Wood knows, it's creating scenes that crackle with suspense, fascination, and copious action. . . . He creates the kind of taut drama that makes the pages fly. . . . You're going to enjoy this top-notch killer drama." —Critical Mystery Tour

"Tom Wood is the new master of the dark, intricately plotted chase thriller, a genre he's turned into a witty, if violent, cross between Robert Ludlum and Lee Child. . . . Few writers have taken us as deeply into the nuts and bolts of the spy world with such an entertaining sense of skepticism about those who seemingly secretly protect us." —*The Australian*

"*The Game* is a strongly plotted story, exciting and thrilling from beginning to end. [It is] full of international intrigue, [and] one is never quite sure what Victor will do next. . . . Cool under fire and always the professional, Victor is a compelling 'good bad guy.' Definitely recommended for readers who enjoy their action nonstop and unpredictable." —Mysterious Reviews

continued . . .

Praise for
The Enemy

"Tom Wood has done his research and it shows. Tactical accuracy, globetrotting locales, and plenty of twists to keep you guessing to the last page. *The Enemy* makes James Bond look like a wannabe."

—Brad Taylor, *New York Times* bestselling author
of *The Widow's Strike*

"A hard-hitting and exceedingly smart thriller that races along with intensity and intrigue. Tom Wood grabs the reader from the opening scene and delivers a powerhouse of a novel with equal measures of high-octane action and fascinating details, creating a world for his characters that feels as real as it does dangerous. . . . Fans of Lee Child and Vince Flynn will not want to miss *The Enemy*."

—Mark Greaney, national bestselling author
of *Dead Eye*

"From Bucharest to Bologna, and from Minsk to Moscow, the action is riveting. *The Enemy* is a thriller on steroids. . . . In Victor, [Wood] has brought to readers a character to rival Jason Bourne." —Gulf News

"A truly great read featuring an unforgettable character . . . this is a thriller to the nth degree. . . . Readers will crave to see this one appear on the big screen."

—*Suspense Magazine*

More Praise for the Thrillers
of Tom Wood

"The scenes are vivid and the plot revelations parceled out at expert intervals . . . an impressively intricate thriller . . . exciting." —*The New Yorker*

Also by Tom Wood

The Killer

Bad Luck in Berlin
(A Penguin Special)

The Enemy

The Game

NO
TOMORROW

...

TOM WOOD

A SIGNET BOOK

SIGNET
Published by the Penguin Group
Penguin Group (USA) LLC, 375 Hudson Street,
New York, New York 10014

USA | Canada | UK | Ireland | Australia | New Zealand | India | South Africa | China
penguin.com
A Penguin Random House Company

Published by Signet, an imprint of New American Library, a division of Penguin
Group (USA) LLC. This is an authorized reprint of an edition published by
Sphere as *Better Off Dead*. For information address Sphere, an imprint of Little,
Brown Book Group; 100 Victoria Embankment; London, England EC4Y 0DY.

First Signet Printing, September 2014

ISBN 978-0-451-46965-6

For my parents

A Price Worth Paying

Bonn, Germany

· Chapter 1 ·

Today was all about waiting. Some things could not be rushed. Patience and preparation were necessary for the successful completion of even the most routine professional killings. Such jobs could be considered routine only because of the preparation that went into them and the patience displayed in their execution. If corners were cut in the lead-up to the job—should any contingency not be considered and planned for—mistakes would surely follow. Mistakes would also occur if the job was undertaken with anything less than the requisite calm and diligence. In this instance, considering the target, adherence to these two protocols was not only necessary but imperative.

He was a man somewhere in his mid-thirties, but maybe older, maybe younger. It was hard to be sure because almost all of the intel on him was unverified. It was either speculation or hearsay, rumor or guesswork. He had no name. He had no residence. No friends or family. His background was nonexistent. He was not a politician or drug baron or war criminal. He was not military or intelligence—at least actively serving—but he could not be called a civilian either. The only thing that was known with any certainty was his profession. He was a killer. The client had referred to him as *the* killer, warning that he had recently dispatched another team sent after him. If a book had been written on the art of professional assassination, he would have authored it. No such book existed, of course. If it had, the team getting ready to murder him would have memorized every word.

He had an unremarkable appearance. He was tall, but no giant. He had dark hair and eyes. The team's women could not decide if he was handsome or not. He dressed like a lawyer or banker in good-quality suits, though ones that were a little too big for his frame. When first they saw him he had been clean-shaven, but he now sported a few days' beard growth. The only notable thing about him was his slight limp, as he favored his right leg over the left. Not severe enough to take advantage of, they agreed.

A million euros sat in a Swiss escrow account. It was theirs upon providing proof of the killer's death. His intact head, preferably, or at the very least irrefutable photographic or video evidence.

They were a tight quartet—two men and two women. All Scandinavians: two Danes, a Swede, and a Finn. They had worked together for years. Always the four of them. Never using anyone else. Never operating if any of them could not be present. They were friends as well as colleagues. It was the only way to guarantee trust in the business of contracted killing. When they were not working, they socialized whenever they could. They took turns hosting the others for barbecues, dinner parties, and movie nights. They had been more than friends at various times, but those times had passed. Interteam relations were bad for business, they had eventually agreed. Their assignments were inherently dangerous. They could not afford to be distracted.

There was no leader because they each had unique skills and talents and therefore inherent superiority in their own fields of expertise. When a bomb was used it was used under the instruction of the Danish demolitions expert, who named his devices after former lovers. When performing a long-range kill the Finnish woman, who had the most rifle experience, held seniority. When poison was required the Swedish chemist made the decisions in his authoritarian baritone. When shadowing a target the second Dane, who was an exceptional actress and knew the most about surveillance techniques, gave the orders. They operated democratically when no single team member held obvious authority. The arrangement worked well. Egos were kept in check. Jobs ran smoothly. No one got hurt—except the target. And never more than they were paid to be. The Scandinavians were not sadists. Except when they were hired to be.

It had been a unanimous conclusion that today they could only wait. The target was even more difficult to corner than they had been led to believe from the intel provided. He had no idea he was under surveillance, but his routine preventative measures bordered on the obsessive. Yet he was smart to use them. He was, after all, being hunted, and so far had given the team no opportunity to strike. Not only was he reputed to be an exceptional killer, but he was also proving exceptionally hard to kill. A good combination of talents, they all agreed, similarly agreeing that they should adopt some of his precautions into their own repertoire when this was over. Like him, maybe one day they would find themselves on the wrong end of a contract.

He was staying in a grand hotel in the city's central district. Aside from the main entrance, the hotel had three other ways in and out. They could watch them all, given their number, but in doing so spread themselves out too thinly to act when he showed. He never departed via the same exit nor returned through the same entrance twice in a row—until he did, obliterating any chance they had at predicting his next choice. The Finn, who was something of a statistician in addition to being an accomplished sniper, snapped a pencil in annoyance.

The target had a deluxe guestroom on the second floor. He had also booked the room next to it. That made it problematic to know in which he slept. The door that joined the two rooms made it impossible. It seemed he slept during the daytime. At least, he spent most of his time at the hotel during daylight hours, though never for a duration that would be conducive to a proper sleep pattern. The single longest period of time he could be verifiably in either of his rooms was five hours. Often he was in the hotel considerably longer, whether in the bar, restaurant, fitness center, or just reading a newspaper in the lobby. He never arrived at or left the hotel at anything close to the same time. The only habit he showed was in opting for the stairs, never the elevator, despite the limp.

Not that the hotel was a good strike point. The rooms he'd booked were located near the elevators, where foot traffic was common. They had little to no chance of orchestrating a kill without the interruption of other guests. It was hard not to become frustrated. They were used to choosing where and when to finish a job, not having their target decide for them where not to make it. They kept their annoyance in check, reminding one another to stay cool. This was all to be expected. Preparation and patience.

He appeared to have no routine outside the hotel. Sometimes he patronized street vendors peddling artery-clogging junk food. At other times he dined in restaurants serving the most exquisite and expensive cuisine. One afternoon he might spend several hours browsing exhibits in a single museum. The next he'd read a book, moving from café to café with it, never staying in any one establishment for more than an hour at a time, and sometimes for only a matter of minutes. When they had figured him so impersonal as to be almost a recluse, he then spent an evening charming women in a cocktail bar.

He had no mobile phone, but at what the Finn deemed random intervals he used Internet cafés or pay phones. They found no traces of his activities when the Danish surveillance specialist then used the same terminal or phone booth. They debated whether such activities were even necessary for him or if they were merely for show, to trip up and distract any undetected tail.

"It's working," the Swede said.

They had no idea why he was present in the city. It could be for any number of reasons. Perhaps he was preparing for a job of his own, getting to know the city and his area of operations. Maybe he was on the run and keeping incognito where he hoped his enemies could not find him. Or could this even be how he lived day-to-day when he was not himself working? It was no life, they all agreed, however many zeroes he could command for his services. If every waking moment had to be spent in a perpetual sense of alertness, then there had to be better ways to make a living. It made them appreciate how fortunate they were. They looked forward to this job's completion and their next get-together. It was the Swede's turn to host and his wife was universally adored. She taught physics but could be a professional party planner, as they would often tell the Swede to his pride.

A hit on the move proved just as troublesome to organize as one based on location. The target used buses, taxis, subways, aboveground trains, and walking with no discernible pattern. Distances were irrelevant. He might walk three miles to visit a coffee shop, yet take a cab for two blocks or spend an hour on the subway only to exit via the same station. How much the limp bothered him on such journeys, they could not tell.

In open areas he stayed in crowds and never walked in straight lines. When on narrow streets he kept away from the curb and close to storefronts. His hands were always outside his pockets. When he drank coffee on the move he did so by holding the cup in his left hand.

"So his primary hand is always available," the Finn observed.

"What if he's ambidextrous?" one of the Danes asked.

The Finn replied, "Less than a one percent chance of that. For all we know, he uses his left hand to make observers think he's left-handed."

"Let's assume he is ambidextrous," the second Dane said. "Whatever hand is occupied, we consider him just as dangerous."

The other three nodded.

They operated from a vehicle that was changed daily, renting a different van each morning. They would take turns sleeping in the back compartment while the others worked. They had multiple changes of clothes and other accessories to make sure he never recognized who followed him on foot. Sometimes they lost him in order to maintain their cover, but that was to be expected. *Take no risks*, they would tell one another. They knew he would return to the hotel at some point, because the Danish surveillance expert had hacked into the hotel's registry system. They knew how long he was staying, how much he was paying for the two rooms, even what he ordered from room service and that he had requested feather-free bedding and smoking rooms.

"But he hasn't smoked a single cigarette in all the time we've watched him," the Swede noted.

"No assumptions," the Finn reminded him. "This guy's only consistency is inconsistency."

"You sound like you respect him."

"I do," she said. "He's a lion."

"A lion?"

She nodded and grinned. "His head will look great mounted above my fireplace."

· Chapter 2 ·

Two days later the voice of the female Dane, who was one of the pair shadowing on foot, sounded through the speaker of the mobile radio unit set up in the back of the rental van.

"He's buying camping supplies."

The Swede pressed the SEND button on the radio control panel and spoke into the microphone. "What kind of supplies are we talking about?"

"A stove, solid fuel, waterproof sleeping bag, bungee cords, padded sleeping mats, a walking cane . . . items like that. I can't see everything he's loaded into the trolley."

The Finn was also shadowing, but currently outside the store. Her distinctive red hair was hidden beneath a wig. "Any cold-weather gear?"

The Swede waited for the Dane to respond when there was no danger of being observed. After a moment's silence she answered, "Not from what I can see. Shall I get closer?"

"Maintain a safe distance," the Swede replied. "This could be a ruse to draw out potential surveillance. We make no assumptions about this guy. Take no risks. Okay?"

"Got it."

The Finn said, "I think he's planning for a job."

"You can't be certain of that," the Swede replied.

She responded without pause because while outside the store there was no danger of being exposed. "He's not going camping for the fun of it. I know that much."

"We can't be sure he is going camping."

"Talk quieter," the male Dane said, and rolled over.

• • •

The next day was the same: more waiting. During that time they had witnessed him buying used mobile phones from a market trader and top-up credit from two different stores. The Finn had point for the foot surveillance. She enjoyed watching the target from relatively close proximity. She enjoyed pitting her skills at remaining unseen against such a careful mark. She didn't take risks, of course, however much she wanted to impress the others. Particularly the Swede, who aroused her and frustrated her in equal measure in those moments when she did not think of her boyfriend or the Swede's lovely wife.

The Finn wanted to be the one that ended this. Not necessarily with the kill itself, but by providing that advantage they had so far struggled to acquire. Perhaps if she did not lose the target, as the others often did, she would be led to somewhere that could be used as a strike point, or learn some extra intelligence that they could exploit to create one.

Gunning him down on the street wasn't their style. They wanted to live free and enjoy their hefty tax-free commissions. It was rare they even left a body behind. A combination of the Swede's cocktails of flesh-dissolving enzymes and acids and the Finn's willingness to use power tools ensured that after they had made a kill, not enough of the target remained to be identified. They charged extra for such cleanup, but would do it regardless. The Finn kept her thrill at putting to use circular saws and belt sanders a secret from the other three. As a girl, gutting reindeer had always been her favorite part of hunting with her father.

She inspected such tools while following the target around a hardware and DIY superstore. They had on sale a handheld circular saw produced by her preferred manufacturer. It had a 1900 mm blade and used 1300 watts of power. Fun times could be had with that, providing one wore the right protective clothing. So much mess.

"He's bought himself an oxyacetylene torch," she whispered into her lapel mike. "It's a good one too."

The deep, sweet voice of the Swede responded in her ear: "What's this guy up to? I know you're going to say he's preparing for a job."

"Maybe he's building something."

"But what?" the Swede said in return.

She kept the target at the limits of her sight and observed as he added a set of protective goggles, fuel tank, and heavy-duty gloves to use with the cutting torch. He then went on to buy a small generator, diesel, and a folding four-wheel trolley to transport his purchases. At the till, he spent a minute flirting with the much older woman who served him. The smile that lingered on her face long after he'd gone told the Finn she had enjoyed the experience.

The Finn didn't follow the target outside. She updated the Swede on his new acquisitions, and the Danish man was put into rotation, wearing smart business clothes—the opposite of the casual jeans and leather jacket he'd worn the previous day. Though arguably more attractive than the Swede, the Dane didn't endure in her fantasies. She didn't feel that electricity between them. The Finn took her place at the radio to let the Swede sleep. She watched his chest rise and fall beneath the sleeping bag.

While the male Dane kept them updated on the target's movements, the female Dane drove the van around the city, always staying at least a street or two away from the target's current whereabouts, but never staying so far away that they would be unable to exploit an opportunity. That opportunity never presented itself, of course; or, more accurately, the target never allowed himself to give one away.

It must be exhausting, the Finn decided, to live such a careful existence, in which one's guard never lowered and each and every movement had to be not only considered but executed with perfection. The Finn couldn't do it, and she was thankful she didn't have to. She would never work alone. It was suicide. There was safety in numbers. No individual, no matter how good, could be as effective as a team. They were about to prove that on this particular job.

"I think we have something," the male Dane's voice announced through the speaker.

"Go on," she said.

"He's entered a storage facility."

The Finn's back straightened. "Interesting."

"That's what I thought."

"He's spending a lot of time in the reception area."

"So he's likely renting a unit."

"Again," the Dane said, "that was my take. Hang on. . . . Yes, he's following an employee out. I can see keys and paperwork. He's being taken to his unit." He couldn't hide the excitement in his voice.

The Finn clapped her palms together.

"What is it?" the Swede asked, stirring.

The Finn smiled at him. He looked so cute and disheveled. "We might have something."

The female Dane used a laptop to remote-hack into the storage company's system and discovered some useful information. The unit rented was four hundred cubic feet in size and situated in the middle of a row of similarly sized units. There were more than two hundred in total at the facility, all ground level. It was a typical facility—a chain—though not a high-end one. The security was adequate but nothing special. There were a few cameras, but plenty of blind spots because they had used the minimum they could get away with. The target had signed a twelve-month agreement, which was standard, and registered under a different name than he was staying at the hotel with.

"Check flight manifests," the Swede said.

She did, and learned the target had an economy-class ticket booked for the day after he was due to check out of his hotel.

"Checkout is at eleven hundred hours," she said. "His flight is at nineteen hundred the next day. Check-in two hours before that means thirty-one hours for him to hang around."

"Too long," the Swede muttered.

The Dane said, "He's going to stay at the storage facility. That's why he has the camping equipment."

The Finn nodded. "He's establishing a safe house. He's not storing anything there. He's keeping it stocked with the essentials so when he's in town he has everything he needs to lie low."

"But why stay at a hotel for the past week if his intention was to set up a safe house?"

The Finn shrugged. She didn't know.

The Swede clicked his fingers. "Because he's coming back to town. He's got a job lined up here. It must be a big one too, or one that is high risk. One where he wouldn't be able to slip out of the city straightaway and won't be able to risk staying at a hotel or guesthouse. But now he's set up a safe house, he can lie low there until the dust settles while the cops waste their time quizzing receptionists."

"Man, this guy is slippery," the Dane said.

"Like an eel," the Finn added, impressed. "But in two days' time he's going to slither into a trap of his own making."

"You sound like you feel sorry for him."

"I do." She smiled. "Almost."

The target checked out of his hotel as scheduled. They followed him to the storage facility, as they had done twice before while he deposited his various purchases. This time he dropped off a small suitcase, but then left.

"Don't worry," the Swede said, because the disappointment in the van was palpable. "We know he's coming back."

"Patience," the Finn added.

"Do we lie in wait for his return?" the Danish woman asked. "He has the door secured with a state-of-the-art combination padlock, but give me a few minutes and I can crack it. Easy."

"No," her countryman replied. "He's bound to have any number of anti-intrusion indicators on or around the door. We disturb the wrong mote of dust and he'll know we're inside."

The Swede said, "Plus, does anyone really want to trap himself in a dark, confined space just waiting for him to return?"

"Not my idea of a good time," the Finn answered.

The Swede smiled at that, then said, "So, we're agreed? We wait it out. He'll come back at some point to sleep. He's not going to stay awake for thirty hours straight when he doesn't have to."

"How do we get the door open without him knowing about it?" the male Dane asked.

"We don't need to," the Finn answered. "We stealth it into the facility, nice and slow and quiet. He won't hear us coming if we keep it smooth. Obviously, he can't engage the padlock while he's inside the unit, so once we're over the fence, he's defenseless. One of us opens the unit's door—so maybe two seconds. The other two breach, fast, flashlights on to locate him in the dark and blind him as he stirs. Then: *bang, bang.* It's over."

"Nice," the Swede said.

Feeling warm from the praise, the Finn turned to the others. "So, it's settled?" She raised a hand. "The storage facility is our strike point?"

The other three raised their hands in unanimous agreement.

"But let's make doubly sure every particular is solid," the male Dane said. "We need this to be one hundred percent."

"Have we ever gone to work with anything less?"

Chapter 3

Shortly after midnight they made their move. The night sky was clear. The air was mild. The male Dane stayed behind the wheel of the van, parked on the same side of the street as the storage facility, but between the wash of streetlamps and out of line of sight of the security cameras. At a distance the vehicle looked parked and unoccupied. He was the getaway driver, providing surveillance and possible backup while the others were inside the facility. They all wore earpieces so he could warn them of anything happening outside that might compromise the job. It was unlikely. The storage unit was located in a quiet commercial area with all businesses closed at that time of night. Little traffic—whether pedestrians or vehicles—passed through the neighborhood. The only people around were them and *him*.

The Danish woman, the Finn, and the Swede would complete the hit as the Finn had suggested—the Swede using his strength to open the door in the shortest possible time, the Finn as the shooter, and the Dane watching their backs. The Finn had earned the role of killer because not only was she a fine shot but she was also considerably shorter than the other two team members. The Swede was the better marksman with small arms, but his height meant he was not the best choice. As the target would be prone, a tall shooter would find acquiring the target in the dark more difficult. A split-second delay could prove disastrous. Everyone was happy with their roles and knew what to do and when.

The target had returned to his storage unit a few minutes before nine p.m. At ten, the staff manning the facility's front desk packed up and went home. The team had no way of knowing how long it would be before the target went to sleep, but they figured waiting a couple of hours made sense, just to be certain.

"He's not going to sit in there reading a book," one of the Danes had said. "He'll get his head down and get out as soon as possible. We know this guy doesn't like to sit still. He knows he's vulnerable in there."

After the kill was completed the storage locker would provide enough privacy for the Finn to go to work with power tools. The target even had a generator to plug them into.

"Thoughtful," she had joked.

They wore lightweight body armor under their jackets and were armed with suppressed pistols and several magazines of spare ammunition. They each carried their own preferred sidearm. No one was expecting anything more onerous than a double tap to the head—certainly not a firefight—but it was essential to prepare for events beyond the worst-case scenario.

The Dane moved toward the storage facility first and alone. The brim of her cap was pulled down low to shield her face and the hood from her jacket hid her hair. She had an aluminum ladder in her hands and a stepladder strapped to her back with bungee cords—purchased from the same store their target had used. She rushed up to the facility's gate, extended the ladder, and hooked the support hooks onto the top of the gate. Both the ladder's hooks and feet had been wrapped in foam. In seconds she had climbed over and dropped down to the other side. She wore athletic shoes with thick soles.

She released the slipknot attaching a set of bolt cutters to her belt and used them to disable the gate's lock. The locking bolt was accessible only from the inside.

The stepladder—similarly silenced with foam—was set in place, and she used the height it provided to reach a wall-mounted security camera. It covered the gate and space behind it. She coated the lens cover with black paint from a spray can.

"Move," she whispered into her radio.

The Finn pushed open the gate and hurried into the facility, followed by the Swede. While this happened the Dane used the stepladder and spray paint to disable more cameras. No risks. The camera recording her climbing over the gate had been unavoidable, but her identifying features were appropriately hidden and no record of the Finn or Swede—nor of their activities within the facility's boundary—would exist.

The target's unit sat in the approximate center of a row of eight units—four units to the closest end, three to the farthest. They took up their positions. Their soft-soled shoes and skill at stealth ensured they made as close to no noise as was possible. The Swede took a parabolic microphone from his rucksack, held the earpiece in place, and pointed the microphone at the unit's doors. He listened for a moment, sweeping with the device.

He nodded at the other two and mouthed, *He's asleep*. Then he pointed to the right side of the door. The Finn and the Dane nodded back. The Finn shuffled over to the right and held up her pistol. Two seconds to get the door open; another one to acquire the target. No way he could wake up and react within three seconds, the Finn thought.

The Swede set down the parabolic microphone, and the Dane readied her gun: an FN P90 automatic weapon. A long sound suppressor was affixed to the muzzle. It was a beast of a machine, but only backup. The Finn would do the shooting with a .22-caliber Ruger pistol. The low-powered slugs would still kill if they struck vital organs—which they would, because the Finn was an expert shot—but they would stay inside the head or torso. No exit wound meant less mess. Less mess meant less evidence. They had rolls of plastic sheeting waiting in the van, ready to be unrolled before her power tools came out to play. The P90 was in case the Swede couldn't get the door open. It seemed unlikely that the target could—or indeed would—secure the unit's door from the inside, but they were taking no chances. If he had rigged some locking mechanism to the inside and the Swede could not wrench the door open within three seconds the Dane would hose the unit down. The P90's magazine held fifty rounds that would be unleashed in a matter of seconds. Even with indirect fire, there was no way the target would survive.

The mess would be absolute, which was why it was purely a backup plan. A nice, clean kill was how they preferred to operate, but with a target such as this they were prepared to accept that some corners might have to be cut.

The P90 now clutched in both hands, the Dane nodded to confirm her readiness to the Finn and the Swede. He edged into position, squatted, and took hold of the door. He nodded to the others. The Finn clicked on the red-dot optic of her pistol and the under-barrel flashlight.

The Dane, gun in her right hand, held up three fingers of her left hand to the others. Then two.

One.

· Chapter 4 ·

The Swede heaved open the rolling door, launching from a squat to standing, arms extended above his head, the metal creaking and clanging—loud and echoing.

The beam from the Finn's LED flashlight illuminated the inside of the storage unit—the camping supplies and equipment, gasoline and cutting torch, and a man-sized shape in a sleeping bag in the far right corner.

A GEMTECH suppressor and naturally subsonic ammunition meant the Finn's double tap was muted to two concentrated sneezes, inaudible beyond five meters. The sleeping bag rippled from the bullets' impact.

She stalked forward into the unit, Ruger still at eye level, and aimed down at the prone target, seeking confirmation of the kill.

"Wait," the Swede said from behind her before she could reach close enough to identify the target.

She did as instructed, surprised at the volume of his voice and utterly trusting that he was justified in his instruction.

"It's not him," the Swede said.

The Finn could not see the body in the sleeping bag from her distance, so he would not be able to either.

"Left," the Swede said.

She looked. "What the—"

The unit's walls were corrugated metal sheeting rising two and a half meters to the flat roof. Where the left wall met the floor was a hole, one meter square. The cutout piece of metal lay on the floor next to it. Cut with the oxyacetylene torch.

"Cover it," the Swede said as he moved forward into the unit.

The Finn trained her gun on the hole, the beam of the flashlight showing the blackened edges where the metal had been scorched by the torch. The Swede kicked the sleeping bag twice, then knelt down to check what was inside.

"Shit," he said, feeling pillows stuffed into the bag to create a man-sized shape. He felt something square and hard. A mobile phone, set to speaker, playing a sound file of recorded breathing.

"He knew we were coming," the Swede said, a slight edge of fear in his voice. "He was waiting for us."

"Where is he?" the Finn asked.

The beam of the flashlight shone a little way through the hole in the wall and into the next unit, which seemed empty.

The Swede pointed at the wall—at the next unit. Then he held out his left hand, palm down, and lowered it as he crouched into a squat, indicating for the Finn to do the same. She did, and the flashlight beam illuminated more of the unit beyond as his eye level descended to see into it. It was as empty as it first appeared.

"Oh no."

"What?" the Finn said, the volume and pitch of her voice rising. "What is it?"

On the far wall of the next unit was another hole and another sheet of metal lying before it. The Swede lowered himself onto his hands and knees to get the angle and saw the same was true of the unit after that. And then again. He could see all the way through and the spill of artificial light beyond the final hole that led outside.

The Swede said, "Watch the flank." He glanced toward the Dane, who was still outside the unit.

No Dane.

He let out a panicked exhale and snapped up his pistol. The Finn saw him do so and spun to where he was looking. The female Dane, who had been there mere moments before, was gone. They hadn't heard a thing.

"Stay calm," the Finn said.

The Swede didn't seem to hear. "He led us here. He wanted us to come after him. Shit. *Shit*."

"Stay calm," the Finn said again.

"He picked this spot to attack us and we watched him do it. It's a fucking trap."

The Finn didn't argue. She used her lapel mike to radio the male Dane. "We need backup, right now."

No answer.

She repeated herself.

The Swede stared at her. "Not him as well . . ."

A voice came through the speaker: male, but not the Dane who was supposed to be waiting in the van. The voice was deep and low. Calm. Terrifying. "I'm afraid no one is coming to help you."

"You bastard. I'm going to—"

The voice continued: "It's nothing personal, but I

can't let any of you live. I know you understand that. You would do exactly the same in my position."

The Finn pulled out her earpiece and smashed it beneath a heel. *"Bastard."* She whispered to the Swede, "We need to move. Right now."

"He's at the van. If we're fast—"

The Finn shook her head. "No, damn it. Think for a second. He could have killed Jans and taken his mike the second we were through the gate. He could be anywhere by now."

"Then what do we do?"

The Finn thought about this for a moment, then pointed at the hole in the unit wall and made a walking action with her index and middle finger.

The Swede shook his head. "No way. That's suicide."

"Then what do you suggest?"

He didn't answer.

The Finn inched closer to the hole.

"I'm not going through there," the Swede whispered.

"Fine." She pointed to the open roller door. "Stay here and cover that entrance until I get to it."

"We can't split up. That's what he wants us to do."

"We have to do *something*. Do you want to end up like the others? If we wait here, we're playing into his hands."

He nodded. "Okay."

"It's going to take me no more than a minute to crawl out and come back round the front. If I'm any longer than that, I haven't made it."

"Don't say that."

"Listen to me, please. You wait one minute for me. If I'm not in front of you by then, he's got me. So you need to take advantage of that and run. Just run. He can't be in two places at once. You count to sixty, and at sixty-one you run for your life. Do you understand me?"

He nodded and swallowed.

She exhaled, then kissed him on the lips. It surprised him, but he kissed her back.

"Don't be late," he said.

She didn't want to be late. *Late* meant *dead*.

"I won't be."

· Chapter 5 ·

The ground was cold beneath the Finn's elbows and knees. She crawled through the first hole and into the unit next to the target's. It was empty. When she stopped, she could hear the rapid breathing of the Swede. She wanted to shout back and tell him to be quiet, but she daren't give her position away. The target—not that he could still be thought of as such—could be anywhere in the facility, but he was close. The Finn knew that. Had their roles been reversed she would stay near, within eyesight or hearing range. She'd called him a lion before. Now she pictured a lion stalking through tall grass.

She crawled through the next hole. Only one more unit before she was outside. The cool air on her skin made her more aware of the sweat coating her face. The current unit was full of musty-smelling cardboard boxes crammed with magazines and books. The Finn stepped around them.

The final unit was empty. She released a breath and crept over to the hole leading outside. If the killer was waiting to ambush her, it would be here. But there was just as much chance of him covering the unit where the Swede waited, which meant this hole would be safe to crawl through. There was no way to know for certain until it was too late. At least for one of them.

Thirty seconds remained until the designated minute had been depleted. What had she told the Swede? *You count to sixty, and at sixty-one you run for your life.*

She stopped. There was no need to crawl through the last hole and risk an ambush, because in less than half a minute the Swede was going to run. Then either he wouldn't make it or he would. If he did, the Finn would know the killer wasn't covering his rented unit and therefore must be watching the hole. However, if the Swede didn't make it, then the hole was safe because the killer couldn't be in two places at the same time.

The Finn waited.

She didn't want him to die. But she wanted to die less. She breathed in shallow exhales and inhales to limit the noise. She needed to hear. She needed to hear whether the Swede made it or not. She willed him not to make it. *Sorry, my sweet.* Twenty seconds remaining.

With ten seconds left, she tensed, readying herself to make a break for it, or if it sounded like the Swede made it, to turn around and hurry back the way she had come. She wondered if the Swede had come to the same conclusion. She wondered if he was silently willing her to die like she was him.

At four seconds she heard the Swede move. He had counted too fast. Not unsurprising, given the heightened circumstances. Or maybe she was counting too slow. It didn't matter.

She heard the scrape of the soles of his shoes on the ground as he launched into a run, as she had instructed.

She heard the urgent footfalls. She pictured him powering out of the unit, veering left toward the exit, sprinting down the alley of space between the rows of units, reaching the—

Two muted clacks reached her ears. The footfalls stopped.

Bad news for the Swede. Good news for the Finn.

She dropped to her knees, crawling fast, not worried about noise, knowing the killer was out of line of sight, over near the facility's reception building and main gate. He couldn't be in two places at once.

The Finn crawled through the final hole and out onto the far side of the last unit. The cool night air felt magical on her sweat-slick skin, but there wasn't time to enjoy it. She had a single moment of opportunity—a single advantage—and she needed to make it work. She rose to her feet.

The killer was at one side of the facility, she was at the other. All she had to do was—

She felt something brush against her face—fast and surprising—then pressure on her throat as it tightened. An image flashed in her mind: the killer buying bungee cord.

It formed a noose around her neck, closing off her windpipe, sending burning pain and panic flooding through her. The Finn grasped at it, dropping her gun, trying to dig her fingers behind the cord, but there was no room. The slack had been stretched out of it by her own weight and the killer above her—on the roof of the unit—pulling upward.

Her feet struggled for purchase. Her face reddened. Her eyes bulged. She tried to speak, to beg, but only a gurgling wheeze escaped her lips.

The upward pressure of the noose kept her jaw locked

shut and the cord away from her carotids. Otherwise, she
would have passed out within seconds as the blood supply
to the brain was cut off. Instead, the bungee cord suffo-
cated her, extending the agony to over a minute. Her
teeth ground and cracked. Her lips blued. Capillaries
burst in her eyeballs.

Eventually, oxygen deprivation induced a euphoric
state of calm and well-being. The pain ceased. The Finn
stopped fighting. Then she stopped moving altogether.

· Chapter 6 ·

Victor was still for a moment as the night breeze flowed over his face and through his hair. It slithered down his collar and up his sleeves. Cold, but gentle and soothing. His heart rate, slightly elevated from the exertion, fell back to a slow rhythm. He opened his hands and let the bungee cord fall away. Below him, the body collapsed to the ground. He felt nothing except a little soreness in his palms. Without the heavy-duty welder's gloves protecting his hands the friction burn would no doubt have taken away skin along with sweat. The bungee cord's inherent slack wasn't ideal for strangulation, but its light weight and flexibility meant it was a fast, maneuverable noose. The proof was in the result. The woman couldn't be any more dead.

He rolled up the padded groundsheets that he'd laid across the unit's roof to muffle the noise of moving back and forth across it and lowered himself onto his good leg. Once inside his rented unit he put on some shoes and began packing up his equipment. He hadn't required all of it, but the more superfluous items he purchased, the less chance there was of the team working out what he really needed and therefore what he had planned. Once it was all loaded onto the trolley—barring the waterproof sleeping bag—he wheeled it out of the unit, through the facility, and out of the open gate.

They'd parked in a good spot. It only took a couple of minutes to transfer it all into the back of the team's van, alongside where the dead driver lay. The other corpses followed, pushed on the loading trolley and concealed by the groundsheets. Victor took his time. There was no need to rush. They had kindly disabled the facility's security cameras for him. In any case, what few cameras there were had been positioned to cover the doors of the units, not their roofs, and he'd been careful to pick a spot outside of any camera's arc in which to cut the hole with the oxyacetylene torch.

He'd used it to burn over the outer edges of the holes he had cut, and placed the rectangles of metal on the outside of each unit. When the morning shift arrived at six a.m. and saw the disabled gate lock and watched the camera footage they—and the subsequent police investigators—would conclude a break-in had taken place. Upon discovering they could not contact the owner of the thief's—singular, because only one assassin had been recorded by the cameras—target, they would deduce that Victor had been storing something valuable and illegal, hence the false identity. With nothing reported stolen, the police would look no further into what seemed to be one criminal ripping off another. Nothing pleased a cop more. Karma, they would say, and do the deep belly laugh that only true joy could create.

There was little cleanup to do. He removed the man he'd shot first, using the waterproof sleeping bag to ferry him so none of his blood and other leaking bodily fluids would be left behind. Victor had killed him with a sub-sonic .22 to ensure the round stayed inside the body and didn't cause a messy exit wound. He figured the redheaded woman he'd strangled had been carrying a similar gun for the exact same reasons. He liked that. He felt he knew her a little better. There wasn't much opportunity for relationships in Victor's line of work and, even separated by death, he felt a connection with the woman. Maybe they had other things in common beyond consideration of armaments. He found himself wondering if they shared a similar taste in music or books. Perhaps she enjoyed the same kind of food. In another life they might have been friends. Even lovers.

He threw her corpse down on top of the others.

Subject:
I Need Your Help

St. Petersburg, Russia

· Chapter 7 ·

Victor opened his eyes to the view provided by his hotel room's ceiling. No alarm had awoken him. No alarm ever woke him. When his consciousness first booted up and took control of his body he needed his senses. Of those senses his hearing was the most important. He needed his ears to collect every creak of floorboards and brush of shoe on carpet, and the click of a doorjamb and a whisper of released breath that might save his life. Hearing could detect an enemy long before sight. Victor knew this because many times he had been the paid enemy of someone aware of his presence only when they saw him for the first time. By then it was always far too late to matter.

He heard nothing that presented any cause for concern. Regardless, he removed the SIG Sauer from the front of his waistband and kept it in hand after checking it for tampering. He wore a navy suit over a white shirt. The tie was folded and rested inside a pocket. His shoes were oxfords, their soles brushed clean to leave no dirt or telltale residue on top of the bedclothes.

The curtains were closed. The inner folds overlapped to ensure not even a sliver of the outside world could be seen, or could see in between them. A lamp cast the room in a glow of warm orange light, as sight was his second-best defense. Hotel corridors were always lit, so an assassin's eyes would struggle inside a pitch-black room, but technology could render night as day, and a flashlight shone into eyes adjusted in that dark room would be blinded worse than by night alone.

There were three means of entry: the bedroom door, the sash window, and the door leading to the en suite bathroom. The bedroom door was locked and barricaded with the room's wardrobe. It was heavy and awkward, but he was strong and patient and valued his life more than the time and energy it took to move it. It provided a nigh on impassable barrier of greater height and width than the doorframe. He used his sense of touch to check around its feet. The indentations in the carpet did not extend beyond their dimensions. The sash window opened to a gap of less than fifteen centimeters. A skilled assailant could conceivably manipulate it to provide a large enough space to climb through, but the curtains were as he had left them and the postage stamp–sized square of toilet tissue had not been moved by the ripple of fabric or flow of air. He checked the bathroom door. A fine fiber of wool remained in place, stuck across the gap between door and frame, at the very bottom, where it would fall quickly to the floor and disappear against the carpet if the door opened, because that is where he had taken it from. A hair had once been used by professionals for the same purpose, but Victor never chose to increase the chances of leaving DNA behind. For the same reason he had stuck the fiber in place with a tiny drop of shower gel from one of the complimentary bottles and not saliva.

The bathroom window was small, but large enough for a slight man or woman to climb through. Such an entry would be his preferred route. Farther from the sleeping target meant less chance of being heard, especially with a closed door in between.

Victor was not slight, but a lifetime of stretching meant his joints had the limberness of a gymnast. The window's size would not have stopped him.

He positioned himself to the side of the bathroom door and used his elbow to flick on the light switch and blind an assailant who had been waiting in the darkness as he turned the handle with his free hand. He flung open the door and entered fast, gun leading. Seeing it was empty, he focused on the mirror behind the sink directly opposite the open door to check that no one stood behind it. Victor lowered the gun.

He was safe. At least until he stepped outside his room.

He checked the time. He'd been asleep for a little more than four hours. A combination of necessity, experience, and training meant he rarely slept for much longer in a single period. His body required as much rest as the next man to function at one hundred percent, but he spread out his requirement whenever it was possible. Most assassins would elect to strike when the target was most vulnerable, and deep in the slow-wave stage three of non-REM sleep was just about the best way of ensuring that. At that point the target would suffer the highest arousal threshold—the lowest chance of waking. For the majority, that point was halfway through the sleep cycle, four or five hours after drifting off, in the early hours of the morning. He made sure never to be asleep during that time, and sleeping approximately four hours increased his chances of being awake when most killers would think it best to strike.

Victor stripped, stretched, and exercised, then ignored the sensory deprivation of the shower and took a bath. It was freestanding, deep and long, and he could relax without his limbs bunched up. Good hotels were a huge drain on his resources, but the monetary expense was almost offset by the ability to bathe in comfort.

The hotel was a beautiful Regency building with a grand facade, high ceilings, and magnificent chandeliers. Exploring it for the purposes of operational security had been nothing short of a pleasure. The lack of CCTV cameras—presumably for aesthetic considerations—was also to his particular tastes. He checked out, chatting banalities with the friendly clerk so as not to appear rude and therefore memorable, and took a cab deep into the city.

He considered the unexpected e-mail seeking his assistance while he entered a metro station, took the train at platform three because he saw three ticket booths were open, alighted at the second stop because two other people stood like him inside the car, and headed across to the southbound platform because a woman smiled at him as she approached the elevators.

A year ago he had deactivated several e-mail accounts through which independent brokers would contact him in the days when he had worked regularly as a freelance professional. People he had never met either offered him contracts or if he had operated for them before might ask to pitch him for particularly lucrative jobs. He would have more intimate contact with them only if they had misled or betrayed him, and then they would never have contact with him—or anyone else—ever again. It had been a dangerous but profitable existence and one he had believed himself to have mastered, but ultimately the isolation that kept him alive had led to a period of servitude. A slave with a gun, he had thought of himself at that time. After that, an independent contractor. Now he wasn't sure what he was. Unemployed, maybe.

His last client had passed him no work recently. He didn't know if that was noteworthy beyond a lack of jobs that required his particular talents. He wasn't about to ask. Unemployed or not, the fallout from those contracts of the past few years—as well as those of his freelance days—meant he could not let his guard down for even a single day. His enemies were legion, and some possessed great power and means. Others did not, but a solitary bullet was the sum total of all the power any enemy would ever need. He accepted and had expected such threats. Only dead assassins had believed they could operate their trade with impunity. The astronomical fee he charged for his services reflected the danger he lived with on a day-to-day basis.

A teenage girl sitting nearby chewed on the nail of her fourth finger, so Victor disembarked the train at the fourth station. This time he elected to leave, because a keen-eyed security guard watching CCTV monitors might note he had had gone north, then south, then north again. Even a tourist wouldn't make that kind of mistake. Especially one who didn't look like a tourist.

Outside the station he took a cab, pretending he didn't speak the language, mispronouncing landmarks until the driver had some idea of where he wanted to go. He gave it ten minutes, because the last two digits of the driver's license number were five and two, and had him stop the car. The driver pulled over behind a BMW, so Victor took the next two right turns because B was the second letter of the alphabet, then continued walking, following the road he found himself upon, ignoring the next thirteen junctions, as M was the thirteenth letter, before alternating left and right for the next four turnings because W was the fourth letter when reading the alphabet backward.

He had detected no one, but that didn't mean he was unobserved. If he was being followed the shadows would find no significance in his movements and ultimate location because he had never been there before and this end location was as close to a random result as any human could hope to create. The street was pedestrianized and lined with restaurants and bars. The crowd of people was dense and ever moving. It was a good place for drawing out shadows and losing them by entering one of the establishments. It was a poor location for an ambush, and until moments ago he had no idea he would be here, so any aggressors planning violence would have had no time to prepare. Nothing would happen here. For now, he was as safe as he was ever going to be.

He walked slowly along the street, listening to the sounds of joy and merriment surrounding him.

A young boy caught his eye. The kid was too young to be working in the area but old enough to be unaccompanied. His clothes were shabby and unclean, but he moved with purpose, sometimes walking fast, other times slow. The kid was malnourished and thin; the lack of calcium and calories in his diet had stunted his growth. A shame for all the obvious reasons, but beneficial for one.

The boy was a pickpocket. Victor didn't see him make

any attempts, but that was only because the boy was waiting for his best opportunity. He was patient and considered, and used his short height to good advantage. People barely noticed him, whereas in return his eye level was not far above that of trouser pockets and handbags. Victor respected the poise with which the kid conducted himself. He was a survivor. He was just like Victor had been at that age, having broken out of the orphanage, living on the streets, doing what he'd had to. Surviving.

Memories were distraction, so Victor cleared his mind. He moved his wallet from his inside jacket pocket and into the left pocket of his trousers.

The kid was good. He didn't let the opportunity go to waste. Victor respected that.

Using his knuckles, he pushed open the door to a bar he liked the look of and stepped into a wall of heat and noise. It was closer to full than empty and had a pleasant atmosphere. Victor was never concerned by the kind of trouble that bars encouraged, but he tried to steer clear of ones where it was more likely to occur. He did everything in his power to avoid a confrontation with a civilian, but a man drunkenly determined to prove his masculinity would respond with equal aggression to passivity as he would to intimidation. Easier to shun those bars where such a man was likely to pass his time than try to pull a punch so that when it landed it did not kill that man.

He picked a spot at the bar and made eye contact with the barman, noting in his peripheral vision a short-haired Asian woman looking his way. Victor sipped an orange juice while he thought about the e-mail. Subject: *I need your help*. The body of the message consisted of nothing but a coded phone number. He knew the number because he knew the code because he knew the man who had sent it. He didn't have to call the number to know it was a request for a face-to-face meeting. Something Victor rarely did, and rarer still when it was requested of him. It was uncommon for people who knew him to want to spend time in his company. Especially when the previous engagement had not ended well. Victor couldn't help but be intrigued. The person who sent it knew enough about him to know exactly how big a request it was.

The e-mail had arrived in one of the few accounts he kept active. Scattered around the world were a number of contacts that he used to fill the gaps in his skill set that he could not afford to leave blank. Such contacts included document forgers, gunsmiths, language coaches, hackers, doctors, smugglers, and experts in other specialist fields. Of those, only a handful knew the true nature of his profession, and only then because he had encountered them while plying his trade and recognized their value. He maintained certain e-mail accounts so that he could contact them via prearranged means, but also so they could contact him on rare occasions. Some debts could not be paid in money alone.

Those accounts were hidden and protected as any could be, disguised by proxy servers and complex webs of ownership, data redirections, duplicates, decoys, encryptions, and ciphers. Victor never accessed the same account more than once from the same city in the same year and regularly tested the integrity of the anonymity they provided. Any account he had the slightest doubt about would be deactivated.

One crack in his security might be all it took to put an assassin just like him on his trail or bring a police tactical team to his door. *Prevention over cure* was one motto he had no choice but to live by. An enemy first had to successfully track him down. Having done that, the enemy needed to corner him while remaining undetected. And should the enemy manage that, there still remained the difficult task of actually killing him.

He had no doubt it would happen. He conducted himself as though death's touch was only a handsbreadth away. He would never make it to old age. Each job he undertook created more danger and added new enemies. But it was an impossible cycle to break free of. Working kept him sharp. Retirement meant the certain erosion of his skills, and there was nowhere on the planet he could hide where no one could ever find him. Life was short. Time was precious. Which was why he took enjoyment from it whenever he could.

He checked to see that the bar had a card reader and said, "Can I buy you a drink?" to the Asian woman with the short hair.

She smiled. "Sure, why not?"

· Chapter 8 ·

The night air was cold on Victor's tongue. He liked winter. He liked the taste of it. He walked along the path pedestrians had carved through an ankle-high layer of snow that covered the pavement, his footprints blending into those imprinted before him. The snow crunched beneath his shoes. His breath clouded with each exhale but his hands hung loose by his hips; cold, but hands confined in warm pockets were useless.

His destination was close. He knew where it lay at the center of a neighborhood of social housing built during the Communist era. Most had been deserted and derelict when he had last visited years before. Now some of the crumbling tenements had been torn down and replaced by newer buildings that were cleaner but no less unattractive than their neighbors. Cars crawled past, headlights filtering through the falling snow that kept the road white. Black slush lined the gutters, a product of the day's traffic, now frozen.

Victor kept to the shadows, avoiding the spill of streetlights, and stopped when he was sure the two guys waiting outside the bar entrance were not regular door-men. They had the right dimensions but their coats were too expensive. He watched them for a moment. The light coming from inside the bar illuminated them well enough that Victor could estimate their ages and when they had last shaved. They didn't see him in return. He couldn't read their lips because they weren't talking. They were alert and concentrating on the vehicles and pedestrians that drove and walked by.

He had expected to find guards. He would have been concerned if he hadn't seen any. That would mean they were skilled enough to avoid his detection and had the motivation to. The two meatheads would not be the full contingent of heavies. There would be more inside the bar and others out back.

An alleyway took him to the narrow street behind the bar that ran parallel to the one in front. Two more guys stood outside the bar's rear entrance. One leaned against a stack of crates, smoking a cigarette, but he still looked just as focused and wary as his partner or the two out front. Victor couldn't enter the bar without first being spotted. The person he was here to meet did not want Victor get-ting close without being aware of it. But the guards didn't need to be so obvious to do that. They were stationed out in the open to ensure Victor saw them. There were two reasons for this. The first was the most obvious: it was a show of strength to dissuade him from any violent inten-tions he might have. The second was to say this wasn't an ambush. The guards were in plain sight in an attempt to convince him there was nothing to be concerned about.

Victor wasn't convinced. He trusted no one. He alone would decide whether to be concerned or not, but his guard wouldn't drop in either case.

He approached the rear entrance. His contact would have expected that and put his best men before it. Victor usually preferred to do the unexpected, but not this time. The person he was here to meet would be reassured by his calculation proving correct. He would feel confident in his management of the encounter. Victor would seem more predictable and controllable.

Less dangerous. Victor liked people to think that.

He approached the two guards.

When he was twenty meters away the closest spotted him and used the back of a hand to bat the other man on the arm. Both looked Victor's way. They straightened as he grew nearer and they were surer of his identity. They stood with feet shoulder width apart, hands by their hips but tension in their arms. He walked at a slow, measured pace, his gaze moving back and forth from one to the other. Their lips stayed closed. The one with the cigarette tossed it away. There was half an inch of white paper between the burning end and the filter. It landed on the road and extinguished.

When he was ten meters away their nerves showed. One clenched his fists. The other shuffled. Neither had spoken a word since they had spotted him. Which meant they weren't in constant communication with those inside. Which reduced, if not eliminated, the chances of the meeting doubling as an ambush.

They were both taller than him, the first by an inch, the second by three. Both had the wide shoulders and thick arms of guys who spent a lot of time in the gym. He wasn't sure if they swallowed or injected their anabolic steroids, but they were long-term abusers. Growth-hormone users too—they had the telltale good skin but enlarged skulls with prominent eyebrow bones and protruding abdomens full of artificially distended intestines. They were more than just muscle, though. Victor's contact hired only ex-military. He wanted men who could shoot as well as punch.

"Stop right there," the bigger one said when Victor was less than three meters away.

Victor did as he was told. He kept his hands at his side, palms open. A passive posture.

"You're him, yes?"

"That depends," Victor answered back in Russian.

The man nodded to himself. "Yeah, you're him all right."

"If you say so."

"Weapon?"

Victor shook his head.

"I don't believe you."

"Then you'd better search me." Victor held out his arms in invitation.

For a moment no one moved. Then the bigger one gestured at the shorter man to do so. He didn't. He motioned for his companion to do the searching himself. They stared at each other, gazes and facial expressions doing the silent arguing but reaching no mutually agreeable conclusion. So neither man held a position of seniority. No one had to follow the other's orders and neither wanted to search Victor. They had been well briefed.

He sighed loud enough to interrupt the power struggle and began unbuttoning his overcoat. Only the bottom two of the four buttons were fastened. That snapped their attention back to him. They stiffened, unsure what was happening, but Victor was moving too slowly and deliberately to be threatening. The smaller man reached into a pocket regardless, and kept it there when Victor took off the coat and let it fall to the pavement.

He stood there for a moment, passive and docile. Then, just as slowly, he held open his suit jacket. The two guards stared, concentration and confusion in their eyes.

Victor turned around on the spot, lifting the jacket tails as he gave them his back so they had an uninterrupted view of his waistband. He faced them again and exposed the linings of his empty trouser pockets. He pulled up the cuffs of his trousers, one at a time. He did the same with his sleeves.

"See? No weapon."

They looked at each other again, this time more relaxed as they now didn't need to get any closer to him than they had to.

"So are we good?" Victor asked with a lightness in his voice and a half smile, making fun of the situation.

The smaller man exhaled. The other shrugged. Then both nodded.

Victor extended the smile as he retrieved his overcoat from the ground. "Too cold for messing around longer than necessary, right, guys?"

He brushed off the snow with the back of his hand. They were smiling too now—three men finding humor after a moment of unnecessary tension.

He closed the distance to the two guards, still smiling, and held out the coat in both hands, elbows bent and near his waist, and gestured with it to the smaller of the two.

"Hold this for me until I come back out."

He asked no question so there was no need for the man to decide on an answer. They were all smiling and relaxed now there was no threat. The man didn't hesitate. He didn't think to analyze the request. He took a step nearer and reached for Victor's coat, bringing his hand out of the pocket so he could take it in both. His fingers gripped the coat.

Victor released it, grabbed the guard's wrists and yanked him closer.

He stumbled, off-balance, into the head butt that Victor launched at his face.

The strongest part of Victor's body—the curve of the forehead—collided with the bridge of the man's nose. Bone crunched. Cartilage flattened. Blood exploded from the nostrils in two downward jets and drenched the man's shirt.

Victor sidestepped away to let him stagger forward under his own momentum. That he didn't go straight down was testament to the man's toughness, but, unconscious or not, he would be out of the fight for as long as Victor needed him to be.

The larger man was quick to react but slow to move under the enormous weight of his unnatural musculature. He swung a well-executed punch that would break Victor's jaw with a significant bone displacement should it connect, but it was too slow to have any chance of hitting its mark. Victor dodged it, struck the Russian in the sternum with his right fist, hit over the liver with his left, and twisted around the man as he reeled from the blows and tried to grapple, and kicked him in the back of the knee as he turned, trying to follow Victor's movements.

He collapsed onto his knees, breathless and grimacing. Victor wrapped his right arm around the man's neck, bracing with the left, and squeezed until he stopped fighting and fell face-first into the snow.

The other man had turned and was staggering Victor's way, blood streaming over his mouth and raining from his chin. The Russian's eyes were wide in an attempt to see through the haze of pain and tears. He threw a straight punch that Victor slipped, stepping inside the man's reach and hitting him on the point of the chin with an open-palmed strike. His head snapped back and he dropped next to the other guard.

He patted them down, found phones, and crushed them under his heel. Both were armed—Baikal handguns and telescopic coshes. Victor tossed the weapons down a nearby storm drain. The two guys would wake up within a few minutes or not at all. It made no difference to Victor. He hadn't tried to kill them, but he hadn't tried not to.

He pulled open the bar's back door and stepped inside.

· Chapter 9 ·

The air was hot and heavy and loud. There was no music playing, but the dense mass of people, discretion eroded by alcohol, all shouted to be heard over each other. It was warm, heating on full blast to fight off the winter outside, and several dozen people were packed inside, drinking and eating bar food. Coat stands near the main entrance were overloaded. A barman mixed cocktails while flirting with a group of young women in heels that could easily kill if employed with a modicum of skill. He wore a bow tie. An ice sculpture of what Victor guessed used to be a naked woman melted slowly behind the bar. The patrons wore stylish clothes and business attire, now wrinkled and disheveled after a few hours of postwork partying. Victor had never had a day job. He'd never worked nine to five. He knew he would go insane confined in an office all day. Assuming he wasn't already insane.

There were no unoccupied tables and only enough room at the bar itself for one elbow. That wasn't an accident. The man he was here to meet could have selected any number of quieter locations. He wanted to be surrounded by people. This time it was purely for his own protection and nothing to do with trying to convince Victor his intentions were not angled toward violence.

Experience suggested to Victor this wasn't a setup. Had he any intimation that it was, he wouldn't have come this far. But he maintained a heightened vigilance. He kept himself ready to act—to fight and run. In his line of work it was the unexpected that was most dangerous. There was nothing to lose if taken by surprise by innocent actions.

Dropping the two outside had been insurance. If he had to make a fast exit he would not be interrupted going out of the rear entrance. Or, should things go bad before he had the opportunity to get out, there would be two fewer Goliaths to flank him. A quick scan of the room revealed another four guards. They were all as big and serious-looking as the two standing out front or the two prostrate ones out back had been. That made a security detail of eight. A serious display of strength, but Victor had expected more. If there were others here he hadn't identified or if they were hidden elsewhere, things could get ugly. But if eight was the total, then so far the situation was manageable. He'd already disabled twenty-five percent of the opposition.

The closest stood up, surprised and unsettled as he noticed Victor without a heads-up from the sentries outside the rear entrance. The guard called out to be heard over the din of patrons and gestured to a nearby guard, who then did the same to another. Within twenty seconds all four were standing and staring Victor's way. They were aggressive and ready to attack, but restrained—attack dogs behind a fence.

Victor made eye contact with each in turn so they knew he was aware of them and approached the corner booth they shielded in a loose semicircle. He weaved his way through the crowd and between tables. He was intercepted by one of the guards. He was a giant, even compared to the rest of the security detail. He was a shade off six-six and almost three hundred pounds. He'd been around twenty pounds lighter when Victor had first met him a couple of years beforehand. He'd also been somewhat less ugly.

"How's the ear, Sergei?" Victor asked.

To his credit, Sergei maintained an even expression. He pivoted his head to the right so Victor could see his right ear. It was twisted and unsightly where it had been sewn back together, with a ragged knot of discolored scar tissue across the center.

Victor said, "You can't even tell."

Sergei frowned. The bunched-up jaw muscles looked as though they might pop through the skin. He gestured for Victor to raise his arms.

"I was searched outside."

"And now we are inside," Sergei countered. "So raise your hands. Please."

Victor did. He stood motionless while he was patted down. Sergei's hands were huge and his technique was rough but also effective. He now knew Victor had no weapon and to which side he dressed.

Sergei said, a measure of surprise in his tone, "You're clean."

"Then why do I feel so dirty?"

Something resembling a smile creased Sergei's face. "Some of the boys had a bet on whether you'd show."

"Did you?"

"I don't gamble. I'm not stupid. But I didn't think you would."

Victor waited a moment in case Sergei had anything else to say, then asked, "Are we done?"

"I want to tear your face off."

"You'll have to join the queue, I'm afraid."

He stepped past Sergei, who did nothing to stop him, and approached the booth where Aleksandr Norimov sat.

· Chapter 10 ·

Norimov was nearly as big as the guys guarding him but he was more out of shape than Victor had ever seen him. The once huge shoulders now relied on the pads of the good suit to square his posture. That suit did its best to conceal the excess bulk stored elsewhere but couldn't disguise the white shirt stretched taut across his stomach. Light pooled on the Russian's bald head. The face beneath was lined and pale. His expression was blank. He knew how to hide his thoughts as well as Victor. He had been a good intelligence officer before turning to organized crime. He could have been scared or delighted or anything in between. Victor wouldn't know until he started talking. Maybe not even then. He reminded himself that Norimov was perhaps the best liar he had ever known.

The Russian acknowledged Victor with a slight raise of the chin. "You're earlier than I expected."

"Naturally."

"Even after your call I didn't think you'd really show."

"Neither did I."

Norimov nodded, thoughtful. "Thank you for doing so."

Victor said nothing to that.

Sergei stood close by, behind Victor. Within grabbing distance, should he need to.

To Norimov's right, a young woman at least twenty-five years his junior slouched on the cushioned bench. She was barely clothed and heavily made up. Her chin was close to her chest. She didn't look up, but Victor could see the struggle it was for her to keep her eyelids from closing. A few milliliters of a cosmopolitan with a sliver of burned orange rind sat in the bottom of a martini glass on the table before her.

"Give us some privacy," Norimov said to Sergei.

He hesitated. "Are you sure, boss?"

"I said so, did I not?" He didn't wait for a reply. "And take Nadia with you."

Victor stepped aside to let Sergei pass, one arm wrapped around Nadia's tiny waist and carrying her as effortlessly as Victor would an attaché case. She made a low murmur, but no words passed her lips. Her arms and legs hung as loose as her hair.

"Charming lady," Victor said as he slid onto the padded bench opposite Norimov.

The Russian sat back, and in doing so gave Victor the first indication of his mind-set: he was instinctively creating distance because he was afraid. Or pretending to be. Scared, or calculating and manipulative. There was no way of knowing.

"I hate bars like this," Norimov said. "We've adopted the West's pretension with a disturbing amount of relish. A bar should be a hole. It should be a dark, squalid place full of stinking, hairy men. You should go there to get drunk and talk nonsense and fight, not sip cocktails and pose half-naked." He sighed. "I didn't think you would come."

"You've already said that."

"Take it as an indicator of my surprise that you're here. I never thought I'd see you again."

"You said something similar when last we met."

"I did?" He sighed again. "You don't know it yet, and no one ever told me at your age, but eventually you'll reach a point in life where you have no new thoughts, you experience no new sensations. Everything you do, everything you say, you've done and said a thousand times before. And then you have the indignity of spending the rest of your days as a broken fucking record."

He pushed the martini glass to one side, using the back of his hand out of the same habit as Victor had. There were no other glasses on the table.

Norimov said, "I apologize for the language."

"There's no need."

"I forgot how you feel about it. I truly am sorry."

"It doesn't matter."

"What was it you used to say? Swearing is an expression of anger. When we swear we're admitting we've lost control. Something like that, right?"

"Something like that."

"Sounded like rubbish then. Now I'm not so sure. You might have a point. Your Russian is still excellent, by the way. I thought it might have suffered with your absence."

Victor didn't comment. He caught the gaze of a waitress who had finished serving a nearby table and motioned her over. He said to Norimov, "You don't mind if I eat, do you?"

The Russian looked shocked, but shook his head. "You never cease to amaze me, but be my guest."

"Hi," the waitress said.

Victor said, "Can I trouble you for a steak, please?"

"Of course you can. How do you want that cooked?"

"Extra rare."

The waitress raised her eyebrows at him. "*Extra* rare?"

"If it's not still mooing, then I'm sending it back."

She smiled, but he didn't know if she thought he was funny or crazy. Either was acceptable. "Anything to drink with that?"

"Black tea and a large bourbon—whatever's cheapest. No ice."

She scribbled the order down on a little pad. "Sure."

Norimov shook his head when she faced him. After she'd left, he said to Victor, "There's no reason to slum it. Drink whatever you want. I'll get the bill. I'd planned to cover all your expenses. You can have a bottle, if you want."

"That isn't necessary." He gestured to the empty tabletop before Norimov. "It's not like you to be without a Scotch."

"I don't drink."

"Since when?"

Norimov shrugged. "I don't know. A while."

"Then why meet in a bar?"

"You know why."

"I know two reasons why," Victor said. "But they're not mutually exclusive."

"Then why even come if you're convinced I want you dead?"

"Let's call it curiosity."

"Curiosity?"

"You know me well enough to know I'd expect an ambush. And the last thing you want is for me to think this is an ambush. It's far too soon for you to have forgotten what happened when you helped organize that attempt on my life."

Norimov shifted on his seat. "You must know I had no choice."

"You mean when you set me up? There's always a choice."

"If you really believe that, then why are you here?"

"I have nothing better to do."

"If that's true, Vasily, then I feel sorry for you."

Victor started to rise from his seat. "I'm happy to go and find something more fun, if you're so concerned about me. The manager of my hotel finishes her shift soon."

Norimov tensed. His eyes widened. "No, no. I'm sorry, Vasily. . . . Please stay."

Victor sat back down. Test complete and a little more knowledge of the situation acquired.

"It is still Vasily, isn't it?" Norimov asked.

"You know it's not. I haven't used that name for a long time."

Norimov placed his palms on the tabletop and shuffled into a more comfortable position. "You should stick with it. I like it. It suits you."

"It served me well enough in its time, but that time has passed. A name is just a tool and no tool endures forever."

"I don't know how you do it. Who do you see when you look in the mirror?"

"I see the specular reflection of light."

Norimov huffed and almost smiled. A few years ago

he would have laughed. Victor was curious as to what had changed.

"Let me pay for your meal. Please. It's the least I can do after you've come all this way to see me. I know you've put yourself at risk."

"Every day carries risk. This is no different."

"Regardless, I appreciate it." When Victor didn't respond, Norimov said, "So, what shall I call you?"

"Vasily, of course."

"'Of course,' you say, as though there is no other option, as if there is no other name you go by, as if there are not a hundred of them."

"One name is as good as any other."

"Tell that to my father," Norimov said. "He named me after Alexander the Great. He believed that a name defines who we are. He believed naming me Alexander would mean I strived for the greatest."

"And did you?"

Norimov smirked a little. "Maybe once. But it was a heavy mantle to wear across one's shoulders. Maybe I . . ." He stopped himself and regarded Victor for a moment. "I wonder what your father thought when you were named."

"I don't believe I had a father."

"Mother, then."

"I don't believe I had one of those either."

Norimov smiled. "How's that uncle of yours?"

"I buried him a long time ago."

"Did you . . . ?"

Victor shook his head.

Norimov said, "You should have."

Victor didn't respond.

"If I remember correctly you chose Vasily because of

the sniper. Yes? Vasily Zaytsev, wasn't it? I seem to recall you always had your head in some book about some old war or soldier."

"Reading is exercise for the mind."

"People used to be terrified of the name Vasily. Sometimes just saying it was enough to get what I wanted. You were a legend, my boy."

"The reason I left."

"I know." Norimov's gaze seemed to peer through him, as if he could read the lie as easily as he could lie himself. Then the Russian's face softened and he said, "It was the right thing to do. That reputation, that infamy, was going to get you killed eventually. Good that you realized that before it was too late."

"A lesson I'm never going to forget."

"You enjoyed it for a while, though, didn't you? Vasily the Killer. Death himself."

"The arrogance of youth."

"The young should be arrogant. If we're not full of ourselves when we don't know any better, then when can we be?" Norimov sat back. "You're a little bigger than when I last saw you. In a good way, I mean. You look good generally. You look healthy."

"You don't."

The Russian turned up a corner of his mouth. "I stopped drinking. I stopped taking care of myself. I stopped doing a lot of things."

"No wonder you look so happy."

He grunted. "And what about you, my boy? How are you spending your life? And don't say work. Even you take time off now and again."

"In the solace of wine, women, and the certain knowledge that life is pointless."

"That sounds uncharacteristically melancholy of you."

"You haven't seen the women."

Norimov chuckled—a deep, throaty sound.

Victor said, "I thought you'd given up laughing too."

The smile slipped from Norimov's face. Victor stared at him for a moment. Norimov looked old. He was some ten years Victor's senior, but in that instant he seemed double that. His skin had always been pale, but now it was also thin and fragile. His eyes, small and permanently shadowed in deep sockets, were dull. The only sign of life in them was pain and fear.

"What's this about, Alek?"

Norimov didn't answer straightaway. His lips parted and he inhaled, but only a sigh escaped them. He tried again, and said, "Someone wants me dead."

· Chapter 11 ·

Victor said, "I know how they feel."

"I'm being serious."

"So am I."

The Russian stared back. He wasn't angry. He was sad. Sad at the truth in the words. Victor had never seen him like this.

"Tell me," he said.

Norimov nodded and reached down to the seat next to him. He picked up a folded newspaper and unfolded it onto the table between them, revealing the back side of a sheet of photographic paper. He gestured toward it.

Victor didn't need to use just his fingernails to avoid leaving fingerprints on the paper, but he did so anyway. He didn't want Norimov to know that he regularly coated his hands in a silicone solution that dried to leave a transparent waterproof barrier on his skin that prevented oil from his fingertips leaving prints behind on whatever he touched. Norimov knew more about Victor's past than he liked anyone to know, and he didn't want that knowledge updated.

The light caught the glossy surface as Victor flipped it over. It was a black-and-white print, shot from an elevated position looking down on the entrance to a restaurant on the opposite side of the street. Victor knew the establishment. It was one of Norimov's businesses, or at least it had been in the days when Victor called Russia home—as much as anywhere would ever be known as such. It was a daytime shot of a car pulled up outside the restaurant's entrance. A tall, heavy man was approaching the vehicle, coming from inside the restaurant: Norimov. Another, bigger man—his driver or bodyguard—was holding the car's near-side rear door open for him.

It could have been a surveillance photograph taken by the St. Petersburg police or Russian domestic intelligence. But it wasn't, because of the Cyrillic script that had been scrawled across it in red marker.

"Smert," Norimov said. "Death."

"I know what it means." Victor put the photograph down. "Which of your rivals sent it?"

Norimov shrugged. "Any of them. All of them. I don't know. But it doesn't have to be another outfit. This could be personal. It could be anyone. Who knows how many people I've wronged? I'm talking to one of them right this moment." Victor sat still. "Maybe ten years ago I had some dipshit dealer executed for ripping me off. Now his kid's all grown up and he wants payback for his dead daddy."

"It must have happened before. You've made more enemies than me. You're still here, though, aren't you?"

"This is different."

"Why?"

Norimov hesitated. He opened his mouth to speak, but the waitress returning with Victor's order interrupted him. She placed the steak down before Victor and then the tumbler of bourbon and the tea next to his plate. Cutlery and condiments followed. He thanked her.

Norimov stared at the steak for a moment. "I remember you preferred it more burned than bloody." He met Victor's gaze.

"You remember right."

"Extra rare so you would get it quickly?"

"Correct," Victor said and lifted his glass.

"Why the cheap liquor?"

"I hate to waste the good stuff."

Norimov frowned. "Waste it?"

"That's right."

The frown lines deepened. "I don't . . ." He looked at Sergei standing nearby, watching, but from a discreet distance. Then he looked at the back door through which Victor had entered.

For cheap whiskey it really wasn't bad. Victor kept the tumbler in hand.

Norimov clicked his fingers to get Sergei's attention and motioned to the bar's rear entrance.

"Everything okay?" Victor asked.

Norimov ignored him. He spoke to Sergei. "Have Ivan come in here."

Sergei stood to pass on the order to someone else so he could stay in close proximity to his boss. He shouted at the nearby man to be heard over the patrons.

Victor's untouched steak cooled before him. He held the glass in a high grip, his thumb and index finger circling the circumference near the rim.

The back door opened. The bigger of the two men Victor had knocked out entered, hurrying but stumbling, his expression full of urgency and anger but his sense not quite returned.

"What did you do?" Norimov asked, head pivoting to look at Victor.

"What I had to."

Sergei turned too as his hand slipped inside his coat. He made eye contact with Victor in time to see him hurl the tumbler.

The heavy bottom of the glass struck Sergei in the face. His head snapped back and blood splattered on the table next to him. He stumbled and fell into it.

Victor grabbed the steaming cup of black tea—served hotter than coffee—and tossed it into the path of one of Norimov's men as he shot from his chair and rushed to intercept. He screeched and put his hands to his scalded face.

Patrons closest to the commotion sat frozen with shock or backed away. Those farther from the melee were slower to react, the volume of loud chatter and merriment disguising the sounds of violence.

In his time as a government agent Norimov had been fast for his size, but that had been some fifteen years ago. Now he was older, fatter, and slower. He was standing only after Victor had grabbed the steak knife from the tabletop, reaching for his own weapon only as Victor flipped over the table between them, gripping the gun in the underarm rig only as Victor sprang toward him.

With steroid-bloated thugs guarding him for the best part of a decade Norimov was so out of practice that he was powerless to stop Victor from disarming him of the pistol, locking his arm behind his back, and putting the sharp tip of the steak knife to his throat, directly over the carotid.

"*Wait!*" Norimov yelled to his uninjured men, up from their seats and powering forward to aid their boss.

The volume of Norimov's voice commanded the attention of the whole bar. Shocked and horrified faces stared. Norimov's men did as ordered, coming no closer but tensed and ready to charge.

"Are you going to kill me?" Norimov asked.

"That's the only reason I'm here."

A swallow. Heavy breathing. "Then why haven't you yet?"

"I'm in no particular rush."

The Russian was breathing fast because he was scared, but he was keeping his composure because he knew he would never see another dawn if he succumbed to panic. "If you kill me you'll never get out of here alive."

"I killed you just by ordering dinner. Now that I have a gun, I'm pretty sure I'll be okay."

"Pretty sure?"

"I was being modest."

"Just hear me out," Norimov said. "Afterward if you want me dead, I'll make it easy for you."

"I'm not sure you could make it any easier."

Victor could feel Norimov's pulse vibrating through the knife.

"Please, Vasily. Hear me out. Please."

"You once told me that you'd rather die than beg."

"I would. If the choice was to beg you for mercy or have that blade buried in my neck, I would gladly thrust myself upon it."

Victor hesitated. He resisted asking the obvious question and Norimov swallowed, then answered it.

"But I'm not begging for my life. I'm begging for the life of my daughter."

· Chapter 12 ·

Victor, gaze fixed on Norimov's guards, said, "You don't have a daughter."

"She's Eleanor's daughter. From her first marriage. She had her long before she met me."

Victor kept the knife point against Norimov's pulsing carotid artery. "You mentioned no stepdaughter to me."

"I never invited you into my home either. That didn't mean I slept on the street."

It was a good point. Victor's eyes flicked between the Russian guys, telling each one he was watching and would give them no opportunity to act without him knowing.

"Do you mind taking this blade from my throat?" Norimov asked.

"It stays. You're auditioning for your life, so keep talking."

"Okay," Norimov said. "Are you really surprised I didn't tell you about Gisele? I always considered you a friend, Vasily, but that didn't mean I forgot you were a paid murderer."

Victor nodded. He understood. He would never trust

anyone in this business with personal information, least of all about a loved one. But even so, he didn't like it that Norimov had not trusted him in return.

"Under no circumstances would I have hurt your family."

Norimov didn't respond to that. Whether he believed Victor or not was irrelevant now. Sergei and the other heavies were still braced and ready to attack should Victor thrust the knife into Norimov's neck. People were filing out of the bar's front and rear entrances. Some were too scared to move. Others were enjoying the show.

Victor said, "If you didn't trust me enough to tell me about your daughter back then, when I had no reason to harm you, why tell me now when I have all the reason I could ever need?"

"Because this threat is not limited to me. You know how things work here. They aren't just coming to kill me. They want to destroy me. If they have their way they will erase me from existence and anyone I care about too. They'll kill my men. They'll burn down my businesses. After I'm gone they'll rip out the tongue of anyone who dares mention my name. I'll be nothing but a memory. The best way to do that is to take Gisele and use her to get to me. Which will work, won't it? If they have her I'll do anything they want to save her. But that won't work, will it? After they've used her to get to me, then they'll kill her too. I could cut off my own head and they still wouldn't show her mercy. That Gisele does not share my blood is irrelevant. She is my stepdaughter—my daughter—and she is marked for death because she had the misfortune of having a mother who married a criminal."

Victor remained silent.

"Now do you understand why I asked you to come?"

"Yes," Victor said, easing the knifepoint away from Norimov's neck. "You've convinced me. I'm not going to kill you tonight. I can't promise the same will be true tomorrow."

The tension left Norimov's muscles. He looked over the sparse crowd of remaining patrons and bar staff. "Maybe we should find somewhere else to continue this conversation."

"Agreed."

Norimov stepped away from the booth.

"What are you doing?" Victor asked. Before Norimov could respond, he added, "You said you'd pay for my meal."

Norimov's eyebrows rose and his lips parted, but he reached for his wallet.

"Leave a nice tip," Victor said.

• • •

An alley lay off the street at the back of the bar. It was an uneven, twisting gap between two tall buildings. Bags of rubbish were strewn throughout. Victor stood with Norimov in the shadows at its center. Even in the darkness Norimov looked tired and scared. Victor wasn't used to seeing him that way. He didn't like it, but it reminded him why he had no one in his life. He would never look as Norimov did now.

"Whoever is out there thirsting for my blood can take it, for all I care. My whole life I've been a criminal. Whether I worked for the crooks who run this country or for myself. My list of offenses is too long to remember. I am, and always have been, a wicked man. When my death comes, however it comes, I will know with utmost certainty that I deserve it. But not Gisele. She has not committed a wrong in her entire life. When she was young, when I first knew her mother, I kept my business a secret from her. But children are curious and eventually she worked out how her stepfather could afford to buy her everything she desired. Then she hated me. She's never stopped hating me."

"If you don't know who wants you dead, why contact me?"

"I want you to protect her."

"How can I protect her if you don't know where the threat is coming from?"

"Because you are a killer. Because every time you go to work you dance on Death's scythe. Because your enemies are everywhere and your allies nonexistent, yet still you stand before me. True, I don't know who will come for Gisele and me, but I do know that when they do you can kill them before they kill her."

"You have plenty of men working for you. Why do you need me?"

"When you last worked for me I had more than thirty good men in this city and beyond. Men who would risk their lives for me, not just because I paid them, but out of respect. When you came to see me at my train yard there were no more than twenty who would still show me such loyalty. Now I have ten, just ten men whom I can rely on to follow my orders. Of those, only two I trust enough to be alone with. Once I was a general with an army. Now I'm a thug in a suit, trying to convince the other thugs that I'm still worth protecting. I have already been usurped by those with bigger balls and stronger stomachs. The Aleksandr Norimov you once knew would laugh at what I have become. Too old, too weak to rule. Now the vultures circling overhead are not patient enough to wait until I'm dead before they swoop down to feast on my remains."

"You're asking the wrong man to pity you."

"Asking you for pity would be like asking a fox to guard the hens. I'm not asking for that. I'm asking for help."

"Then sell everything you can, take Gisele, and go. Get out of St. Petersburg. Leave Russia far behind. They won't find you if you know what you're doing; I'll tell you how. And they won't try if you don't give them a reason."

Norimov was shaking his head even before Victor had finished. "No. I have to stay here. I must learn who has initiated this vendetta; otherwise Gisele will never be safe. I'm not like you. I can't live the life of a fugitive and I won't ask Gisele to either. And if I did opt to run, she would never come with me. She would not see past her hatred of me to be convinced of the need until she was staring into the barrel of the gun pointed at her head."

"Then you put both your lives at risk."

"Not if you do as I ask." Norimov stared at Victor. "Not if you protect her while I do what I have to do. I have been a bastard all of my life. When I first fell in love with Eleanor, I did so despite her daughter. I never cared for Gisele. I never cared that she grew to hate me. But if I could change anything, I would be a better father to her. I would . . ." He took a breath to compose himself. "I can't change the past. But I can try to change the future. Once this threat has been dealt with, then I'm getting out of this life for good. I'll go somewhere far away and never put Gisele at risk again."

"There's no guarantee you'll find out who is coming after you, nor that you can neutralize the threat even if you do."

"Do you think I don't already know that, Vasily? But

I have to try. My organization may be a crippled shadow of its former power, but I still have eyes and ears spread throughout this city. Given enough time and enough expenditure I can uncover any secret. But I can't do that and protect Gisele at the same time."

"And what happens when you learn who your enemies are? How do you defeat them when by your own admission you have only a fraction of your former strength?"

Norimov said nothing, but his eyes answered.

"I can't fight a war for you," Victor said. "Even if I wanted to."

"Then don't. Just keep Gisele safe until it ends. Whatever that end is."

Victor looked away. "You're asking me to risk my life for someone I've never met, on the request of someone who conspired to have me killed."

"No," Norimov said, reaching out a hand to grip Victor's shoulder but stopping himself—whether through fear of what Victor would do should contact be made or simple hesitation, Victor didn't know. "No," Norimov said again. That's not what I'm asking. At least, that's not how I'm asking."

"You're not making any sense."

"I know you won't help me after what I did to you, even if the distaste of an innocent's death could pierce that black heart of yours."

"Then why ask?"

"Because my dead wife can't ask you instead."

Victor stood as still as he could. He knew what was coming.

Norimov continued: "You have no loyalty to me any longer, I get that. I understand it. I don't blame you. I always told you to never forgive a betrayal. No doubt that lesson has kept you alive more than once. But what did Eleanor ever do to warrant you turning your back on her daughter?"

Victor didn't answer. Eleanor's beautiful face flashed in his mind's eye. Smiling, as always.

"She was kind to you, was she not?"

"That's because she didn't know who I was—who I am."

"And she died still believing you were the good man you pretended to be. I did not tell her otherwise."

"Thank you for that."

Norimov was silent for a moment. The soles of his shoes scraped on the ground as he paced. When he turned back, he said, "She talked about you from time to time."

Victor waited. It took all of his will to keep his thoughts on the present exchange to stop doors opening in his mind that he had shut and locked long ago. He didn't want Norimov to see any more than he wanted himself to feel.

"She didn't understand why you had to leave the way you did. Just like she didn't understand why you never came back."

Norimov stepped a little closer. The instinct to back away was strong. Victor managed to fight it. "From time to time in the first couple of years after you'd gone, although she always denied it, I would catch her crying. I worked out why only once she'd died. At least, I didn't allow myself to before then."

Victor did everything in his power not to blink. In a way, it didn't matter. Norimov knew. Whatever Victor did or said made no difference now.

The Russian stood close enough for Victor to feel the warmth of his breath. "Tell me, Vasily, if Eleanor was alive and standing before you as I am now, would you turn down her request for help? If she stared into your eyes and begged you to save her daughter's life, would you even pause long enough to take a single breath?"

"I . . . I need time to think about this."

"No," Norimov hissed, poking Victor in the chest with a finger he should have snapped but could not bring himself to. "There is no time for fucking deliberation. You answer me now, you piece of shit, or you walk away from here and condemn my daughter—Eleanor's daughter—to death."

He had looked sad and scared earlier, but now he was desperate and angry. He was no longer afraid of Victor because he feared for Gisele above himself. He hated Victor and needed him. Victor could hear the shuffle of footsteps and crunch of snow on the side street between the alleyway and the bar where Sergei and another of Norimov's men waited. They were anxious because of their boss's raised voice.

"Answer me," Norimov yelled.

Saliva struck Victor's face. Around him, the wind howled. The sky above was black and starless.

"Answer me!" Norimov yelled again.

Victor did.

· Chapter 13 ·

"Okay." Victor nodded. "For Eleanor."

"Thank you," Norimov said, words expelled on the rush of a heavy sigh. "Thank you."

"Don't thank me. I'm doing this for Eleanor."

"I don't care why you're doing it. Just that you are."

"Where is Gisele?"

Norimov shook his head. "I . . . I don't know. She lives in London, as far as I'm aware."

"As far as you're aware?"

"She hasn't spoken to me in years, and I don't know where she is. I tried to contact her straightaway but I can't reach her. She's missing."

"Then you need to consider she might already be dead."

"No," Norimov hissed through bared teeth. "Not yet. She's still alive, I know she is. If those bastards who sent me that photograph had killed her, they would mail me a box containing her heart. And if they had her, I would already have received the footage of them torturing her. Until that happens, I have to believe she's out there and okay."

"How am I meant to protect her when you don't know where she is?"

"You can track her down, Vasily. I know you can. Not even the most elusive of targets could hide from you when you had their scent. Go to London and find my daughter before those animals do."

Victor nodded. "After I've done this, I never want to hear from you again."

"Of course. Anything you want. Just please help my daughter."

"I'll take the first flight in the morning. Let me have a number I can contact you on. I'll update you as and when I learn anything."

"Yes, yes. Absolutely. We'll do it your way."

"Tell me exactly what has taken place since you received the threat."

"As soon as the photograph arrived I sent one of my men to London. He's been looking for Gisele for the past week, but he's an enforcer, not a detective. When you arrive, he can help you. He'll meet you at the airport. I have a place where you can stay there. Everything will be provided for you."

"No. I'll make my own arrangements. You can give me his number and I'll contact him after I've arrived."

"There's no reason for you to be concerned about me or my men."

"Do you think I would have agreed to find Gisele if I was concerned?"

"Then why the precautions?"

"Because I would be dead without them."

Norimov listened, then nodded. "Sure, I understand. I can give you money to help with your expenses. I don't know how long this will take. I don't want you out of pocket on my account."

"I'm not doing it for you, remember?"

"I'm not likely to forget. If Eleanor was here, she would insist and you would take the money instead of offending her."

Norimov reached into his coat. He had a shrink-wrapped brick of hundred-dollar bills. A glance told Victor the brick contained one hundred bills. "It's clean."

"Regardless," Victor said. "I don't carry that much cash."

"Your choice," Norimov said, putting the brick away again.

"You do realize that they might have her already? They might be keeping her alive while they smuggle her back to St. Petersburg. Better leverage that way, and here is where they are strongest. That's what I would do. I would call you and make her scream down the phone for you to save her, and I would tell you to come alone—and you would."

Norimov put his face in his hands. "For all my crimes, I have never been so sadistic. I am a sickly lamb surrounded by wolves because my compassion is weakness. Ironic, because my criminality bred Gisele's hatred of me. Had I been crueler, she would now be safe."

"Almost certainly," Victor agreed. "You forgot the first rule."

The Russian stared at him, red-eyed and weak. "Survival before everything. I know. I did forget. I allowed myself a life. But is it worth it, Vasily? Is surviving enough?"

Victor thought about all the corpses he had seen, all the dead faces of those who had failed to survive because he had instead.

"Each breath is worth it."

For Eleanor

London, United Kingdom

· Chapter 14 ·

International airports were among Victor's least favorite places. Almost without exception they were teeming with armed security guards and cameras. Each time he passed through passport control he risked being compromised. Either because the identity he was traveling under had been flagged in connection with one of his previous jobs or it had ceased to be clean for reasons beyond his control, or his frequent surgeries had failed to outwit the continued advancements in facial-recognition technology, or a keen-eyed member of staff identified that he simply wasn't *right*.

He'd been in London within the past year as part of a job, but only to discuss it. The time before that, the visit had been what could be called a personal project, and though he'd been involved in serious criminal activity, no one had lost his life by his hand. Traveling anywhere he'd operated before carried risk, but in this instance visiting London posed minimal risk. He had a strong suspicion that once he left again, he wouldn't be returning for a long time.

He arrived at London City Airport after a smooth Rossiya flight that took a little more than four hours, getting out of his seat when about half of the cabin had already departed, to reduce the chances he would be picked out for scrutiny. Those in a hurry to disembark were more likely to be noticed, as were those in no hurry. The center of the bell curve was where Victor always preferred to lurk.

A smiling woman asked him a few routine questions as she checked his documents and smiled wider after she'd wished him a pleasant stay. He circled the terminal twice as part of his routine countersurveillance, paying particular attention to those waiting with a view of where his arrival lounge connected with the terminal proper.

He had an overnight bag but no other luggage. Victor preferred to travel light. He would travel with no luggage at all if not for the fact it would mark him as someone to pay attention to. The case was a cheap knockoff purchased from a market trader in St. Petersburg. It contained similarly counterfeit clothes. Victor had no intention of wearing them or keeping hold of the case any longer than necessary. Though the case and the clothes had not been used as part of any criminal activity, they connected him to St. Petersburg, to Russia. Therefore they were compromised. Not solely because of his relationship with Norimov or his enemies in the country, but because they were evidence of his movements. Any connection with his past, whether a day ago or ten years ago, had the potential to cause him harm.

A Polish woman fixed him a coffee and he sipped it while sitting on an uncomfortable plastic chair. Abandoning the half-empty cup on the table, he found a pay phone near an information kiosk, inserted coins, and used the knuckle of his left middle finger to punch out the international dialing code, then number.

It took a few seconds for the line to connect.

A voice said, *"Privet?"*

"I'm in London," Victor replied in English. "But we might have a problem."

"What kind of a problem?" Norimov asked, switching languages too, tentative but curious.

Victor watched travelers walk by, wearing shorts and T-shirts, limbs browned by holidays in sunnier climes.

He said, "You need to answer a question for me, and you need to be honest."

"Of course."

"Did you tell anyone to wait for me at the airport?"

The answer was a resolute "No."

"Okay," Victor said. "That's good and bad."

"Why both?"

"It's good that you respected my wishes. But bad because it means a third party is interested in me and knows enough about my movements to have a watcher in place for my arrival."

"A watcher?" There was hesitation in Norimov's voice.

Victor looked over to where a large, dark-haired man in a padded jacket and jeans loitered near a concession stand.

"Don't worry," Victor said as he watched the man trying to act casual. "I'll deal with it."

More hesitation. "What do you mean . . . you'll *deal* with it?"

"I mean I'll neutralize the threat, of course. I'll call again when I've news about Gisele's whereabouts."

"Wait."

Victor did, then said, "Is there something you want to tell me?"

"Wait," Norimov said again. "Don't hang up. You don't have to neutralize any threat. He's my man."

"I know that. Did you honestly think I wouldn't know that the second I saw a pumped-up gorilla hanging around near my arrival lounge? I'm offended you have such a low opinion of me."

"I . . . I don't know what I thought. I wasn't thinking. I should have known better. I'm sorry. I truly am. I panicked, okay? I just wanted to make sure you arrived. That's all. You'll appreciate that I'm on the edge here, don't you? Dmitri wasn't going to follow you, I swear."

Victor said, "He couldn't follow me if his life depended on it. When you hire people for their muscle mass you really shouldn't be surprised when they stand out in a crowd. I could smell the stink of steroids in the air before I even saw him. Where's the other one?"

Silence on the line.

"Don't make me ask you again, Alek. You have two men in London. I'm looking at one of them. I'm asking you where the other is. Don't even think about lying. Gisele's missing. You haven't been simply praying that I'd show. You said yourself that you didn't believe I would meet you. You also said you have ten good men on your payroll. There were eight guarding you in that bar. That leaves two. Which isn't a lot to send if you're concerned about your daughter. But I take it the two in London now are the only ones who could get visas in time, or at all."

Norimov took his time responding. When he did, "I'm sorry" was all he managed to say.

"You said that already."

"I'm not trying to f— I'm not trying to screw you

around, Vasily. I'm scared. I'm not thinking straight. I should have told you about Dmitri and Yigor. I'm sorry. I know you work alone. I didn't want to risk you saying no. They won't bother you. They won't get in your way."

This time Victor didn't respond.

"Are you still going to find Gisele for me?" Norimov asked after a moment.

"If I were here for you I would now be boarding the first flight out, and the next time you heard from me would be when I was standing over your bed in the middle of the night." A pause. "But I'm not here for you, am I?"

"I'm not likely to forget."

"But that doesn't mean I will tolerate your interference. Consider this your first warning. Do you understand what the second will be?"

"Yes. I—"

Victor hung up.

Fourteen seconds later the large man with dark hair fumbled to retrieve his phone from a pocket of his jeans. He held it to his ear and Victor watched the movements of his lips.

Privet? Yes?

Then: *Nyet, kone no, on ne videl menja.* No, of course he hasn't seen me.

The man listened for a moment, then glanced at Victor. *Oder'mo. On smotrit prjamo na menja.* Shit. He's looking straight at me.

Victor watched as the man ended the call and forced the phone back into his jeans pocket. They were tight. Victor approached the man. He stared at Victor as he crossed the space, his back straightening and his shoulders squaring, maximizing his already significant height and bulk as a show of defiance and ego.

"Dmitri, right?" The man responded with a single slow nod. "Do you speak English?"

Dmitri nodded again. "We met two years ago in St. Petersburg. Your name is Vasily. You broke two of my ribs."

His English was good, as Victor had expected. Dmitri wouldn't be much use searching for Gisele in London otherwise.

"I meant to break only one," Victor replied.

Dmitri frowned. He had a wide but low forehead and the same prominent eyebrow bone from growth-hormone abuse as the guys outside the bar. They were probably gym buddies.

He said, "I had to have two surgeries to fix them. And they're not properly fixed. I have to sleep on my back or on my left side. I snore if I sleep on my back and my girl kicks me in the shin until I wake up and stop. Sometimes, when I'm already asleep, I will roll over onto my right. I don't know it at the time, but then I wake up and I'm in agony. The pain is unbelievable. It's the nature of the break, they tell me."

"I could have killed you. I didn't. You should be thanking me."

"Fuck you," he said with a small smile.

"It's good to catch up, but we really don't have time for this while Gisele is missing. I take it you've been trying to find her—checking where she lives, speaking to friends, and so on?" A nod. "Good, then you can help me."

"Why would I want to help you?"

"This is about Norimov's daughter, not me. He sent me here because you've failed to locate her. Either you can assist me or you can refuse. Whatever you decide, I'll find her. If you help me track her down you can share the credit, assuming she's still alive. If you don't help me and I find her too late, then Norimov will know you put your personal feelings before the life of his daughter."

"You're an asshole."

"That's what people always tell me."

"I don't like you."

"No one likes me."

Dmitri took a step closer. "I don't take orders from you."

Victor could smell the coffee on the man's breath. "I never said that you did. But I recommend you stand down before you say something you'll feel compelled to back up."

"Do you remember what happened when you fucked up my ribs?" He didn't wait for an answer. "We just asked you to leave, that was all. No big deal. You pretended to comply. You acted like you were an okay guy. Then you hit me with that cheap shot."

"A succinct summation."

"You're a coward. I didn't know that then, but now I do. So I'm never going to give you that same opportunity again."

"Good for you. But you probably shouldn't have told me that. Better if your opponent doesn't know your intentions. Like when I broke your ribs."

Dmitri drew a sharp inhalation of air through his nose. It wasn't quite a snort, but equally unpleasant. "It doesn't matter. All that matters is you're nothing but a little man who acts like pussy. In a fair fight, I'd snap you in half."

"Then I guess it's good for me that I never fight fair." Victor stared into Dmitri's eyes. "So, if we're done with the bravado, what's it to be? Are you going to help me or not?"

Dmitri edged closer: aggressive but short of an out-right challenge. He wasn't about to start a fight in an airport, whatever his level of dislike. "I'll help you find Gisele, assuming you're not bullshitting that you can. But I'm doing this for Norimov, because he's a good man. I'm not doing it for you."

"I appreciate that. I'd also appreciate it if you watch your language."

"Excuse me?"

"Don't swear."

Dmitri thought about this for a moment, then shrugged as if it didn't matter. He said, "No swearing, sure. And I'll do whatever you need me to do. Then when this mess is all sorted out"—a little smile played on his face—"we can . . . settle our differences."

"Sure," Victor replied. "If you're that keen to sleep on your back for the rest of your life, I'm more than happy to oblige you."

· Chapter 15 ·

Victor's hotel was located only a few minutes' drive from the airport. Dmitri drove fast, but not fast enough to draw attention. He was urged on by purpose but not to the detriment of caution. He may have been looking for his boss's daughter, yet he was still a career criminal. Victor ignored protocol and sat beside him in the passenger's seat, instead of in the back. It gave him less protection and fewer options should Dmitri's animosity take on a darker hue, but he wanted the Russian to work with him, not against him, and the less he did to potentially antagonize the man, the sooner he could effectively use him.

Victor spent the short journey asking questions and paying close attention to the answers Dmitri gave. Much of the information he had already garnered from Norimov. The hunt had not produced any leads. Dmitri had canvassed the local area, stopping people in the street to show them an old photograph of Gisele and to ask if anyone had seen her. They hadn't.

"The rest of the time I've been driving around, trying to spot her. I didn't know what else to do."

Victor nodded. "Has anyone else been looking for her? Other Russians?"

Dmitri shook his head. His neck was so thick Victor was almost surprised he was capable of even the slightest rotation. "I haven't seen anyone. What does that mean?"

"If they're coming after Norimov, they have strength and resources. It wouldn't be hard for them to find out that Gisele lives in London. So either they're here looking for her too and you didn't see them, or they've found her already."

Dmitri sighed and chewed on his bottom lip. "Bad times."

"Have you checked her home?"

"She's not there."

"I know. I mean, have you been inside?"

Dmitri shook his head. "It's a flat in a building. People are there. We'd have to break the doors down. No keys. Norimov said not to. He said keep the profile low."

Victor nodded again.

"What do we do first?"

"I'll check in and take a quick shower. After that, we start looking for Gisele."

The hotel was located in a cluster of other hotels, all serving the nearby airport and a huge exhibition center. Dmitri pulled up outside the front entrance.

Victor said, "I'll be about half an hour. Use that time to get me a good-quality multitool and a box of big paperclips."

Dmitri stared, confused, but decided against asking why. He shrugged. "Sure. Whatever you want. Multitool and paperclips. Big ones."

• • •

Inside, the hotel was as spare and modern as its glass-and-steel facade suggested. Victor checked in, declining the offer of having someone take his suitcase to his room, and took the stairs up to the third floor. He'd required only a standard room to sleep in, but he had other requirements that necessitated a junior suite. He placed his suitcase on the floor next to the bed, examined the suite briefly to make sure it fulfilled his needs, and went into the bathroom to turn on the shower. He unwrapped a packet of soap and dropped it into the bath beneath the flow of water. He unscrewed the tops of the mini bottles of shampoo and shower gel. He poured a quarter of each into the bath. He left the shower running and took the freestanding magnifying mirror from the bathroom. He opened the curtains and placed it on the windowsill, adjusting its position so it sat exactly where he needed it and with the mirror at the required angle.

His suitcase contained some clothes and other effects, which he distributed throughout the room—a suit and shirts hanging from the door of the walk-in wardrobe; shaving kit, toothbrush, and toiletries in the bathroom; underwear on the bed.

He unfolded a bath towel and briefly held it underneath the shower's flow. He dropped it on the tiled floor. He shook a can of deodorant, pointed the nozzle upward at the ceiling and sprayed for a count of six.

His suitcase contained, aside from the items he'd already taken from it, an attaché case, which he removed. He positioned the suitcase on the bed and zipped it closed. He took the attaché case with him as he left the suite.

By the time he'd reached the ground floor he still had twenty minutes of his half hour remaining. He headed away from the main entrance on its east side and walked to the hotel's business center, passed it, and carried on past the fitness suite. He pushed open an exit that took him to the hotel's south side, where a trio of hotel employees on a break were smoking cigarettes and drinking hot drinks in the chill sunshine. An elevated railway with a road underneath lay before him.

He crossed the road to the other side and walked between the sparse line of trees that marked the boundary to another hotel.

He went inside via its north entrance and made his way to the lobby, where he smiled at the thin gentleman behind the front desk.

"I'd like to check in, please."

His room was on the fourth floor. It was a pleasant enough guest room but nowhere near the standard of the other hotel. He spent a minute familiarizing himself with its layout and then he opened the curtains. The view was a poor one. He looked out at the elevated railway to the north. Between its tall concrete supports he could see the south facade of the first hotel. Directly in his eyeline lay the hotel's third-floor windows. Some had their curtains open. Others were closed.

Only one had a freestanding mirror positioned on the windowsill.

• • •

The warehouse used by Norimov's men as a safe house was located in an industrial park in East London. It was a dirty building with decades of grime and pollution staining the brickwork. It contained more than sixteen thousand square feet of space that had once been used to store plumbing and heating equipment and goods. According to Dmitri, it had been empty for some years. He didn't know if Norimov owned it or rented it, or if they were there illegally. A huge corrugated steel gate stood on the south facade, high and wide enough for trucks to back into. Next to the gate were two stories of offices that protruded from the otherwise square warehouse.

The second of Norimov's men introduced himself as Yigor. He wore synthetic sports trousers and a worn sweatshirt. His shoes were big white trainers that glowed in the light. He was a weight lifter, like Dmitri, like all of Norimov's men. But he was the biggest of them. His arms were as thick as Victor's thighs. His hair was long and greasy and his face was pinched and fat. Eyes the color of the Baltic Sea stared out from hooded, half-closed lids. He smelled as bad as he looked, but was always smiling. It was a happy but half-crazed grin that showed an upside-down mountain range of uneven teeth.

"You the bad man, yes?" he said in broken English, his South St. Petersburg accent thick and coarse.

Victor said, "That's me."

They shook hands. Yigor's hands were massively broad, making his fingers seem short and stubby. They were rough and calloused from years of lifting heavy weights.

"I heard all about you," Yigor said. "Dmitri and Sergei say you baddest mother."

"You shouldn't believe everything you hear."

Yigor's grin widened. "I like you. I can tell you are the bad man. Like me. Bad men together, yes?"

"We'll be best of friends in no time."

The warehouse's office annex had its own entrance—a glass door set perpendicular to the steel gate. A reception area stood on the other side, with a long, fixed counter topped with glass. The carpet had once been blue but was now stained with dirt and oil. The polystyrene ceiling tiles were stained yellow with nicotine from the days when smoking was allowed in the workplace. Downstairs, the interior office walls were wallpaper-covered aluminum, fronted by plate glass and glass doors. Some had lowered strip blinds. Most offices were kitted out with desks and chairs and filing cabinets—all cheap furnishings that had been well used in their time. There were a number of old computers, printers, and other obsolete and worthless pieces of electronic equipment, and a telephone landline in every room, discolored from age and use. The ground-floor offices had been left untouched, but Dmitri and Yigor had occupied the first floor. The offices there were similar to those below, except much larger and therefore less numerous.

There was also a boardroom and kitchen. Norimov's men had claimed an office each to serve as a bedroom, complete with folding cot, sleeping bag, and other small luxuries. What had once been a boardroom now served as a communal area for Dmitri and Yigor. One half of the large oval table was covered in soiled pizza boxes, greasy take-out containers, empty cigarette packs, crushed cans, and warped bottles of soft drinks.

"You can have that one," Yigor said, pointing to an empty room. "No need to pay for hotel. Save your money. I will get you a bed. Norimov pays for everything. Then you have more of the cash to spend on the women. This town is full of it. Buy them fancy cocktail that tastes of kids' sweets; they like you lots. Good deal, yes? Norimov pay you plenty of the money, yes?"

Victor shook his head. "There is no payment. This is not a job."

Yigor pulled a face. "Then you crazy. This war is going to be danger everywhere. Norimov's enemies going to kill everyone he knows. They kill you too, if they can. You should ask for lots of money. So, you want a bed?"

Victor said, "I'll pass."

"Suit self. Waste all your money on that hotel."

Two hotels, Victor thought.

They kept their outside jackets on inside the warehouse because there was no heating. There was electricity, so there were at least lights. Most of the bulbs and fluorescent tubes were missing or burned out, however, leaving many offices unlit and large areas of the warehouse floor in darkness. One corner had a collection of crates, pallets, and chains that served as makeshift weights for the two Russians to work out with.

Yigor said, "What do we do first, Mr. Bad Man?"

"Take me to where she works."

Chapter 16

Norimov hadn't spoken to his daughter in years, but he kept track of her life as much as he was able. She went by her mother's maiden name: Maynard. Gisele was twenty-two years old and had studied law in London and was a couple of months into her yearlong pupilage at a law firm prior to qualifying as a barrister. The firm was located in the heart of the city's financial district. Dmitri drove. Victor opted to sit in the backseat because he didn't want to be surrounded by giants. The drive was short and Yigor told jokes for the entire journey. He was the only one who laughed at them.

"I've already tried here," Dmitri said as he found a spot to pull in to.

"That's good," Victor replied. "When?"

Dmitri shrugged as he applied the emergency brake. "Soon as I arrived in London."

"A lot can change in a week. Wait for me."

"Sure." He relaxed in the seat and set the back of his head onto the rest. "I sleep."

"Don't get a ticket."

Dmitri didn't respond. Victor climbed out of the relative quiet of the car interior into the noise of London: traffic and people creating the urgent breaths of the city around him. He didn't like London but he didn't dislike it either. Its ancient identity had been warped and changed and divided into many disjointed pieces. It was huge and dense but low and suffocating. There was so much to enjoy but so much not to. From an operational perspective, he couldn't ask for a better metropolis. It was always busy, always congested with crowds to hide among, and intercut with irregular alleys and side streets. The saturation of CCTV cameras was far from ideal, but British police officers did not carry firearms as standard.

He crossed the street, passing slow-moving cars and rounding a red bus collecting passengers. The buildings were all grand and centuries old, adding an air of importance, respectability, and wealth. He walked at a leisurely pace, taking a circuitous route through neighboring throughways, searching for watchers. A tall order in such a busy area, but if Norimov's enemies had put her workplace under surveillance, those watchers would be Russian gangsters. Every person in this part of the city was either a suited professional, overworked and always rushing, or a tourist, walking slowly and taking photographs. Watchers would stand out.

He saw none. He wasn't sure what that meant. If they already had Gisele, they wouldn't need to look out for her at her place of business, in the hope of kidnapping her on her way to or from work. But after making Norimov aware of the threat, they would expect his forces to mobilize. If their intention was to wipe him out, it would be smart to ambush anyone he had sent to look for his daughter.

Low stone steps led up from the street. Victor used his knuckles to push through the revolving brass-and-glass door. The lobby was vast and high-roofed and starkly modern. He approached a curved counter and explained to the receptionist he was a visitor to Gisele's law firm. After using his left hand to sign the guestbook, he was given a pass and used it to get through the electronic turnstiles that shielded the elevators. A big security guard nodded at him.

On the second floor, he approached the law firm's reception area. Both receptionists—one male, one female—smiled at him as he approached the boomerang-shaped desk. The smiles were good, if false. The smiles said: *So lovely to see you again.* They had been well trained. In his good suit he looked like a client, maybe even an important one.

"Good afternoon, sir," the male receptionist began. "How are you today?"

"Tremendous, thank you. What about yourself?"

"Wonderful. How might I be of service?"

Victor said, "I have a four p.m. appointment with Gisele Maynard. I'm sorry to say I'm a little late."

The receptionist didn't check the system for the appointment. He didn't break eye contact. "I'm sorry, sir. Ms. Maynard isn't in the office today."

Victor made sure to appear taken aback. "Oh," he said. "That's terribly disappointing." He sighed and drummed his knuckles on the desktop. "I've come into the city specifically to see her. I've wasted a lot of time." After checking his watch, Victor added, "Are you expecting her back tomorrow?"

"I'm afraid I don't know." The receptionist did a reasonable job of looking sympathetic. "I really am terribly sorry for your inconvenience."

"Is she unwell?"

The receptionists looked at one another. The woman said, "She hasn't been in the office since last week."

He pretended to think, to remember. "I spoke to her last Wednesday and we agreed to this meeting then. When was she last in? If she had planned to go away, why would she arrange to see me?"

"I don't think it was planned," the male receptionist said. "It's probably just the office bug."

The woman added, "She was in on Thursday, but we haven't seen her since then."

Victor made a big deal of sighing. "This is extremely frustrating."

The man said, "Sir, I am very sorry. When she does come back to the office I'll of course let her know you came in today. Can I take your name?"

He said the alias he'd signed in with.

The receptionist made a note of it. "Is there anything else I can do for you?"

Victor raised an eyebrow. "Anything *else*? No, that's everything."

The receptionist's smile never faltered. "You have yourself a lovely day."

· Chapter 17 ·

Gisele lived in southeast London in a top-floor apartment of a converted Georgian town house. The building had once been two residences of wealthy Londoners with three aboveground levels and a semi-subterranean one. Like many similar houses, these two had long ago been converted into flats for the city's ever-expanding populace. The facade was painted cream and kept clean and bright. A U-shaped driveway of loose gravel provided access from the quiet street. A small garden and huge oak tree sat in the middle of the curve. Four cars were parked on the driveway. All were well maintained. Norimov hadn't known if his daughter owned a vehicle, but Victor saw that she did. It was a maroon Volvo. Less than three years old. It was the only one of the four cars that did not have tire-width grooves in the gravel leading up to it because it hadn't been used in more than a week.

He would have liked to have examined it more closely but he was illuminated by the sodium orange of streetlamps, and an observer inside could see him from behind blinds or net curtains without his knowledge. It was only seven p.m. but sunset had been more than an hour ago. Lights were on in most of the windows. Gisele's were dark, as were a few wherein the occupiers were still at work or commuting from it. Londoners worked long hours.

Victor wore a charcoal business suit, sky blue shirt, and no tie. A suit was his preferred outfit, for many reasons, for the majority of situations his work put him in. He spent most of his time in cities where suited men were common and anonymous. A suit also provided an instant air of respectability. A man in a suit rarely seemed suspicious. If that man was running, he would appear late, not fleeing. Police wouldn't stop that man near a crime scene unless they knew who they were looking for. Security guards would not check closely when that man flashed credentials. Civilians would be more easily convinced of that man's lies.

And when that man was seen within a building where he didn't belong, residents would believe he had reason to be there.

I'm an estate agent, Victor said inside his mind as he approached the front door. *I've been asked to value Miss Maynard's flat.*

Broad steps led up to the two front doors—both painted in a fiery red—one leading to the flats on the left, the other to those on the right. Victor veered to the right-side door. The garden flat had its own entrance at the side. The buzzer fixed to the right of the main front door had three buttons and numbers corresponding to each of the aboveground flats. The door had a dead bolt. He'd have preferred not to have to pick it with people inside the building but he couldn't afford to waste time waiting until midmorning, when most would have left for their day jobs.

He reached into a pocket and took out two of the paper clips that Dmitri had sourced. Victor had cut, bent and manipulated them using the multitool, forming a torsion wrench and rake. He inserted the wrench into the bottom of the lock and applied gentle pressure. The rake went into the top of the lock and he dragged it back toward him, bumping the tumblers. Using proper tools the lock would have taken less than ten seconds to open. With the improvised wrench and rake it took thirty-three.

He pushed open the door, stopping when he saw no one in the hallway on the other side. It was a neat, simple space, clean and organized. Function over aesthetics. A door led to the ground-floor flat. A staircase led up.

A pile of mail sat on the carpet near the front door. There were letters and obvious junk mail and free newspapers and circulars for all three of the flats. Victor sifted through them, separating out the ones for Gisele Maynard or those that were addressed to different names but the same residence.

He ascended to the top floor. He heard music emanating from the first-floor residence. Some kind of dance music. Victor was glad he couldn't recognize the song. Music had peaked more than a century ago. He didn't understand why people couldn't just accept that.

Gisele's front door was double locked. A minute later Victor pushed it open. The smell hit him first. It was a clean, neutral fragrance. He wasn't going to find a body here. He felt relief. He'd never met her. He'd known of her existence for less than twenty-four hours. But he was glad he wasn't going to lay eyes on her as a corpse. At least not yet, anyway.

He eased the door closed behind him. Conversion

flats had thin floors. The resident below might hear otherwise, even above the incessant thump of electronic drums. When the door clicked shut, the hallway fell into darkness. Victor stood for a moment, letting his eyes adjust to the gloom and listening. He'd seen no evidence of another intruder but that didn't mean a skilled operator was not already inside the apartment. Victor knew nothing about the threat Norimov and his daughter faced, but he also knew it could materialize at any moment.

He maintained his vigilance, but moved on when he was as close to sure that he was alone as he could be, clearing the rooms one by one until he was certain he was the only one there. Then he made sure all the curtains and blinds were closed and turned on the lights.

Gisele's apartment consisted of a narrow hallway with doors on either side that led to two bedrooms, a bathroom, and a storage room before leading into an open-plan lounge and kitchen. French doors led out onto a small balcony that overlooked the shared garden. She had simple but expensive tastes. The furniture was functional but high quality. He liked the minimalist approach. If he had his own taste, this would be it.

There were no signs of a confrontation. If Norimov's enemies had found and taken Gisele, it hadn't been from here. He sat down on a bespoke couch to examine Gisele's mail. The couch was as comfortable as it looked, but he sat perched on the very edge, head in line with his hips, ready to spring to his feet should the need arise.

He'd ignored the flyers and other hand-delivered circulars, leaving them by the entrance downstairs. There were a couple of letters to the previous occupant, but he paid attention to them as he did the ones addressed to

Gisele. He wasn't interested in the contents of the letters but the postmarks. The earliest date was the ninth—two days before Norimov received the threatening photograph. The postmark stated the letter had been sent first class. At the earliest it would have slid through the mailbox on the tenth, but could have arrived on the eleventh or even twelfth. So he knew Gisele hadn't been home for at least seven or eight days.

On the opposite side of the lounge, an ergonomic mesh chair sat before a desk made of glass and chrome. A computer rested on the desk. It would no doubt be able to tell him when she had lasted logged on, but he didn't have to power it on to know it was password protected. He was no hacker. Instead, he turned his attention to a three-tier document tray next to the computer monitor. On the bottom level were bills and statements, all at least two weeks old. The middle tray contained more recent correspondence. Unopened letters sat in the top tray. The most recent letter had a postmark for the eighth. It had most likely arrived on the ninth or tenth, narrowing down Gisele's absence to no more than seven days. She hadn't been home since the day Norimov received the photograph.

In Gisele's bedroom, Victor went through her things. He wasn't sure what he was hoping to find, but time spent being thorough was never wasted. Her clothes were good-quality garments. She had a large, sliding wardrobe. The dresses, blouses, and suits inside were hung on wooden hangers and coordinated by color and type. She liked color, but there were few daring items. There were four trouser suits: gray, charcoal, brown, and black. Victor appreciated their quality. An empty hanger hung between the brown and black suits, so he knew she'd worn her navy on the day she didn't return home. There was too much color elsewhere in her wardrobe for her not to have that classic shade.

He searched through all her drawers in every room. He opened every box and case. He had a glass of water in the kitchen area of the open-plan lounge, washing and drying the glass after he had finished and putting it back exactly as he had found it. The kitchen was at the rear of the building, overlooking the garden. The blinds had fat wooden slats. Even closed, Victor could just about see the world outside.

Her phone sat on a table near the couch. He used the knuckle of his little finger to punch out Norimov's number. He answered after a few rings. It was after midnight in St. Petersburg.

"Have you found her?"

"You have a lot of faith in me," Victor replied. "But even I don't work that fast. I'm in her apartment." He explained what he'd found—and hadn't. "She's been gone for a week. You need to accept the fact they have her. Or they tried to take her and something went wrong. She could very well be dead."

"I won't believe it until I see her body."

He didn't press the issue. "Have you had any further threats? Any attacks on your businesses? Any of your men assaulted?"

"Nothing since the photograph. The only men injured are the ones you hurt."

Victor thought about this for a moment. He looked between the blind slats. "You can relax for the time being. She's not dead."

"But you just said . . . How can you know for sure?"

"Because I can see three men climbing over the wall of the garden."

"What?"

"They must have been watching from the street behind and saw the lights on in the flat. They think I'm her."

Norimov's voice was quiet when he said, "Then I almost feel sorry for them."

· Chapter 18 ·

Victor replaced the handset and switched off the lights. The apartment fell into darkness. He judged the angle and cracked open the curtains covering the balcony doors. He looked over his shoulder to check. A swath of dim light cut through the darkness of the lounge, illuminating the opening where it joined the hall leading to the front door. Outside of the swath there was almost no visibility. He wouldn't see an enemy two meters away. But they wouldn't see him either.

They had probably been waiting in a car, interior lights off, eyes adjusted to the night. But the communal hallway and staircase were well lit. By the time they reached Gisele's apartment they would have lost their night vision. That put them on even footing with Victor. In a few minutes his eyes would adjust to the lack of light and he would see as well as he needed to, but by then it would all be over. They would be across the garden by now and moving past the entrance to the garden flat, circling around to the front of the building.

Victor heard the muted crash of the door being forced open below. He felt the vibration, which had traveled up through the building, in the balls of his feet. He pictured the startled face of the resident below.

Streetlamps outside cast a dull orange glow between the open curtains. Motes of dust drifted lazily across the path of light. He stood motionless in the darkness, listening. Ready. Content.

His ears captured sound from many different sources: the rumble of traffic outside, the soulless melody thumping its way through the floor below, the murmur of a heated argument far away. He concentrated to pick out the footsteps hurrying up the stairs. Initially faint; phantom sounds that grew and intensified with speed as the men ascended to the first floor, then the second. They were moving fast. This was no stealth operation. They were aggressive and loud. Not professionals.

He counted three sets, so none of them were staying back to protect their escape route from interfering residents. Few, if any, would respond to the noise of the forced door. They would be shocked, then scared, then would convince themselves it wasn't as they had first thought. They would seek to rationalize the danger away. Humans put their heads in the sand just like ostriches. Victor exploited that often.

They stopped outside Gisele's front door. They weren't about to pick it. They were passing on last-minute instructions because they didn't have anything that resembled a proper plan. Sloppy. Nowhere near professional standards. They were street criminals. Thugs. They could even be psyching themselves up. Maybe: *On the count of three* . . .

The front door burst open and smacked into the wall.

Victor remained standing in the same position. He didn't have to move. The three guys were going to do the hard work for him.

They had kicked in the door. It made a lot of noise. Even submissive residents might not talk themselves into thinking there was a reasonable explanation. The police could already have been called. Now they were against the clock and they couldn't know where Gisele—or who they thought was Gisele—was located.

So they had to move fast. They had to spread out. There was no danger in that.

They were three dangerous men after one civilian female. Easy.

Wrong.

He stood motionless, listening. He didn't have to do anything yet. He had only to wait. They would come to him. He could hear the urgent exhales of the three men. They weren't out of breath but were breathing hard as they rushed through the apartment. One would check left—the two bedrooms. The other would check right—the bathroom and storage room. Which left the third to head straight into the lounge, into the swath of light and into—

Victor, as he leaped from the darkness onto the guy from behind as he hurried forward, wrapping his right arm around the man's neck, the crook of his elbow pushing against the trachea, applying pressure on the carotid arteries on each side of it, shutting off the blood supply to the brain. His left palm covered the man's mouth and nose, muffling his cries, inaudible over the heavy footfalls of his two companions.

Ten seconds without oxygen was sufficient for the brain to shut down nonessential functions like consciousness, and the man slumped to the ground. There wasn't enough time to induce brain death and a snapped neck was too loud to risk, so Victor left him where he lay.

With two rooms each to check, the other two would arrive in the lounge in close succession, but not together because one had two bedrooms to check with space to hide in—under the beds, in wardrobes—while the other had smaller, barer rooms to clear.

He took down the next man in the same way as the first, but the six seconds of the choke hold weren't quite enough to induce unconsciousness before the third man appeared behind him.

He didn't have to look back to know the third man hesitated when he saw his two companions prostrate and Victor standing over them, and hesitation was as good as surprise in Victor's line of work.

It enabled him to close the distance before the man could grab the handgun from his pocket and point it Victor's way. A snapshot from the hip might have had some success, but the man didn't have the reflexes, skill, or even courage to try.

Victor used a forearm to push the muzzle clear, grabbed the wrist and triceps to lock the arm, but the gunman knew how to fight and was throwing an elbow with his free arm before Victor could break the joint. He caught the attack on a raised forearm, pushing it up, exposing the man's chest for an elbow of his own that he drove into his enemy's ribs. He didn't have the leverage to crack any, or the room to aim for the solar plexus, but a whoosh of air left the man's mouth. In that moment he didn't have the strength to stop Victor from ripping the pistol from his hand.

He tossed it away because he had no need of it—and it would only make noise and mess Victor could do without—and there wasn't time to adjust his grip on the weapon and get his finger inside the trigger guard and have the muzzle pointed at his enemy, because the man had recovered from the elbow to the chest and was fighting back. He was good. He had speed and strength but Victor had more of both.

He backed off to avoid a head butt, slipped a hook and the elbow that followed it, blocked a kick to his thigh with a raised shin. He retreated another step, encouraging his attacker to continue the assault and tire himself out as he increased the ferocity of his attacks in an effort to make up for the gulf in skill until fatigue and frustration created an opening to—

Snap his opponent's head back with an open-palmed blow to the face, breaking his nose and sending him stumbling backward.

Victor easily knocked aside the man's panicked defensive punches and shoved him to keep him off-balance until he tripped on the leg of one of his unconscious companions. His arms splayed in an attempt to stay standing, but in doing so left him defenseless.

Victor's takedown dropped the man facedown onto his head and his whole body slackened.

He stamped on the back of the man's neck. The crack told him he'd broken vertebrae. His enemy's limp body told him he'd transected the spinal cord.

The second man—who had not quite been rendered unconscious—had managed to get to his hands and knees.

A kick between the legs put him back on his stomach.

Victor switched on a lamp and squatted down next to the man to wait until the pain had subsided enough for him to be useful.

"Who sent you?" Victor asked when the man finally stopped writhing and opened his eyes.

"No Anglais."

"Then I'm afraid to say that you're no use to me."

Victor put a hand on the man's throat and squeezed. A raspy scream escaped his lips. He stared into Victor's eyes.

"*Wait* . . . I'll talk."

"I should be a language teacher."

The man was average height but solid and strong. He stank of body odor from sitting in a warm car for perhaps hours, the morning's shower long ago. He seemed about twenty-five. Prison tattoos were visible on his neck. He had a scar on his cheek.

"If you promise to cooperate," Victor said, "I'll take my hand away. Deal?"

The man nodded as much as the hand around his throat would let him. "Deal."

Victor removed his hand, pretending he didn't notice the man's right fist in his jacket pocket; pretending he hadn't noticed it slide inside the pocket when he'd begun strangling the man.

The instant Victor took his hand from the man's neck, the man pulled a knife from the pocket and stabbed up at him. He didn't know whether the man was going for his spleen, stomach, or heart, or even whether he was just thrusting with little care to where the wound ended up. It didn't matter. The blade didn't get anywhere near Victor's skin.

He caught the knife-holding fist, applying pressure with his thumb while twisting with his fingers to lock the wrist joint and relieve the weapon from the man's weakened grasp.

Victor said, "That was a really bad idea."

• Chapter 19 •

He reversed his grip on the knife so the blade protruded from the bottom of his fist and drove the point down into the man's abdomen.

It made a popping, sucking sound as the skin was pierced and sliced. The man's face contorted in shock and horror more than from pain. Adrenaline kept the agony away. That respite was temporary. The pain would come soon.

The man gasped and bucked as Victor tugged the blade free of the vacuum's hold.

Blood so dark it was almost black bubbled out of the wound. It soaked his shirt, spreading fast, glinting in the gloom.

Victor said, "I don't suppose you believe me when I say that in less than one minute you're going to beg me to stab you again."

The man just stared. Shock was pulling the color from his face. Beads of sweat were appearing over every inch of skin. His hands pressed flat over the wound. Both were drenched with blood.

Victor showed him the blade. "The blood's dark because I've stabbed you in the inferior vena cava. Don't be fooled by the name. It's one of the most important blood vessels you have. It carries all the blood from your lower body up to your heart. The blood's dark because it's de-oxygenated because it hasn't reached there yet. Now it's pouring out of your belly. It can't enter the right atrium of your heart. It can't be pumped to your lungs. It can't pick up oxygen. In about four minutes there's not going to be enough oxygen in your blood to keep you alive. Your whole body is going to crave it. But you're going to lie there and bleed to death. The pain is going to be hor-rendous. I can't stop the pain, but I can keep you alive. Do you want me to keep you alive?"

The man nodded frantically, the whites of his eyes large and bright and full of tears.

"Then I have to put the blade back inside the wound. It'll create a vacuum and stem the bleeding. More im-portant it will let the blood flow up to your heart. Pres-sure on the wound won't be enough. Look." Victor gestured to the blood coating the man's hands. "Do you want me to stab you again?"

The man didn't answer. He stared and cried.

"I'll give you a few seconds to think about it," Victor said.

He left the man for a moment to break the neck of the first one he'd choked because he was coming round, then returned.

"It's a straight choice," Victor continued. "There are no variables. Either the blade stays in my hand and you bleed to death in a matter of minutes, or I slide it back in and you make it to the hospital. London has some great trauma surgeons. They deal with knife wounds a lot. This is a routine job for them. But you need to decide right now which way it's going to be. Each second you delay is a minute less you'll have to live when you eventually decide there really is only one option. You don't want to die. You want to live. So, shall I put the knife back in?"

"*Yes,*" he begged.

"I won't say I told you so."

Victor slotted the knife blade directly into the wound. The man bucked and thrashed and screamed. The adrenaline was all used up now.

"You made the right choice," Victor said. "The blade has plugged the hole and will slow the bleeding long enough for me to ask you some questions and for me to call an ambulance and for the paramedics to arrive and keep you alive until you get into an operating room with a surgeon to stitch you up. But you don't have a lot of time, so you're going to have to answer me without hesitation or stalling. You need me to believe you. If I have a single doubt about any answer you give, then I'm going to pull the blade out again and I'll only put it back in when you convince me you're telling the truth. That's fair, isn't it?"

The man's face was pale and soaked in sweat and tears. "Yes," he yelled. "Hurry the fuck up and ask me."

"Tell me you understand."

He nodded. "I do. I understand. Please hurry."

"Just so we're clear: who are you here for—me or Gisele?"

"The woman. We saw the light on. We thought—"

"I don't care what you thought. And you should care about answering my questions only because you haven't got enough life left to waste even a second of it."

"Okay. Okay."

"How long have you been looking for her?"

"A few days."

"Be more specific."

He thought for a moment. "A week."

"Be more specific," Victor said again.

"I don't know. Christ . . . Since last Tuesday."

"Eight days?"

"Yes. *Fuck*. Eight fucking days."

"I'll forgive you the language because of the circumstances. But don't push it. Who are you working for?"

A half moment of hesitation. "Blake Moran." He spoke the name with reverence and fear, even with a knife in his abdomen.

"That's nothing but a name. Who is he? Tell me about him."

"I don't know. . . . He's the boss man. He's . . . God, it hurts so much."

"A drug dealer?"

The man nodded. "The biggest."

"I doubt that," Victor said. "At this moment who are you more afraid of: him or me?"

The man didn't answer fast enough so Victor took hold of the knife's grip and twisted it—just a little, but enough. He muffled the resulting scream with a palm over the man's mouth.

"You!" he yelled when Victor removed his hand.

"Remember that before you answer my next question. Where can I find Moran?"

"He has a big house in Bromley. Like a fucking fortress, with guards and dogs—"

"Yeah, yeah. I get the idea. What about businesses? Clubs, bars . . . ?"

The man grimaced and gulped. "A café. In Lewisham. Near the station."

"What's it called?"

"I can't remember. *I'm sorry.*"

"It's okay. I'll find it."

"Please, that's all I know. Call me an ambulance."

"Remember what I said about not having time to waste?" The man nodded. "So stop wasting it. Who told Moran to find the woman?"

"No one. No one tells him what to do."

"Everyone takes orders," Victor said. "Even men like Moran. What were you going to do with the woman, had you found her here?"

"Secure her and take her someplace safe."

"Where?"

"One of Moran's sites. A derelict house. The address is on my phone."

"That's bad form. Even someone like you should know that. Once you'd taken her to this house, then what was the plan?"

"Call Moran. Tell him we had her. Wait for further instructions."

Victor patted down the man until he'd found the phone. He checked it, then showed the man the screen. "Is this his number?"

The man nodded. "That's him. I'm starting to get cold. Please, call the ambulance."

"Are you supposed to use a password or some sort of code?"

"I . . . I don't understand. The *ambulance*, man."

Victor slipped the phone into a pocket. He considered for a moment. "I think that's it. Thank you for your honesty. It's saved me a lot of time and hassle. I appreciate that."

"So . . . you'll call me an ambulance now?"

Victor looked down at him. "You didn't seriously believe me, did you?"

The man's eyes widened. "What? What do you mean?"

"I'm not going to call you an ambulance. And even if I did, they're not going to be able to keep you alive."

"But you said . . . What about the surgeons?"

"If you were on the operating table at this very moment, maybe. But even that would be a long shot. The wound is mortal. That was the point."

"Please. Don't kill me," the man pleaded.

"I already have," Victor said.

"But . . . you told me—"

"I lied," Victor said. "I'm not a very nice person."

The man began crying and reached out when Victor stood. "Don't leave me."

"If you pull the knife out, the pain will be over sooner. Otherwise you have maybe five minutes. If you believe in God, now would be a good time to start begging him to forgive your many sins. And even if you don't, it can't hurt, can it?"

Victor walked away.

Behind him, the man prayed.

· Chapter 20 ·

An hour later, Nieve Anderton climbed out of her black Audi. Two police cars were parked outside the building. Another sat on the gravel driveway. Parked next to it was the ambulance. The Audi was a solid, powerful sports car. The door was big and heavy. She made sure it didn't slam. Not to avoid the noise, although she preferred to remain quiet and unheard, but to stay in control. Being in control was important.

A brown leather blazer covered the blouse that hung loose over her belt. The blazer was smart and of a tailored fit. The blouse carried a designer's stitched logo on the chest pocket. Her jeans were similarly labeled. Her boots were made from polished rattlesnake skin. She liked to dress well. She liked to make a statement.

The street was quiet despite the police presence. Residents kept to themselves. They didn't make a fuss. A few silhouettes at windows were about as obvious as they were going to get. A paramedic stood on the pavement outside the driveway, looking at his phone—texting or checking e-mail or watching funny cat videos. He was in no hurry, no more than the various cops and crime-scene techs. There was no need to rush. Everyone was dead. Three corpses, Anderton had been told. So far unidentified.

They looked like criminals, apparently. Burglary gone wrong, people speculated.

"One's bled out from a knife wound to the abdomen," the crime-scene coordinator was telling her as she slipped on plastic overshoes. "The other two have broken necks. One's facedown; looks as if he's been stamped on. The other has had his head wrenched." He did the action. "Like this. Nice, eh?"

"How many assailants?" Anderton asked, zipping up her overalls.

"That I can't tell you. No footprints in the blood. No other obvious signs. We'll know more once the nerds have finished."

"Nerds?" Anderton echoed.

"Hey, I'm allowed to say it. I used to be one."

Neighbors were being questioned by police constables. No one seemed to have seen anything, but plenty of people heard doors being kicked open and sounds of a struggle. Then screaming.

Anderton left the crime-scene coordinator to attend to the various plastic-bagged exhibits that were being ferried out of the building. She squeezed her way past a couple of detectives who looked at her with measurable disdain, and entered the building.

"All the way up to the top, ma'am," a uniform offered.

"Thank you."

She ascended the stairs. It was difficult. The overalls were far too big for her frame, and the shoes had little grip on the carpetless steps. Anderton reached the top, slightly out of breath. She was in shape, but didn't hit the gym anywhere near as much as she used to. Age was catching up with her. Life would begin in a couple of years, she'd heard plenty of times.

"And who the flying fuck are you?"

A burly detective in a poorly fitting suit stepped out of the apartment. He looked about forty years old and smoked about forty a day. Even without the aggressive attitude, she knew he would be trouble. She could read people well enough to know that just from the way his shoulders sat, bunched and widened, attacking because he was defensive. Not the smartest man to show his hand so easily.

"My name's Nieve Anderton," she said, offering her hand. "I'm from the Security Service. And who might you be?"

"The guv'nor. Detective Chief Inspector Crawley. And you're on my crime scene, Ms. Anderton, so I suggest you piss off back to the salon. This is a *police* matter."

She smiled through the insult. "Are you always this personable, or is it only with the ladies?"

"Oh, this is me in first gear, love, I assure you. I haven't even begun to turn on the charm." Crawley rested his hands on hips. His beer gut was bigger than his ego.

She met him at his own game. "When you do turn it on, be sure to let me know. I wouldn't want to miss it. Now, if you'll excuse me, I need to go in there." She pointed to the open front door.

Crawley looked astonished. "You do? Well, why didn't

you call ahead? I could have had the red carpet brought down and rolled out for you. Guess we'll have to make do without. Tell you what—I'll lie down and you can walk over me instead."

"I assure you, I'd like nothing more than to trample you with my four-inch Pour La Victoires, but I wouldn't want to pop you open like a balloon." She glanced down at his distended stomach. "So I guess we're both out of luck. Therefore, why don't you save us a lot of time and give me your cooperation and access to your crime scene? I'd certainly appreciate it."

"I'd very much appreciate it if you would get lost and let me and my men do our job. You MI5 clowns can balls it up after we're done. How's that sound?"

Anderton took a breath and stepped close enough to smell the fried chicken on Crawley's clothes. "I'm sorry you didn't get many hugs as a child, Inspector. But this really has gone beyond a joke. You're obstructing official Security Service business, and if you don't let me in there, then I make a call to your superintendent. David, isn't it? We're on first-name terms, you see. Lovely wife, he has. Beautiful kids too. His eldest has a bit of a crush on me, I think. Do you get what I'm trying to tell you? Or should I make it clearer? How's this? Back off, or I'm going to have to bend you over and fuck your career up the arse until you're shitting blood." She smiled at him. "Okay?"

He stepped back. "Nice mouth you have there, sweetheart. And you called me charming!"

"Oh, I assure you, this is me in first gear. Do you understand me, DCI Crawley?"

"*Yes*, I understand you." He sighed and shook his head. "You're the guv'nor."

"That's correct," she said, and stepped around him. "Walk me through it."

He followed and gestured. "Door kicked in. All three were killed in the lounge over there. Other rooms have been tossed. Nothing taken, far as we can see."

The bodies had yet to be removed. The forensic people were milling around them and the rest of the flat. Tape placed by the crime-scene coordinator marked areas of interest. One of the corpses lay facedown on the laminate flooring. He looked as though he had suffered a hell of a beating. The back of his neck was red. Underneath the skin, the spine was broken, but the exterior wound was almost nonexistent. The second corpse, again with a broken neck, was more obvious in the manner of death: the head was at an unnatural angle to the rest of the body. There were no other injuries.

The third body was drenched in blood, originating from a wound to his belly, and soaking his clothes and forming a pool around him. Anderton almost couldn't believe the amount that had come out of him. His skin was so white it looked as though he was wearing makeup—a vampire in an old horror flick.

Interestingly, the knife that had killed him was clutched in his right hand. He had pulled it out. Which was about as stupid as it got. Anderton thought every man and his dog knew never to remove a blade. It was suicide.

"Some blokes messed 'em right up," Crawley said from behind her.

She turned to face him. He was scratching at his crotch. He didn't stop when he saw she noticed. No brains. No manners. No class. She spotted a ring on his finger and felt enormous sympathy for the man's wife.

"So," he continued. "Are you going to tell me what

a supersecret agent from MI5 is doing at my crime scene?"

Anderton smiled. "You surely don't expect me to answer that, do you?"

He rolled his eyes. "Defense of the realm, national security, need to know—blah, blah, blah."

"Couldn't have put it better myself, Inspector."

"You do realize that if you showed me the courtesy of sharing a little intel that, A, it would encourage cooperation and, B, help us both out?"

"You mean the same courtesy you showed me in the hallway?"

"Yes, well. Call me psychic, but I knew exactly how this was going to turn out, and I'm not keen on me and my boys doing all the legwork on this investigation so you can swoop in at the end and steal all the glory."

"I'm not in the glory business, Inspector. I'm in the protecting-this-country business. The same business that you should be in."

He looked away.

"Any evidence left by the killer?"

"Killers," he corrected. "And no. Nothing so far."

Anderton pivoted on the spot, analyzing the scene. She pointed. "He stood there, close to the door and out of sight. When they came in, they had split up, searching the other rooms. The one farthest away from the door was the first to die. We can see that because there are absolutely no signs of a struggle. He rushed straight past the killer—had no idea there was any threat—and was attacked from behind before he could get farther into the flat. Pressure on the carotids from behind. A classic rear naked choke would have taken him out in seconds. Killer then waits for the next one to show. That's when it gets a little messy, because the third one must have been following close behind."

Crawley was shaking his head. "Excuse me, but what the hell are you talking about? What's all this about one killer? The CSC doesn't know how many attackers there were. And these weren't plastic hard men. No way one guy took them all out."

"Look around this place," Anderton said. "There's barely any mess aside from the three corpses and the blood. How did that happen if there were multiple attackers? There would be multiple signs, wouldn't there? This flat would be a bomb site. But it's not. We have a ridiculously neat arrangement of bodies, all in this area just inside the lounge entrance. How did multiple attackers hide well enough to catch three men by surprise and then kill them without leaving a single trace? If you know, I'm all ears."

Crawley was still shaking his head, but he didn't respond.

"And look at the way they're lying," Anderton said. "Two of them have their feet pointed at the hallway."

"And?"

"That means two of three were taken down without even having the chance to turn around. No way that happened unless a single attacker took out the first without the second one knowing about it."

Crawley shrugged, defeated. "All right. You might have a point. We'll look into it."

"Who owns the flat?" Anderton asked.

"One Gisele Maynard. Twenty-two years old. Lives alone. Neighbors we've spoken to haven't seen her for days. I hope you're not suggesting a girl—sorry, a woman—beat seven shades of shite out of these three, are you?"

Anderton acknowledged the ridiculousness of his question with a smirk. "I think you would be surprised what we're capable of, Inspector, when we're allowed out of the kitchen. But in this case I'm with you. No, I don't see it."

"Wow, you agree with me. It's like all my Christmas mornings rolled into one."

"I wouldn't get used to it, if I were you."

Anderton smiled at him and he matched the smile. She handed him her card and he took it without the slightest hesitation. This pleased her. Not because she wanted him to like her, but because he was a once-disobedient hound now loyal to his new master.

"Let me know if you turn up anything else, Inspector."

· Chapter 21 ·

Blake Moran's café was located between a kebab shop and a narrow single-lane road, on the other side of which lay a bowling alley. Like the kebab shop next to it, the café was no chic eatery or coffee shop. It looked the kind of place that nonregulars hurried past, concerned by the hordes of unsavory men that hung around inside all day long. Metal tables and chairs stood outside on the pavement. A freestanding blackboard listed today's specials in indecipherable script. Victor thought he made out the word *soup*.

He waited at a bus shelter thirty meters away, on the other side of the street. He pretended to study the route and timetable listings while he performed the last stage of his surveillance. The cover was probably excessive. No one inside the café seemed to pay any attention to the goings-on outside. Intermittently, men would come out to smoke. Often they had lit up before they made it to the door. Victor didn't envy the public-health inspector who would have to give the proprietor a verbal warning.

He'd operated against, and been around, enough organized criminals in his time to recognize a front. The café was a bad establishment in a worse area, and filled with gangsters. Any hapless passerby who had the misfortune of stepping inside for a drink or meal would never elect to go back a second time. But the custom, or lack thereof, didn't matter. Cafés had a high percentage of cash turnover, which meant they were good places to launder money. Every cup of surprisingly expensive espresso or bottle of mineral water the goons inside ordered would be delivered with a receipt. No money would change hands, but the day's take equivalent in illicitly gained cash could be put through the books and come out the other end clean and declarable.

The same went for the kebab shop next door, judging by how friendly those who ran the two establishments were. Combined, the two likely gave Moran a tidy legitimate income that covered his everyday expenses and kept the tax man and the police off his back. So, he was reasonably smart. The three men he'd sent after Gisele had one pistol between them. If they regularly carried guns, they would have had them on them in the apartment, or at least in their car. If those four had only one gun between them, Moran's crew members were not universally armed. A few knives, blackjacks, and brass knuckles, no doubt, but light on firearms. That made things a little easier for Victor.

As was typical for London, there were a couple of CCTV cameras in the immediate area, but neither would impede his plan. From what he could see, the men inside the café seemed relaxed. They were joking and drinking coffee: killing time between actions. The man Victor stabbed had called Moran a drug dealer. That seemed an inaccurate term. The thugs in the café didn't look like dealers, and in the time Victor had been conducting surveillance he had seen only a handful of men come or go. That didn't equate to dealing drugs. The men were thugs, like the four in Gisele's apartment had been. They were muscle. Soldiers.

Moran was a trafficker, not a dealer. His men could sit around in the café all day because the work was irregular. They would go into action when a shipment was due— whether coming in or going out. Moran bought in bulk and shipped in bulk. He needed his men to protect his business from being ripped off by those above him or below him in the pyramid. No business would be done in the café. That was just a front. And no wholesaler could ship product as soon as it was received. So Moran had a distribution center.

Like his residence, it would serve as a better location to confront him, but there was no telling when he would head to either. Each hour that passed meant more chance of him finding out about his three dead men. In some ways that might help, as he was likely to mobilize his soldiers to find out what had happened. The number in the café would certainly fall as a result. But those that remained, and Moran himself, would be alert and on guard. Maybe not thinking further attacks were imminent, but a natural rise in awareness and readiness would be an automatic response.

More problematic, though, would be what Moran might do. He was no small-time dealer, but he wasn't about to expand his territory to St. Petersburg. He wasn't preparing to usurp Norimov. He hadn't been the one to send an old Russian blood threat. Someone had asked him to kidnap Gisele. Either that person was the direct threat to Norimov or he was a link to it. Regardless, when

Moran discovered he'd lost his crew because of that he would report this fact and whoever was targeting Norimov would know they had competition to find Gisele. Victor wanted them to know that only when he was ready.

He crossed the road and headed toward the café. There were a dozen of Moran's soldiers inside. There might be others scattered around the rest of the establishment. Guns or not, they created a near-impassable barrier. An easier way existed. He entered the access road adjacent to the café, walking on the same side of the road as the bowling alley. Across the narrow street was the side of the café. A quick glance gave Victor an accurate picture of numbers, positions, and their readiness. So far so good.

The street was a single lane. No sidewalks flanked it. The bowling alley occupied the entire side Victor stood on until the road turned after about seventy meters. There were a few shabby signs for businesses farther along on the opposite side, all closed. Between them and the café was a short driveway for deliveries and a high metal gate blocking access to the uneven area of asphalt that lay behind the café. Victor could see two vehicles parked there: a van and a Mercedes-Benz. The soldiers' vehicles had to be parked elsewhere, either along the access road or similarly close by. A single CCTV camera overlooked the gate.

Victor doubted it would be manned full-time, but scaling the gate under full view of the camera was still too much of a risk. He walked along the access road. A three-story office building stood adjacent to the metal gate. The ground-floor windows were reinforced with mesh and covered in posters for local nightclubs and events. They were several layers thick. Frayed corners flickered in the breeze. There were no lights on anywhere in the building but the premises were protected by a security firm, according to a couple of signs. Maybe that meant there was a guard somewhere inside or it could just refer to an alarm system. Next to the office building was a row of small businesses. Three of the four businesses on the same side of the street as the café had either obvious alarm boxes or security grilles. The odd one out had neither. It had whitewashed windows because it had closed down. A long time ago, judging by the rental agent's faded sign. No lights were on, either on the ground floor or two floors above. Perfect.

The improvised picklocks were still usable. The torsion wrench would last a good while longer, but the pick was marked and bent a little from the previous usage. Victor used his fingers to bend it back into shape as much as he could and crossed the street.

No one was around to witness him pick the closed-down business's front door. There were two locks. He was inside within forty seconds.

Dust and mold spores reached his nostrils. He stood in the darkness and let his eyes adjust and his ears take in every sound for his brain to separate and analyze. He could hear the tick of pipes and the noise of the outside city filtering in.

He was in a short hallway. A frosted-glass door led deeper into the ground floor. He ignored it and ascended the stairs, making his way to the back of the building as soon as he reached the second floor. A pebbled window let in a little light. He unlatched it and heaved it open. It took some effort. The paintwork had eroded and the wood had swelled and warped.

He opened it as far as he could without risking damage, creating a gap higher than necessary for him to slide through, headfirst, on his back, until his hips lay across the sill. Cool wind ruffled his hair. He looked around.

Below was a narrow alleyway, barely shoulder width across, marked on the far side by a spiked metal fence. On the other side of the fence lay a loading bay for a removal firm. The alley didn't link to the open space behind Moran's café, because the office building was deeper than the two businesses next to it. Victor had expected as much. He set his fingertips on the top of the outside window frame and slid backward and up into a sitting position. He then pulled up his feet and set them on the windowsill, shuffling back until his heels had reached the edge of the exterior sill and hung over it. He stood, walking his palms up the wall until they gripped the lip of the flat roof above.

Victor set one foot against the inside of the brickwork surrounding the window and pushed off with both feet at the same time as he pulled with his hands, muscles straining all along his forearms, biceps, and shoulders, until he was high enough to swing a leg around onto the roof to make the last heave easier. He rolled onto his back and stood.

He'd reduced his profile to a crouch by the time he reached the roof of the office building. It was about a meter higher than the current roof. He stepped up onto it and over the small parapet. Skylights dotted the roof. He moved across until he overlooked the rear entrance of Moran's café and the parking area behind it.

A back door was open and music from a radio drifted out through it. From the little he could see from his elevated position it looked as though it led into a kitchen. There were no windows on the ground floor at the rear of the café, but several on the two floors above. Some had lights on. Behind the closed blinds would be the headquarters of Moran's organization. Probably no more than an office or two with an air of legitimacy. The man himself would be in one of the lit rooms.

Victor changed position so he could see the van and the Benz parked outside the café. The space led behind the office building. Parking spaces were clearly defined in white paint but all were empty, aside from broken pallets and other junk presumably dumped there by Moran's men. A fire escape was fixed to the office building's back wall. A useful way of getting down, except Victor had no plans to.

He used the grip of the handgun to chip away at the roof's concrete parapet until he had a handful of fragments. He hurled them at the Mercedes-Benz.

It was Moran's car, Victor was sure. With all his men in the café a few meters away and protected by a locked gate, there would be no need to engage the alarm. But the car had a huge price tag. If he parked it anywhere else he would do so only with the alarm switched on. That would become habit.

The concrete chips pelted the Benz's bodywork.

The alarm blared. Lights flashed. Habit.

Victor moved back to where he overlooked the café's kitchen door. Within seconds Moran's men began rushing out of it—fueled by espressos and excitement from the break in monotony that the alarm's excruciatingly loud wail provided. It wasn't a ruse to draw Moran out of the building. It wasn't to distract his men. It was to mask the noise he was about to make.

Victor backed off a couple of meters, ran, and leaped off the roof.

· Chapter 22 ·

The gap between the office building and the café was about four meters. The office building was three stories high; the café was only two. For a moment, Victor sailed through the night air, right foot extended, left trailing behind, arms out at right angles for stability, then arching forward as he tilted his head and gravity pulled him down, bringing his feet together and bending at the waist so when the balls of his feet hit the roof he was absorbing the fall's energy and using it to bounce into a roll, moving onto his shoulders and elbows, hips and legs following over his head, and coming back onto his feet.

Below him, the alarm ceased.

He heard a voice—Moran's or one of his lieutenants—shouting, "It's nothing. Get back inside and make sure you're ready. We're moving out in ten."

The sound of Victor's landing had been reduced by the roll but would have been registered by everyone outside if not for the car alarm. Someone in a room directly below him might still have noticed it. But he had leaped to and landed on a room without lights on at the windows. He'd stacked the odds in his favor as much as he could hope to.

There were no skylights, but Victor hadn't expected to find any. There was no fire escape either. But there was a drainpipe.

He tested its stability. Good enough. He lowered himself off the roof, pressing his shoes to either side of the pipe, then took hold. He felt it give a little as his weight pulled on the screws, but it held. He climbed down, taking his time to both limit noise and avoid putting any sudden strain on the pipe. When he was level with the sash windows, he took a hand from the pipe to try the window to his left. He wedged his palm beneath the center crossbeam and heaved. It didn't budge. He tried the one to his right. This one didn't lift either, but he felt less resistance. He braced himself and tried again. His arm shook under the strain, but the window rose a couple of inches. He took a breath and tried again. This time it rose farther and he felt warm air from inside flow out. Sounds followed it—music and talking, but both muted, from beyond a closed door.

Victor pushed the window as far up as it would go, then lowered himself farther down the pipe. He reached through the gap with his right hand and gripped the inside sill. Then he pulled himself across as he pushed off the pipe, jerking his left arm over to grab hold too. A moment later, he was inside the room.

It was an office. Two desks occupied opposite corners. Filing cabinets lined one wall. Maps of London tacked to corkboards filled the other. Victor eased the window until it was nearly closed, but left a couple of inches to slip his hands under. He straightened his jacket and brushed the grit and dirt from his suit. He didn't want his appearance to give away how he'd entered.

He waited at the door, listened, and slipped outside the room when he heard no one in immediate proximity. The music from downstairs was louder now. It drifted up a staircase at the end of the hallway. Between the staircase and the office was another door. It led to a room where he'd seen lights on.

Two voices on the other side of the door.

He drew the pistol, cocking it as he turned the handle so the click of the door opening disguised the noise.

The two men were both looking at him as he stepped inside. They were slow to react because the last thing they expected was for an armed stranger to walk through the doorway. Moran sat on a leather sofa, slouched back with his feet up on a glass coffee table. He was stripped to the waist and wearing a pair of spotted boxer shorts and sports socks. He faced a huge but switched-off TV mounted on a wall. Next to the dirty soles of his socks were bags of cocaine, a mirror smeared with residue, and a slim chrome tube. Another man stood near the doorway. He was talking about:

". . . The importance of maintaining a unified front when dealing with—"

Victor dropped him with a backhanded pistol whip, and brought a finger to his lips. "Shh."

"Who the fuck are you?" Moran breathed. His eyes were as red as his nostrils.

Victor eased the door shut with his free hand and stepped forward. "I'm all your nightmares rolled into one."

"How did you get in here?"

"Magic."

Moran hadn't moved. He hadn't even sat up. "Do you have any idea who the fuck I am?"

"You're the man who wishes he were anywhere else but here."

"I've got fifteen hard fucktards downstairs. You pull that trigger and you're dead. Do you get me, boy?"

"No, if I squeeze the trigger, you're dead. And you have twelve men downstairs, not fifteen. The other three won't be coming back."

"What are you talking about?"

"Do you recognize the gun in my hand?"

Moran didn't speak, but his eyes answered for him.

"You may have twelve men downstairs, but they've done you exactly zero good so far. And once you're dead, what does it matter to you what happens next?"

Moran said, "What do you want?"

"That's better. I want to ask you a few questions."

Moran sat up, pulling his feet from the table and setting them on the floor. "Go on, then. Ask."

"Gisele Maynard. I take it you recognize the name?"

No answer.

Victor said, "It's really not in your interest to play games with me."

"So what are you going to do about it? You've showed your hand, boy. You want answers. I have those answers. You can't torture them out of me. You can't risk the noise or the time. Not unless you want my lads charging in here. You can't shoot me either. You've gone to all this trouble for answers. Kill me, and you'll get none." He smiled. "I think I've just owned you."

Victor nodded. "You're right. But your outfit is already down the three-man crew you sent after Gisele." He took a step and stamped his heel down hard onto the temple of the unconscious man. "Now you're down four men."

Moran shrugged away his shock and kept himself composed. "They're company assets. You think they're irreplaceable? You think I can't put more guys on the payroll?"

"Again, you're right. So I'll tell you what I'm going to do."

"I'm all ears."

"I can't shoot or torture you, so if you don't answer my questions I'm going to turn around and walk out of here."

"*Quelle surprise*. Run along now, bitch. Consider this a free lesson in who not to fuck with. Next lesson, I'll have to charge. The price is your worthless life."

Victor continued. "Then, after I've disappeared into the night, you're going to hear from me again. The four you've lost so far will become ten by this time tomorrow. And I won't stop there. I'll keep picking them off. On the streets. In their homes. When you're collecting product. When you're delivering it. You're going to struggle moving and protecting the same quantity as before. You'll be spread thin. *Thin* means 'vulnerable.' You can hire more men, sure, but as quickly as I can kill them? And before word hits the street that your organization is hemorrhaging numbers? Can you rebuild your strength before your rivals decide it's the right time to move in and take over? How are your suppliers going to react when they learn you're being picked apart? How are you going to convince more men to put themselves into my crosshairs when new guys don't survive the first twenty-four hours in your employment? How are you going to keep the loyalty of your existing men when you're willing to let them die? And for what? To protect whoever hired you? Did they really pay you that much? Are you that scared of them?"

Moran didn't blink. "You're nuts."

"There's a good chance of that, yes. What's it going to be? Am I going to walk out of that door, or am I going to walk out of that door and come back later?"

"Sod it," Moran breathed. "It's just a job. I didn't get paid that much. It was a favor, okay? Whatever this is about, whoever you are, I've got nothing to do with that girl. I was asked to snatch her. That's all. Bundle her into the back of a car and drop her off."

"Who asked you for this favor?"

"Andrei Linnekin."

"Who is that?"

"One of my suppliers. My main supplier. He ships the shit over here from wherever the hell it comes from. Afghanistan or some other hole. He asked me to get the girl as a favor."

"Where can I find Mr. Linnekin?"

"I don't know. I swear I don't know where he lives or operates from."

"Then how were you supposed to contact him when you had Gisele in your possession?"

"Phone him, of course."

"Give me his number."

Moran hesitated. "Look, if I do that and you go and fuck up his shit, he's going to know I told you, isn't he?"

"And?"

"What do you mean *and*? He's Russian mafia, isn't he? He's with one of those commie outfits that own half of London."

"So?"

"Are you soft in the head? You mess with him and he's going to put a straight razor through all my tendons and leave me in the sewer for the rats to eat. Do you know how I know he'll do that? Eh? Because I've seen him do it to someone else who betrayed him. Why do you think he had me there to see it? So I would know to never do the same."

"You've already told me his name, so my incentive for keeping you alive is rapidly diminishing. Either you give me his number or I look for it myself while you try to keep your guts inside your body."

Moran picked up the mobile phone from the glass coffee table and tossed it to Victor. He caught it in his free hand.

"His number is in there," Moran said.

"You've made the right choice."

"You are crazy, aren't you?" Moran asked. "You kill my men, break into my place of business, threaten me, and now you're going after the Russian mafia. And all for some woman. I take it she's your girlfriend or your sister, right? She has to be, for you to do this."

Victor shook his head. "I've never met her."

Chapter 23

The morning was cold and damp after the night's down-pour. Puddles reflected the diseased sky above. Andrei Linnekin climbed out of his silver custom Bentley. He sipped from a tall take-out cup of coffee—latte with a double shot of hazelnut syrup. Two of his men were already on the pavement, one facing each way. He was glad to see they were alert. They had better always be alert. He paid them enough to ensure they never blinked. He was a powerful man. One of the handful of men that were trusted by the bosses back in the old country to run London. That brought him enormous wealth and influence, but also made him a prime target for all manner of criminals. Two more of his men exited the Bentley after him.

"You and you," Linnekin said, pointing. "Stay here and keep an eye on my baby." He stroked the car's hood, reveling in the squeak of skin against the polished paint-work. "I want her kept safe. She's delicate."

He crossed the road. Traffic was almost nonexistent in this part of the city, especially at this time of day. The street cut through an abandoned industrial complex. It was huge. A chemical plant of some sort. Linnekin didn't know the specifics and he didn't need to know. What mattered was it had closed down more than a decade ago. The whole neighborhood was industrial. There were no residences or other commercial properties. It was as close to isolated as anywhere in the godforsaken metropolis could be. The complex was the Russian's favorite place in which to conduct the occasional torture or execution. His men could work over some poor hapless soul for days on end without concern of discovery.

A chain-link fence surrounded the complex but there were several holes made by junkies looking for somewhere to shoot up or smoke crack. They didn't do so anymore. Not since Linnekin's men had put half of them in the hospital and the other half in the morgue. Word of these things spread. There were safer places to get a fix. The first of Linnekin's men held open one such hole for his boss to climb through.

Linnekin wore designer jeans and a short-sleeved shirt. The shirt had three buttons unfastened at the top to show off the solid gold jewelry glinting among his chest hair. His thick wrists were similarly adorned. His open-toe sandals kept his feet cool and dry. There was no sun for his sunglasses to filter but he rarely took them off. He was unarmed, because he was always unarmed. He didn't need to carry a piece when all of his men did.

He made his way across the wasteland lying between the fence and one of the complex's factory buildings. The ground was made up of uneven concrete slabs, cheaply laid and now cracked and warped. Grass had sprung up along the joints. There was a bad smell in the air: old chemicals and rust. He checked his watch. He was five minutes late and counting but he didn't care. Linnekin owned the city. People waited for him, not the other way around. Sometimes he would be deliberately late to meetings with men of no small worth to show them he feared no one—to show them, in turn, who should be feared.

One of his men walked ahead, the other behind, footsteps loud on the hard ground. He passed a perforated oil drum blackened by soot. Litter had collected along the factory wall. London was a dirty town, made filthier by its inhabitants, who didn't give a shit about it. *No pride,* Linnekin thought, tossing his mostly empty coffee cup to the ground.

The lead man stepped through an open doorway. There was no door. Linnekin followed. He took off his sunglasses. The smell of chemicals was metallic and pungent. He'd never grown used to it. Concrete rubble from a collapsed ceiling covered the floor. The hole above was huge. Steel reinforcement bars hung down from around the opening, twisted and rusted. Linnekin heard the scurrying of rodents as he walked through the rubble, careful where he placed his feet. He should have thought about that and worn better footwear. He wore sandals, as his feet would sweat even in a snowstorm. He glanced up through the hole in the ceiling. A square shaft rose straight upward until it disappeared into the darkness. Water dripped on his head. Linnekin cursed and rubbed his hair. He cursed again, brushing his palm against the thigh of his jeans to wipe off some of the styling product.

In the adjoining room, he followed his man through a gap in a wall. Sunlight found its way into the room through smashed-out windows. Glass crunched underfoot. More rooms, more rubble, and Linnekin passed through another doorway without a door and into a large open area. There were holes in the floor and ceiling.

Their footsteps echoed. He noticed he could hear only two sets of footsteps and glanced over his shoulder. There was no one behind him.

He stopped and turned around. After ten seconds, nobody had come through the doorway. Linnekin called for the lead man to stop. Now the only sounds he heard were his own breathing and the crunch of grit beneath his sandals. He moved back and through the doorway. The corridor on the other side was empty. He tried to think when he'd last seen or heard the man following him. He didn't know.

The corridor was long and dark. Skylights ran along the ceiling but were caked in grime. Piping ran along one wall. Linnekin peered into the gloom.

"Peta," he called.

No answer. He'd better not be taking a leak. Idiot had the bladder of a thirteen-year-old boy. Linnekin called again, louder. Still no answer. He went back through the doorway.

"Get Peta on your cell," Linnekin said to his lead man. "Find out—"

His man wasn't there. The room was empty.

He sighed. "What is it with everyone wandering off?" he shouted. "You stay at my side, remember? How can you protect me when I can't even see you? *Morons.*"

There was no reply. Heads were going to roll for this. He was in no mood for this kind of incompetence. One day it might cost him his life. His men knew that. They knew better than to leave him. He paid them never to . . .

His eyes widened as he began to understand. His pulse quickened. His breathing grew faster. He swallowed.

Linnekin panicked. Now he knew what was going on. This was it. This was the day when every brutal act he'd

committed was answered for. This was the day he looked
his brother in the eye before he was murdered. Linnekin
knew it, because that was how he had gained his position
of power, influence, and wealth: by killing men who believed him unquestionably loyal.

He fumbled for his gun before remembering he
hadn't been carrying one. He never carried one. The days
when he needed to had long passed. He tugged his phone
from a pocket.

His hands were shaking so much it took three attempts to enter the correct code. Why did he even have
it locked? Who was going to steal from him? He found
the number for one of the two guarding the car.

The line connected after a few seconds but the reception was terrible at the center of all that concrete and
metal.

"Hello?" he said. "Can you hear me? Get in here now."

There was a garble of static in response.

"Get in here now," he shouted. "I need you. *Hurry.*"

The call disconnected.

No one was going to save him. He had to save himself. He turned around to rush toward the doorway and
run for his life back the way he had come. But he didn't
move because a man stood in the doorway.

He was tall and wore a charcoal suit. His hair was
short and black. His eyes were just as dark. The expression was blank and unreadable, but Linnekin knew what
kind of man he was staring at. He recognized a killer
when he saw one.

The man's hands were down at his sides. He stood
casually. No weapons. No aggression. But implicitly
threatening by nature of his presence. He may have been

unarmed but Linnekin feared him no less than if he held a silenced pistol in his right hand.

Linnekin couldn't take his gaze from the blank face and cold black eyes. "Who are you?"

The man in the suit stepped forward. "Who I am is not important."

Linnekin glanced around desperately. There were people nearby—his men outside and Moran and his crew already here. They had to be close. He could call for help, but what good was it going to do? If the man had got this far, then what had happened to them? Linnekin thought of the two men by the car and was furious at himself for leaving them to protect his precious Bentley. Would they hear if he screamed? Would they get here in time if they did?

Then Linnekin realized what had happened and felt like a fool. "Moran isn't here, is he? He sent you to kill me."

"No one sent me."

"Then he gave me up, didn't he?"

"Without much of a fight, I have to say."

Linnekin exhaled. His mouth was dry and his tongue felt thick and coarse. "What are you waiting for, then? You believe I'm scared of you? Do you think I'm going to piss myself? I've been expecting a bullet my entire life and lived twice as long as I ever believed." He stood straight and squared his shoulders. "I won't beg."

"I don't want you to beg."

"Then why don't you tell me what you do want with me? You won't get any money. I'd rather die now than give you the change in my fucking pocket."

"Keep it," the man said. "I don't want your money. But there are two things I do want. The first is for you to watch your language."

"You can't be serious."

"I bet you your knees that I am." The man adjusted his suit jacket to show the grip of a pistol protruding from his waistband. "Shall we find out if I'm serious?"

Linnekin caught his response before it left his lips. He then shook his head. "The second thing?"

The man stepped forward again. There were about three meters between them. He said, "I want answers."

"And what do I get in return?"

"You're in no position to negotiate."

"I'm a businessman," Linnekin said. "I'm always negotiating. The moment you told me you wanted something, you opened negotiations. You want answers. I want to walk out of here. So let's cut a deal."

"Now I know where Moran learned his technique. Okay," the man said. "I like your style. Let's deal. You tell me what I want to know and I let you walk out of here."

"What about my men?"

"They'll have headaches."

Linnekin considered, then said, "Okay. Then we have a deal."

"Good. I want you to start by telling me why you've been trying to kidnap Gisele Maynard, aka Gisele Norimov."

"Who?"

The man didn't answer.

Linnekin said, "Who?" again, then: "I don't know who you're talking about."

"I can see that," the man replied, a note of surprise in his voice. "You had Blake Moran's men watch her apartment for over a week. Last night, they broke in expecting to find her. They intended to kidnap her. Instead they found me."

"I heard Moran lost some men. Good. A small price

for betraying me to you, but I appreciate the sentiment. You have my thanks."

"Was Moran telling the truth about you asking him to kidnap Gisele?"

Linnekin shrugged. He let his shoulders relax. "When I ask someone for a favor, I'm not asking; I'm telling them they have no choice. I didn't remember the girl's name at first because I didn't pay any attention to it."

"Explain."

"I'm not into kidnapping. Such things are beneath me. Do I look like I'm struggling to pay the bills?"

"Then why?"

"Because, like Moran, I was asked to. Why are you even here if Moran's men found you and not the girl?"

"My reasons are my own," he said by way of an answer. "What is the name of the man who asked you?"

"Who said anything about a man? *She* didn't give me her name."

"A Russian?"

Linnekin shook his head. "British."

"Describe her to me."

"Tall. Well dressed. Blond. Green eyes. All business. I'd never met her before or heard from her since."

"Why did you take a risky job from someone you didn't know? You said yourself that you don't need the money."

"Because it wasn't in my interests to turn the job down."

"What makes you say that?"

"Because I know what the f— I know what I'm talking about. This woman knew all about me. She knew my name. She knew the names of my men. She knew which town I was born in and when I came to this shithole of a country. She could name every front company we use and had the license plates of every truck. She even knew when my next shipment was due to arrive. You don't say no a person like that. Just like people don't say no to me."

The man considered this. His expression didn't change.

Linnekin added, "Whoever she is, she's dangerous. I could tell that in the same way I can tell you are too. Only you're a very different kind of animal to her. You're more direct. She's smarter."

"I doubt that."

Linnekin smirked. "Really? She got me to do what she wanted without even having to threaten me. *And* I left with a smile and wished her well. You, on the other hand, I'll spend every waking moment of my life hunting down."

The man said, "A brave thing to say when you're at my mercy."

"We made a deal, remember? I'm talking, so when this is over I'm walking. That was the deal. Your word is on that. People like you and I are the worst of the worst and we know that. We're happy with that. But we keep our word. That's the only humanity we have left. I'm telling you everything straight, just like I said I would. You're going to let me go, just like you said you would. We didn't negotiate about what happens later. Don't pretend you thought this would be the end of it. You know very well that I can't let this lie."

"Fair point," the man said. "What were you supposed to do when you had Gisele in your possession?"

Linnekin smirked again. He was starting to enjoy himself. "Nothing. She told me she'd know when I had Gisele."

The man in the suit remained silent.

"So," Linnekin continued, "she's watching me, isn't she? She's watching my whole network, my men, everything we do. Everyone we meet. Which means she's now going to know all about . . . you." Linnekin grinned. "Still think you're so smart, tough guy?"

· Chapter 24 ·

Victor returned to the old plumbing supplies warehouse a little after eight a.m. He entered through the door leading into the office annex and followed the sound of grunting into the main warehouse space. Dmitri was working out—squats—with an improvised barbell weighted with sand-filled buckets and chains. Yigor spotted him. Both men were drenched in sweat. The air stank.

Dmitri noticed him and walked over. "Why have you got blood on you?"

Victor explained in as few words as possible.

Yigor grinned. "I knew it. You *are* Mr. Bad Man."

"What's the next move?" Dmitri asked.

Victor didn't answer. He made his way back into the office annex and upstairs to the first floor, where he used a landline to call Norimov.

When the line connected, Victor said, "Do you know a man named Andrei Linnekin?"

"No. Who is he?"

"A Russian mob boss. He had a drug trafficker named Moran put a crew out to look for Gisele. They were the guys who I encountered in her apartment. They'd been looking for her for the past week."

Norimov said, "Why did he tell Moran to kidnap my daughter?"

"Because he was too lazy to do it himself."

"I don't recognize the name Linnekin. I would have thought when my rivals were identified they would be men I knew, men I had broken bread with. He must be following orders for someone back here."

"Not necessarily," Victor said. He summarized what he'd been told about the blond woman with green eyes.

"So she's just another link in the chain."

"I'm not so sure. According to Linnekin, she knew everything about him and his operation."

"Because she was told it by the bosses. Linnekin may be a boss in London, but he'll answer to someone in Russia. That's how it works."

"Then why didn't they go straight to Linnekin? Why trust the job to a foreigner only for her to go to a Russian? Unless things have dramatically changed in recent times, the Russian mob isn't exactly trusting of outsiders. Or women."

"So who is she and why is she after me?"

"Smart enough not give Linnekin her name. Smart enough to convince him to take on a job he neither needed nor wanted. She wants Gisele, but couldn't do it herself. Either because she doesn't have the resources—which can't be the case if she knew so much about Linnekin—or she didn't want to get her hands dirty. Linnekin created a buffer between her and the kidnapping."

"Why?"

"Again, I don't know. She's careful. She wants things done in a particular way. She didn't expect Linnekin to palm the job off to someone like Moran. She won't be happy when she finds out he did and it's exposed her."

"How will she find out? Don't tell me you didn't kill him."

"We made a deal. If nothing else, I'm a man of my word. Besides, he's not my enemy. He's a middleman. If I killed him, I would need to kill his entire network. And I don't have the time for that."

"If he finds you—"

Victor said, "You of all people should know that I'm more difficult to kill than I like to appear. Linnekin's smart. He won't come after me so soon. He knows nothing about me. He's going to enjoy being alive first."

"You're taking a huge risk, my boy. That's most unlike you. Better not to take any chances, and kill Linnekin."

"When, and only when, I deem it necessary," Victor said. "But for now I have more pressing matters."

There was silence on the line for a moment. Victor could hear the heavy footfalls of Dmitri and Yigor climbing the stairs nearby.

Eventually, Norimov said, "If this woman you speak of doesn't have Gisele, why is she missing?"

"I'm starting to think that maybe she's not."

"What?"

"Something doesn't make sense. Gisele has been missing for a week—the same length of time since you were threatened—but if they have her they're not saying so. If they don't have her, where is she?"

"That's what I want you to find out."

"There's a chance they've already come after her."

"I know that. You don't have to keep telling me."

"I don't mean they have her."

"Then what do you mean?"

Victor said, "What if they tried to kidnap her before you received the photograph? Because then you wouldn't be able to warn her. That way, the first you'd know about the threat was when they told you they had your daughter or when you opened a box and found her head inside."

"What are you getting at?"

"It's a hypothesis," Victor said. "Perhaps this woman tried to kidnap Gisele and failed. When she couldn't locate her, she went to Linnekin for help, to look for her in London. At that point you were sent the threatening photograph because the attack had begun and she didn't realize you two were estranged. The photograph was sent so you would know who was behind the kidnapping attempt, so that you would divide your forces to protect Gisele. Which is what happened. Maybe the attempted kidnap happened right outside Gisele's building. She was too scared to return home and so is staying elsewhere. There was a gap in her wardrobe that would fit a medium-sized wheeled suitcase."

Norimov thought about this for a moment. "But where would she go?"

"How would I know? I've never met her. I know next to nothing about her. I don't know who her friends are or who she would stay with."

"Please let it be so. You've got to find her before they do. Please, Vasily. You must protect her."

"I'm aware of the objective. But she might turn up in a few days, blissfully ignorant of what's been going on in her absence."

"I'll pray that she does," Norimov said. "Some more of my men are on the next plane to London. An old friend in the FSB came through and managed to get them visas."

"I don't want any help. I'm only using Dmitri and Yigor so I can keep an eye on them."

"You're in charge, Vasily. My boys can sit on the sidelines until you need them."

Victor hung up. He stood in the gloom, thinking. Something wasn't right. He didn't believe everything he'd told Norimov. But he wasn't sure what he did believe.

• Chapter 25 •

Anderton's contact was a heavyset man with skin as black as the silk shirt he wore beneath a tailored charcoal suit. The only color came from a folded pink pocket square protruding from the suit jacket's breast pocket. He lounged at a corner table, his feet up and resting on a stool before him. Black loafers rested on the floor. Toes wiggled beneath socks.

A glass was raised Anderton's way as she approached through the clutter of tightly packed tables and chairs. The bistro was small and hot and close to capacity. The air was full of the sound of loud chatter.

Anderton said, "Marcus," and smiled as she took a seat opposite.

Marcus Lambert smiled in return: a flash of large bright teeth. "My dear. How are you keeping?"

"I'd like to say as tremendous as always, but I'm afraid I have a delicate situation."

Marcus responded with a slow nod. "So soon to the meat of the matter? No sexy waltz of chitchat first? I'm heartbroken."

"I'm afraid so. Time is not my friend today."

"And here I was thinking it was my caustic wit that brought you here."

She said, "The pleasure of your company is why we're not doing this over the phone."

"I shall accept that little lie. Why don't you tell me what kind of trouble you're in?"

She didn't respond. She held his gaze.

"Ah," Marcus said eventually. "It's about that."

"It was never going to be anything else."

Marcus placed his wineglass on the table between them. He laced his fingers together. "Correct me if I'm wrong, but you said it was under control. And that was after you told me we were never supposed to mention it again."

"Right on both counts. But I'm not mentioning it. Neither are you. Someone else is."

"Oh," Marcus said.

"Yes, *oh*," Anderton said back.

"I thought that was solid. You told me it was."

"That was then. This is now."

Marcus sat back. "We don't work together any longer. How is this still my business?"

"Because your business only exists because of what I—*we*—did. And you've done so very well out of it, haven't you?"

He looked away while he considered. Anderton left him to it because there could be only one conclusion.

"What do you want me to do?" Marcus asked.

"I need your company. Specifically, I need some of your assets."

"I don't like where you're going with this."

Anderton smiled. "That's irrelevant, Marcus. You run

a private security firm and I'm your new client. I'm asking for a team. Off the books, of course. Only your best."

"What exactly do you intend to use them for?"

"You know what I need them for. I have my own people for eyes and ears, but we're past that stage now. I can tell you specifics if you like, but I'm guessing you don't want to know any more than absolutely necessary."

Marcus thought about this. "How much more damage must be done before this is over?"

"An old Cambridge tutor of mine—Professor Vaughn—used to say, 'If you poke a bear once, you may as well keep poking.' Do you understand what that means?"

Marcus said, "I'm afraid I had a very different level of education than you have. In inner-city London, you count yourself lucky if your teacher shows up. Riddles were never on the agenda."

"My point is that we've already crossed so many lines with our little indiscretion—"

"Indiscretion," Marcus echoed. "You make it sound so harmless."

Anderton ignored the interruption. "So what use is there in debating how far we go now?"

Marcus finished his wine and poured himself another glass. "Does Sinclair know about this?"

She used her nails to lift a Sicilian green olive from a little bowl on the table. "Of course. He's been assisting me. He understands the importance of cleanliness."

"Is he still crazy?"

Anderton bit a piece from the olive and chewed. *"Mmm,* that's divine. I love it here. They use only the best."

"Well?"

She finished eating and wiped her fingers on a napkin.

"He's who he's always been. Just like you, however much you try to hide it behind all this aspirational decadence."

"Always has to come back to class with you, doesn't it, Nieve? If I so chose I could buy this here restaurant you're so partial to. Today. In cash."

She smiled at him. "That's the thing about class, Marcus: the more you try to buy it, the more you find it's sold out."

He swallowed some wine. "Sinclair's a liability. You know I had to fire him, don't you? The man took far too much pleasure in his work than is healthy, even for a mercenary. Using him for this makes me very uncomfortable. He's a dangerous dog who should have been destroyed long ago."

"There's some merit in that analogy, granted. But he has as much stake in this as you and I. And you're forgetting the essential fact about our dear friend: I hold his leash."

Marcus considered this. He toyed with the gold Patek Philippe on his left wrist. "I have a team in North Africa. They're good. More important, they're reliable."

"They sound perfect," Anderton said.

"When and where do you want them?"

"Here, in London. And I need them here yesterday."

· Chapter 26 ·

The United Kingdom has the highest rate of violent crime in the whole of Europe, but even so a triple murder in a leafy London street is a big deal. However, not even a day after Victor had killed three of Moran's men in Gisele's apartment there were no outward signs that any crime had been committed. The street seemed as quiet and peaceful as it had before. He expected there to have been a police car stationed outside the building last night, parked against the curb where it was visible to the residents, to reassure them. The two officers unlucky enough to have pulled that duty would have complained to each other about the waste of manpower, but the decision was for public relations. A triple murder, yes, but the three dead men were all criminals. Whoever had killed them wouldn't be coming back to butcher the neighbors.

Victor made sure his tie was straight and the knot tight as he walked up the gravel driveway. The same three cars were parked there as had been on his first visit. Gisele's sat in the same place as before. At the front door, he knuckled the buzzers for the two flats below Gisele's. No one answered. He descended the steps and moved around the side of the building to where the garden flat was located. He knocked on the front door.

There was no answer, but he heard someone inside so knocked again.

A chain clinked in place and the door opened a few inches until it became taut.

"Yes?"

A narrow segment of a woman's face was visible in the gap between door and jamb. She looked in her late fifties or early sixties.

Victor flipped open his wallet to give the woman the briefest snapshot of the ID inside. Her limited line of sight helped. "How do you do, ma'am? I'm Detective Sergeant Blake with the Metropolitan Police. I'd like to ask you a few questions about the events of the other night."

"I already spoke at length to a DCI Crawley."

"I know, ma'am. But the inquiry is ongoing and with new information comes the need for new questions. May I come in?"

She chewed her lip for a second. "Now really isn't a good time for me."

"I won't keep you long, I promise. The sooner we can fill in all our blanks, the sooner we can catch those responsible."

"Those? Inspector Crawley gave me the impression you were only looking for a single perpetrator."

That gave Victor a moment's pause. Whoever DCI Crawley was, he knew how to read a crime scene. "We can't rule anything or anyone out at this present time.

But the quicker they're off the streets, the better. As I'm sure you'll agree."

"Yes, I suppose so."

"May I come in?"

Deliberation. A sigh of defeat. "Okay. Yes. Come inside."

She shut the door to unhook the chain and opened it to allow him to enter. He stepped through the doorway into the hall. The ceiling was only a few inches above his head.

"This way, please."

The woman led him through to a lounge and offered him a seat. Floral paper covered the walls. Ornaments and antique oddities adorned every sideboard, of which there were many. Oil paintings hung from every wall. The floors were all carpeted and overlaid with colorful rugs.

He sat down in an armchair that gave him the best view of the door and the window. The curtains were closed. The flat was half-sunk into the ground, and even with the closed curtains he knew the driveway would only begin halfway up the window. Natural light would be a problem, especially in winter. Two lamps were switched on. The room had a warm, soft glow. The woman looked ten years younger than she had in the hallway. He didn't know her name. He'd been looking out for letters but there had been no mail by the door or left on sideboards.

"So, Sergeant. How can I help?"

"I wonder if I might trouble you for a glass of water first. Please."

"No problem," she said, sounding like it was. She left him to go to the kitchen.

He stood and slid open the drawers of a corner bureau

until he found utility bills and bank statements. He was back in the armchair when she reentered with a highball glass of water.

"There you go."

"Thank you. . . . Is it Miss or Mrs. Cooper?"

"Miss. But call me Yvette, please."

"Thank you, Yvette."

He sipped the water and set the glass down. "As I'm sure you're aware by now, there was a violent crime in the top-floor flat two nights ago."

"Three murders."

"That's right. I'd like to talk to you about the flat's occupier."

"Okay."

He saw she was suspicious and holding back, perhaps not believing he was who he said.

"Do you know Gisele Maynard?"

"We're neighbors. I knew her about enough to say hello in the morning. That kind of thing."

"Do you know where she is?"

Yvette shook her head. "I haven't a clue."

"When was the last time you saw her?"

"Oh, I really don't know. Obviously, before she went missing."

Victor nodded. "So you believe she is missing?"

"I . . . Well, no one's seen her, have they?"

"That's what we're trying to establish. She hasn't been to work in more than a week now. Does she have a boyfriend she might be staying with?"

"No. There's hasn't been anyone like that in her life for a while."

"What about friends?"

"I don't think she had many. At least, proper friends. All she did was work. She was very passionate about her job."

"And family? She has a father in Russia. Might she be visiting him?"

Yvette shook her head. "Definitely not. She had nothing to do with him. He's not a nice man. Shouldn't you be writing all this down?"

"I have a good memory for these things." He smiled and tapped the side of his skull while thinking the woman knew a lot about Gisele for someone who only ever said hello in the morning. "On the night of the murders, did you hear or see anything?"

"No, I was at work that night. Thank God."

"What kind of work do you do, Miss Cooper? I'm sorry—Yvette."

"I do shifts at the delivery office. I hate it." She smiled and laughed. "Don't have much choice at my age."

Victor nodded. Yvette sat with her knees close together and her hands in her lap.

"Do you live alone, Miss Cooper?"

"Yes. Why?"

"If there was another resident, I would have to speak to him or her about the other night. That's all."

"I had a flatmate once. Years ago now. I prefer living on my own. Not sure how much longer I'll be able to afford it, though. It's so expensive in London."

"I know what you mean," Victor said. "My partner and I are struggling to save for a deposit."

"Take my advice and go somewhere where you'll get a place twice the size for the same money. But good luck with it."

Victor said, "I think that's everything. Thank you for

your time." He stood, and said as she went to do the same, "Don't worry. I'll see myself out."

"Do you have a card? In case I think of anything else."

He patted the left side of his chest, over his inside jacket pocket. "Not on me, I'm afraid. But someone will probably pop round to see you again."

"Great," she said without enthusiasm.

"Cheers. May I use your bathroom?"

"If you must."

Like the rest of the flat it had a low ceiling. A ventilation fan buzzed on when he flicked the light switch. He closed the door behind him. He stood for a minute. He didn't move. He didn't need to do anything because he had seen what he had come into the bathroom to see.

When he stepped out and back into the hallway he found Yvette standing there, waiting for him. Her face was stern and frowning. "Are you really a copper? Let me see your ID again. You'd better not be a bloody journalist after scraps. You people make me sick."

Victor didn't bother arguing. He opened the closed door.

"Hey," Yvette called, "what are you doing? That's my room."

On the other side of the door was a bedroom. It was as full of ornaments as the lounge. The bed was immaculately made. There was no en suite or sliding door or walk-in wardrobe. He approached the second door. Yvette stood in his path.

"I'd like you to leave."

Victor said, "You claim to live alone yet there are two toothbrushes in your bathroom. You told me you weren't here the other night but I saw your lights were on. You also know a lot about her for someone who is just a neighbor."

"I said I'd like you to go now. Get out of my home."

"I will have no choice but to move you if you don't let me pass."

She squared herself in front of him. "If you do, I'll call the police. The *real* police."

"Last chance," Victor said. "Move."

She glared at him. "Get. Out. Now."

"It's okay, Yvette," a voice said from behind the closed door.

It opened and a young woman appeared.

"Hello, Gisele," Victor said.

Chapter 27

At five-six she was a little shorter than Victor had expected. She had an average build with strong shoulders and hips. Her skin was almost white and dusted with freckles across her nose and cheeks. Her hair was dyed a darker red than her natural color, making her eyes all the bluer. They were large and the shape of almonds, but half-hidden by a pair of designer glasses. Though she didn't have the height, in every other respect she looked like her mother. She tried to ignore it but he saw her stiffen at the sound of her name. She saw that he knew.

"If you don't leave," Yvette said, "I'm going to call the police."

Victor ignored her. He kept his gaze locked with Gisele's. Her eyes were beautiful, whites intense to the point of glowing and irises bluer than any ocean he'd ever seen. Her mother's had been the same.

"Who are you?"

Yvette said, "He's says he's a policeman. But he lied. He's a stinking journo."

"No, he's not," Gisele said.

"No, I'm not," Victor agreed. "I'm here because your father sent me."

"Stepfather," Gisele corrected. Norimov had been right. She did hate him.

He nodded to concede his mistake. "I don't have time to explain. It's important that you come with me."

She shook her head. Once. "No chance."

That caught him off guard. He hadn't considered that she would be an unwilling player. But it made sense. She was smart, educated, and she hated Norimov. Victor felt foolish for thinking she would behave otherwise. He was as much a stranger to her as she was to him.

"Your stepfather is concerned for your safety."

"Then maybe he should have chosen a less dangerous way to earn a living."

"He loves you," Victor said.

She laughed. He didn't know whether that was because she considered such a thing funny or because of the clumsy way he delivered it. He was unused to saying such things.

"What did you say your name was?"

Again, Yvette answered for him: "Blake, unless he's lying about that too."

"If he works for my stepdad, then everything he told you was a lie."

Victor said, "You can call me Vasily, if you like."

"Okay, Vasily. My stepdad sent you. Great. Now fuck off."

"Seconded," Yvette added.

"I don't want to scare you, Gisele. But I don't know how else to say this: you're in a lot of danger. I'm here to protect you. But you have to come with me."

She leaned against the doorframe, arms folded in front of her chest in a show of defiance. "I'm going nowhere."

"Your life is at risk."

The blue eyes widened. "You think I don't know that?"

"I think a week ago something happened that scared you and you've been staying here ever since. Am I right?"

Yvette said, "You shouldn't trust him."

She stood close to him, closer than he usually allowed people to get, but he saw that she did this out of protectiveness of Gisele—standing between him and her—and so made no move to reposition himself or her.

"Oh, don't worry. I won't." She stared at Victor, hands on her hip bones. "You'll forgive me if I have an issue taking your word for that, seeing as I've known you for two whole seconds."

"I understand that. I do. I can imagine how all this sounds to you. I'm a stranger, but I'm an old friend of your father's. He sent me because there are people who are seeking to do him harm. And you, by association."

She thought about this for a moment. "If you and my . . . if you and Alek are old friends, how come I've never met you?"

"That's a good question. I suppose I should have said we were business associates instead of friends."

"Ah," she said, "so you're a gangster too. Now I really don't trust you."

"Gangster?" Yvette said, eyes wide.

"I'm not a gangster."

Gisele said, "If you know Alek, then you're a criminal. Feel free to deny it, if you like."

"That is true enough," Victor said. "I am a criminal.

But that doesn't change the fact that you are in danger and I'm here to keep you safe."

"Why am I in danger?"

"Perhaps we can sit down in the lounge and talk this through," he suggested.

"I'm fine where I am," Gisele said. She settled against the doorframe as though it was the most comfortable place in the flat.

Yvette added, "There's no point sitting down. You'll be going soon. *Alone.*"

"Okay," Victor said. "You're in danger because your stepfather has enemies. We don't yet know who they are, but they're targeting you by virtue of your relationship to him."

"I have no relationship with him. I've *never* had a relationship with him."

"That doesn't matter to them. What matters is your stepfather loves you and they can get to him by getting to you. He believes they'll try to use you as leverage against him. I'm here to stop them doing that."

"What do you mean, use me as leverage?"

"They'll kidnap you first and use you to draw out your stepfather."

"And then?" Gisele said, a challenge in her voice.

There was no point in lying. Hiding the truth wasn't going to convince her to trust him. He said, "They'll kill you."

He saw the defiance falter in her expression as whatever anger toward Norimov and distrust of Victor she had was replaced by fear. He didn't like scaring her, but there was no other way of making her understand the danger she was in. He saw that she believed him.

Yvette said, "Gisele, we must call DCI Crawley. He has to know about this."

"No," Gisele said while still looking at Victor. "Not yet. Not until I know more."

"But you need—"

"I don't need to do anything, Yvette. I don't want anyone knowing about Alek and his bullshit. It's taken a long time to distance myself from all that. The moment it gets out that I'm the stepdaughter of a Russian mob boss my career is over before it's even begun. I'm not letting that happen until I absolutely have to. God, I fucking hate him for putting me through this shit again." She exhaled to calm herself down. Then to Victor she said, "How am I supposed to trust you? Why are you here to protect me, and not those juicers he hangs around with?"

"I don't expect you to. You shouldn't trust me. You shouldn't trust anyone you've just met, even me. But I am here to help and I suppose we can say your stepfather trusts me to protect you more than he does his men."

"So, what? You're like a professional bodyguard or something?"

"Let's say that I understand how an enemy might come after you and how to stop them."

She rolled her eyes. "This is such bullshit."

"I'm not going to argue. The point is there are dangerous people who want to do you harm. And they will, unless I stop them. I can't do that unless you agree to do as I say. Okay?"

"No, it's not okay. I don't know who you are. All I have to go on is what you're telling me. Which isn't a lot. For all I know you're one of Alek's enemies, trying to trick me."

"How can I prove myself to you?"

She considered for a moment. "Are you carrying a gun?"

He nodded.

"Oh, my God," Yvette breathed. "You brought a gun into my home? How dare you."

Gisele said, "Give it to me."

It was a stupid mistake to have made, to ask her how he could prove himself. She had her mother's power to make him trip over his words and fail to think before speaking.

"I can't do that," he said.

Gisele wasn't surprised by his answer. "Then get lost. Go back to Alek and tell him that I wouldn't go with you. While you're at it, tell him I said I hate him."

"Please," Victor said. "If I worked out that you're here, then it's only a matter of time until your stepfather's enemies do the same. They won't ask you to come with them. They'll just take you. I might not be around to stop them."

"Holy shit. *You* killed those three guys in my flat?"

He didn't react but he was surprised how well she could read him. Maybe it was a family trait.

"Gisele, please. We don't have time for this."

"I'm calling the police," Yvette announced, and strode into the lounge, where Victor remembered a landline sat.

He didn't try to stop her. He could render her unconscious in seconds, but then Gisele would never trust him. He had to leave Yvette alone. He had to convince Gisele to come with him before the call connected and local units were dispatched. But there was no time left.

He drew the handgun. Gisele gasped and Yvette turned in response and screamed.

Victor racked the slide to eject the chambered round,

caught it in his other hand, and released the magazine. He held out the weapon by the muzzle.

"Okay," he said. "You win. Take the gun."

She stared at it. "It's real, isn't it? I know. I've shot a few."

"You have?" Yvette asked, repelled.

Gisele shrugged. "Back in Russia. Alek's idea of quality time with me. No wonder I'm so fucked up." She snatched it out of his hand. "Please put the phone down. Everything's cool."

Her voice was quiet and soft but carried enormous strength and persuasiveness. Yvette paused, then nodded. She replaced the handset.

"I still want him out of this flat."

"Me too," Gisele said. "He'll be gone in a minute. Won't you?"

"Only if you're with me."

She turned the gun over in her hands. She was examining it, maybe comparing it to those she had fired in the past. He could tell she was equally fascinated and appalled by it. "Why are you so keen to be my bodyguard? You don't know me. I've never even set eyes on you before today."

"I know your father."

"But you said you're not his friend. So why are you helping him?"

"Okay," Victor said. "Your father asked me to help you, but I didn't say yes because I used to work with him. I agreed because I used to know your mother when I worked with your father. She was a nice woman."

Gisele swallowed. "She's been dead for years."

He nodded. "I know. It was a long time ago when we knew each other. I liked her. She was always nice to me. If she needed my help, I would help."

Gisele studied him, her eyes searching his for the truth—for something to believe in. She was still staring when she said, "What color were her eyes?"

He didn't blink. "Blue, just like yours."

"Easy enough to find out. How tall was she?"

"Taller than you are. Five eight and a half. You must have your biological father's height."

"Left or right handed?"

"Left. But right-eye dominant."

"I didn't know that part." She paused, frowning. "You could be lying and I wouldn't know."

"I'm not lying. I couldn't have known that you didn't know that information."

"Then you know more about my dead mother than I do. Thanks for pointing that out."

"I taught her how to use a bow and arrow. That's how I know."

He watched Gisele's eyes angle to look again at the gun in her hand. She said, "You told me if she wanted your help you would say yes, but she's dead. She's not asking you to help me."

Victor nodded. "If she were alive now and she asked me to protect you, I wouldn't hesitate. She isn't alive to ask me, but that doesn't change my answer."

Gisele took a deep breath and exhaled through her nose. She held his gaze with her blue eyes full of strength and intelligence. He felt as if he were looking back in time.

"Okay," she said, eventually. "I'll come with you."

"Don't do it," Yvette said. "You can't possibly believe him." Her own eyes were large and accusing, gaze flicking between Victor and Gisele.

Gisele's eyes never left Victor's. "I grew up surrounded by liars. Now I work in a profession defined by lies. I *know* liars. He doesn't sound like one to me."

"Don't be so naive, dear," Yvette added. "This one is bad news."

Gisele said, "Maybe. But I have my phone. I'll call you later and let you know I'm okay."

Yvette was aghast. She frowned. "If he hasn't murdered you by then."

Gisele ignored her. She held the gun out to Victor. He took it.

"You've made the right choice," he said. "Let's go."

· Chapter 28 ·

Gisele sat in the passenger's seat of the man's car and tried to stop herself from becoming overwhelmed by what was happening. She was voluntarily in a car with a strange man who claimed to have been sent by her father because his enemies were after her. Enemies who had tried to kidnap her a week ago. It was crazy. It was madness. This kind of thing didn't happen to people like her.

"Holy fucking shit," she said, following a big exhale.

She saw the man who clearly wasn't named Vasily frown. He didn't speak, however. His gaze never left the road ahead. She didn't like the silence. It gave her too much time to think about how stupid she was being. He had a gun.

A deep breath calmed her down a little. She had believed him before. There was no reason to reverse her opinions just yet.

When it became obvious he wasn't going to speak for the entire journey unless spoken to, she said, "I guess we should get to know one another."

He didn't look at her. "That's not necessary."

"Not necessary? Are you joking?"

"I don't make jokes."

"Good to know, Mr. Serious, but I'm going to go ahead and disagree with you on that whole 'necessary' thing. If you're going to be my bodyguard, then it makes sense to know you better, and vice versa."

The lights changed and he accelerated. "I'm not a bodyguard."

"Okay," she said. "But—whatever—you asked me to trust you, and I've taken a huge risk getting into a car with you. You don't want me to regret my actions already, do you?"

He didn't respond.

She said, "Let me put it another way: if you want me to come with you and stay with you, then I need to feel comfortable with you, and right now you're not making me feel very comfortable. I'm about thirty seconds away from digging my nails into your eyeballs and calling the police."

That made him look at her. She saw that he understood she was not joking. He hesitated, not sure how to respond.

"I'm down to about twenty-three seconds," she said.

"Fine," he said. "Let's get to know one another, if you like."

"I'd like you to want to too."

"Fine," he said again. "I do. Tell me about yourself."

"That's better. That's much better. Not so hard to be friendly, is it?" She didn't wait for an answer because she knew she would probably be waiting a while. Whoever this guy was, he wasn't a talker. "You know a bit about me already, yeah? But did you know I can touch the end of my nose with the tip of my tongue?"

That made him look at her, eyebrow raised. She laughed at his reaction.

"Not even a hint of a smile? Man, you're cold. I can't really," she admitted. "Just trying to take the edge off what is an extremely stressful situation."

"This is not exactly the time for humor, Gisele."

"So you're saying there *is* a time for humor?"

He glanced at her. She took this as his way of saying yes. She said, "Are you married?"

"No."

"Kids?"

"No."

"Girlfriend?"

"No," he said for the third time.

She exhaled. "Loving the one-word answers. Really getting to know you. Let me try changing tactics. How old are you?"

"I'll keep that to myself."

"Ah, like that, is it? Youth fading, old age creeping up on you? You're over thirty, right? What are you, nearly forty?"

He looked at her.

She smiled. "Just joking. A bit. Where do you live?"

"I move around a lot."

"So do I. I walk, run, ride a bike, take the bus. That's not an answer. Where are you from? I don't think you're Russian, but your accent is hard to place."

"That's the idea."

"So, where were you born?"

"I don't know."

"What do you mean, you don't know?"

"Exactly what I said. I don't know where I was born."

"What does it say on your birth certificate?"

"I didn't have one."

"What does it say on your passport?"

"I have lots of passports."

"Okay, fine. What does it say on your very first passport?"

"Like my age, I'll keep that to myself."

She rolled her eyes. "I knew you were going to say that."

"Then why ask?"

She shrugged. "It doesn't matter, does it? If you don't want to tell me anything about yourself there's nothing I can do about it."

"It's not a case of want but necessity. The less you know about me, the better."

"The better for you, you mean."

"For both of us," he said.

She saw an honesty in his eyes despite his evasiveness. He refused to open up about himself but made no effort to lie or pretend. It would have been easy enough to lie to her. She wouldn't know what was true and what was not. She liked that he didn't do that.

"Okay, I'll give up getting to know you for the moment. But only because by saying so little about yourself you've actually told me quite a lot."

"I have?"

"Oh yeah, bud. But now it's your turn to ask me something. And before you say you don't need to, I'm telling you that you do. Remember what I said about these here nails and your eyeballs."

After a moment, he said, "What happened a week ago?"

Gisele took a deep breath. "I knew you were going to ask me that. And I don't exactly want to relive it."

"It's important."

"Fine. I guess I have to sometime, right? Might as well be now. I was working late at the office. There was a lot to be done, as my boss wasn't in that day. I was the last to leave. I barely made the tube home. When I got out at my station I noticed there was this guy hanging around. He looked at me. You know, stared. I thought he was going to ask me for money or a light or something, but then he looked away and started playing on his phone. I didn't think anything more about it, but I was walking fast, just in case. Which was pretty dumb, because all I could hear was my own footsteps. I couldn't hear his behind me." She took another breath. "I guess I was lucky, because his phone went off and I didn't look back but I *knew* it was him. So a minute later when this car pulls up next to me I'm already alert and I start running. What I didn't know was that the man behind me had tried to grab me at that exact moment. But I was already running so he only caught a handful of hair and yanked it out." She rubbed the back of her head.

"Did he chase you?"

She nodded. "I guess. I think so. I didn't look back and I'm quite quick. As well as a self-defense class, I jog and take a spin class. I like keeping fit. Even if I could still lose a couple of kilos."

"Where did you go when you ran away?"

"Not far. I ran into the first place I could find: an Irish pub. Soon as I was inside, I called the police. No one followed me in."

"That was smart. You forced them to back off. They might have gone straight to your flat to wait for you there."

"The detective said the same thing."

"Did you see the driver of the car?"

She shook her head.

"What was the car like?"

She shook her head again. "I have no idea. I'm sorry."

"There's nothing to be sorry for. Was there anyone else in the car beside the driver?"

"I don't think so."

"What did the police say?"

"That I was very lucky."

"Did they have any idea who the two men were?"

"No. They asked me lots of questions, of course. Do I have any enemies? Do I owe anyone money? That kind of thing. They said they might have been looking to rape me. Fuck, can you imagine? It's a cliché, but you never think it will happen to you. Well, you don't want to believe it could. Otherwise you'd never leave your house, would you?"

"Did you tell them about your father?"

"Why would I? I haven't seen Alek for years. I haven't had anything to do with him since I've lived here. I say that, but I still take his money. And, yes, I know that makes me a hypocrite. But you know what they say: not everyone can afford to have principles."

"Did the cops tell you to stay with your neighbor?"

"The police said they would have a patrol car drive by to keep an eye on me, which they did. Exactly one time. When I realized that they weren't going to do anything else until after I was raped or murdered, I decided I would take the week off work and stay with Yvette. She offered. Well, insisted. She's nice. A bit paranoid, though. She wouldn't open the curtains in case *they* came back looking for me. That's why I hid when you knocked on the door. I hope you didn't scare her too much."

"Please apologize on my behalf when you see her next."

"So the guys who tried to grab me are enemies of Alek?"

Victor nodded. "He believes another outfit is seeking to wipe him out."

"Good. He deserves it."

"You don't mean that."

She shrugged.

Victor said, "Regardless, you don't deserve this."

"How do you know I'm not exactly like him?"

"I can tell. You're a good person. Like your mother."

"How good could she have been if she married him?"

"Norimov kept her in the dark as much as possible. She knew he was a criminal, but she didn't know what that meant."

"Then she should have found out."

"She loved him long before she knew he was a criminal."

"That's not a very good excuse."

She saw him consider this for a moment. "Maybe not."

He slowed to a stop at an intersection. Gisele saw his eyes never stopped moving while they waited for the light to change. Not just at the roads ahead and to the left and right, but also to the road behind. She saw it for what it was—vigilance—and felt comforted by it. She knew next to nothing about this man, but somehow trusted he would keep his word to protect her.

She relaxed in the seat and let her eyes go unfocused on the city outside, blurring the sharp lines and glare into softness and light.

• Chapter 29 •

Through the cabin windows, the city was a seemingly infinite blanket of orange dots glowing in the darkness. The plane touched down at London City Airport shortly before seven p.m. local time. It wasn't a commercial airliner but a private charter jet. It was a Gulfstream G550, capable of seating up to nineteen people. Tonight it carried eight passengers. All men. The cabin crew, more accustomed to serving oil tycoons, bureaucrats of the European Union, and Arab sheikhs, were not sure what to make of these eight unkempt passengers onboard the luxury jet.

Instead of suits, they wore jeans and khaki trousers, T-shirts and hooded sweatshirts, sports coats and leather jackets. They were all tanned and had varying amounts of facial hair. Most were well built, ranging in age from early thirties to late forties. They had boarded the Gulfstream with few words at Tripoli International Airport, declining offers of help with their luggage. Their bags were a far cry from Louis Vuitton and Prada. They were sports bags and rucksacks, as dirty and weatherworn as the men who carried them; instead of being stored away in the luggage hold or even in the overhead compartments, they were placed on the fine leather seats next to their owners.

The Gulfstream was equipped with a bar stocked with a range of wines, spirits, and liqueurs. The crewman stationed behind it spent the flight bored and restless with nothing to do. Each of the passengers ignored the complimentary alcohol, instead drinking only bottled water, tea, or coffee. They accepted the food, however, emptying the stock of gourmet meals and making a horrendous mess in the process. They had no taste and no class, eating smoked salmon pâté from the same plate as steak tartare, asking for crème anglais to be poured over strawberry semifreddo. The crew was appalled.

It was a three-hour, forty-minute flight from Tripoli. The televisions and other gadgets were ignored. The men seemed to have neither interest in their surroundings nor the need to pass the time. They did little more than eat. And after they had eaten they slept. One even lay sprawled on the long couch, booted feet up and leaving smears of dirt on the suede. Only one stayed awake, reading and making notes in a small notebook, undisturbed by the snores around him.

The comfort and facilities of the luxury charter jet were wasted on the group. Their very presence was an insult to the expertise of the cabin crew. They whispered among themselves, sampling the bar's drinks to pass the time and speculating on who the eight men could be, the conclusions becoming more and more outrageous as blood-alcohol levels rose. They had the look of men who performed tough manual work. One of the crew suggested they were soldiers, but it was agreed with their lack of uniforms, manners, and nonmilitary haircuts, they had to be otherwise employed. But how could these men afford to travel in such an expensive aircraft? If they were not rich themselves, who was footing the bill for the charter? And, more important, why?

The men exited the aircraft with barely any acknowledgment to the crew. Only one bothered to express his appreciation. If he noticed the inebriation of the cabin crew, he did not comment on it. A woman waited for them on the tarmac. She shook their hands in turn and led them to where a couple of black Range Rovers were standing by. The men boarded the vehicles, and the crew watched the brake lights disappear into the night.

· Chapter 30 ·

Gisele shifted in the passenger's seat. Her jeans were digging into her stomach. They were high-waisted to keep her tummy in. The sweater helped too, and its geometric pattern added some breadth to her otherwise modest bust. She liked to look nice but drew the line at such patriarchal shackles as high heels and underwear that encouraged yeast infections. Women shouldn't have to torture themselves in order to look their best. Men wouldn't stand for it—literally—so neither would she.

She thought of herself as an attractive woman—not as hot as she would have liked, but she received enough compliments and pickup attempts to have a positive self-image. Her companion, stone-faced and unblinking, didn't seem to notice. This irritated her. She noticed him. He was tall and in shape and had an aura of unshakable confidence bordering on arrogance. She found that to be a particularly attractive quality in a man. A shame, then, that he had no personality.

She wanted to be taken seriously as a lawyer and dressed appropriately conservative and tried to act older than her years. She wasn't prepared to flirt and flatter to get ahead, even if the opportunities seemed to be there. Men at her firm clearly liked her, especially the older men. She already had the weight of her stepfather's criminality hanging around her neck. The only way she would ever be respected was by showing people she knew what she was doing. Problem was, she didn't yet know how to do her job. Studying law and practicing it couldn't be more different. For now, she was happy to assist and watch and learn. Her time would come eventually. She knew that.

Gisele wanted to make it as a lawyer, to earn respect and pay the bills and do some good to distance herself from Alek and the life he led—the life that had paid for the nice house they had lived in and bought her everything she ever wanted and nothing that she had needed.

Feeling herself getting stressed thinking about her stepfather, she rubbed her arm and said to the man next to her, "Where are you taking me?"

"Your stepfather's men have a warehouse where they're holing up. We'll stay there until we know our next move."

"What do you mean, *next move?*"

"You let me worry about that for the time being."

She nodded, then examined him. Fit, but slim. Decent clothes. Well groomed but not stylish. "You don't look like a bodyguard."

"I've told you. I'm not a bodyguard."

"Then what do you do for a living?" she asked.

He didn't answer. He acted as though he hadn't heard her.

"Well?" she said after a moment's silence.

"I'm a security consultant."

"No, you're not."

"Why do you say that?"

"Because if you were, then you wouldn't have pretended not to have heard my question."

He remained silent.

"We've already established you're a gangster," she said. "I just wanted to know what kind."

"How many kinds of gangster are there?"

She shrugged. "I know only two kinds. There are guys like Alek who wear a suit and act respectable, like they're a CEO or something, and there are those who do the heavy lifting so people like Alek can get rich. So, which kind are you?"

"I'm a different kind."

"The security-consultant kind?"

He nodded.

"Which of Alek's guys are there?" she asked.

"Dmitri and Yigor."

She smiled. "Cool, I haven't seen them for ages. It'll be great to catch up."

"You like them?"

"Sure I do. Why wouldn't I?"

He said, "Because they're gangsters working for the stepfather you hate."

She shrugged. "It's not their fault I hate him, is it? Growing up, they paid me more attention than he did. Yigor used to drive me to school and let me play the same stupid music every day. Dmitri, he's a sweetie. Once you've spent some time to get to know him, anyway."

"Then I guess I haven't had the time."

"You don't like him?"

"It's more the other way around."

"He doesn't like you? I can only assume he has good reason. What did you do?"

"I suppose you could say that we had an altercation a couple of years ago. One that he still holds a grudge over."

"Like a fight?"

"Of a kind."

She looked shocked. "And you won?"

"It wasn't a fight per se, so there wasn't what you'd call a winner and a loser. But he came off worse, if that's what you mean."

"So, are you one of those guys who knows that cage-fighting MMA stuff?"

"Not exactly, but I know a little about self-defense."

Gisele smiled, impressed and intrigued. "Me too. I told you about my class, right? Can you show me some cool moves?"

"I'm afraid I don't know any cool moves."

She eyed him, suspicious. "Why don't I believe you?"

· Chapter 31 ·

I t was cold in the aircraft hangar. Outside it was less than ten degrees Celsius, according to her car's thermometer. Inside it had to be even colder, Anderton thought. She wore her long winter coat and scarf. There was no heating, obviously, and the domed ceiling was at least thirty meters overhead. Forty thousand cubic feet of space for aircraft was almost empty. The only vehicles inside were Anderton's car and two black Range Rovers. Men climbed out of the four-by-fours. Eight of them in total. Anderton knew their faces only because she had seen the files Marcus had supplied. She knew each man's name and particulars because she had studied those files and memorized every detail. She had never worked with them before.

They dropped out of the vehicles, boots loud on the hard floor and echoing around the hangar. It took them a few minutes to assemble before her because they unloaded bags and rucksacks. Most eyeballed her a little, sizing her up and coming to all sorts of judgments and conclusions. They would have worked with intelligence officers before. They had probably all been screwed over or put in danger because of bad intel. She would be the whipping girl for their collective distrust and dislike of what they referred to as green slime.

But that was before, back when they had been serving their respective countries and risking their lives for far less money than anyone who gets shot at for a living should make. Now they earned a lot more and didn't have to answer for their actions. They were mercenaries. According to Marcus, his best. And if not his best, his most reliable. In Marcus's world, on the Circuit, as private security contractors called it, *reliability* was code for "willingness to do jobs that other mercenaries would not." *Don't worry about this guy. He'll do what needs doing. He's reliable.*

That's what Anderton required above all else. "What do you think?" she whispered to the man next to her.

Sinclair shrugged by way of an answer and folded his arms in front of his chest. Ropey muscle tightened beneath the tanned forearms. Normally, the stance would have indicated defensiveness to Anderton, but coming from Sinclair it could not be read as such. Marcus had referred to him as a dog that should have been put to sleep, and he was at least half-right. Sinclair was an animal, and therefore his behavior could not be interpreted by human standards.

He was a white South African. Dangerous and unpredictable, but he was loyal and excelled at doing the kinds of things that turned even Anderton's stomach.

Overhead fluorescent tubes bathed the mercenaries in harsh, unforgiving light. When they had formed a loose line, she closed the distance between them. The heels of her snakeskin boots clattered on the floor.

The hangar air was crisp and stank of diesel and engine

grease and jet fuel. When she was three meters from the men it also stank of body odor. She reminded herself that a few hours before they had been in Libya and then on a flight. There was no lack of discipline in their hygiene. They simply didn't have the time or opportunity to pay attention to activities like regular showers, shaving, and using deodorant. Plus, she had been in some of the same parts of the world these men had recently operated in, and most natives there didn't either. They were all tanned from time in Tripoli, North Africa, and the Middle East. Most had been in that region for months. She had winced when reading reports of some of the things they had done. But that was good. She didn't want heroes.

They had been stationed in Libya for the last three weeks, working for Marcus as they had all done numerous times before. They were running a number of simultaneous operations for several different clients who had hired them through Marcus's company. They had provided close protection for VIPs. They had conducted surveillance. They had trained and advised. And they had killed.

Anderton took a breath. She was well-read. She was well prepared. Now it was time to get to work.

"Gentlemen," she began. "Thank you for such a speedy arrival. I know Marcus hasn't told you much about why you're here."

"A job," one said.

His name was Wade, the team's unofficial leader. The eldest and most experienced of them. He meant the kind of job that men like him and the others were qualified to complete; the kind of job that was discussed at night in aircraft hangars. Anderton didn't know why Wade had given up a life of service to his country to work as a private security contractor, but she guessed it was in no small part influenced by the extra zero on his yearly income.

"That's correct," she said. "It's a single-objective operation to take into custody a civilian female. I've prepared a detailed dossier on the target, but the salient facts are: she is twenty-two years old, she's—"

"You're hiring the eight of us to snatch one girl?" said another—Rogan. "You've got to be fucking kidding."

"I'm about as far removed from kidding as it's possible to be. Taking this girl into custody is the least you have to be concerned about, I assure you."

"What's that supposed to mean?"

"It means I am not the only party interested in her. Her father is the boss of a Russian organized-crime network and he's dispatched some men to protect his daughter. To get to her, you'll have to go through them."

The mercenary snorted. "We eat Russian mafia for breakfast."

Others smiled or smirked.

"That's great to know," Anderton said without inflection. "But I suggest you take them seriously. These are not street thugs we're talking about."

"No offense, missy," Wade said, "but you're not giving us a lot to go on besides your opinion. And you'll forgive me if I don't settle for the opinion of a desk jockey whose closest run-in with danger is using a pencil sharpener. We've been working round the clock down in rag-head land, and we're a week into prepping our next action. We're shipped off to London and all that work has gone down the drain like a turd. No single girl, even one with some gangsters guarding her, requires the eight of us."

Another of the mercenaries said, "True story."

"Maybe you've all been in the sun too long," Anderton countered in a calm and reasoned manner. "Forget what you've been doing. *This* is the only job you should care about. Clear?"

"Waste of talent is what it is," one of the men said.

Anderton smiled at him. "Then no doubt you'll finish it in double-quick time."

The hangar was quiet for a moment.

Wade straightened. "London is not like Libya. We fuck up in the slightest way and we find ourselves in the epicenter of an almighty shit storm."

"Which is why you get paid so much, sport," Sinclair said.

Wade looked at him. "And who the fuck are you?"

Sinclair didn't bother to answer with words. His gaze locked with Wade's and his mouth stretched into a sardonic grin.

Anderton answered for him: "He's an associate of mine. He's part of the operation."

Wade, clearly not liking Sinclair staring at him, said, "Can't he answer for himself?"

Anderton said, "He'll talk as and when he's ready. But I'm in charge here and we have things to discuss."

But Wade was in no mood to forget. He was still looking at Sinclair. "What's the matter, boy? Too chicken to talk to me?"

Anderton saw that the barb had been only half-serious, but Sinclair immediately tensed up and his fists clenched. When he spoke, his voice was quiet and menacing.

"If I'm a chicken, then I'm the meanest fighting cock you ever saw. And I'll peck those eyes right out of your skull."

He began walking toward Wade, who, not wanting to appear weak before his men, stood his ground.

When Sinclair's face was inches from Wade's, he said, "Wanna see how hungry I am?"

Wade said, "Back off."

Anderton kept her cool. These guys were wound up tighter than she'd figured. She was all too aware she was standing in a room with nine trained killers who were a spark away from exploding.

"What my esteemed associate was trying to say," Anderton continued, as if the standoff weren't happening, "is that this job may not have a hard target but it is in a hard environment—one of the most heavily surveilled cities in the world, wherein there are many difficulties that can multiply into innumerable unknown factors that can potentially impede our ability to complete our objective and emerge on the other side with our skins intact. Hence the need for a large, experienced team."

Sinclair, still in Wade's face, nodded. "What she said."

Anderton put a hand between them. "Gentlemen, if you're done, we have a lot to go through before we move out. . . ."

· Chapter 32 ·

Gisele was quiet for the rest of the journey. She was quiet when Victor parked Dmitri's car two hundred meters down the access road from the plumbing supplies warehouse. Victor climbed out first and scouted out the area. He saw and heard no threats and returned to the car. She looked at him expectantly.

"It's clear."

"What's clear?" she asked.

He realized he had been thinking out loud. No, he corrected himself. He had been acting as part of a unit—on point—informing the rest of the team about the path ahead. It had been a long time since he'd thought and acted in such ways. He didn't particularly like that Gisele had brought that behavior out of him.

"Nothing," Victor said.

He drove the remainder of the way and parked outside the warehouse.

"It's not exactly the Ritz," Gisele said as she closed the passenger's door.

He didn't respond because his first thought was that

she was complaining, but then he saw her face and understood she was joking. For a moment it seemed as if she were enjoying herself, but he understood the humor to be a distraction—a front because she was nervous. She believed her life was in danger, but she didn't want to believe it. Anything that eased the reality was a welcome diversion. If he could keep her safe while Norimov solved the problem, she might never have to know anything beyond that.

"I'll think of it like we're going camping," she said, looking around. "Only without the scenery."

"Don't be scared," he said.

"Well, I wasn't until you said that."

Victor frowned. He wasn't sure if he had been wrong in his assessment or if she was still joking. But this time, he remained silent. He let her in through the glass door next to the huge steel gate. He drew the pistol because he heard voices other than Dmitri's and Yigor's, but tucked it away again when he realized they belonged to more of Norimov's men, newly arrived from Russia.

"This way," he said to Gisele, and took her up the stairs to the first floor of the office annex.

"When do we eat around here? I'm getting a little peckish. These hips won't grow themselves, you know."

"Dmitri or Yigor might have some food, or they can go and pick something up."

"What are you, their boss?"

"No. But I'm not leaving your side. So they'll have to do the grunt work."

"You said you weren't a bodyguard."

"I can't protect you if I'm not with you, can I?"

She looked him over. "No offense, but you're not exactly massive."

He took no offense. "You'll have to take my word that in keeping you safe my body mass will be the least important factor."

"Gisele," Dmitri roared when they reached the board-room.

He leaped to his feet and rushed her way. Victor moved to block his path but she stepped around him and embraced the big Russian, who lifted her up as he hugged her.

"Ugh, don't crush me."

He was grinning as he gently lowered her down. Also in the room were Yigor and three other of Norimov's men. Victor recognized them all from the bar. The two he'd disabled outside the rear entrance were there, the smaller one sporting a nose splint and the larger one a scowling expression. The third man was Sergei. His scarred ear was bright red in the cold.

"You found her," he said to Victor, who nodded.

The Russians all looked at him for an explanation but didn't press when he failed to present one. Some knew Gisele. Others did not. They spent a few minutes introducing themselves or catching up. Victor pretended not to notice the stares he was getting from Aleksei and Ivan—the two he'd dropped outside the bar. Yigor was the only one of the five Russians Victor had not fought. He was glad to have avoided that. Yigor was the biggest of them all, and the one Victor saw knew how best to handle himself.

There were lots of happy faces and backslapping. Gisele looked uncomfortable being the center of attention.

He took the opportunity to ask her, "Why do you want to be a lawyer?"

Apparently relieved to be lured away from the jovial

Russians, she said, "Because I believe in the law and I want to be part of it."

"But why?"

"Oh, look at you, wanting to find out how I tick. I'm flattered. Nay, humbled."

"That's not answering the question."

"You're a pushy one when you want to be, aren't you? Wish I hadn't let you off the hook so easily beforehand, but fine, I'll justify myself to you if that's what you want. Everyone hates lawyers, don't they? That makes no sense to me. Sure, there are some sharks out there, but aren't there in any profession? And how many of those professions are more essential? Not many, I'll tell you that. We need lawyers to ensure the law is followed, because the law is the very definition of society's morality. It should be formidable and scary and vengeful, but also understanding and gentle when required. It doesn't always work and it almost never achieves true justice, but it's all we have and it's better than the alternative."

"Which is?"

"Barbarism."

"Very articulate."

Her eyes narrowed. "Are you being sarcastic?"

"Not at all."

"Okay. Good. Thank you, then. I think." After a pause, she grinned. "Also, you can earn a decent living. Which is useful because I like nice things. I'm not all about the altruism, you know. Let's call that Alek's influence. I'm trying to shake it off. Might take a few more years. What about you? You said your name is Vasily, yes?"

He nodded. He felt the accusation in her tone.

She affirmed it when she said, "But you're not Russian."

"It's the name your father knows me by."

"So what's your real name?"

He didn't answer.

"What? You're joking, right? I come here with you, trusting you, and you won't tell me your name? That's ridiculous."

"I don't expect you to trust me. I said I hope that eventually you will. It's safer for you if you don't know who I am."

"That's a lie."

He said, "It's as close to the truth as either of us needs."

She frowned, openmouthed, trying to decipher the comment. He was spared further interrogation because she heard Sergei say to Yigor, "We'll take her back in the morning. No one will get to her between the five of us."

"Hey, hold on a minute," she said. "Who's this you're taking *back*? If by *her* you mean me, then I hate to rain on your parade but there isn't a snowball's chance of my going to Russia with you."

"Gisele, please," Sergei pleaded. "You have to come with us. We're going to keep you safe. Okay?"

She pointed a thumb at Victor. "I thought that was his job."

Sergei said, "He's done his job. Now it's our turn. You don't need him anymore. You have us. Your father wants you at his side. It's safer there."

"He's not my father. And if you try to take me to Russia I will scream all the way through passport control. Try it. Let's see if I'm joking."

Sergei turned to the other Russians for backup. They looked away or shrugged. They were well used to beating cooperation out of people, but had no clue how to handle their boss's rebellious stepdaughter.

She turned to Victor. "Are you going to back me up, or what?"

He realized he didn't know how to handle her either. He said, "We can discuss the particulars tomorrow," to put a halt to further discussion or potential argument. He wasn't yet sure of his next move. He had to rest and recharge.

Gisele said, "Whatever. But I'm not going anywhere, just so you know."

"I'll go get food," Yigor announced with a clap of his hands. "We should celebrate, yes? Eat lots of bad food and drink lots of good vodka, yes?"

"No one drinks alcohol," Victor said, "until this is over."

Gisele looked at him. "Wow, you're a party animal, aren't you? Personally, I could use a few shots to help forget all this life-and-death stuff. It's getting a bit old."

"When this is over," he insisted.

"I'll hold you to that. You can buy me a cocktail."

Yigor sneered at him as he put on his coat. "Yes, Mr. Bad Man. You the boss." He saluted. "Just the food."

Chapter 33

Victor left Gisele with the Russians and performed a circuit of the warehouse. It was a huge space but almost entirely empty. He took his time, searching for anything out of place, any signs of intruders or danger. He didn't envision Norimov's enemies launching an attack, but he couldn't rule out that they were aware of the warehouse. He was confident he had not been followed since his arrival in London, but he couldn't say the same for Norimov's men.

He cleared the first floor of the office annex and then the floor below, and finally the warehouse proper. As expected, there were no signs of any forced entry.

Upstairs again, he found Gisele sitting in the darkness on an old office chair.

"Where have you been?" she asked.

"Checking the perimeter."

"Why?"

He stopped himself from launching into an explanation of the dangers of operational complicity, and instead responded: "Habit. Why aren't you with the others?"

She shrugged. "Needed some me time. Those guys can be pretty intense. Are you going to join us?"

"I have to call your father."

"Stepfather. Tell him to go to hell for me."

He waited until she had gone back into the boardroom, then called Norimov.

"She's safe," Victor said.

For a moment, there was silence on the line. He pictured Norimov holding the phone away from his face, perhaps pressed against his chest, while he controlled his emotions.

When Norimov spoke, his voice was full of happiness. "I don't know how to thank you."

"You don't need to. I did this for Eleanor, not you."

"I understand. I do. Regardless, you will forever have my gratitude."

"Keep your gratitude," Victor said. "It's worthless."

Norimov sighed. "I guess I deserve that. Put Gisele on the phone, please."

"She doesn't want to talk to you. She doesn't like you very much. Can't say that I blame her."

There was a long pause. "This horrible business will push her even farther away from me."

"No doubt."

"Thank you for not placating me."

"I wouldn't begin to know how to," Victor said.

"I know I have wronged you, my boy, and when you return to St. Petersburg with Gisele I will do my very best to get back into your good books."

Victor said. "I'm not coming with her."

"Right," Norimov breathed. "Of course. Your task is over. She's safe now. So I guess this is good-bye."

"It is," Victor said.

He hung up before Norimov could say another word and stood in the semidarkness of the room. His reason for being in London was over. Norimov's men could take over from here. He could hear laughter coming from the boardroom at the end of the corridor. One of the Russians was telling a story about when Gisele had been a child. Victor stood, looking at the closed door framed by lines of light.

He turned away and approached the nearest staircase. Within a couple of hours he would be on a flight to mainland Europe. By tomorrow, he could be anywhere in the world. He pictured a tastefully decorated hotel room and crisp white sheets, far away from anyone who knew anything about him.

Behind him, the boardroom door opened. Dmitri.

The Russian caught up with him. "There's something you need to see."

He waited.

"The electrical box," Dmitri explained. "I think it's been tampered with."

Victor didn't hesitate. He wanted no reason to stay, but he was not prepared to leave Gisele if anything was unaccounted for.

"Show me."

Dmitri led him to the far end of the corridor and into a room full of pipes and cables.

"Over there," he said.

The box was fixed to a wall, two meters from the ground. Victor opened it up. It took him a second to realize it hadn't been tampered with. A second later he heard the three other Russians enter the room behind Dmitri.

He faced them. Dmitri stood a little ahead of the rest.

They occupied the other half of the room with their combined massive bulk, forming an impenetrable wall of muscle by virtue of just standing there, side by side. The door was behind them. Yigor was the only Russian not present; he hadn't returned yet with the food.

They were silent, but words could not have added to what their body language told him. Victor knew he should have seen this coming, but he'd believed they cared more about Norimov and his daughter than their pride. He realized he should have known that a wound to a Russian's pride took far longer to heal than any physical injury.

"We don't need to do this. I'm on the next plane out of here."

Dmitri said, "Not until we've settled our differences."

"This is a bad idea."

There was a vicious smile. Russian pride.

Dmitri shook his head. "No, it's not. We have Gisele. She's safe."

"Okay," Victor said. "Let's work this out."

"There's nothing to work out. We're going to beat the shit out of you."

"I don't think so."

Dmitri laughed. The others didn't join in. They were too pumped up and focused on violence to find any humor in the situation. "Don't worry. We're not going to kill you. Just hurt you like you hurt us. Make things right."

"I understand," Victor said. "But I didn't know you were so selfless."

Dmitri smiled, then frowned. He hesitated for a moment, then asked—as he had to—for an explanation. "What are you talking about?"

"There's four of you," Victor said. "And you're all a lot bigger than me, so we all know you are going to win."

"Yes . . ." Dmitri said.

"And you all must know that the first of you to enter my reach is the one I'll be able to kill before the other three put me on the floor."

Dmitri said nothing.

Victor continued. "As you orchestrated this little revenge mission, these guys will expect you to make the first move. So you must be prepared to sacrifice your life in order to let the others have their revenge. Like I said: I didn't know you were so selfless, Dmitri."

He said, "You won't have time to kill me."

"There's only one way to find out." Victor turned his attention to the other three men. "Unless there is someone else who wishes to die in your place?"

He held their gaze, one at a time, until each had looked away. Then he stared back at Dmitri.

"Well?"

The door opened. Gisele entered the room, saying, "There you all are. What are you guys doing in here without me? I thought I was supposed to be the guest of honor."

Everyone looked at her. No one responded. She read the tension in the air. "What the hell is going on?"

Before anyone could answer, the lights went out.

• Chapter 34 •

A single small window let in some ambient light from the streetlamps outside. The Russians were slow to react, faces a mix of shadow and orange glow, looking to one another for an explanation, for someone to take the lead. Victor pushed through them and dragged Gisele to the floor, below the level of the window.

"*Hey,*" she said. "What are you doing? You're hurting me."

Victor stayed quiet for a moment to listen. He heard nothing.

Gisele pulled her hand free of Victor.

"Stay down," he said.

"Okay, okay. You could have simply asked, you know?"

Dmitri said, "What's happening?"

Victor gestured at the window and the orange glow filtering between the aluminum blind slats. "We're the only ones who have lost power."

"Then it's a circuit breaker," Dmitri said, but without conviction. He stepped closer to Victor—farther away from the window—and squatted.

"Please," Gisele said. "What's going on? Why are we on the floor?"

Victor didn't answer. He didn't yet know. Maybe it was nothing, but he didn't believe in coincidences.

One of the Russians—Ivan—stepped toward the window, curious, investigating. No tactical sense.

Victor said, "I wouldn't do that if I were you."

He glanced back, an incredulous expression contorting his face for a second before it exploded.

Blood and tissue splattered against the far wall. Shattered glass from the window flew across the space and rained down over the floor, pelting Victor as he shielded Gisele. The shot Russian dropped into a heap, the left side of his face missing, blood quickly pooling around him.

Gisele gasped and some of the other Russians yelled in surprise or horror. Victor paid no attention as he concentrated on listening for the sound of the shot, to work out how far away the shooter was positioned. It never came.

A suppressed rifle, then, shooting subsonic ammunition from enough distance for the city to swallow up the noise, but with a heavy round to inflict that kind of damage. Victor pictured the shooter across the street, maybe one hundred meters away, on the roof of the building on account of the difference in height between the hole in the window and where it had struck the target. Any farther, and the slow round's inaccuracy would have made such a shot too problematic to take.

Regardless, the sniper was an excellent marksman to have made a head shot from a cold bore with a slow round when the target had only just appeared and had been partially concealed by blind slats.

Dmitri and the others dropped to the floor to join Victor and Gisele. She kept her palm over her mouth as she breathed in huge, panicked breaths. Victor avoided the growing pool of blood draining from the exit wound in the dead Russian's head and took the pistol from his coat along with the spare magazines.

"What do we do?" Dmitri asked, eyes wide in the darkness, a brave man but one succumbing to panic.

"First thing: calm down. Second: we have to defend the staircase outside this room. That's the best place to assault. Come on. We don't have long."

Still in a crouch, he opened the door and stepped out of the room, Dmitri and the other Russians following him, making more noise than he would like, but there wasn't time to instruct them on better operational procedure. The warehouse was vast, but mostly open on the ground level. The first-floor office section was narrow, located on the building's west side, accessible via two sets of stairs.

Victor whispered to the Russians, instructing them on the best positions to take to cover the nearest staircase. They nodded and spread out as they were told.

"That's their primary assault route," Victor told them. "If you hold your positions here, you'll drive them back. You'll have them in a crossfire."

"How do we know there are more?" Sergei asked. "Maybe just one man with rifle."

Victor looked at him. "If you believe that, go down those stairs and make your way outside."

Sergei said nothing further.

"What are you going to do?" Dmitri asked Victor.

"There are two staircases leading up, remember?"

He motioned for Gisele to come over to him. She did, walking as fast as she could while still crouched.

"Where are you taking her?" Dmitri demanded.

"Out of the line of fire. If you and your guys can contain them at the first staircase, I can do the rest. Okay?"

Dmitri nodded. "Do it."

With Gisele following close behind, Victor headed toward the farthest set of stairs at the far end of the office floor, straining to see in the darkness where the artificial ambient light failed to reach. A single corridor spanned the entire length, a staircase at either end, with doors leading off to offices, a kitchen, toilets, and walk-in storage. He opened each door as he passed, improving visibility as the outside light seeped from the rooms' windows into the corridor. The sniper had shot from the south. He couldn't shoot through these windows.

Victor paused when he reached the open reception area at the far end of the corridor. The staircase lay out of sight around a corner. He listened. He didn't know how many were out there. He didn't know anything about their skill or armaments beyond the fact that they had a sniper with a suppressed weapon who was a fine shot. He had to assume the others were as capable. They wouldn't assault with sniper rifles, though, but automatic weapons—submachine guns or assault rifles. His handgun would come off second in any firefight, but he knew the location better than any attacker, and those attackers knew nothing about him.

Behind him, the Russians were nervous as they waited at the defensive positions he'd assigned them. They were gangsters now, not soldiers as they had once been long ago, but they had guns and he had no reason to doubt their ability or willingness to use them. Whether they would be able to repel whoever came up the staircase, he couldn't be sure. But they would slow them down, and that's all he needed them to do. He cared only about Gisele's survival and his own.

He hand signaled her to follow and whispered, "Hide behind that desk and keep down until this is over. Don't come out. Okay?"

She nodded, breaths coming fast and quick. "Okay."

He watched her get down to her hands and knees, then moved on. A floor-to-ceiling window covered the wall adjacent to the staircase. Victor saw no reflections of movement within. He gestured for Gisele to stay put, then hurried across the reception area, gun up and leading, sweeping around the corner as he stayed in partial cover. The staircase was clear. He heard nothing from below.

Victor checked that Gisele was staying in her hiding place and then took up a position farther into the room, from which he could cover the staircase. He felt no fear because fear was an emotional response to danger. The brain learned to fear before it learned how to solve problems. It was a survival mechanism: running from danger increased the probability of living through it. Emotion was older than thought, and stronger, but Victor had learned that the best way to survive was through cold logic and lateral thinking. He suppressed the part of his brain that wanted him to be afraid. He allowed no emotion to cloud his judgment and survived many times because no fear ever slowed him.

• • •

Behind him, the Russians waited in the darkness, breathing heavily and sweating. Their gaze passed over each other when they weren't staring at the stairwell and its descent into blackness. They were tough, brave men, but all were scared of what was coming. Adrenaline made them shake. Sweat shone on their faces. The thump of their racing hearts filled their ears. No one wanted to end up like poor Ivan with half a face.

They didn't hear the shuffle of feet on the floor below, near the staircase, didn't see the figure that peered up from the darkness and made a swinging motion with his arm.

Something small and metal hit the polystyrene ceiling tiles above their heads, bounced off a wall and clattered and rolled across the thin carpet.

"What was that?" someone yelled.

A second later the grenade exploded.

Chapter 35

Light flashed in the darkness, sparks and flames rushing out from the epicenter, shrapnel hissing through the air, burying itself into walls and melting ceiling tiles. Debris rained down, clattering on the floor. Smoke billowed, filling the corridor, swirling and snaking to fill the space. Sound, powerful and excruciating, pulsed outward, consuming all.

The dull thump of the explosion was colossal, the burst of light so bright it reached all along the corridor and illuminated the room around Victor for the briefest of instants, blinding him while the overpressure wave reverberated through his body.

A disorientation grenade. Or flashbang.

The Russians grimaced and squinted, their ears ringing with a high-pitched whine, their eyes, streaming tears from the smoke, seeing nothing but impenetrable white.

A black-clad figure emerged at the top of the staircase, moving fast and assured in a half crouch, picking out the closest target and hitting him in the chest with a burst of submachine-gun fire. The Russian stumbled backward into a doorframe, sliding down it, lifeless by the time he reached the floor, clothes soaked red.

The gunman swept his weapon away even as the Russian was still stumbling backward, seeking targets, shooting at the next nearest enemy, but missing as he backed off through the doorway of another room. Nine-millimeter rounds took chunks out of the door and wall.

The Russians returned fire, sporadic and desperate, blinded by the flashbang.

The gunman kept moving, firing in bursts, taking cover as behind him another black-clad figure followed, reaching the top of the stairs, sweeping the other way, covering the lead man's blind spot, seeing no live targets but double-tapping the Russian slumped against the doorframe when he saw him twitch.

No enemy could be too dead.

• • •

The noise of the shooting was monstrous. The lights flashing were as bright as fireworks illuminating the office around Gisele in staccato strobes. The barrage of noise and light overloaded her senses. She sat huddled in a ball behind the desk, as the man had told her.

Smoke hung throughout the room. The air was a thick gray gloom that deepened shadows and dulled the orange glow of outside streetlamps.

She had her palms pressed over her ears in an attempt to muffle the incredible amount of noise. She kept her chin down, almost pressing against her chest, and shoulders hunched.

Gisele flinched and gasped and trembled but didn't scream or cry out. Despite her fear she knew she had to stay as small and quiet as she could manage. There was nothing else she could do.

. . .

Victor pictured what was happening because he couldn't yet see. He knew about disorientation grenades. He knew how they worked. He knew what they did. He knew it had been thrown in ahead of an assault. The Russians would be deaf and blinded if they were fortunate, or injured or killed if they were not. In either case the staircase would be undefended. The assaulters would advance up it without risk and begin the massacre.

The positions he had assigned them would help. The flashbang would not have rendered them all incapacitated. If they had an advantage in numbers they could fight back. It was possible that they could still pin the assaulters long enough.

Victor's world came back into focus as the noise of the gunfire grew louder. In between the semiautomatic shots from the Russians' handguns, he recognized the distinctive click of the MP5SD, almost inaudible thanks to the integrated suppressor. He picked out two rhythms for two shooters. Such firepower was expensive and hard to source. These guys were better than well armed and had breached the warehouse without making a sound. They were no mere street thugs or enforcers but a well-equipped, well-trained assault team.

Bullets blew through the partition wall Victor was using as cover, easily penetrating the cheap material, showering his face with dust and debris.

He ducked and moved away, farther into the room, eyesight improving with every passing second. Though barely able to see and hear, the map of his environment in his mind was unaffected, as was his understanding of what was happening behind him.

He switched the pistol to his left hand and stuck it out of cover to let out a few blind shots toward the far staircase, knowing the Russians were out of the line of fire. The *pop-pop-pop* registered in his ears, but far quieter than it should, masked by the incessant ringing from the explosion.

He turned to cover the closest staircase, but there was no sign yet of any other assaulters. He switched back again, seeing muzzle flashes flare bright through the smoke and darkness. The Russians were returning fire. Whether they had their senses back was irrelevant. Indirect fire could kill just the same as an aimed shot.

Rounds hit the ceiling somewhere above him. A light fixture exploded.

He shielded himself with an arm as chunks of polystyrene from the ceiling tiles and shards of glass rained down over him.

If the sniper and the two assaulters were the sum total of their attackers, Victor and the Russians could force them to withdraw with their superior numbers. But the team's intel had to be accurate for them to know about the warehouse. Then they would have a good idea of the number of defenders. If there were only three, then they would have attempted stealth, silently picking off their enemies. They hadn't. The sniper had taken the first opportunity to reduce the number of enemies because the assaulters were already in the building. And they weren't going for stealth. They were going strong. Because they had the firepower and, more important, the numbers.

The two at the far staircase were just one two-man fire team. There would be more, sweeping through the warehouse to clear it in a slick military assault. The Russians weren't going to keep the two upstairs occupied long enough before the other team or teams joined the battle and overwhelmed them. If another fire team attempted to flank them using the near staircase, Victor couldn't stop them.

The gunfire would eventually draw the attention of the Metropolitan Police, but the warehouse was in an industrial area with no residences and no through traffic. By the time they arrived, this would be over.

The plan had been to defend. It wasn't going to work.

Victor hurried over to Gisele. She was shaking and even in the dark looked white with fear. He held out the pistol he had taken from Ivan's corpse.

"Is it true what you said before about knowing how to use a gun?"

She managed to nod and he passed her the weapon. She took a deep breath then released the magazine to check the load before pushing it back in place with her palm. She racked the slide.

Victor said, "If anyone approaches without identifying themselves, you shoot. Don't hesitate."

Her eyes were wide. Fear. Disbelief. But she nodded.

He didn't know if she would. He didn't know if she was capable of taking a life. He hoped that neither of them would have to find out if she was.

Victor descended the near staircase, fast but quiet, gun up and sweeping. He reached the ground-floor offices. There were multiple rooms and corridors, leading both outside and into the rest of the warehouse. He paused and listened. He heard nothing.

The attackers must have entered the building from the west side, at the farthest point from the offices, where they wouldn't be heard breaking in. There were rolling doors and loading bays along the west wall. They could have entered through any one of them or any number of them at the same time, either staying together or splitting up. They knew there were people in the offices upstairs, but they couldn't know where else threats might wait, so had to move with some caution, but it wouldn't be long before they reached the office segment. From the main warehouse, there were multiple ways in, but still only two staircases up for the attackers to converge on. Victor didn't know where they were now, but he knew where they had to end up.

Shooting the attackers in the back wasn't complicated. Doing it without getting caught in the Russians' line of fire was far from simple.

He hurried, because there were no enemies at this staircase.

He was behind them.

• Chapter 36 •

Victor heard the second team before he saw them. A door—leading to the warehouse itself—was kicked open in a room behind him. He spun around and moved laterally because that room was divided from his only by glass. He managed to snap off two shots before the assaulters spotted him, but missed because he was moving and so were they.

MP5s opened fire, bullets following him, punching holes through the glass until it gave way and collapsed in a shower of glittering shards. He shielded his face with an arm as he ran and slid through a doorway, shooting back under his armpit to buy some time.

He gained only a couple of seconds before he heard, then saw, a grenade bounce off the doorframe and then a wall, and then roll along the floor toward him.

He dived over a table, trailing a hand to tip it over as he fell, bringing the tabletop down on its edge behind him.

The flashbang exploded.

His eyelids were already squeezed shut but still he saw white. The overpressure wave thumped against the table and pushed it, and him, across the floor.

Shrapnel embedded in the tabletop. The plastic veneer melted and the chipboard beneath smoldered and burned. The grenade wasn't manufactured to kill, but at close range could do so or maim. Had the table not protected him, he would now be out of the fight.

His eyes could just about focus and he heard nothing, but knew the two men were moving the second after the explosion, thinking him incapacitated.

He waited a moment, picturing them headed through the doorway, fast and well trained, hesitating because they couldn't see him behind the table, then rolled to his side, arms and head coming out from behind it, squeezing off rounds.

The first man was hit in his center mass, falling backward into the second assaulter, bringing him down too as he fell.

Victor was up and moving, not risking further engagement because he had to get back to Gisele.

• • •

Muzzle flashes illuminated the first-floor corridor in intermittent bursts of light. The loud reports of the Russians' handguns drowned out the suppressed automatic fire from the submachine guns that hissed through the air and tore through the thin interior walls.

Lumps of polystyrene fell from the ceiling. Dust swirled with the smoke from the flashbang. The air stank of cordite and fear.

The Russians backed off under the relentless stream of

automatic gunfire, shooting back blind as they darted between doorways.

The lead assaulter ejected the empty magazine, slipped it back into the assigned pocket of his tactical vest, pulled out a full one, and slammed it home. He worked the breach and resumed shooting.

The second put down suppressing fire while the other man was vulnerable, then reloaded while the first covered him.

The Russians were not elite but they had picked their positions with a frighteningly good tactical sense. The two-man fire team had expected to clear the office floor within sixty seconds. That wasn't going to happen. This was going to drag on for at least another two minutes before the inevitable victory was achieved.

• • •

Victor hurried through the ground-floor offices, staying in the center of rooms and corridors despite the natural inclination to seek safety near walls, because in close-quarters battle it was along walls that bullets tended to travel.

He took a circuitous route through the offices to avoid any pursuers and to prevent rushing blindly into another fire team.

The din of the shooting upstairs intensified as he neared it—the loud pops of the Russians' handguns above the suppressed automatic fire of the submachine guns, the clinking of expended brass and the thump of bullets striking walls, urgent commands and desperate screams.

He could tell the assaulters had taken the stairs and were fighting back the defenders. It wouldn't be long before the Russians were killed—or fled. He didn't know the strength of their courage or how deep their loyalty to Norimov or Gisele went.

Victor slowed as he neared the hallway where the staircase was located. He saw no one on the ground level.

He approached the staircase, gun leading, aiming up as he moved before it, stepping through a swath of orange gloom spilling through a window on the west wall. He smelled the acrid odor of cordite and the sulfur of the flashbang smoke. The assaulters were out of sight above him, but the suppressed fire of their submachine guns was loud and distinctive to his ear. The return fire from the Russians was sporadic.

"Gisele," he called. "I'm coming up."

There was no response. He didn't know if that meant she couldn't hear him over the gunfire or because she was dead. He ascended the first step but stopped. A noise.

Footsteps in the hallway leading to the rest of the ground-floor level—where he'd come from a moment before.

He made out a man-sized shape in the darkness, realizing at the same time that with the nearby window he was more visible than the new arrival—who would have seen him first.

Victor leaped from the staircase as another MP5SD opened fire. Rounds buried into the wall and staircase where he'd been standing, blowing out splinters of wood and a cloud of paint dust.

He hit the floor in a roll to disperse the impact, scrambling into the cover of an arrangement of office desks and chairs. Bullets chased him, taking chunks out of the cheap veneer-and-plywood furniture.

He dodged out of the line of fire, popping up to shoot back as his attacker moved forward to the mouth of the hallway, driving him back. Bullets sparked on steel supports.

Victor moved again—staying in one position would only make it easier for his assailant—and aimed where the gunman would next appear.

· Chapter 37 ·

On the upper level the two assaulters moved positions, putting bursts along the hallway, outnumbered but not outgunned, suppressing the Russians until they were in cover. At random intervals the Russians returned fire, shouting indecipherable instructions to one another, maybe coordinating their attacks or just keeping the others informed that they were still alive.

Another one was hit as he popped out of cover, caught in the throat and face with a long burst that made the Russian dance, a geyser of blood spurting from him, before he dropped. That left two. There was no danger of not triumphing, but they were burning through time they didn't have. This warehouse may be empty but other units in the industrial estate were not. Each second the firefight continued increased the chances of a passerby or a worker on a cigarette break hearing the gunshots.

The police would be on the way soon after that, if they weren't already.

• • •

Victor waited, drawing a bead on the darkness where the room met the hallway. Any movement would be greeted with a double tap. Another flashbang exploded on the floor above him. He was unable to move to the stairs and ascend to help the Russians above because he had to cross through the path of his attackers' vision. But five seconds waiting became ten.

He moved because he knew his enemy was in the process of outflanking him. The gunman was the aggressor, better armed and with allies nearby. He would press the attack, not wait for a defender to engage him.

There were two other ways into the room—one door on the west wall leading directly into the main warehouse, and another to the north that fed into a series of storerooms that were also accessible from the rest of the warehouse. The gunman could come through either.

No way to know which, and it wasn't possible to cover both effectively. Victor dashed toward the hallway, away from both, throwing himself into a dive when he heard a door kicked open behind him.

Bullets whizzed over Victor's head and sparked where they struck the steel supports. He zigzagged as he ran, knowing his attacker would be in pursuit. He weaved ten meters along the hallway, shouldering a door open and half running, half falling into the room on the other side.

Nine-millimeter rounds cut through the air behind him. He could feel the change in pressure and air temperature on his neck. Splinters of doorframe caught in his hair.

The firing stopped, the shooter no longer able to keep him in his gun sights. He could be in pursuit, closing fast, but had already proven himself smart enough not to rush into an ambush.

Victor grabbed anything he could and threw it in the direction of the door to create obstacles to slow his enemy.

He needed time. He had to maintain distance. He kept moving, utilizing the cover provided by desks and tables, chairs and cabinets, running in diagonal lines, ducking as he heard the rapid spit of the MP5SD opening fire somewhere in the darkness behind him.

Glass smashed. Metal sparked. A fluorescent ceiling light exploded.

Victor ran, relying on speed, distance, and angles to make himself a target too hard to hit. He hurried, knowing his way through the offices better than his pursuer, who would move at a slower pace, expecting an ambush.

"Gisele," he called as he powered to the top of the staircase.

He exchanged glances with Dmitri, who had retreated here from his original position.

Victor said, "The others?"

The Russian shook his head in way of an answer. He was drenched in sweat and bleeding. "Get her out of here," he panted.

Victor nodded, knowing what Dmitri meant and respecting his sacrifice. "There are others downstairs. They'll breach this staircase soon."

Dmitri said, "Then hurry," and squeezed off some rounds down the corridor.

Victor hurled the desk aside, expecting to see Gisele dead from a stray round, but instead she lay in a huddle, hair disguising her face, and for a moment Victor saw not Gisele but her mother, Eleanor. She had Ivan's pistol clutched in both hands but her eyes were shut. She didn't even know he was there.

He pulled the gun from her grip before he touched her on the shoulder so she didn't shoot him by mistake.

"Are you hurt?"

She shook her head.

"We have to go."

She nodded and he heaved open a window. "Climb through after me," he said.

She nodded again.

He hauled himself through and dropped. It was four meters to the ground. Far enough to break bones, but he slowed himself with the wall and rolled to disperse the energy of the impact.

"Hurry," he shouted up. "I'll catch you."

He figured she would take some coaxing, but she didn't need any. She dropped and he caught her, falling with her into a half roll to spare them both injury. She took a second longer getting to her feet.

"Come on," he urged. "It's not over yet."

· Chapter 38 ·

Victor had to assume Dmitri's car was disabled or covered. At the very least reaching it would put them both at risk. Instead, they ran. They headed away from the warehouse, steering clear of the main roads, sticking to alleys and side streets. He stayed behind Gisele, both to shield her from any pursuers and to better listen out for them, guiding her with his hands, forced to move slower as a result. But he couldn't risk it the other way and have her falling behind or taking a bullet in the back. Sirens blared in the distance.

She was fit but already slowing under the pace Victor was pushing her to. After a few minutes she was breathing hard and stumbling as much as running, but they had covered a lot of distance.

"Stop," he said. "Catch your breath."

He pulled her into an alleyway before she could rush past.

"Okay?"

She nodded but couldn't speak for a moment because her heart was racing and she'd lost her fine motor skills.

"Are . . . we . . . safe?" she managed to ask between gasps.

Suppressed gunshots echoed off the buildings, answering for him. Brickwork crumbled at the mouth of the alley.

"Move."

There was no crack from the bullets so they were subsonic, but the muted bark from the muzzle wasn't the distinctive click of an MP5SD. It was louder, duller. A handgun. Whoever was behind them wasn't part of the assault force that had stormed the warehouse. They had probably been watching the perimeter or providing surveillance or backup and had chased them the whole way, or were sweeping the area and found them.

He risked a glance behind—saw two men—and pushed Gisele onward, knowing their enemies were catching up with every step. Alone, he could outrun them, but she limited his pace and enabled their pursuers to stay close enough that he knew they would never create enough distance to hide.

"That way," he hissed, and pushed her down a bisecting alley.

At the end was a chain-link fence on top of a low wall. He slipped ahead of Gisele and interlaced his fingers, palms up.

He didn't have to tell her what to do. She understood and used his palms as a step as he propelled her upward. She was no athlete, no climber, but she caught hold of the top of the fence and pulled herself over. No hesitation. No asking for aid.

Victor followed, leaping, grabbing hold, hauling himself up and over, dropping down to the other side a split second behind Gisele and pushing her to the ground because he knew their pursuers were right behind them and lining up their sights.

The twin gunshots were louder in the alley's confines. Gisele flinched, but they were already lower than the wall. A bullet hit a fence post and made the chains rattle and sway.

Victor waited until he could hear the scrape of feet running before pulling Gisele up and away. They were on a railway track siding, overgrown and uneven. He led her over the tracks, not looking out for trains because it was easy enough to hear a hundred-plus-ton locomotive. On the far side of the tracks stood a number of train carriages, stationary and disused, covered in graffiti and stinking of rust and decay. A bullet pinged off the exposed frame of a carriage, far enough away that Victor had no immediate concern, but a reminder that their pursuers were relentless and had lethal intent.

He came to a stop and ushered for Gisele to follow suit. He pointed. "Get on your stomach and shuffle under that carriage and crawl so you're hidden by the wheels."

She nodded. "What are you going to do?"

"Don't get out under any circumstances, unless it's me telling you to. Anyone who tries to crawl under the train after you, wait until you can see their face and go for their eyes. Okay?"

She nodded again and dropped to her stomach and did as he instructed.

He stood and moved to the corner of the carriage, settling into the darkness, waiting for their pursuers to follow.

• • •

The two men hurried across the train tracks, arms out, eyes peering along the barrels of their handguns. Unlike the others who had assaulted the warehouse, these two wore civilian clothes. They'd lost sight of their targets but knew where they had to be. The abandoned train carriages formed the only concealment. The two men would have seen them had they tried to make a break for it along the tracks. The alternative was a nine-meter drop that would surely kill them. No one was that stupid.

Communicating with hand signals only, they split up, one going left while the other went right, intending to approach the rusting carriages from either flank. They had no concern for the woman. She was a civilian. Which meant there was only her protector who offered any threat, and he couldn't ambush them both if they split up. They were cautious because they were professional, but neither was scared.

The thrill of the chase was strong in both.

They lived for moments like this.

· Chapter 39 ·

Dmitri staggered away from the wall, unable to see with his blinded eyes the blood that stained his shirt, but capable of feeling the intense burn caused by the two bullets in his chest. He reached one hand to the wall in an attempt to stay on his feet while the fingers of his free hand crept along his chest, touching warm, sticky liquid and ripped clothes. He coughed bloody foam.

Slowly his own wheezing cries grew louder than the ringing in his ears and he realized he was lying on his back, the grimy ceiling tiles coming into view through the whiteness, but then strangely turning gray, as if stained, then black.

• • •

Victor waited in the darkness. London was too low-rise and built up for the night to ever be truly black. Even here, away from streetlights and other illumination, there were varying degrees of gloom. This side of the carriage was in shadow, the primary ambient light coming from the buildings and streetlamps from the east, from Victor's left. He crouched low, where it was darkest, listening to the quiet crunch of shoes on gravel and vegetation, noting when they broke apart and formed separate sounds, one growing increasingly quieter while the other grew louder.

They had split up. A problem, but Victor never expected it to be easy. The footsteps were cautious but not slow; they were still in pursuit. Wary, but still the aggressor. Still in charge of the situation.

That would soon change.

• • •

The first man leaned forward as he approached, lowering his eye line in an effort to peer beneath the first carriage. Did something catch his eye? He wasn't sure. It would be a stupid place for someone to hide—trapping himself somewhere with no easy means of escape—but desperate people made mistakes. The thought of scaring someone to stupidity appealed to him.

He moved on, slowing as he reached the carriage, checking the ground ahead for anything that might make noise underfoot and give away his position. He kept close to the front of the container, brushing the weather-beaten metal with his shoulder, blending his own shadow that extended before him into the carriage's own.

The gun rounded the corner first, moving fast but smooth, his hands and arms following as he turned through ninety degrees until he was facing along the shadow side of the carriage. His eyes had adjusted to the gloom, but the darkness was still dense.

He didn't see the girl's protector—crouched no more than two meters in front of him—until he was springing forward, coming up from below the pistol's muzzle. By then it was too late to aim and get off a shot.

With both hands gripping the pistol, he had no way to defend himself after his attacker pushed the barrel to one side as he closed the distance between them and snapped out a straight punch to the man's throat.

He gasped—airless and soundless—trachea crushed, and had no strength to resist as his attacker hyper-extended his right wrist, pulled the gun from his grip, and dragged him to the ground and held him there. He spent the last seconds of his life in silent agony.

• • •

Victor held him prone while he struggled. His mouth was wide open in a vain attempt to suck in air. A knee pinned his legs and a hand on each arm kept him from writhing too much and making more noise than could be avoided. At the far end of the carriage the silhouette of the second man appeared against a backdrop of over-grown vegetation. Victor watched the man, uncon-cerned, knowing that if the dying man hadn't seen him at a distance of two meters, the second wouldn't at twenty. Noise posed more danger of discovery, but every passing second meant the dying man grew weaker and struggled less.

When the man on the ground became limp, Victor released him. He checked the gun—a 9 mm SIG Sauer—and the load. The magazine was full and a subsonic round was in the chamber. He made sure the suppressor was screwed on tightly, and stood.

The second man had already passed out of sight, mov-ing between two carriages as he continued his search. Victor didn't follow. Whether the man had seen him or not, he wasn't prepared to funnel himself between the carriages, leaving himself exposed at both flanks as he emerged. There would be no way of knowing if the man had doubled back or was setting an ambush.

Instead, Victor stalked parallel, rounding a clump of long grasses and discarded oil drums until he was on the far side of the next two carriages. He peered into the darkness, but couldn't pick out a human shape in the mix of shadows. He waited, focusing on the sounds reaching his ears, disassembling the ambient noise until he identified the quiet footsteps. Twelve, maybe fifteen meters away.

Then they stopped. Victor pictured the man waiting in the darkness, until he heard another noise—quieter, shuffling.

He realized his enemy was crawling under a carriage. But which one? He could be moving either to Victor's left or right. No way to tell without moving himself, but it would be down to chance if he chose the right direction. He opted to stay put. He lowered himself into a crouch, scooped up a handful of gravel, and hurled it forward.

The gravel pinged off the metal hulls of some carriages and scattered on the ground.

It wasn't meant to sound like someone moving to tempt his enemy to move back, but it would distract him and disguise the noise of Victor dashing to the right. He peered around the edge of the carriage, seeing and hearing no one. He grabbed another handful and threw it up into the air so it rained down on top of the carriage.

Again, he used the noise to disguise his movements as he hurried back to his previous position. He reached down to grab and throw more gravel, then went to the left, moving fast because he now knew where the man had to be, and rushed around the back of the carriage, into darkness. He saw the man's silhouette against the distant vegetation.

Victor squeezed the trigger three times and the silhouette dropped into the shadows.

He approached, walking fast, to check that the man was dead, as he hadn't seen where the bullets impacted or even if they had all hit. When the man came into view he saw one had struck him high on the chest, shattering the clavicle, while another had drilled a hole in his face through the left cheek a couple of centimeters below the eye.

The man was alive. The subsonic bullet hadn't had the velocity to pass all of the way through the skull and blow an exit wound out of the back. Victor figured it had deflected as it passed through the cheekbone and followed the curve of the skull, missing the brain. A fatal wound if left untreated, but the man was at no immediate risk. He probably couldn't even feel it. A miracle he was still alive, some might say. His good fortune would be short-lived.

He lay on his back, breathing rapidly, arms straight by his sides, either not daring to move or believing he couldn't. He wasn't screaming, so the adrenaline surge hadn't yet faded.

Victor walked closer.

"Help," the man said. British accent.

"You're asking the wrong guy."

"Please."

"I heard you the first time."

Victor squatted next to him and searched through his pockets. The man didn't try to stop him. Unsurprisingly, he was clean. Operating sterile. A pro.

It took a moment of searching in the dark until Victor found something appropriate to his needs. He would have preferred a piece of wood, but the square of rotting cardboard would do. He folded it in half and then again. The man watched him.

"Aren't you going to ask me anything?"

"In due course."

Victor squeezed the cardboard in his hands, making it thinner and denser.

"If you let me live," the man said, "I'll tell you everything."

"You don't know everything," Victor replied, compressing the cardboard one last time, forming it into a small plank about five centimeters wide by ten long and two centimeters thick. "And I don't have the time to make sure what you say is truthful. We need to act fast, don't we?"

The man swallowed. "I won't lie to you."

Victor held up the cardboard. "It'll save me a lot of time and you a lot of pain if we make sure of that at the very start."

The man shook his head. "We don't need to make sure."

"Bite down." He lowered the piece of cardboard to the man's mouth.

"Please . . ."

"Trust me, you want this."

Breathing hard, the man opened his mouth. Victor lowered the cardboard between the man's teeth. He bit down on the cardboard.

"Ready?" Victor asked.

He didn't wait for an answer. He used the edge of his palm to strike the shattered collarbone.

The man's scream was louder than even Victor expected. It was a high-pitched wail that echoed between the carriages. The man tensed and went into spasm.

Victor checked his flank while he waited for him to finish, then took out the cardboard. The man had bitten through it. "Are you going to lie to me?"

"*No.*"

"You see, now I believe you. What's your name?"

"Joe."

"Joe what?"

"Forrester."

"What the fuck are you doing?"

Victor looked over his shoulder to see Gisele approaching. He said, "I'm interrogating him."

"You're torturing him."

"No, I've tortured him. Now I'm interrogating him."

She came closer. "I don't think the distinction is important."

Victor said, "I assure you that it is to him."

"I won't allow it. It's a war crime."

"I don't suppose there is any point reminding you that we're not at war here?"

"You could have fooled me, and you're being facetious. I won't let you commit torture in my name."

"Fine." Victor rose to his feet.

He shot the man named Forrester between the eyebrows.

Gisele startled. She stood gasping, hand over her mouth. She glared at him, angry and disgusted despite the surprise and revulsion. "*What did you do that for?* You murdered a defenseless man. What the fuck is wrong with you?"

"I'll tell you all about it some other time. Right now we need to get out of here."

· Chapter 40 ·

The air smelled divine—blood and gun smoke. Perfume of the gods. Sinclair sucked in a big lungful as he stepped forward. Spent brass cartridges crunched underfoot. The insidious blare of sirens grew ever closer. The mercenaries were getting restless. They were keen to withdraw. Sinclair was unhurried. He had no fear of the police, even without Anderton's power over them.

Besides, he required answers.

Peering through the scope of his rifle from across the street, he had watched the flashes of gunfire play out through the windows of the first-floor offices and listened to the radio chatter of the assaulters with keen interest.

He'd dropped the first Russian as soon as the opportunity had presented itself—and a fine shot, if he did say so himself—much to the irritation of the assaulters, who would have preferred more time to get into position. Sinclair operated on his timescale, not on the whims of fools.

That first kill had elevated his bloodlust, but the Russians had refused to cooperate, annoyingly staying out of the reach of his rifle. With enormous self-restraint he had avoided taking shots based on muzzle flashes alone, to avoid killing one of the assaulters by mistake. No tragedy in itself, but Sinclair didn't want the hired mercs questioning his skills as an exceptional operator. He wanted only praise. Only glory.

"It's time to get the fuck out of here," Wade was saying.

"Soon," Sinclair said.

The plan had not been for a prolonged firefight. Two two-man fire teams were supposed to clear the warehouse and overwhelm the Russians with flashbangs and automatic fire. A two-minute assault. Three, tops. Based on the assumption they were up against an outgunned and surprised resistance. But that was not what Sinclair had seen or heard. The Russians were not supposed to put up much of a fight, if any. Certainly not engage the assaulters into a prolonged gun battle.

Sinclair had intervened to save the attack.

Want a job done right . . .

Only it hadn't worked out like that. Sinclair wanted to know why. He wanted to know about the man he had fought—the man who had escaped with the girl.

Rogan said, "This one's still alive."

Sinclair turned and approached. One of the giant Russians lay slumped on the floor, unmoving, but his eyes were open and alert.

"Dmitri, yes?"

The Russian didn't respond, but Sinclair knew he'd understood.

He squatted down next to him. "I'll give you a choice, sport. Tell me who your friend in the suit is and I'll put you out of your misery." He drew his KA-BAR combat knife and began cutting. "Or don't, and we'll get to find out just how much pain you can take."

· Chapter 41 ·

The car was a rust-stained Ford that was almost as old as Gisele. It barely looked roadworthy but her companion selected it over newer, better vehicles. At first she didn't understand why, but then she knew: it had no alarm as standard and was too neglected to have acquired one. She watched, a little in awe, as it took him six seconds to jimmy the lock and less than twenty to cross the wires beneath the steering column to get the engine started. She'd known cars could be hot-wired, but had never seen anyone actually do it. The ease with which he managed it surprised her.

"Get in," he said.

She didn't care for the way those two short words sounded suspiciously close to an order, but now was not the time to discuss his manners. She did as instructed, reluctantly at first because she knew it was stolen. She saw that he noticed she didn't like getting into a stolen car any more than she'd liked him torturing and executing a man. He didn't comment, though.

Gisele slumped in the passenger's seat and closed the

door. She fastened her seat belt and he pulled away from the curb, accelerating hard. Cars and buildings flashed past the window. She glimpsed smudges of people and the blur of bright signs glowing through the rain and night. Her companion drove like a race-car driver—fast but in control, effortlessly weaving through the traffic while Gisele braced against the forces trying to fling her from side to side. He braked sharply to avoid a turning bus and the seat belt stopped her from hurtling forward. Before she had taken a breath the force of the car's acceleration pushed her back into the seat. From the corner of her eye she saw him glancing at her—concerned for her or what she might be doing, she didn't know. She kept her own gaze forward and her mind on making sure the contents of her stomach stayed where they belonged. Thank God she hadn't eaten for hours.

She looked at his face. It was as blank as it had been when she had first met him in Yvette's flat, as if nothing had happened between then and now.

"Aren't you scared?" she said.

He didn't answer her. It didn't matter. She was scared enough for both of them.

"I . . . I've never seen anyone die before. I've never even seen a corpse. . . . This is crazy."

"There'll be time to reflect later. For now we need to put as much distance between us and the warehouse as possible."

A horn blared as they overtook another car. She looked over her shoulder to see the silhouette of the car's driver gesticulating his anger. She turned back, reaching out to grab the dashboard in an effort to steady herself as he performed another fast overtake.

A moment later, Gisele noticed the car was slowing down.

"Why are you . . . ?"

She stopped because she saw lights flashing ahead, and seconds later the wailing of sirens reached her ears and a police car sped past them in the opposite lane. She twisted in her seat to watch it disappear into the distance.

"Do you think they're heading to the warehouse?"

"Most certainly."

"Will those gunmen still be there?"

He shook his head. "They'll be long gone by now. Like us. That's why we have to keep moving."

She thought of the terror she'd felt hiding behind the desk, waiting to be killed.

Tears welled in her eyes and she wiped them away with a sleeve before he could notice. She was determined not to cry. She didn't want to be weak. Tears were losing control of emotions and she had to stay in control. She felt strange, not exactly scared but hyperalert and aware of every sound and sight and sensation assailing her. She'd experienced something similar while experimenting with drugs at university. This was real, though, not some chemical artificially changing her consciousness. Her ears were hot. She placed a thumb to her neck to feel her pulse. The bursts of pressure were so fast she couldn't count them.

"Are you okay?" the man asked as he accelerated again now that the police car had vanished into the distance behind them.

A moment ago the answer would have been yes. Now she felt panicked. "My pulse," she said. "My heart is beating too fast. I'm scared."

He reached across and put the tips of two fingers over

her carotid artery, driving one-handed. He held the
fingers there for a few seconds. "Your pulse is about one
hundred and thirty-two beats per minute. That's fast, but
nothing to be scared of. Breathe deeply and hold before
releasing slowly."

She did. *Nothing to be scared of,* she repeated in her
thoughts.

"There you go," he said. "It's dropping already. You're
fine."

She nodded. She didn't feel fine but she felt slightly
better.

"What you're feeling is perfectly normal."

"Then why aren't you going through the same?"

"This isn't my first time in combat."

"Are you saying you're used to it? *How* do you get
used to it?"

"Like anything else: with experience."

Gisele stared at him. She wanted to ask what other
experiences he'd had, but at the same time she also didn't
want to know. She kept her lips closed.

She watched the man as he drove, studying his expres-
sionless face and rigid posture. Whoever he was, whatever
his name, however he claimed to be protecting her, could
she really trust him? *No,* she told herself. He glanced her
way and she had been too lost in thought to look aside
before their gazes met. His eyes were as black as the night
outside. She didn't know who he was. She didn't know
where he was taking her. She swallowed her fear before it
could smash through her facade of composure.

She sat upright. If he wasn't going to suggest it, then
she was. "We ought to go to the police."

"Why?"

"What do you mean, why? Because of what just happened. The shooting. The *killing*. Armed men attacked us. This is a huge deal. We were involved. We have to explain what happened."

"It won't do any good."

She stared, incredulous. "How did you work that out?"

He said nothing.

She looked at him. "You mean it won't do any good for you, don't you?"

He didn't answer.

"Because you killed two men. Shit, you tortured one too. Oh God, this is crazy. You're psychotic."

"I did it to protect you."

"Then tell them that. I'm a witness. I can back you up—"

He was shaking his head. "I'm not going to the police under any circumstances."

"And what about me? I can go. I'll explain what happened."

"They'll work it out eventually by themselves."

"That's not the point. It's our civic duty to report a crime. We have to. It's the law. They can help us. They can help me."

"No, they can't."

"That's what they do. That's the point. Slow down."

"Soon," he said.

"Slow down," she insisted. "Now. You're going to get us both killed."

"When we're far enough away from danger, I will. Not before."

She thumbed the button to release the seat belt. It swiftly glanced across her chest.

He saw. "Put that back on."

"No," she said. "It stays off until you slow down."

He took his eyes from the road to meet with hers. She fought not to blink under the intensity of his gaze, but she held firm. She needed to make this stand.

He looked away and the car began to slow to something approaching the speed limit.

"Engage the seat belt," he said.

She reached for it. "If you drive crazy again, it comes off. Understood?" He nodded and she pushed the clasp back in the receiver. "Alek used to drive like a maniac when I was a kid. I hated being in the car with him. That's probably why it took me so long to learn to drive."

"Understood," the man said.

"Now, please, if you don't mind, take me to the police so I can sort this mess out."

He said, "There is no way to sort it, at least not for the police. You need protection and the police aren't going to protect you. They're going to take your statement and drive you home and leave a car outside your building overnight. And then what happens if they don't catch whoever is after you? Do you think that car will stay outside for the rest of your life? What about at your office?" She said nothing. "The police are not bodyguards. They will investigate thoroughly and completely, but only once you're dead. Until then, you're a waste of their resources."

"So you're saying I'm helpless?"

"No. I'll help you. We'll get through this together."

She was shaking her head before he had finished. "No. Just take me to a police station, please."

"Not now. We have to create some distance first. If you still want to later, I will."

She nodded because she didn't believe him and she didn't want him to know. "Fine," she said. "Then we call Alek. We need to find out if the others are okay and let Yigor know what happened."

He didn't respond.

"Did you hear me? I want to know if Dmitri and the others got away."

"Later."

"Fine," she said again. "In the meantime, I have to use a bathroom."

"Soon. You'll have to hold it."

"I can't."

His eyes flicked between the road and hers. She felt as though he would see through the lie had he not had to keep glancing away.

"Okay," he said finally.

• Chapter 42 •

The car stopped a few minutes later and Gisele was opening the door before he had finished applying the hand brake.

"I'm leaving the engine running," he told her. "Be as fast as you can. If you hear a horn, I want you back here fast. Understand?"

She nodded without looking at him. "I've got it."

The garage forecourt was empty of other cars. He'd parked close to the entrance of the store and she hurried the short distance to the doors, pushing one open with a shoulder and stepping into the warmth. The bright fluorescent lights made her squint after so long in the car. She searched with her eyes for the sign to the bathroom. A small sign was affixed to the wall above a door near the counter.

"You have to buy something," the young man said from behind a till.

"I just want to splash some water on my face. I'll be quick. Please."

He was shaking his head before she'd finished talking. "You have to buy something."

Gisele sighed and fished around in her pockets and collected some coins in a palm. She turned over her hand to set them down on the counter and headed for the bathroom.

"What are you buying?" the man asked.

She pushed open the door. "Anything. It doesn't matter. You pick."

Inside, she engaged the lock and leaned back against it. She took big, urgent gulps of air, then remembered what her companion had said and slowed her breathing and felt calmer. She didn't need to use the toilet. She didn't want to splash water on her face. She didn't know what to think or do. She figured she had about five minutes before he would come looking for her. Gisele studied her reflection in the small mirror mounted above a sink stained with lime scale. The harsh light wasn't doing her skin any favors. She was always struggling with her complexion, but now her makeup was smudged and her mascara had run. She was pale and drawn and her eyes were red and puffy. Her hair was a mess. Not that any of it mattered now.

She took her phone from her coat pocket. Gisele thumbed the screen and tapped in her code to unlock it. There were numerous texts and messages and updates and notifications that competed for her attention but she ignored them all and tapped the icon to make a call. Then she tapped 999.

Her thumb hovered over the dial icon.

We can't go to the police, he'd said. He would say that. He'd killed at least two men, torturing one of them. Whoever was after her, he was just as bad as they were. She didn't know who he was. She didn't even know his name. He'd rescued her, but from whom? For all she knew, the men chasing her might be the good guys. Her companion certainly wasn't. The police hadn't been much help before, but she understood why. Nothing had actually happened to her. No crime had been committed. But they would help her now that people were dead. They would believe her. They would protect her. Like her nameless companion had.

"Shit," she whispered aloud.

Whoever he was, whatever he had done, he had risked his life to protect her. The two men who had chased them to the train yard had shot at them, or at least him. If it hadn't been for her companion, who knows where she would be now? Captured? Dead?

Gisele pushed the HOME button to cancel the call and slid the phone back inside her pocket. She wasn't prepared to sell him out to the police after what he'd done, but she had spent enough time in his company. She stood on her tiptoes to unlatch the window lock and push the window open. She slid off her coat and pushed it through the gap, climbing up as it fell out of sight and wriggling through after it. It was only a short drop to the ground outside. It felt like nothing after the drop from the warehouse window.

He was waiting for her. She didn't see him straightaway as he was standing with his back to the wall, out of her line of sight until she turned her head. Startled, she put a palm to her chest.

"Come on, Gisele," he said. "We don't have time for this."

"Get away from me, you fucking psycho."

"We've been through this," he said, stepping toward her.

"You're a psychopath. You murdered a defenseless man."

"You wouldn't let me torture him. So no logical reason to keep him alive. He'll be one less enemy to potentially deal with at a later time."

"You call that logic? He was wounded. He wasn't a threat. He was shot, for God's sake. And you could still have questioned him."

"To no gain," he said. "You took away his incentive to tell the truth. Any answer he gave would have been a lie."

Her eyes were wide with shock and disgust at his blunt logic. She didn't know how to respond at first. "You . . . you can't be sure of that."

"Hence the necessity of torture."

"That's no justification. Torture does not work. In my research—"

He cut her off. "When all this is over I'll happily debate with you the merits or demerits of torture. But we don't have time. We need to go. I'm here to protect you, Gisele. And to do that, you have to stay with me until this is over."

She stepped away from him. "Until what is over? What *is* this?"

"Until the threat against your father is over."

"Stepfather. Those guys back there, they weren't Russian gangsters, were they? At the train tracks, that man was British."

"He was. As for the others, I don't know. But you're right, they're not Russian mob."

She kept backing away as he approached. "Then who are they?"

"I have no idea."

"What do they want with Alek?"

"I don't know that either. But they want you for it."

"And you can stop them?"

He hesitated. She hadn't expected that. She ceased backing away because he was no longer coming toward her.

"I can't promise that," he said, finally. "But there's nothing I won't do trying."

She saw the sincerity in his eyes even if she couldn't bring herself to believe him.

He continued: "The police can't help you. We have no evidence. We have no idea who these people are or what it is they're after, beyond you. The police can't do anything with that. By the time they work out what's going on, you'll be dead. I can't allow that. I won't allow it."

"It's not up to you," she protested. "It's my life. I'm in charge of me. However much you care about it, you don't care about it as much as I do. I'm not a child. I don't know you. I don't have to do what you say. If I want to go the police, then you should respect my decision."

"It's not about respecting you or not. In this instance, I know more about these things than you do and I'm the best person to make decisions on how to keep you alive."

"Maybe so, and I will carefully consider your advice. But, ultimately, I make my own decisions. You can't force me to do what you say." She read his look. "Are you telling me I don't have a choice?"

"I'm telling you that it's better if you come with me willingly."

"So you're prepared to kidnap me to stop them kidnapping me?"

"It's not like that."

"What is it, then? What else do you call it?"

"Protective custody."

"With emphasis on the word *custody*."

He said, "For your own good. So I can make sure no harm comes to you."

"You say it as if you really mean it."

"Please, Gisele. Stay with me until morning. Let me protect you until then, at least. Get some sleep, and at first light if you want to go to the police then I'll drop you off at the nearest station. By morning the police will have a good idea of what happened at the warehouse, so you're more likely to be believed than if you go now. But until then you need to be at my side. Whoever attacked the warehouse is still out there, and if they tried that hard to get to you, they will be looking for you now. So we have to get off the streets."

She eyed him, suspicious but failing to find a lie. "You'll really take me to the police in the morning if I want?"

He nodded.

"Swear?"

He nodded.

"Say it."

"Okay," he said. "I swear."

"Okay," she said. "I'll stay with you tonight. But only because I can't get my head around any of this and I don't even know what I'd tell the police. You're right—I need to sleep and I have to think."

"Good. First we need to destroy your phone. Before you protest, it could be traced. I'll buy you a new one."

A sigh. "Fine."

He led her back to the car and they climbed in.

After a moment, Gisele said, "What would you have done if I hadn't come with you willingly?"

He turned, released the hand brake, and checked the mirrors. He didn't look at her. "It's probably best if I don't answer that."

Chapter 43

They drove through run-down areas that looked worse for the night and rain. Rubbish bags were piled up near lampposts, graffiti-covered walls and bus stops were vandalized. High streets consisted of betting shops and 99p Stores and a multitude of fast-food outlets.

The café Victor selected was open all night and had the red-and-white bands of the Polish flag in the signage. The air inside seemed thick with the smell of grease, and loud with an argument in the kitchen that flowed through the fly strips hanging down over an open doorway.

Victor took a seat so his back was against the far wall and stopped Gisele when she went to sit down opposite him.

"That one," he said, pointing to the chair next to her.

She glanced over her shoulder at the large plate-glass window at the front of the café and didn't comment as she took it. He liked that she understood without being told that he wanted a clear view of the street outside. She was no professional, but she was a fast learner.

Victor ordered the soup of the day and a coffee and

wouldn't allow Gisele to just have the tap water she asked for.

"She'll have a Coke," he said for her.

When the waiter had gone, she said, "Don't do that again."

"Do what?"

"Order for me. Don't tell me what I can and can't have."

"You need the sugar, Gisele. It'll help calm you down."

She studied him. "Then say that. Don't treat me like I'm an idiot."

He nodded. "I'm sorry. I'm not used to having to explain myself."

She shrugged. "It's okay. I can see you're not good with people."

He didn't respond to that. They waited in silence for a moment.

Gisele said, "I have a friend from uni days. She lives in Chiswick. We could stay with her."

"No," the man said. "Now they've lost us, they could be watching people you know, expecting you to seek refuge."

"Shit," she said.

"It's okay. It helps us."

She nodded, understanding. "So they'll be spread thin."

"Exactly."

"Then I wish I had more friends." She sighed and stood. "I have to use the bathroom." When she saw his look, she added, "Don't worry, I'm not going to try to sneak off again. Lesson learned and all that."

"The thought never occurred to me."

He watched her walk to the bathroom.

The soup and the Coke arrived while Gisele was in the bathroom. The soup was Polish tomato and it was served hot enough to make an excellent projectile weapon, should it come to it. Victor ordered a second bowl of it and a ham sandwich for Gisele, figuring she'd gain her appetite when she saw it.

"Don't be thinking I'm eating that," she said as she sat down. "I have a rule about not putting anything in my mouth that had four legs and a face. Or two legs. Or fins. Anything that was alive, basically."

He looked at her.

Before he could respond, she snapped, "Don't give me any shit about it or I'll tear your head off. I kid you not."

"I can tell, and I assure you I wasn't going to give you any"—he left a pause—"about it. I respect your self-discipline."

"Really?"

He nodded. "Yes, really. Any willing sacrifice is worthy of respect."

"Why do I feel like you're trying to take the piss?"

"I don't know why you feel like that. Maybe I'm not very good at giving out compliments or you're not good at receiving them."

Gisele's face softened and she said, "Probably both." She popped the tab of the can of Coke and took a gulp. She burped. "Sorry."

Victor ate his soup while keeping his gaze on the passing foot and vehicular traffic. There was only one other customer—an old guy in a huge trench coat who dipped biscuits into a mug of tea. The argument in the kitchen flared up intermittently. Victor's Polish was rusty, but he got the gist of it. The new hire wasn't working hard enough but didn't much like being told so. Victor guessed they were members of the same family.

"Good?" Gisele asked.

"The soup?"

"Yeah, the soup."

He nodded. "Make sure you drink all of that Coke."

"Yes, Dad. What's next?"

"We'll ditch the car and take public transport. The more we vary our route and our mode of transportation, the harder we'll be to track. A moving target is a hard target."

She sighed. He saw that the enormity of the predicament was weighing on her so he asked, "How long have you lived in London?"

"Half my life, I guess." The distraction worked. She relaxed a little. "I used to board in a private school in Buckinghamshire. My mother had been taught there and wanted me to have the education she'd had. I don't know why. She grew up to marry a gangster. Great use of her education there, right? Maybe she wanted me to reach the same lofty heights. On the holidays I would go back to Russia. Within a few years it didn't feel like home anymore. I always hated Alek and couldn't wait to come back to England. Then when Mum died I stopped flying back on the holidays and stayed with friends. I barely heard from Alek and made no effort to contact him. He carried on putting money in my bank account every month, and I even hated him for that. I still spent it, of course. I figured he owed me for what he put me and my mother through. Now I feel like a hypocrite for taking his money when I know how he made it. I put the deposit down on my flat with his money. I intend to pay it back eventually, when I'm actually earning a real wage."

"Commendable of you."

"Maybe. It seems to me I have to work twice as hard to be a good person because of who he is. Not that it makes any sense."

"Is that why you want to be a lawyer?"

"I guess so. I originally wanted to be a lawyer so I could go after Alek." She laughed. "I'll put that down to teen angst, though. Now I've calmed down a little and I don't want to use the law against people but for them. I'm not sure why I'm telling you all this when you're a criminal like him."

"I'm nothing like him."

Her forehead creased. "Yeah, right. How are you so very different, then?"

He thought for a moment. "I keep my word. I would never betray an ally."

She studied him. "So Alek betrayed you?"

He nodded.

"Then why are you helping him?"

"I told you: I'm not doing it for him."

She rolled her eyes. "Yeah, I remember. It's all for my wonderful mother. I hope I'm as great as her one day." She looked away and finished the can of Coke, then tapped her nails against it. "Last night, I saw this moth with only one wing trying to fly. It made me so sad."

Victor had no idea how to respond.

· Chapter 44 ·

London was a twenty-four-hour city. Taxis and buses flowed along its arterial streets all through the night. The bus's route wasn't important. After leaving the café they had taken the first that had arrived at the stop. Victor paid cash for his ticket while Gisele had a prepaid travel card she touched against the reader. The driver was an old Jamaican with two thick strips of white hair above his ears. He didn't hide his annoyance at having to pick up the handful of coins Victor had paid with. A few tired souls occupied seats on the bottom level, all sitting as far away from one another as the seating arrangement would let them. A woman in a green coat looked up from her book at Victor as he passed her.

He directed Gisele to the back of the bus, where they sat down near a man in work boots and a padded jacket, enjoying the extra warmth generated by the bus's engine. When the man alighted two stops later, Victor took his seat so he was next to the emergency exit. He gestured for Gisele to follow him.

"Precaution," he explained, and she nodded.

He liked that she didn't ask him to explain his actions any more than he had to. A group of rowdy young guys boarded and stood in the center of the bus. They had the loud voices and exaggerated movements of inebriation. They laughed and joked about their evening so far and were expecting more fun when they reached their next destination. One looked Gisele's way and Victor smelled the trouble in the air as easily as he could smell the alcohol and cologne. Even a drunk man could see that Victor and Gisele were no couple, with the age gap and lack of intimacy. He was tall and well built with perfectly styled hair, shiny, tanned skin, and shirtsleeves rolled up to reveal forearms covered in elaborate ink. He took a step forward, swaying under the bus's movements, holding on to a bar for support.

No, Victor mouthed.

The young guy stopped, doing a double take, not quite understanding the situation initially, but his lizard brain knew danger when it saw it, despite the alcohol, and he snapped his eyes away. Gisele glanced across at Victor but said nothing.

In part to hide his embarrassment and in part on the hunt for further amusement, the young guy with the perfect hair turned his attention to the nearest available alternative: the woman in a green coat who sat near him, reading a paperback book, doing her best not to attract the attention of the group.

He lifted it from her hands, asking, "What you got there, darlin'?"

She stiffened under the sudden violation of her personal space and property. The fear in her eyes was as obvious as the menace had been in Victor's. She pushed herself back in her seat to create space between her and the man with the forearm tattoos.

"Men can be such idiots," Gisele said. "Can't he see he's frightening her?"

Victor said nothing. He watched the scene before them.

The woman in the green coat didn't answer. The young guy flicked through the book, saying, "Haven't read one of these since school. Any good?"

Undeterred by her silence, he took the seat next to her. She recoiled and tried to stand up to get past him.

"Hey, don't be like that. I'm trying to be friendly here."

He grabbed her by the wrist to pull her back onto the seat and she slapped him.

"Shit," he hissed.

The slap and his reaction stunned the rest of the bus, including his friends, into silence.

"Give me my book and leave me alone," she said.

One of the friends said, "You didn't have to hit him."

"Don't be such a prick tease," another added.

"This is going to get bad," Gisele said to Victor. "Do something."

He shook his head. "We don't draw attention to our-selves."

The young guy with the perfect hair and shiny tanned skin stood and the woman backed away from him, but into his friends. They didn't restrain her, but they didn't get out of her way either. He rubbed his cheek and threw the book to the floor.

"How would you like it if I slapped you?" he asked.

"What's going on back there?" the bus driver shouted.

"Do something," Gisele said again. "You can stop this."

Victor didn't respond.

The woman said, "Just leave me alone. I didn't ask you to sit next to me."

"I was trying to be friendly," the young guy responded. "And you fuckin' slapped me."

"You scared me."

"Do I look like a scary bloke to you?" he asked, stepping forward until he was inches from her face, then leaning closer, using his height and size to best advantage, threatening by proximity, making her recoil down and away.

"Stop that, you dickhead," Gisele said, and stood. "Leave her alone."

She took Victor by surprise and he wasn't fast enough to stop her. She'd already taken a step forward before his hand had grabbed her coat.

The young guy turned toward Gisele. "Stay out of it."

"What exactly is your problem?" she said in response. "Are you that pathetic you have to feel like a man by intimidating women?"

Victor tried to pull her back but she resisted. "Let go of me."

"No."

The young guy, seeing the chance to distract from the insult, laughed. "Looks like this is the party bus tonight, boys."

His friends joined in the laughter.

Gisele turned to face Victor. "Let go of me right now, or this is nothing to the amount of attention I will bring on us."

He saw the strength of will in her eyes and released her coat. He knew better than anyone that some battles could not be won by force alone.

She turned back and approached the young guy with perfect hair. "Get off at the next stop and teach yourself some basic manners. You'll thank me in the morning."

"You don't get to tell me what to do. Who the fuck do you think you are?"

Victor stood and moved closer, keeping out of the way in respect for Gisele's wishes, but close enough to intervene should it prove necessary. Including the tanned guy with the tattoos, there were five. They were young and fit; the latter because they went to the gym to look good, not for health, but building muscle to attract women built strength too. A reasonable level of endurance could be expected, based on age if nothing else, but no fighting experience beyond the occasional street brawl that was over in a punch or two. They didn't yet know how exhausting real combat could be. They wouldn't find out either, if it came to it, because it would be over long before they tired.

Gisele said, "I'm not telling you what to do. I'm telling you what you should do."

He frowned, confused and insulted and embarrassed in front of his friends. "Ah, fuck off," he said, and shoved Gisele.

Victor was already moving but she snapped out her hand, grabbing the guy's fist, her thumb across his knuckle line, and twisted clockwise, rolling the fist and wrist and elbow until the arm was pointing up and locked and all the pressure was in his shoulder, trying to torque the joint past where the socket would let it go. Her free hand pushing down against the guy's upturned elbow increased the pressure and forced him down until he was on his knees, grunting and wailing.

The speed and violence of the move stunned his friends, but only for a second. One stepped forward. Then another. The others would soon follow.

Victor said to them, "Of all the times in your life that

you need to make the right decision, this is the most important."

One said, "What does that mean?"

"It means I'm giving you all the chance to go home tonight without a detour to the hospital. Take it."

They hesitated. He stared each one in the eye, seeing each fighting the internal battle between courage and fear and showing them that in turn he fought none.

"Let go of me," the young guy with the tattoos yelled at Gisele.

"Once you've apologized to her."

The woman in the green coat, wide-eyed, said, "That's . . . that's really not necessary."

Gisele applied extra pressure to the lock and the young guy yelled, "Okay, okay, I'm sorry."

"And you'll get off at the next stop?" Gisele asked.

"Yes."

Victor used a knuckle to ring the bell and the bus came to a stop a moment later. The doors hissed open and Gisele released the hold. The young guy with the no-longer-perfect hair struggled to his feet with the help of his friends and they disembarked. Victor didn't take his gaze from them until the doors had hissed closed again and they were throwing insults from the safety of the pavement outside.

"Are you okay?" Gisele asked the woman in the green coat.

She nodded with enthusiasm. "You totally kicked his ass. Thank you."

Gisele smiled in response. "You're welcome."

Victor said, "We have to get off this bus."

· Chapter 45 ·

What a day. Andrei Linnekin sipped from a bottle of Peroni and took a bite from his take-out burger. He sat behind his desk in the office above his club. He had not gone out to get the food, of course; one of the idiots working for him had fetched it. The idiot was not only stupid but slow. The burger was barely lukewarm. Still, Linnekin was hungry and wolfed down the food. The man he'd sent was one of the ones busted over the head by the asshole in the suit. He looked ridiculous with bandages wrapped around his skull. Linnekin was making him and the others jump through hoops, keeping them on their toes with fear of what he might do in retribution for their failure. He didn't let on that they would not be punished, that it was he who felt responsible for what had happened to them. He hoped that soon the matter would be satisfactorily resolved.

Moran had wisely fled the city, if the rumors were to be believed. Linnekin had all sorts of pain planned for him if he ever returned. True loyalty could not be bought. It had to be enforced.

There were practical considerations too. His men expected him to be strong. His enemies would fear him only if they believed him to be strong. His bosses would remove him if he was shown to be anything but strong.

He didn't feel strong, but he kept that to himself. He finished the last of the burger—leaving the gherkin—and washed it down with the rest of the Peroni. *A king's banquet,* he thought to himself.

Commotion from beyond his office door made him sit upright and reach for the sawed-off shotgun he kept behind his desk. He held it out of sight as a precaution. It would not do for his few remaining able men to see him with a gun in hand unless it was unavoidable. If they thought him scared, they would be scared in turn and he needed them to be fearless.

They had pistols in shoulder rigs or tucked in waistbands, plus shivs, brass knuckles, and an assortment of other tools for killing and maiming. Linnekin didn't pay too much attention. His only concern was that his men were better equipped than London's police force. He couldn't quite believe it when he had first arrived in the city and been informed of this. *Don't insult my intelligence,* he had said, thinking he was being played for a fool. Then, when he realized it was the truth: *Are they trying to make it easy for us? Imbeciles.* He'd subsequently learned about the armed-response teams, but knowing that the regular cops carried nothing more fearsome than a club was a source of constant amusement.

The door opened. A figure stood in the doorway. A woman with blond hair and green eyes. *Her.*

"Hello, Andrei," Anderton said, pleasant and courteous. He toyed with the beer bottle. "I find it funny how you English speakers use that word to greet one another in person when it was invented specifically for use with the telephone."

"How educational," she said, stepping into the room. "What do you want?"

"I see I've interrupted your dinner."

Linnekin brushed the greasy burger wrapping to one side. "I'm done. Why are you here? You told me that I'd never see you again."

"This is true. But circumstances have *evolved* since our last conversation."

"I haven't got the girl, if that's what you mean. I delegated it to a man named Blake Moran. I—"

She interrupted him. Linnekin hated such disrespect, but managed to maintain his composure.

"I know. I've known the whole time. But I'm not here because of the girl. I'm here because I'd like to talk to you about the man who came to see you."

Linnekin took his time before responding. She had interrupted him. Now she could wait.

"You mean the man who cracked open the skulls of two of my men and threatened to kill me? The man who only did so because of the—how did you put it?—*favor* you asked of me."

"There was no favor. You were well paid for your services."

"We'll have to disagree on that," Linnekin said. "I'm not in the kidnapping business, as I told you before. But you didn't leave me any choice, did you? With all those thinly veiled threats."

Anderton took a seat opposite him.

"I don't remember asking you to sit down."

She smiled at him. "You must have forgotten your manners. Momentarily, of course. And, yes," she said, in answer to his earlier question. "That's the man I mean. He's caused me a lot of problems tonight."

"I'll shed a tear for you later."

She pursed her lips and nodded. Linnekin was glad of any offense he could cause. He both feared her and hated her and was determined not to let this woman think she had any control over him.

One of Linnekin's doormen stumbled through the doorway behind her. His face was bloody.

"I'm sorry, Mr. Linnekin. They—"

He waved his hand. "Just get out."

The doorman left.

"Did you have to do that?" Linnekin asked.

She smiled. "I assure you, I was most polite."

"Can we get to the point?"

"Of course. May I have something to drink? I'm a little thirsty."

Linnekin said, "Sure. My bladder's full." He reached for his fly.

"I'll let that one go, but only because I know what you're doing. You don't like me. I understand. You're not used to taking orders from anyone. Least of all a woman, yes? And especially not when that results in you being embarrassed in front of your men. But you need to understand who I am. You need to understand that you only exist in this city by the grace of me and me alone. With one e-mail I can have every one of your men arrested."

He shrugged to hide his anger and fear. "So what? You have nothing on me. You're a devil, but you're a government succubus. You wouldn't dare coming after me head-on."

She considered for a moment. "Perhaps, but why

should I when with one phone call I can have your poppy fields in northern Helmand burned to ashes?"

He stiffened at the threat.

She saw it and smiled. "How will you explain that one to the bosses back home?"

Linnekin, teeth clenched, exhaled through his nose. "What do you want?"

"I've told you: information about your visitor. Six-two, dark hair and eyes, suit. What is his name?"

"He didn't give one."

"What did he say to you?"

"He was looking for the girl. He thought she'd been taken."

She absorbed this. "What else?"

"That was about it."

"I'm sure there was more to your discussion than that. He killed three of Moran's men and disabled two of yours. That's a lot of damage just to ask one question."

"He didn't say who he was and I wasn't in a position to interrogate him, okay?"

"Did you tell him about me?"

Ah, the point.

Linnekin said, "I don't know anything about you, do I?"

"That's not answering my question."

"He had a gun to my head. I was at his mercy. What did you expect me to do?"

She nodded, false sympathy and faux understanding smeared across her perfectly made-up face.

"Do you know why I hired you in the first place?"

Linnekin shrugged. "Because you're lazy?"

"Cute. I hired you because I didn't want any blow-back. I didn't want to be connected. I wanted someone to kidnap the girl for me, someone who didn't know why and didn't know who she was."

"And your point is?"

"Now you do. Now I'm connected because you're connected. My point is that means we're either enemies or friends."

"Which would you prefer?"

"I think it's more a case of which would you prefer, Andrei."

"What do you English say about *with friends like these* . . . ?"

"We also say 'The enemy of my enemy is my friend.'"

"What are you proposing?"

"We work together to solve this problem. I believe this man is still in London with the girl. Your network has eyes and ears. Keep them open. That's it."

Linnekin considered. "And if we spot them?"

"Inform me. My people will do the rest."

"Aside from his face, I know nothing about him."

"That's no problem. He's with the girl. Look for her and you'll find them both."

Linnekin nodded. "Okay. Deal. I know what he did to warrant my vengeance, but what is this girl to you?"

Anderton didn't answer. She stood up and left. Linnekin watched her go, hoping the suited man would kill her to save him the bother. But he wanted the man for himself. He had given his word.

Chapter 46

I t was still raining when they alighted a few stops later, leaving enough of a distance between them and the group of drunk guys to ensure they did not cross paths again, but not staying on the bus for any longer than they had to. He found another car to steal, this time a twenty-year-old Vauxhall station wagon.

"That was a nice move back there," Victor said when they were both inside. "But you really shouldn't have gotten involved."

"I'm not like you. I wasn't going to let him hurt her."

"He didn't hurt her."

"Not physically, at least not at that point. But no one deserves to be intimidated like that."

Victor said, "But when you intervened you couldn't have known what the end result would be. Had I had to become involved, things could have turned out very differently."

"Or maybe I knew that as soon as that greasy prick was challenged, he would back down. Maybe you need to start giving me a little more credit. I've been taking self-defense classes for months. I knew what I was doing. Plus, I carry a can of pepper spray, just in case."

"It could have escalated into something very bad for both of us."

"But it didn't, did it?"

"No," he admitted.

"And it didn't put us at any additional risk, did it?"

He hesitated, then had no choice but to agree. "It did not."

She stopped and looked at him. "So what exactly is your problem?"

He considered her, and if not for the danger they were in might have smiled. "You'll make a good lawyer someday, Gisele. Of that I have no doubt."

"I'll take that as you conceding the argument."

He didn't answer. Out of the corner of his eye he saw the beginnings of a smile, but it disappeared within a heartbeat and she said, "Maybe you need to start trusting me."

He nodded to placate her. He didn't trust her—not when their lives were in danger. But he was impressed with her resolve. She was calmer than any civilian should be in such a situation. For now, at least, he did not have to be concerned with Gisele's actions or inactions further complicating his job.

Except this was no job. It was a favor on behalf of a dead woman. He focused on the road ahead to prevent the memories from surfacing. This wasn't the moment to let himself be distracted. Both for his sake and the sake of the young woman sitting next to him.

She didn't ask where they were going, but he guessed that was because the enormity of what had happened was hitting home. He expected her to cry, but she didn't. His eyes flicked between the mirrors as he drove, watching out for pursuers, but after ten minutes he was sure there were none. After another ten he allowed himself to think about what to do next. The immediate danger may have passed but a whole new level of threat had materialized. Whoever these guys were, they were not Russian and they were not gangsters. They were mercenaries. Good ones.

Eventually Gisele said, "We can't wait any longer. We need to find out if Dmitri and the others made it. Back at the warehouse, I mean. We shouldn't have left them. We need to contact Alek or Yigor."

"No," Victor said.

"Don't be a bastard. They were trying to protect me just as much as you were. Maybe more so. I need to know they're okay. I'm worried about them."

"They're all dead, so stop worrying."

"I can't believe you just said that. You can't be sure they're dead."

Victor said nothing to that. Apart from Yigor, the Russians were all dead. He stayed quiet because Gisele wasn't ready to accept it.

"As you killed my phone, let me borrow yours for a minute so I can call Alek."

"I don't have a phone."

Her eyes widened with disbelief. "What? Then you're the only person who doesn't."

"I came to the same conclusion myself."

"This is ridiculous." The annoyance turned to despair. "I need to know if they're all right. I need to know . . ." She exhaled sharply. "You don't give a shit about them, do you?"

He saw the hostility in her eyes. He was used to such

looks but it was essential to keep her on his side. He couldn't protect her if she saw him as an enemy. "Okay, I'll call your stepfather."

A few minutes later he stopped the car next to a pay phone and left the engine running and the driver's door open while he went inside to call Norimov.

As soon as the line connected, Victor said, "She's okay."

Norimov breathed a huge sigh of relief. "Put her on the phone."

Victor looked at her sitting in the passenger's seat, rubbing her shoulder, staring expectantly at him, waiting to hear about Dmitri and the others. He shook his head and he watched as she put her face in her hands.

"Not now," Victor said. "What do you know?"

"Only what Yigor told me. He called not long before you did."

"Which is?" Victor asked.

"That when he tried returning to the warehouse it was swarming with cops."

He thought about this for a moment, then summarized the attack and subsequent escape, finishing with "Dmitri sacrificed himself."

"That hurts me. My poor boys. They were good men."

"No one who works for you is a good man."

"They died for me—for Gisele. Whatever wrongs they did before then are irrelevant. When Gisele is safe I will grieve for them. They deserve that of me, at least."

"Gisele is far from safe. The assaulters were mercenaries— pros—with suppressed MP5s, body armor, and flashbangs. I killed two of them, maybe three, but there are as many more still alive. What aren't you telling me, Alek?"

"I . . . I don't understand what you mean."

"A rival organization is not going to hire a team of professional mercenaries just to kidnap your daughter. That seems a little excessive, don't you think?"

"I agree. They must have known I sent men to London to protect her."

Victor didn't respond. "If there's something you're keeping from me, then you should know I'm going to find out what it is, and you'd better pray that I don't learn that you've put Gisele or me in danger as a result."

"Vasily, I'll swear on my life, if that's what it takes. I've told you everything."

"It is your life you're swearing on."

A pause; then, "In time you'll see I'm telling the truth. Until then, I implore you to get Gisele out of the country. Bring her to me, to St. Petersburg, where I can protect her."

"Negative. You can't protect her from these people. Four of your men just died to prove that fact. Until I know more, we're not moving."

"But—"

"The decision is not yours to make. Your safe house was blown. If your enemies knew about that, they know everything. Gisele stays with me until I've figured out exactly what is going on."

Norimov was quiet for a long moment. Eventually, he said, "Okay," because there was nothing else he could say.

"Where's Yigor now?"

"Driving. He's waiting to hear from you."

Victor said, "He can stay waiting."

"What are you and Gisele going to do next?"

"I'm not telling you."

"Excuse me? I'm her father."

"And I'm protecting her. That means I do things my

way. My way is the reason you don't yet have to organize her funeral."

A sigh. "Okay. Fine. You can handle this however you see fit. I'll go along with whatever you think is best."

Victor said, "You don't have a choice," and hung up.

· Chapter 47 ·

They ditched the car, leaving the engine running and the lights on. It was only a matter of time before it was stolen, Gisele's companion had explained. What the thief or thieves did with it was unimportant, but they would add another layer of defense against their enemies. They caught a bus, then alighted to board the tube, then another bus before a taxi took them the rest of the way to a hotel. He paid the fare and left a modest tip.

He guided Gisele into the lobby and up to the third floor, and she followed him to where she assumed he had been staying, as he already had a keycard. She watched in silent confusion as he went into the bathroom and spent a few minutes pouring shampoo and body wash into the bathtub, then rinsing it away before unwrapping soap and wetting towels. She wanted to know what he was doing but had no energy to ask. She left him and flopped down onto the bed.

He entered a moment later and said, "Get up."

She lay there, eyes closed, hoping he would just let her rest.

A strong hand gripped her by the wrist and wrenched her to her feet.

"What the fuck . . . ?"

He didn't answer. She looked on as he messed up the neatly made bed and squashed and punched the pillows.

"What did that bed ever do to you?"

He ignored her—infuriating her in the process—and went briefly back to the bathroom, returning with a free-standing mirror that he then placed on the windowsill, painstakingly positioning it as if it were the most important thing in the world.

"You have serious issues."

"Let's go," he said.

"Go? We just got here. You said we were going to rest."

He held open the door and ushered her through it.

Back on the ground floor he steered her away from the lobby when she headed in that direction. She was looking around and becoming increasingly confused as he took her through the hotel's ground floor, past the business center and fitness suite, and out the southern exit.

"Where are we going now?" she asked.

"We're nearly there."

He checked the traffic and crossed the road beneath the railway and cut between the sparse line of trees.

"Here?"

They entered his other hotel and used the stairs to ascend to the fourth floor. He unlocked his room with another keycard and led Gisele inside. She stepped in slowly, brow creased and eyes wide as she looked around, trying to understand what they were doing. This made no sense at all.

"You can sit down," he said.

"Are you going to tell me to stand up in three minutes' time?"

"No."

"Promise?"

He nodded, and she lay down on the bed. After a moment she asked, "What was wrong with the previous room?"

"This one is better."

"If you say so," she sighed. "I've given up trying to understand you."

She watched as he closed the curtains. As with the mirror, he spent a bizarrely long amount of time adjusting them. He turned around. She realized there was only one bed. Her pulse quickened, as she feared he would want to share it. It disgusted her to think of him lying next to her.

"You can sleep in the bed," he said. "I'll take the armchair."

She wondered if he'd seen in her face what she'd been thinking and felt bad for it. She pushed herself up onto her elbows. "Funnily enough, I'm not actually tired now. My brain is fried. Deep-fried in crazy, that is."

"Nevertheless, you should try to get some rest. First rule of soldiering: sleep whenever you can."

"In case you hadn't noticed, I'm not a soldier. I'm about as far from a soldier as you are from a normal person. Well, maybe not *that* far."

"You still have to sleep," he insisted. "You may not feel like it now, but if you don't, it will catch up with you tomorrow. That's how it works."

"And we need to be alert, right? Because they might come after me again?"

"That's right."

"God, it's so much work."

She sat up and pushed herself off the bed. She had to walk off some of the nervous energy. She paced and watched him as he wedged the back of a desk chair underneath the door handle. It seemed such a simple precaution to take, but she would never have thought to do it. Her mind was racing at one hundred miles an hour, but she couldn't think clearly. In comparison, his calmness was unnatural and unnerving.

Stepping away from the door, he said, "Whoever these people are, they are heavily invested in you, Gisele. They're skilled and they have numbers. And they will succeed unless we do everything right. Even then, it might not be enough."

"Thanks for the reassurance."

"I'm not attempting to reassure you. I'm telling you how it is, because you can't afford to relax for a second."

"Then how am I meant to sleep?"

"Stop trying to pick a fight with me. It won't work."

"I don't like you," she said.

He nodded. "I know. But I don't need you to like me. I just need you to do what I say."

"You sound like Alek."

He didn't respond. He went to step around her on the way to the bathroom and she flinched. He saw it and backed away, seeing her fear even though she was trying to hide it. For a moment they stood in silence, her afraid and him surprised, until he said, "There's nothing to be nervous of, Gisele."

"You killed two men. You tortured one."

"I did what was necessary," he explained.

"Says you. I don't know what's necessary or not. I

don't understand any of this." She rubbed her arm. "All I have to go on is what you tell me. How am I supposed to know if what you're saying is true? I look at you now and you don't seem any different from when I first met you. But so much has happened since then. I can barely keep a lid on what I'm feeling. I can only just about stop myself screaming at the top of my lungs. Yet you . . . nothing. You said you were used to it, but it's more than that, isn't it? What happened doesn't bother you at all. Getting attacked. Killing those men. The blood. The violence. None of it has even the slightest effect."

She was staring at him intently and saw that he thought about lying, but a second's deliberation was all it took for Gisele to see the truth.

She said, "Man, you *are* a fucking psycho," and backed away.

"It didn't bother me—that's true. But you don't have to worry about me, Gisele. I won't hurt you."

"Again, says you." She backed away another step until her shoulder blades were against the wall next to the door. "What's the word of a murderer worth?"

He didn't respond.

She said, "If you wanted to, you could kill me just like that," and snapped her fingers. "Couldn't you?"

His black eyes didn't blink. "I'll never want to."

"But you could. If you are lying and turn on me, there's literally nothing I could do to stop you, right?"

He had no choice but to nod. They both knew it was the truth. Denying it would have been ridiculous.

He said, "I'm here to protect you, Gisele. To that end I'll do everything I'm capable of to make sure no one harms you. If that scares you, then I'm sorry."

She noted he was careful to create as much distance as

possible between them as he passed. He flicked on the
light switch.

"You don't scare me," Gisele said from behind him.
"You terrify me."

He paused and nodded without looking back.

· Chapter 48 ·

The night had always been Victor's friend. He guessed he had spent more of his waking life during the night than the day. He had learned to know the night and to use it, but now it was an enemy because he was not alone. Gisele was finally still beneath the duvet after tossing and turning for a while. She complained about the lights being left on but Victor was insistent. She lay on her side at the very edge of the bed—as far away from him as possible. He didn't blame her.

Victor stood by the window, gazing outward. He was relaxed yet vigilant. He was used to waiting. Waiting was half his work: waiting for people to show; waiting for them to leave; waiting for it to get dark. The most undervalued skill of the assassin was patience. Those who didn't have it didn't survive for long. Now that patience might keep Gisele—and him—alive.

He'd said he would take the chair but he stood. The chair was wedged against the door handle. He was positioned by the window, looking out between the curtains but from an acute angle. Across the street on the other side of the concrete posts supporting the elevated railway line he saw his other room and the mirror set on the windowsill. He could see nothing in the reflection. If he could, it would mean someone was in the room.

Gisele woke with a start, bolting upright in the bed, gasping when she saw him but then relaxing slowly once she had processed the situation.

"I fell asleep," she said.

"That's good," Victor replied. "Try to go back to sleep. Get as much sleep as you can."

"First rule of soldiering?"

"Something like that."

"What are you doing by the window?"

He shrugged, as though it was nothing. "Just passing the time."

"You can't sleep?"

He shook his head.

"What time is it?" she asked.

"Almost three thirty."

"Have you had any sleep?"

"Yes," he lied.

He looked at her. She was massaging her left triceps. That was the third time he'd seen her rubbing her arm. As far as he knew, she wasn't injured.

"Are you okay?"

She huffed. "Never better."

"What's wrong with your arm?"

She looked back at him, at first confused, then understanding. "I get somatic pain when I'm stressed. Nice how my body turns against me at the very worst possible times, isn't it?"

If she had been injured, he could have used his medical knowledge to help, but she had no physical ailment he could treat. He was powerless.

"You almost look concerned about me," she said. "Don't worry, I'm used to it."

"Tomorrow," Victor said, "you're going to have to cut your hair."

She stopped rubbing her arm. "Seriously?"

"It's a precaution. Your hair stands out as it is."

"It's not exactly long. If I cut it shorter then I'll be more memorable and noticeable, surely."

"True, but they already know who you are and what you look like. If it takes them an extra second to realize that the young woman with short hair is actually you, that might save your life."

She frowned. "What can happen in a second?"

"Let's hope you don't find out."

"Fine, you win. It's the middle of the night. I don't have the energy to argue with you anymore. In the morning I'll cut my hair off and go all nineties lesbian."

"A few inches off the length will do fine."

"You want me to color it too?"

"Ideally, yes. We'll pick up some dye tomorrow."

"Sounds great. Can't wait. Why don't we go the whole way and I'll get dreadlocks? Perhaps a few facial piercings? Maybe bleach my eyebrows white?"

"I'm glad you're able to keep your sense of humor in all this."

"One of us has to." She smirked and pushed her fingers through her hair. "I'll give myself a pageboy cut. Will that do? I think I can pull it off."

He nodded. "That sounds perfect."

She looked away, fingers still in her hair. "I'm going to miss you."

"You are?" Victor said, surprised that anyone would miss him, least of all someone he'd known for such a short time.

Gisele's gaze met his. A line of confusion separated her eyebrows for the moment it took her to process what he'd said. "I . . . I was talking to my hair."

"Of course," Victor said, feeling foolish. "But it'll grow back."

She nodded as if she hadn't already known that, as if the misunderstanding had gone unnoticed, to spare him any embarrassment. Then she said, "There's no way I'm going to fall asleep now. Why don't we play a game or something? Otherwise I'll spend the rest of the night awake, staring at the ceiling, panicking at every sound."

"You don't need to do that. I'll stay on stag until first light."

"Stag?"

"British Army term," he explained. "Means 'on duty.' In this case, on guard duty."

She sat forward. "You were in the British Army?"

"That's not what I said."

"So you weren't?"

"That's not what I said either."

"Are you going to tell me anything about yourself?"

"Not if I can help it."

She raised her eyebrows—annoyed but not enough to pursue the issue.

He could feel her working up to saying something. He didn't prompt her. He let her say it in her own time.

"I haven't thanked you for what you did for me earlier tonight. I thought I was going to die back there."

He said, "You don't have to thank me."

"You've saved my life."

Not yet, he thought.

Chapter 49

The two big Range Rovers raced through the dark streets, rain pelting the bodywork, tires throwing up rainwater. In the first vehicle were five of Marcus's mercenaries. In the second, Anderton sat in the passenger's seat while Wade drove. Sinclair sat in the backseat, chewing gum as he adjusted the straps of his Dragon Skin vest to get the most comfortable fit. The windshield wipers swung back and forth, flicking away rain, each time presenting Anderton with a glimpse of her reflection on the glass. A pretty sight once, but not now, with the creases of dishonor cutting through her flesh.

She finished her phone call with a curt, "Keep yourself available," and directed Wade to take the next turn. He drove fast, pushing the limit of what they could get away with without drawing the attention of the police. Her credentials would get them out of any bother, but better not to get into it in the first place.

She updated the two men with what she had learned.

Rogan's voice came over the radio: "This is Unit One. We're nearly there. ETA six minutes. Over."

She thumbed the send button: "Confirm, Unit One. When we arrive I want you to split up and secure the perimeter while we enter and establish location. Make sure you have eyes on *all* exits. I don't want them slipping away." She released SEND.

"Copy that."

The Range Rover exited the bridge, following the road as it meandered to the right. Wade decelerated as they came to a traffic island.

From the backseat, Sinclair said, "I can handle it. Alone."

She didn't bother to reply.

"I said I can handle it."

Anderton met Sinclair's gaze in the rearview mirror. "Like you handled it at the warehouse?"

He frowned. "That was different. No one told me about the assassin."

"So he would not have bested you had you known he was there?"

The South African's voice was clipped and sharp. "Correct."

"For your own sake, I hope you're right," Anderton said. "I don't want any more mistakes."

"There won't be," Sinclair assured.

She nodded. "I know. Because this time I'm leading."

He looked away and continued chewing his gum.

Next to her, Wade's gaze was locked on the road ahead, but Anderton saw the fear the man was trying to hide. She could smell it on him. He was thinking of his two dead teammates.

Anderton felt nothing. The death of the two mercenaries had no effect on her except to elevate the stakes of the game. She had a worthy enemy. One who would soon be dead.

· Chapter 50 ·

As she had predicted, Gisele couldn't get back to sleep. She tried. She really tried. Bedclothes rustled as she attempted to get comfortable, and there were sighs of frustration when she failed to drift off. But no matter what she did to relax and clear her mind, images and sounds assailed her consciousness: flashes of grenades, gunshots, and cries. Then the fear would rush back into her and her heartbeat would thump in her ears and she found herself panting and more awake than ever. Eventually she gave up and pushed herself into a sitting position against the headboard, pulling the bedclothes high up over chest even though she was fully dressed.

He stood near the window, as before. He didn't acknowledge her. He was so still and focused he didn't seem alive. She couldn't decide whether this was a good or bad thing. She did know that it was freaky.

When she couldn't stand it any longer she climbed out of bed and padded over to where the room's phone sat on a desk. She lifted up the receiver. That broke whatever spell he was under. He faced her and she said:

"What's Yigor's number?"

"Put the phone down, Gisele."

"Give me Yigor's number."

"No," he said. "Put the phone down and go back to bed."

"I really don't like your tone. I never knew my real dad, but you're not him. You're not even my stepfather. So don't talk to me like that. I want to speak to Yigor. Now."

"That's a risk I'm not prepared to take."

"What do you mean by that? Yigor's on our side."

"Perhaps," he said. "But at this present time I don't know how those men found us at the warehouse. There's a good chance one of your stepfather's men sold you out. Only one of the men he sent here is still alive. And that man conveniently happened to have been absent from the warehouse when it was attacked."

She stared at him, wide-eyed in disbelief. "No way. You can't possibly be serious. Yigor would *never* do that."

"Then the team must have been shadowing you this whole time and for some reason opted to wait until you had armed guards before moving in."

Her mouth hung open for a moment. "What was that—sarcasm? Great time to find your sense of humor. Don't mock me, okay? And you don't need to be dismissive of my opinion either."

"Okay," Victor said.

"It's ridiculous to think Yigor had anything to do with that. He used to drive me to school, for fuck's sake. Trust me, he wouldn't."

• • •

"Drive nice and slow," Anderton told Wade. "Don't pull up directly outside. Park like we're guests. He might be watching."

The mercenary nodded and steered the Range Rover through the hotel's large parking lot at the building's east side. He drove as instructed: slowly.

"There," Anderton said, pointing to a free space some twenty meters from the hotel.

Wade guided the vehicle to a stop.

She radioed Unit One: "Okay, we're here. Wait ninety seconds and join us. Park farther away and secure the perimeter. Don't break cover unless I explicitly say so." She released the SEND button and looked at Sinclair. "Ready?"

Inside the lobby, Anderton led the two men straight to the front desk. They all wore civilian attire, jackets done up to hide weapons.

"Let me do the talking."

A pretty blonde with too much makeup smiled at them. Before she had a chance to say a word, Anderton said, "Get your manager. Now."

He was a short man in his fifties with a pronounced gut. Anderton showed him her credentials and he read them with eyebrows raised.

He said, "You'd better come with me."

In a small office behind the lobby, he asked, "What is it that I can do for you?"

"I'm here because of a potential threat to national security."

"My God, do you mean terrorists?"

"I can't divulge that information at this stage," Anderton said. "I need the room number of one of your guests. A single man, Caucasian, early to mid-thirties, short dark hair. Tall. Well dressed. He'll have a young woman with him."

The manager swallowed. Nervous. "What . . . what's his name?"

"We don't have a name, but we do know he checked in yesterday morning."

"Madam, we have hundreds of guests at any one time. I'm sure there are dozens who match that description. Most of whom are accompanied by a lady friend. Some don't even stay the night, if you know what I mean. So I'm not sure I can help you without more information. Would you like me to print you off a list of guests?"

Anderton smiled to put him at ease. "Show me the footage from your security cameras."

• • •

In a small, claustrophobic room, Sinclair and Anderton stood behind a big hotel security guard who sat in front of a bank of video monitors and equipment. The manager had shown them to the room, then hurriedly left.

"So," the guard began as he manipulated the controls, "what's this guy done?"

"That's classified," Anderton said.

"What camera did you want to take a look at? We've got twenty-two to choose from. I can give you Car Park A, Car Park B, Car Park C, Lobby A, Lobby B—"

"Lobby. Whichever one covers people passing through the main entrance."

"Gotcha." He pressed a few keys on the keyboard before him. "And what time code did you want me to look at?"

"Go back five hours," Sinclair said. "And cycle through from there. It's not complicated."

The guard sighed and shook his head as he rewound the footage from the hotel lobby. "Hey, chill out, man. You don't have to take that tone with me. I'm only doing my job here."

"Then shut up and do it."

He looked back over his shoulder. "Shit, you can't talk to me like that." He took his hands from the controls in a show of defiance. "You're not my boss, you"—he put on a bad imitation of Sinclair's accent—"you South African prick."

In a second the guard was off the chair, face forced into the floor, his right arm twisted behind his back, Sinclair holding his wrist and elbow, ready to break the arm with an ounce more pressure. The guard yelled in pain.

"Easy," Anderton said. "Easy, we don't have to do it that way. He's sorry." She looked at the guard. "Aren't you?"

"*Yes.*"

Sinclair released him. "Then work faster and keep your lips shut or I'll chew them off your face."

The guard pulled himself off the floor and slid back on to his chair. Grimacing, he returned to the controls. He rewound the footage to the requested time code and then played it forward.

"Take it to eight times speed," Anderton said.

He did so and they watched the rapid, jerky movements of guests and staff entering the hotel and passing through the lobby. Anderton noticed Sinclair's teeth were grinding together.

"*Stop.*" Anderton snapped her fingers. "That's him. Play it."

On the screen a man entered the lobby, only his back visible. He was dressed in a suit and had short dark hair, but no other features were obvious. Trailing a few meters behind him was a young woman.

Anderton left the room. She gestured for the blond receptionist to follow her. Back inside the viewing room, she pointed at the screen.

"Who's that man?"

The receptionist leaned forward and looked closely, her brow furrowed. The monitor showed two figures walking past the reception desk and heading for the stairs.

"He walked past you three and a half hours ago," Sinclair prompted.

"Oh yeah," she said. "I remember him. He was a nice guy. Thompson, I think his name is."

"What room is he in?" Anderton asked.

"Three ten. Why? What did he do?"

The guard said, "Don't ask, Layla."

Anderton frowned as she left the room with Sinclair in tow. "This is too easy. Something's not right."

Sinclair said, "I like easy."

Chapter 51

"**T**hey could have been following you, for all we know," protested Gisele. "You could have led them straight to me."

"That's better," Victor said. "That's the kind of critical thinking you should be using. You can't work on the simplest assumption. You have to consider every eventuality."

She stared at him. "Oh, very clever. Nice way to get me to come round to your way of thinking and make it seem like it was my conclusion. But I'm not dumb enough to fall for it, so I'd appreciate it if that was the first and last time, all right?"

"I chose the most straightforward way to make my point. I don't have time to teach you everything."

"*Teach* me? Are you fucking serious? Teach me what?"

Victor took a breath. "Easy on the language, okay? I've given you a pass until now because of the circumstances, but I don't appreciate it."

"You think I care what you appreciate? I don't appreciate you killing people in front of me either."

"Would you prefer it if I only killed people when you weren't looking?"

She took a breath like Victor had, only a deeper one that she held longer and let out slower. "I'm not going to allow myself to be pulled into these stupid arguments. You're protecting me, sure. Thanks. But I won't be treated like an idiot."

"Good. It's not my intention to treat you like one. I'm trying to teach you how to survive this. The men after you are extremely dangerous. They are ex-military and they will kill us both if we don't do everything right. Do you understand that?"

Gisele said, "Like they killed Dmitri and the others. Not that you care what happened to them."

"I happened to them," Victor said. "I left them. You're my priority, not your father's gangsters. I did what I could to help them, but the only thing that mattered was getting you out of there. They provided a useful distraction for our enemies."

"You're saying you used them as human shields?"

"Would you prefer to be dead in their place?" She looked appalled but didn't answer. "Bear that in mind. And don't waste your compassion on those men. Each and every one is—was—a killer. They don't deserve it."

"You killed people too. I saw you. Does that mean you don't deserve my compassion either?"

"I deserve it even less than your father's men."

She didn't respond.

"If you're going to survive this," Victor said more quietly, "you've got to have an utterly selfish mind-set. If you have to run over a street full of people to live another day, then you do it."

"I would never do that."

"Then if comes to it I'll have to do it for you."

"You're a disgusting excuse for a human being. Do you know that?"

"I've had a niggling suspicion."

"And it doesn't bother you?"

"Very few things bother me."

"You can't honestly believe the things you say."

"We're programmed to survive. Whether you believe that was instilled into us by evolution or God, that's who we are. We're survivors. Civilized society exists only when survival is not at stake. Put a person in fear for their life and see how much attention they pay to morality. You said yourself that morality needs to be enforced by the law."

"Yes, because there are bad people out there. I didn't mean that all people are inherently evil. I'd say you have a very pessimistic view of the world, but if you ask me it's a thinly veiled justification to do terrible things. But you don't have to be that way. You have a choice. It's never too late to change who you are. Make a fresh start. Be a good person. You never know—you might find you prefer yourself like that."

"If I were a good person we'd both be dead by now."

• • •

While four of the mercenaries maintained the perimeter, jackets zipped up to hide their body armor and weapons, Rogan joined Anderton, Sinclair, and Wade in a corridor leading out of the lobby.

"The target's location has been identified," Anderton reiterated to the men outside. "We're moving up. Be alert, but maintain your distance."

She didn't want to alarm people unnecessarily or risk the target spotting them from his window. It was the middle of the night but the area was far from empty of people.

The reply came: *"Copy."*

"Okay," she whispered to the three men with her. "Unit One has the perimeter, but it's loose. We don't want them getting past us on the way, so let's do this nice and fast but smooth. Sinclair and I will take the lift. Rogan and Wade, you guys ascend the far staircase so we come to their corridor from either end. Don't get jittery, boys; there are too many people here to risk a negligent discharge. All set?"

The elevator arrived at the third floor and Anderton and Sinclair entered the corridor. Both had pistols drawn and ready. Anderton whispered into her radio: "Unit Two in position."

She signaled to Sinclair and they moved down the corridor, Anderton on the left, the South African on the right.

Wade's voice came through her earpiece: "This is Unit Three. We have reached the third floor."

They turned a corner and saw the two mercenaries at the far end of the corridor. Simultaneously, the two groups moved with caution toward the door marked 310.

"Okay," Anderton whispered. "That's near enough. Wade and Sinclair go in first and secure the main room. Rogan and I follow. Wade, clear the bathroom. I'll watch your backs. Okay, close in."

They crept forward. Wade and Sinclair took up positions on either side of the door, with Rogan and Anderton behind them. She could taste sweat on her lips. This was it.

"Green light."

· Chapter 52 ·

Wade aimed at the room's lock with a twelve-bore pump-action shotgun fitted with a nine-inch Hush-power suppressor. The blast disintegrated the lock and Sinclair charged in through the busted door. Rogan followed him, each man sweeping a different half of the room. Wade entered last, disappearing into the bathroom.

"Clear!" he shouted.

"Clear," Rogan stated.

Sinclair, lowering his gun: "Crystal."

Anderton stepped into the lit room. No Gisele. No killer. She was annoyed, but not as surprised as the three men. It had felt too easy.

"Check under the bed," Sinclair said.

Wade shook his head. "There's not enough room."

"Do it."

He squatted down and made a play of lifting up the skirt. There was only a two-inch gap.

Anderton radioed the mercenaries outside. "They're

not here. Be alert." She walked over to the window, rested her palm on the sill, and whispered, "Where are you?"

• • •

Across the street, Victor turned around from arguing with Gisele to see a woman with blond hair in his other hotel room. He remembered Linnekin's description of her: blond, tall, well dressed, all business. He couldn't see whether her eyes were green, but he was sure this was her.

He stood still, watching. She did not look happy in the slightest. He felt a small measure of satisfaction at her anger, but that didn't change the fact Gisele's enemies were closer than he wanted.

With the curtains almost fully drawn he wouldn't be seen in return. He could see men in the room behind her—two or three. The mercenaries.

The others must be elsewhere, but nearby. They would be here in force.

For now, they didn't know the room was a decoy.

Victor looked at Gisele. "Get dressed."

"Where is this fucker?" Sinclair asked to anyone who was listening.

Anderton ignored him. She said, "Clear out and search the hotel. They might still be on the premises: bar, restaurant, fitness suite. Look everywhere."

Sinclair, Wade, and Rogan withdrew, leaving Anderton alone with her thoughts.

She had sensed something wasn't right beforehand. Now her instincts had proved correct. She circled the room. The bedclothes were mussed. In the bathroom, a towel was damp. Complimentary toiletries had been opened. All suggesting the room had been used and they'd missed them. Yet . . .

She approached the bed. She stared at the pillow. It was squashed in the center. The pillowcase was the perfect white of hotel-laundered linens. She looked closely, leaning in.

"No hairs," she said to herself.

Neither short dark hairs from the assassin nor longer red hairs from Gisele.

Anderton turned to face the window. The curtains were not fully closed. Interesting. More significant than that, though, was the freestanding mirror sitting on the sill.

She was careful in her actions to appear casual, as if she had not realized what was happening. This was not the killer's room. This was a ruse. This was a shield. A decoy. And Anderton had fallen for it.

Seemingly in an idle wander she approached the window. She placed both hands on the windowsill once again and gazed out, emitting a long sigh of frustration and annoyance. She resisted shaking her head. That might be overkill.

There was a hotel on the other side of the street.

Anderton judged the position of the mirror and the angle and pictured him across the street, standing at one of the windows of the hotel opposite.

• • •

"What do we do?" Gisele asked as she slipped her shoes on, voice high-pitched between rapid breaths.

"It's okay," Victor said, watching the blond woman sighing in frustration at the window opposite. "We're safe for the moment. We wait for ten minutes to give them time to extract. Then we go."

She stood. "Where to? How did they find us?"

"Anywhere. We'll work it out on the way. And they haven't found us. Stay calm."

• • •

Making sure to look as if she weren't looking, Anderton scanned the hotel across the street. There were dozens of windows, each belonging to a room. Norimov's assassin would have to set up a surveillance point at least at the same floor as the current room. Third or higher. She discounted those rooms on the first two floors.

Logic would dictate that the room's lights would not be on, or if not the curtains would be drawn. Mentally, Anderton dropped those rooms that did not apply. That left five rooms. Three on the fourth floor; two on the third. One of the fourth-floor candidates was at the far left of the building, almost on the corner. A height advantage was no good if the horizontal angle was acute. Anderton crossed it off.

Four left.

She picked up the room's phone and called the information desk. She told the operator the name of the hotel opposite and hummed quietly while she waited.

A man answered and asked her what he could do for her.

Anderton said, "This is Detective Chief Inspector Crawley from the Metropolitan Police. I need your help with a case."

"Oh, okay, what can I do for you?" was the nervous reply. Anderton pictured someone not dissimilar to the manager of the current hotel.

"It's quite simple, so please don't be nervous. A confidential informant of mine is staying in your hotel but I don't know which room he's staying in."

"What's his name?"

"Hooper, but he'll be using an alias for safety reasons. Trouble is, I don't know what the alias is and I can't get through on his mobile."

"How can I help, then?"

"I think we'll be able to work out what name he's using if you bear with me. He'll have checked in within the past forty-eight hours on his own and won't have checked out yet."

"I'll have a look at our records and get the names of those people."

Anderton could hear him tapping on a keyboard for a few moments.

"Right," the man said, his voice confident now, happy that he could perform this role and help. "I've got over . . . uh, well over twenty single men . . . John Belamy, Peter Cochrane—"

"Did any of those guests request anything specific in their choice of rooms? My CI has . . . how shall we say? *Quirks.* He would want a room with a north-facing window. Can you see if anyone asked for such a room?"

There was silence for a moment. "I'm afraid such a request might not be noted on the system. The operator might simply have given him a room that met that criteria. Let me see . . . uh, no. Sorry. There's no such request on any of the reservations. I'm not sure what else I can tell you."

"Okay," Anderton said, sounding like it wasn't that big a deal. "Of the single men who checked in during the time period, how many ended up in a north-facing room?"

There was a half-exhaling, half-whistling sound. "I can see . . . Let me count. Yeah, nine single men in north-facing rooms."

"Great," Anderton said, encouragingly. "That narrows it down. My guy doesn't like to be near the ground, so which of those nine men is in a room on the third or fourth floor?"

"We're getting close," the man said. "Down to two. One on the third floor and one on the fourth: Roger Telfer and Charles Rawling. If you want, I can put you through to them one at a time so you can see which is your man. It's no bother. I'm happy to help. They are—"

"Which had the earlier check-in?"

The man made a clucking noise. "Uh . . . that would be Charles Rawling. Room 419. Is that your guy? Would you like me to put you through to his room?"

"That won't be necessary," Anderton said. "I'll see him in person. But thank you for your assistance, er . . ."

"Nathan."

"Thank you, Nathan. You have yourself a good night."

"You're very welcome."

Anderton hung up. She knew they were in the fourth-floor room and not the third. Both had been available when Norimov's assassin had checked in. He would have taken the fourth-floor room as a preference, for the height advantage.

She radioed Sinclair: "Listen carefully. They're in the hotel across the street. This room is a decoy. He's in 419, repeat, 419. Charles Rawling. If I'm right, he knows we're here and he's looking at my back as we speak. But he doesn't know I know. He's going to wait until we clear out and vanish with the girl. So long as I sit here, he thinks they're safe. Don't tell the others. He might notice their reactions. Make your way over there while he's watching the rest of us. Do what you do best."

"With pleasure."

• Chapter 53 •

Sinclair exited the hotel via the main east entrance and cut through the parking lot, moving south. He crossed the road beneath the overhead railway line and headed for the other hotel, where Anderton assured him the killer was waiting. He made sure to avoid the north-facing facade of the new hotel and therefore the watchful gaze of the girl's protector.

If Anderton was right, it wasn't a bad trick. Not Sinclair's style, but he could see the merits of it. He preferred to meet his threats head-on, on his terms, not those of his enemies. Hiding was weak and it was stupid.

He felt liberated without the cumbersome presence of the mercenaries. He was on his own in the hunt. Just the way he liked it.

Wade's team had been useful in taking out Norimov's retinue of thugs, but they were no longer required. Two of them had gotten themselves killed already. It proved what Sinclair had known from the start: the others were B-team quality. They had served in elite military units, sure, but they had lost the edge that came with constant training and discipline. Sinclair had never lost that edge because he had possessed it long before his time in the armed forces. He wouldn't have survived the slums of Johannesburg without it.

He had learned early on to rely on himself alone. Sinclair could operate from the shadows, unseen and unheard; by the time his adversaries noticed him, it was too late. Sinclair felt only excitement. Combat jacked him up like nothing else in the world. A perfect drug.

He entered the hotel via its east entrance and took the elevator to the fourth floor.

• • •

From his position at the window Victor could see little of the happenings across the street at the other hotel. The mirror told him the woman and the mercenaries had exited his room. He pictured them searching the hotel in case he and Gisele were in the fitness suite or business center or bar. Once they realized they weren't in the building, what would they do?

He couldn't be sure. No doubt one or more would be left on site as watchers in case they returned, the others waiting nearby for the order to move in.

"Talk to me," Gisele said. "I'm freaking out here."

"Don't worry," he said. "We'll go now. We'll slip out of the hotel via the south entrance. Chances are, the bulk of them will be gone. Those who're left won't see us."

She gulped and nodded. She looked terrified.

He put a hand on her shoulder. "We'll be fine. Okay?"

She relaxed a little at his touch. "Okay."

There was a knock at the door.

Gisele startled. Victor snapped a palm over her mouth to catch any noise.

Shh, he mouthed. *It's okay.*

It wasn't. He didn't believe in coincidences—he couldn't afford to—but the knock could be innocent. His enemies were in the wrong hotel. He could see two of them watching the perimeter. They didn't know he was here with Gisele. No one did. He approached the door, stopping two meters away, out of a direct line of sight from the fish-eye spy lens. The gun was in his right hand.

"Who's there?"

A voice answered. Male. South African accent. "Mr. Quinn, sir. I'm from hotel management. I'm sorry to disturb you at this late hour."

"What can I do for you, Mr. Quinn?"

"I'm afraid I need to perform a quick check on the smoke detector in your room. It's purely routine."

Victor made a cursory glance behind him at the device on the room's ceiling. It was a small white plastic box containing a CO_2 detector. "It looks fine to me."

The man called Quinn said, "I'm sure it does, but we've had a few false alarms and I wouldn't want it going off by mistake and interrupting your sleep."

The tone was of a man with too much work to do and not enough time, a little impatient at the holdup.

"Like you're doing now?" Victor said.

"I'm terribly sorry, but I'm afraid it is important. I'd hate for it to go off and startle you."

"I'll risk it, thanks."

A pause, then a second knock. "I promise, I'll be quick as a flash."

Quinn didn't sound as if he would take no for an answer, and each second Victor had to deal with him meant time he wasn't watching out for his enemies. Unless that was the point. He approached the door, footsteps silent on the room's carpet. He gestured for Gisele to stay still and stay quiet.

She nodded. Looking at her, he understood how they had been caught off guard. He was at his best operating alone. Alone, he was always aware, always ready. He could rely on himself to do what had to be done. He'd relied on allies in times past, but Gisele was no professional. She was a civilian. But that wasn't it either.

He was responsible for her. More than that, he wanted to be responsible for her. He'd known her a matter of hours but he cared whether she lived or died. That made them both vulnerable. He'd told her she had to have a totally selfish attitude to survival. He no longer had that.

• • •

Sinclair waited on the other side of the door. He stared at the pinprick of light at the center of the spy hole. It was impossible to see through it from his side, but he didn't have to. All he needed to see was that dot of light extinguish when the killer brought his eye to the lens.

Then he would know exactly where the killer's head was located. Sinclair had his pistol drawn and pointed at the spy hole, index finger on the trigger, ready to squeeze.

A guaranteed kill shot.

• Chapter 54 •

Victor stood to one side of the door to keep his body protected by the interior wall. He used his hand to signal to Gisele to move back and away from the door so she was out of the line of fire. He swapped his gun into his left hand and with his shoulders to the wall aimed it at the door.

"Can you come back later?"

"I'm afraid not, sir. It has to be done now."

Victor angled the muzzle to where he thought the man stood, based on the sound, but it wasn't an exact science. Without looking he couldn't be sure of his position or even if he was an enemy.

"Look," he said, "I haven't long come out of the shower. How about you come back in ten minutes when I'm dressed?"

He pulled the hammer back with his thumb.

"All right," the South African said. "I'll return in ten minutes."

Victor listened to footsteps quieting. He peered through the spyhole. No one stood in the corridor outside. He stepped away from the door and eased his finger off the trigger.

"Oh, my God," Gisele breathed. "How have they found us?"

"Yigor."

"He wouldn't. I know him. Shit. What are we going to do?"

"Get out of here. Fast."

He moved away from the door and over to the window. The two Range Rovers were still there. There were still gunmen positioned nearby, trying to look inconspicuous. Victor didn't understand why they were there and not in his hotel. To distract him, maybe. But then the mercenary at the door wouldn't have needed to knock to find out if he was inside because they would already know that to have men positioned to distract him.

Which meant the man at the door and those outside were not operating together. At least at this moment. The South African had seen through Victor's ruse, but the others had not. He would no doubt be passing on his discovery, but it would take a few minutes for the other mercs to arrive. That delay gave Victor and Gisele a chance.

He returned to the door and peered through the spy hole. The corridor outside was empty but he knew the South African was out there, either waiting for Victor and Gisele to show themselves or preparing to attack.

Inside the room, they were vulnerable. It was small and impossible to defend. The window didn't open. It would be toughened glass and hard to smash. The noise of trying would alert his enemy. Even if Victor and Gisele could get through it without taking a bullet in the back, they were too high up to drop and the hotel exterior would be almost impossible to climb with any speed. At any moment the mercs across the street could spot them or the blond woman would lean out of the window to shoot him and Gisele while they descended.

He needed another way out. He needed a distraction. There was a plastic kettle on the sideboard along with cups and packets of coffee and sugar and tea bags. Victor unplugged the kettle, laid it on its side on the floor, and stamped on it with his heel until he could pull it apart to expose the element at the bottom and the electric thermostat integrated into the base. He pried the thermostat away and tossed it aside. He plugged the kettle's remains back into a socket and switched it on. Without the thermostat to regulate the temperature, the element would eventually become so hot it would melt. Victor didn't require it to get that hot. He dropped a handful of sachets onto the element.

Gisele watched him.

After ten seconds the paper began to smolder and smoke. Victor kept his gaze on the door and the gun aimed and ready to shoot. He didn't have to watch the smoldering paper. He knew what would happen. He grabbed both robes from the bathroom and pushed them into Gisele's hands.

"Hold these and follow my lead," he said.

She nodded.

An excruciating wail filled the room as the smoke alarm on the ceiling detected the elevated concentration of carbon dioxide gas in the air.

Victor waited. He knew alarms would be sounding throughout the hotel. Behind him, the paper sachets caught fire. He let them burn.

He figured thirty seconds would be long enough and approached the door. A glance through the spy hole told him what he wanted to know. He opened the door. The alarm's wail was even louder with those in the corridor and from other rooms sounding simultaneously. Several guests were in the corridor, having exited their rooms. They wore pajamas and robes. They were sleepy and squinting. Others were following. The same scene would be unfolding in every corridor on every floor of the hotel.

"This is outrageous," someone was saying.

Another said, "It'll be a false alarm."

Victor looked past the guests, all shuffling in the direction of the elevators and stairs, to where, at the end of the corridor, stood a man not in pajamas or a robe. He wasn't sleepy or squinting. He had a strong, stocky build and was around six feet tall. He was tanned and dressed in khaki trousers and a leather jacket zipped up to his neck.

He stared straight at Victor.

• • •

Sinclair's unblinking gaze burned into the black eyes of the killer. Bastard had pulled off a good trick with the alarm. Lots of people were between them, shielding the killer and the girl and preventing Sinclair from taking a shot.

The corridor extended around the hotel floor in a rough square. The section where Sinclair stood was on the opposite side to where the elevators and stairwells lay. That was the only way out, but the killer would no doubt try to play hide-and-seek. Sinclair had no intention of letting him do that with the girl.

They backed away because—presumably to their surprise—they saw Sinclair reach under his leather jacket. Through the shifting mass of guests, he saw the killer and the girl turning, then running.

Sinclair drew his weapon, a Glock 18 fitted with an

extended magazine and long suppressor. It was a handgun, but one capable of fully automatic fire. A single squeeze of the trigger would release five bullets in the same time that a conventional pistol fire took to fire one.

An elderly woman in front of Sinclair gasped when she saw the gun.

"You might want to duck," he told her.

· Chapter 55 ·

Despite the civilians between them, the South African mercenary opened fire. The wailing alarm drowned out the noise but Victor saw bullets taking chunks out of walls and sending blasts of dust and debris. Behind him, a woman was caught in the line of fire. Atomized blood misted in the air. A round caught the shoulder pad of Victor's suit jacket.

He half fell, half slid around a corner, pushing Gisele ahead of him, a hail of bullets following, noiseless but no less deadly. A wall-mounted light fixture exploded.

He scrambled back to his feet, drawing the SIG, waiting for the firing to stop. Even with an extended magazine the Glock expelled its load in five short bursts. Victor didn't waste the opportunity.

"Stay here."

He rushed back out into the corridor to catch the target as he reloaded.

• • •

But Sinclair wasn't reloading. The empty Glock was in his right hand and he had drawn his backup handgun into his left.

I knew you were going to do that.

Both men moved and fired at the same time, bullets smacking into walls around them. Guests were already down on the floor or had fled back into rooms. Their screams were silent with the alarm blaring. One of the killer's bullets caught Sinclair's handgun and sent the weapon flying out of his fingers.

He dived around a corner.

• • •

Victor took the opportunity to scramble backward, trying to get out of the corridor before his enemy returned with a fully loaded weapon in his primary hand.

"Come on," he said to Gisele.

He dodged around and pushed past terrified guests, reloading the SIG as he ran. The magazine wasn't empty but he wanted it at full capacity if he faced the mercenary again.

He was aware of people looking at him, the ripped suit jacket, the gun. He couldn't do anything about that. Getting out alive meant more than going unnoticed. He hurried to the end of the next corridor, leaned round the corner.

Bullets struck the wall next to him, sending plaster exploding into his face. He recoiled, eyes filling with water. He wiped them furiously on his sleeve until he could see.

He pushed Gisele clear, dropped into a crouch and leaned round again. The South African was at the far end of the corridor, the Glock now in both hands.

Victor managed to squeeze off a single inaccurate shot before more rounds came his way. Chunks were blown out of the floor and wall around him. A man, emerging from his room because of the alarm but unaware of the firefight, walked straight into the path of bullets. He was hit twice and fell to the floor in a tangle of splayed limbs.

Victor fired, but his target was already moving, dodging back into cover, an empty magazine falling from his gun, Victor's bullets striking the wall where his enemy had been a moment before.

He moved, firing as he did so to keep the South African pinned down while he made for the stairwell, ushering Gisele to follow him. People were screaming and shoving each other out of the way to escape the gunfight.

Victor took a robe from Gisele and touched her on the arm. "Put it on and hurry to the bottom."

She nodded.

He put down covering fire in the mercenary's direction until Gisele had descended a couple of floors, then charged through the panicking crowd, vaulting over the banister to drop down to the next level. He did the same again and again, until he landed on the ground floor a moment after Gisele, stumbling to keep his balance, then throwing open the stairwell door and dashing through into the lobby. He heard his enemy above, yelling at people to get out of his way.

Victor slipped on the robe and kept moving, Gisele, also robed, at his side. They couldn't exit out of the front with the other mercenaries likely to approach from that direction so he headed for the rear of the hotel, slowing down to attract less attention and avoid signposting his route. Panic from the floors above was spreading fast. The crowds of guests were agitated and becoming scared. The fire alarm continued to wail.

He eased Gisele and himself into a mass of people wearing dressing gowns and robes and let them both be crowded toward the exit. Security personnel were as panicked as the guests. They didn't know how to deal with a gunfight. For minimum wage, they had no intention of getting involved. He kept his eyes moving, looking out for threats, but no one paid him or her any attention. They were lost in the anonymity of the crowd.

The rear doors were held open by hotel staff to let the guests out faster.

"Keep moving, keep moving," one was saying. "We'll have you back inside soon. There's nothing to worry about."

He stepped outside into the cool night air. It was raining but not heavily. The hotel was shaped like a letter V and they stood in the courtyard between the wings where vehicles were parked and guests were gathering. To the north a line of trees shielded elevated train tracks. On the other side of the tracks, some seventy meters away, stood the other hotel. It had been approximately three minutes since the South African had knocked at the door. If they weren't here already, the other mercenaries soon would be.

"This way."

They set off to the west, keeping people all around them, scanning for threats. The chaos of the ever-expanding crowd of guests helped keep them hidden but simultaneously hindered his attempts to spot his enemies before they spotted him or Gisele.

Victor made sure to act like the people around him— walking at a frightened pace, distressed expression, wide eyes. Gisele didn't have to pretend. He led her in a zig-zagging path through the melee so they didn't provide easy targets for someone taking aim. After a minute they had passed the west wing of the hotel. It was quieter on the far side. A sparse crowd of mostly hotel employees had gathered here. They were happier than the guests because this was an extra break from work. They didn't yet know why they had been told to exit the building.

Another line of trees marked the boundary of the hotel's grounds. Victor and Gisele cut across to them, walking at a casual pace so they did not catch the eye of enemies looking on as easily as they would if hurrying. On the other side of the trees lay a long parking lot of maybe five hundred spaces. Most seemed occupied. Beyond the parking lot stood a huge hotel complex.

Victor disrobed and gestured for Gisele to do the same. He tossed the garments aside.

Within a minute he had selected a medium-sized Renault that was too old to have an alarm as standard. He used the SIG like a hammer and smashed out the window of the driver's door. He reached inside and opened it, then leaned across the glass-covered seat to open the passenger's door for Gisele.

"Get in."

She did while he tore off the covering from the steering column and hot-wired it blindly, his gaze constantly sweeping the area for mercenaries. The engine rumbled into life.

Two men were running their way.

Chapter 56

They converged on them from two sides—one twenty meters to Victor's left, the other twenty-five to his right—weaving their way between parked vehicles with fast, confident movement. The closest man had a tall, bulky frame but was faster than the other man, who was small and lithe.

Gisele was already shuffling lower in her seat before Victor could say, "Stay down."

He put the car into reverse and backed out of the parking space, swinging the wheel clockwise to put him facing in the direction of the nearest exit while he cranked down what remained of the driver's window.

The big guy, now sixteen meters away, reached under his sports jacket. The smaller man continued to sprint their way.

Victor changed into first gear, keeping hold of the wheel in his left hand while he drew out the SIG with his right. The tires squealed and smoked. He extended his arm out of the open window next to him and fired twice.

Both bullets struck the door panel of a large SUV

inches from the big guy, who startled at the impact, momentarily slowing him as he pulled out an MP5K from under his jacket. Victor would have shot at him again but he had already accelerated out of the line of sight.

Automatic gunfire roared in response.

Holes puckered the safety glass of the rear windshield and blew out the window of the backseat behind Victor. Gisele covered her head with her arms and hands.

The road brought them closer to the second man, who had braced himself into a firing position, crouching and leaning on the hood of a small car.

Victor didn't hear the pistol shots over the noise of the MP5K but he felt the reverberations of bullets thumping into the car's bodywork. The side-mirror glass exploded and showered Victor with tiny shards that struck his arm, shoulder, and face. He flinched and squinted to protect his eyes, lurching in his seat away from the spray of glass, involuntarily turning the steering wheel.

He recovered in time to stop the car from crashing, but dented a wheel well against a parked minivan. Metal screeched against metal.

Victor ducked down in his seat, returning fire as he passed the closest gunman. Rounds continued to strike the Renault. In his rearview mirror he saw the big guy with the MP5K rush out into the road fifteen meters behind him and flames spit out of the weapon's muzzle.

Holes blew through both windshields, spreading cracks across the safety glass, impeding Victor's view. He felt a tire blow.

"Brace yourself."

He waited a few seconds until he had put some distance between the Renault and the two gunmen, then slammed on the brakes and pulled the hand brake, and was jumping out of the car before it had stopped moving.

He kept low and ushered Gisele to follow him out of the same door because it was farther away from the gunmen than her own. She crawled over the seats and Victor pulled her out.

"Go."

He fired off a couple of shots while Gisele ran as fast as she could for the count of five; then he ran after her, heading for the exit, counting off seconds in his head, picturing the smaller gunman giving chase. Then he stopped, spun around, and dropped to one knee as he extended the SIG and brought his left hand up for stability, the iron sights of the gun lining up over the pursuing mercenary, who had moved out of cover to give chase.

The man's momentum carried him forward as bullets hit him in the chest, shoulder, and finally face. He dropped to the ground, leaving blood, brains, and chunks of skull sliding down windshield glass.

Victor moved to intercept the guy with the sub-machine gun, but he wasn't there.

Instead there was nothing but rows and rows of vehicles.

He stopped and signaled for Gisele to do the same. He motioned for her to get down between vehicles and he dropped into a push-up position, lying on his front to peer beneath the cars. The asphalt was cold and hard and wet under his palms. He saw no feet or legs, but his line of sight was interrupted by numerous wheels.

If he couldn't see his attacker, then the reverse must also be true.

He stayed down for a moment, thinking. The big guy

wasn't stalking closer, keeping low and hidden until he initiated his attack, because that would work only if Victor was stationary. Once he ran, he would quickly get out of range with his enemy too low to see him. So the gunman wasn't trying to get closer for an ambush. He was trying to stay alive.

No point dying for a paycheck that couldn't be cashed. Victor lived by the same principle. But the merc would still want his fee, which meant he was calling for backup.

Victor hurried over to where Gisele waited.

"Are you okay?"

Gisele nodded. "I'm fine."

He stood and looked around. Still no sign of the gunman but he saw a man frantically trying to unlock the door of an old MG convertible, but he was too scared by the recent gunfire to get the key in the lock. Victor dashed over, coming up behind the man and relieving him of his keys. The man stood trembling with fear. Victor put a hand on his shoulder and forced him to the ground.

"Hide," Victor told him.

It was advice that could save the man's life. A fair trade for his car, Victor thought. He waved Gisele over, but it was too late, because he saw a black Range Rover pull into the parking lot.

· Chapter 57 ·

They ran, heading south, away from the Range Rover, turning to the side to get between cars until they were clear of the parking lot and facing a dock where the vehicle wouldn't be able to pursue. Either those inside would be forced to jump out and chase on foot, or the four-by-four would turn around and try to get ahead of them—or both. Any of the scenarios worked for Victor, because it would mean a divided force.

He followed the waterline to the east, Gisele at his side, passing the hotel again but out of sight of the crowds and potential onlookers. They crossed the dock on a footbridge that ran alongside the road bridge, ending up on an empty strip of concrete that continued along the elevated road to his right but finished at a dead end of steel fences and vegetation. A foot tunnel led east under the road.

Victor glanced back to see a figure running along the far side of the dock, heading to the footbridge. Muzzle flashes glared bright in the darkness but the range was too great for accurate shots.

"Through the tunnel," he said to Gisele. "Hurry."

• • •

The pursuing mercenary made it up to the bridge in time to see the killer disappear. He immediately thumbed his mike. He reported as he ran.

"Targets are on the south side of the dock, entering a tunnel under the bridge. They're going to come out on the east side of the road. Repeat: the east side."

Anderton's voice replied: "Copy that. Stay in pursuit. We'll head them off."

The mercenary kept running. He was fast and fit and had crossed the footbridge in less than fifteen seconds. He cut across the strip of concrete and into the tunnel, gun up and ready for an ambush.

Predictably, the tunnel stank of piss. When he saw it was empty of people he sprinted along it, slowing before he reached the far end, wary of a potential ambush, then moved out fast, gun leading. Directly in front of him was the tall chain-link fence marking the boundary of London City Airport. A footpath beside it extended to the north and south. He swept left as he emerged from the tunnel— no one—then right, seeing the girl running, twenty or so meters ahead.

He aimed, but didn't fire as he saw movement in the corner of his right eye, not from the empty tunnel but from above.

• • •

Victor leaped down from the elevated road, crashing into the mercenary, taking him to the ground under his body weight, feeling him slacken from the impact. He ripped the gun from the man's hand, reversed his grip, and ham-

mered the pistol's muzzle down into his eye until it became wedged in the socket and the struggling ceased.

He tore free the dead man's radio, switched it off, and
shouted, "Come on."

Victor and Gisele dashed back through the tunnel,
then headed north, onto the footbridge.

"Down," Victor said, because he heard the roar of a
powerful V8 engine on the nearby bridge.

They went into low crouches and he saw a Range
Rover pass, heading south in the opposite direction. A
few seconds later a second Range Rover did the same. It
wouldn't take them long to work out that Victor and
Gisele had doubled back.

"Run," Victor said.

They sprinted across the bridge and headed north
onto a narrow road that fed the hotel's parking lot. He
left Gisele on the pavement and dashed into the road,
straight into the coming traffic, arms waving, dodging a
minivan that wasn't going to slow down in time, then
moving in front of a small Peugeot that did, tires squealing on the damp asphalt.

The driver shouted, "What the fuck are you doing?"
as Victor circled the hood.

The door opened before Victor could reach for the
handle. The driver—a big Polish man—was climbing out
to confront him, eyes wide with rage.

Victor dropped him to his knees with an uppercut to
the solar plexus. He left the man wheezing and gasping
and grabbed hold of Gisele's wrist to drag her around
to the passenger's door. He opened it and bundled her
into the seat, slammed the door, and rushed back around
to the driver's side, shoving the kneeling Pole to one side.

The door fell shut as Victor accelerated away. He put his left palm on the top of Gisele's head and forced her down in the seat because she was too upright.

"Stay down," he said. "Keep your head lower than the windows."

She didn't respond but she didn't fight or argue. Either she was happy to do as he told her or she was too scared to resist. It didn't matter as long as she was breathing.

In the rearview, the Polish man was climbing to his feet and staggering along the road after them. Victor respected his single-mindedness, but he wasn't about to return the vehicle. He hoped it would still be in one piece by the time the police released it back to the man, but the odds were against it. He cut through the parking lot and then joined the road that ran between the hotels, heading west.

• • •

Wade kept his eyes on the road and the traffic, slowing as they came to a traffic island. Anderton and Sinclair were looking to their left—east—expecting to see the girl and the assassin running alongside the road, having come out of the foot tunnel as reported by Cole, and then heading south because there was no escape north or east.

"Where are they?" Sinclair spat.

Anderton said, "Take the first exit left. That's the only way they could have gone."

"No," Sinclair said, shaking his head. "We should have seen them."

She radioed Cole, who had been pursuing on foot: "We can't see them. Report."

No reply.

"Cole, answer me. We—"

"He's dead," Sinclair said. "They doubled back. They're on the opposite side of the dock by now."

"How do you know that?"

"Because that's what I'd have done," Sinclair answered.

Anderton sighed. "Then we've lost them."

• • •

Victor pushed the Peugeot as hard as it could take. The engine was weak and the handling nonexistent but the car was small and the tires had decent grip. He weaved it through the traffic, ignoring the blaring of horns and minor collisions he left behind. He knew he was risking attracting the attention of the police—whether via an unmarked vehicle or from a call made by a civilian—but better to be chased by cops than killers. Whoever these guys were, he couldn't see them shooting through the police to get to him and Gisele. If they had any sense they would back down the moment the police became involved. He wasn't going to rely on that, however.

Gisele kept low in the seat as he instructed, swaying and sliding as he swerved and braked and accelerated again. When he saw no pursuers he slowed down and took the next turn so he could join the traffic like a regular driver and disappear into the crawl of inner-city vehicles.

Victor glanced at Gisele. "Are you okay? Are you injured?"

"What?" she whispered, eyes open and blankly staring at a point beyond the dashboard.

She was having a panic attack. Her automated nervous system was crashing. Her lizard brain was caught between fight and flight. The result was paralysis.

"Just breathe," he said, "but slowly. Draw in one

lungful of air and hold it in the bottom of your chest for as long as you can. Then let it out nice and slow."

She did. He could feel the fear radiating from her like a tangible energy. He wasn't sure what to say. Nothing was going to make it vanish. Fear was nature's purest form of advice. It couldn't be mastered. To control it took years. He had no advice that could free her from it now.

He put a hand on her arm. The skin trembled beneath his touch. "It's going to be okay," he said, because it wasn't okay and it was the truth that scared her, not lies.

She nodded. Maybe she believed him. Maybe she didn't. She still shook. She had to work through the fear in her own time.

He said, "Are you hurt?"

In his peripheral vision he saw her shake her head, so he concentrated on the road in front of them and his mirrors. There were no men with guns or black Range Rovers. "I think I'm going to be sick," she said.

"I can't stop yet. You'll have to do it into the foot well."

Gisele shuffled in the seat, leaning forward, knees parted. She stayed like that for a couple of minutes but didn't vomit. She asked, "What do we do now?"

"For now we keep moving," Victor said. "After that, I have no idea."

"You won't think less of me if I start crying, will you?"

"Of course not."

"Okay, good," she said, voice breaking. "Because I can't hold it back any longer."

He drove in silence as next to him she cried and cried.

· Chapter 58 ·

Rain lashed the windows and ran down the glass in chaotic rivulets. Gisele stared at the flowing serpent of headlights beyond, twin red eyes glowing in the darkness. They stared back, malevolent but harmless, threatening violence but delivering none. For now. She inched closer to the man next to her, hoping that while she remained there, no one would hurt her. If she'd felt he would respond she would have leaned against him, encouraging a comforting arm to be wrapped around her. But she stayed rigid in her seat. However much she wanted that embrace, she would not ask for it and show more weakness than she had already.

She hated him for his callousness and criminality. She hated herself more because she needed him. He had proved his loyalty and she could cry because of it, even if it was only because he had liked her mother. Whatever their relationship had been or had not been, it gave him an immovable conviction the likes of which she would not have believed possible. How could someone risk his life for someone he did not know on behalf of someone he had once known? It was a mystery to her, but she was okay with that. Whoever this man was, he did not think or operate like other people. It would be easier to fathom the motivation of an alien.

She knew almost nothing about him, and though that had irritated her earlier, now it reassured her because all she understood was that he was someone of strength and resolve who could deliver extreme violence to protect her from it. He was a specter more than a person—made of violent energy more than flesh. Flesh could be destroyed. Energy could not.

But she wasn't like that. She was weak. She was scared.

Gisele stared out at the snaking red eyes blurring through her tears.

• • •

If Gisele moved her right hand he took the next right turn. If she moved her left, he headed in that direction. When her hands stayed still in her lap he maintained the same heading. After fifteen minutes they were far away from the hotel, having taken a random route to an unpredictable location.

Victor said, "You can sit up now."

She took a long time to do so, the adrenaline hangover robbing her of strength. "Are we safe?"

"No," Victor answered, even though he wanted to say yes. "We're anything but safe."

She nodded, bottom lip over the top. He saw that she had wanted a different response. Any different response. Offering comfort and reassurance was not his strong point. It occurred to him that he should have entered this as a character; someone more personable and relatable. But he was sharper as himself. Acting a role took effort.

Keeping Gisele alive required all of his concentration, but he saw now that it would be easier to have her do exactly as she was told if she liked him. If she thought of him as a friend then she would trust what he said without question. That lack of hesitation might be the difference between life and death. But it was too late now to initiate a charm offensive. She'd seen him kill people. She wouldn't be able to look past that. No one could. That was why he'd made sure her mother had never known what he did for Norimov. Now he felt that in deluding Eleanor he had betrayed her.

He noticed that the fuel tank was getting low. He wasn't planning on keeping the car much longer but he couldn't be sure a pair of Range Rovers were not going to appear behind him at any moment. If they did, the Peugeot would need fuel. He pulled into the first twenty-four-hour gas station he saw.

"I'll be as fast as I can."

She was quiet as he climbed out of the vehicle. He didn't know what she was thinking. He could see the fear and uncertainty in her expression but otherwise it was blank.

He half filled the tank and paid in cash, keeping his head angled away from the forecourt's security cameras and face tilted away from the one behind the cashier. He was more obvious than he would usually be because the cameras were well positioned and top-of-the-line and he was being actively hunted. He saw the young guy behind the desk notice his behavior but the kid was confused. He hadn't worked out what Victor was doing. Better to be noted by someone who would forget him within ten minutes than have his face recorded in crystal-clear high-resolution video.

He bought some bags of potato chips and chocolate bars and an armful of bottled water. He noticed the guy behind the counter smiling to himself, thinking Victor was stoned on account of the junk food and avoiding eye contact in an attempt to hide his vacant gaze. Victor did nothing to convince him otherwise.

Before leaving the gas station he scanned the forecourt through the glass. No Range Rovers in sight. No gunmen.

He handed her the plastic bag of supplies as he slid into the driver's seat.

She peered into the bag. "I don't like junk food."

"Eat. It's all full of carbohydrates."

"Carbs are the devil."

"We need them. You especially. Eat up."

She sighed and he heard her rummage in the bag.

"Don't say anything," he said as her mouth opened. "Just eat."

She found a chocolate bar she liked the look of and bit off a small chunk. She chewed slowly. "What are we going to do?"

"Find somewhere to lie low."

"Then what?"

He didn't answer.

"Why don't we simply keep driving?" she asked. "Let's get out of the city. Never come back."

"Where would we go? We don't have a car. Public transport is risky. People are looking for us."

She held up her hands. "We're *in* a car."

"It's stolen. We'll have to ditch it soon."

"Why can't you steal another one? Or we can take a train or go to the airport. Anything."

"Not yet," Victor said. "They'll expect us to run.

They could be watching train stations and airports and following reports of stolen cars. If we're spotted, it's over. First we lie low and consider our next move. We can't risk snap decisions. In the morning, maybe we will leave the country. But it's a choice we'll make when I've had time to think. Do you have your passport on you?"

She shook her head. "It's at the office. In my desk. I went to a conference in Brussels. I . . . I knew I shouldn't have left it there."

"That's a problem, then. They'll know about your workplace."

"Then what are we going to do?"

"I'll come up with something. But for now I need you to think."

She stopped chewing and looked at him, reading his tone. "Me? About?"

"At the hotel, the man who knocked on the door wasn't trying to kidnap you. Neither were the men in the parking lot."

"I . . . I don't understand."

"I'd been led to believe they wanted to abduct you, but that's not what I witnessed. They were trying to kill you. That was an assassination attempt."

Her mouth hung open and her brow was furrowed. Shock. Disbelief. "Why would they want to kill me? You said they wanted to take me to put pressure on Alek. That's why you're protecting me. That's what you told me."

"I was wrong. This isn't about your stepfather. This is about you."

"That doesn't make any sense. *How* can it be about me?"

"I don't know, but with a little time you might figure out why this is happening to you."

"So you're saying it's my fault?"

"That's not what I said."

She pushed her fingers through her hair. "Then please explain what the fuck you're saying."

"That there is a woman who wants to kill you," Victor said. "The people who attacked us in the warehouse and at the hotel are working for a woman with blond hair and green eyes. She's British. Do you know anyone like that?"

"I don't know. How would I, based on that description? I could have met dozens of women like that, couldn't I?"

"Has anyone threatened you?"

She shook her head. "No."

"Any criminals you might have crossed as part of your work? A case you've been working on?"

Her head was still shaking. "I haven't worked a single case yet. Don't you get it? I'm not a qualified barrister. It's not that long ago that I got my degree. I don't handle even the most minor of cases, let alone one that might warrant all this. God, there's nothing I know or have done that could give all these people a reason to try to kill me. If I had, then my whole firm would be under threat too. They wouldn't single me out. I'm not important."

"You are to her. To her you're so dangerous she will risk everything to kill you."

The shaking stopped. The eyes were wide. "But I'm nobody."

• • •

Victor left her in the car while she ate and walked to the edge of the garage forecourt. He reached into his inside jacket pocket and withdrew the small two-way radio transceiver he'd taken from the dead mercenary. It was a Motorola, an expensive model, with a range of up to ten kilometers. It would be less in a dense urban environment. He couldn't be sure it would be in range. Only one way to find out.

He powered it on and thumbed the SEND button.

"Do you know who this is?"

He waited. For a moment, all he could hear was the sound of tires splashing through puddles. Then a woman's voice came through the speaker.

"I do know who this is," she said. "You're Norimov's man. The assassin."

Her voice was distorted and crackling because the signal was weak.

She added: "It's nice to speak to you at last."

"*Nice* is perhaps not the word I'd elect to use," Victor said.

"Even putting luck to one side, I have to admit you're proving quite the troublemaker."

"It wasn't luck that killed four of your guys tonight."

A pause before she replied, "Is that why you're speaking to me now, to gloat? That would be a mistake."

"I don't make mistakes."

"Is that so?" the woman said back. "Except for the fact you're now involved in something that doesn't—*shouldn't*—concern you. That is a monumental mistake on your part."

The voice was becoming more distorted. They were traveling farther away from him and Gisele.

He said, "Would you like to have a wager on that?"

She chuckled. "Sure, why not? I'll humor you. What exactly are we betting with?"

"Your life," Victor said, and smashed the radio beneath his heel.

· Chapter 59 ·

Victor pulled over on a high street in the north of the city where bright signs advertised a multitude of fast-food outlets. There were other shops in between, but all closed at this hour. The street was empty of people.

"Wait here."

Gisele nodded.

He'd left the engine running because hot-wiring was temperamental and he didn't want to risk it not working again, especially if they had to move out in a hurry. He scanned for threats as he walked until he found a rental agent. He examined the properties listed in the window display. He checked the photographs and read through the details. He memorized the two that best matched his criteria: houses, unfurnished, quiet neighborhood, available immediately.

Gisele was sitting very still when he climbed back into the car. He didn't ask if she was okay because no civilian would be in the circumstances.

The display hadn't listed the precise addresses of the properties, but they didn't take long to find with the details provided. Both had signs out front, but the first house—despite its immediate availability—was occupied. The second was empty.

It was an end-of-row terrace, slim-fronted but long. The front garden was overgrown with weeds. The window frames were cracked and warped. The front door was sun bleached. Victor parked the Peugeot half a mile away and led Gisele on foot. Having the car closer would be useful if they had to make a fast getaway, but it was stolen and therefore had more chance of leading enemies to them than saving them if they were otherwise found.

Victor walked ahead to scout for threats. Gisele followed a little behind, as he'd told her to. She needed to stay close to him so he could protect her, but with enough distance to give him time to clear an area before she entered it. He led her down the alleyway that ran behind the row of terraces and separated its back garden from those of the houses behind. Fences rose tall on either side of their shoulders. When he came to the right spot he stood with his back to the fence and linked his fingers in front of him.

"Here," he said. "Climb over."

She stared up at the high fence. "You've got to be kidding."

"Put your foot on my hands and use it as a step. I'll lift you."

"And I'll break my neck falling down the other side."

"No, you won't. The garden will be higher than we are now. The drop will be a short one."

"Says you."

"Come on," he said. "We have to be fast."

She made a big deal of sighing, placed her hands on his shoulders, then raised her right foot and set it down on his upturned palms.

"After three?" she asked, sarcastic.

"Three," he said, and lifted.

She grunted and pushed herself up, grabbing the top of the fence and then hooking an elbow. He hoisted her higher and she struggled up and over. He heard her drop down onto the other side.

"Are you okay?" he asked.

There was no answer.

"Gisele, are you okay?"

"I'm fine."

There was anger directed at him in her tone. It was not an unexpected response to the trauma she had been through in the past few hours. From an operational perspective he would have preferred her to remain quiet and passive, but for her sake it was better to be angry than scared.

He turned, leaped vertically, took hold of the cold wood, and heaved himself up. He dropped down next to her.

"What now?" she asked.

There was no alarm. The house was unfurnished. The landlord had no need of one because it didn't affect him if the tenants were burgled. Victor picked the lock of the back door and ushered Gisele inside. He checked every room, every door, every window. He made sure all the exterior doors and windows were closed and locked and the interior doors were all open so sound would travel through the house easier.

She said, "You've made a draft."

He didn't respond.

"There's no furniture."

"We don't need any."

"Whose place is this?"

"No one's. It doesn't matter. We'll stay for a few hours until it's light and move on. Get some sleep."

He turned around and went to perform checks of the house. He again checked every room and window. Nothing had changed in the past ten minutes and nothing was likely to, but he needed the alone time. The house had been neglected in the way rented properties often were. The tenants were not going to put any time or expense into maintenance when they didn't own it. The landlord didn't live there, so he cared only about the bottom line.

Victor saw its potential. Given two weeks he could reverse the neglect. Given a month he could transform it. But he could never live in the house. It didn't meet his specifications on defense. There were too many neighbors. He would end up getting to know them and they would know more of him in return than he wanted anyone to know. Alternatively, he would have to make a determined effort to keep out of their way and they would talk about him and begin to wonder why he was so antisocial. He ripped off a peeling segment of wallpaper to stop the tear from getting any larger.

• • •

He was standing in an empty bedroom, staring out through the sliver of space between curtain and wall. Foxes were scavenging in the night. He couldn't see them. But he heard their keening on occasion. Red flashed in his mind.

He heard a scrape.

Any hint of fatigue evaporated, replaced by focus. He stood silent and listened. It had originated outside the house. Faint and quiet among the other sounds, but close. A shoe on asphalt, maybe. It was hard to be sure. He peered into the night. He saw nothing. He heard a car passing on the street outside the house's front. He heard an airliner flying overhead. He heard the wind shaking fences and branches and rushing over every surface. Ten minutes passed without another notable sound reaching his ears. He remained poised, listening and watching. If it had been the sound of a killer moving into position, Victor would be ready. If it was nothing, it didn't matter whether he was ready or not.

But it mattered to him. He had to be ready every time, just in case. He had to hear every sound. Not only his own life depended on it, but Gisele's too. He didn't want her to die. He didn't want to let her mother down.

After twelve minutes he decided the noise had been nothing. He would have liked the neighboring house to have a dog that barked whenever anyone came near its territory. But no barking had ensued when Victor and Gisele had climbed over the back fence. Any canines nearby stayed indoors with their owners and any territorialism would wait until the morning. In another life he pictured himself with a dog. He liked dogs. They seemed to like him too. They always wanted to play-fight with him. But owning a dog meant having a home, and he couldn't foresee himself ever having one again. He had to keep moving, whether he was working or not. Trouble would inevitably find him if he stayed in one place too long. A moving target was always harder to hit than a stationary one, as he had told Gisele.

He'd been standing there for two hours when he heard Gisele climbing the stairs. Each step creaked. It would drive most occupiers crazy, but Victor liked it. A silent staircase was a killer's best friend. He willed Gisele to turn around and go back down. He wanted her to rest. He wanted to be left alone. He kept his thoughts to himself.

"I fell asleep," she said from behind him. He knew she

was standing in the doorway because her steps did not disturb the room's floorboards.

"That's good," Victor said. "But you should go back to sleep."

"What are you doing?"

"If they come, they'll come through the backyard. Like we did."

"They won't find us here, will they?"

"Act as though you're always vulnerable and you'll have more chance of surviving when you are."

"If you say so." She hugged her arms. "It's cold."

She was right. It was cold. The outside temperature was below ten degrees Celsius with the wind chill. Inside it wasn't much warmer. The winter air found its way under doors and through cracks. He hadn't noticed until now because the cold wasn't going to kill him in the time he would be here. Comfort meant little to him when survival was at stake. But he understood she was nothing like him. She was a civilian. And young. What hardship meant to him and her could not be more different.

"I know," he said. "There's electricity but the gas must have been disconnected. You can have my jacket if you like."

"No," she said, sharpness in her voice despite the tiredness. "I mean, no, thank you. It's okay. I'll survive. There's no food in the fridge or the cupboards. I woke up starving."

He knew he should have picked up some proper food for her before they arrived. He hadn't thought to at the time because food wasn't a priority. A few high-calorie snacks had been more than enough for him. The body could function at near maximum capacity for days without food, eating itself to stay fueled. But it couldn't survive long pierced by bullets.

"We'll get you something when we move out."

"I'm not sure I can wait that long without eating."

"You can. You just haven't had to before."

"Right." She sighed. "I know I could stand to lose a kilo or two. Might as well start now. It's not as if I have anything better to do."

"You don't need to lose any weight."

She shot him a look, as if he were about to follow the comment with some sarcasm. When he didn't, she smiled. "Thanks."

"There's nothing to thank me for. It's a statement of fact."

"Then thank you for stating the fact." A pause, then: "Is there anything I can do to help? I found a stack of party cups left in the kitchen cabinet. I could get you some water if you're thirsty."

He was. But he wanted her to rest more. "I'm okay. Get some more sleep if you can. We need to move on soon."

· Chapter 60 ·

Daylight came. Slowly, because Victor watched every second of it. The rear bedroom window faced east and he saw the steady lightening of the sky above the distant rooftops, haloed in blue, then yellow and white. Birdsong accompanied the change of colors, then the rumble of engines starting up and working hard, left idling while heaters fought back the cold and frost. When he could see the outline of every paving slab in the backyard, he stepped away from the window. No one would attack now. Their enemies would wait for darkness or the perfect opportunity. This was neither.

They had survived the night. He lay on the floor. There was no carpet, only bare floorboards, but he was asleep in seconds.

When he woke he sat immediately upright, ears collecting sound, subconscious failing to pick out the noise of attack but detecting nothing that concerned him. He descended the stairs. He'd been asleep for just over an hour—the first rest he'd had in two days. The guilt he felt at leaving her undefended twisted his stomach.

She was asleep, curled up into a ball in a corner of the empty lounge. She looked peaceful.

He left and cleaned himself in the downstairs bathroom using only water because there were no toiletries of any kind. He stood at the sink, cupping water in his hands under the running tap, then scrubbing it under his armpits, over his chest and shoulders, along his arms and over his stomach and shoulder blades. He finished by doing the same with his face and hair. The water was so cold it made his hands turn red and brought up goose bumps over every inch of skin it touched. His lower body would have to wait for now. There were no towels and not even a roll of tissue, so he let the winter air slowly dry him.

• • •

Gisele awoke, groaning and squinting. Usually, she was up at six a.m. and out the front door just after seven. She was never at the law firm for less than ten hours a day. Often it was twelve. A few times a month it was more like fourteen. Everyone hated lawyers, but in Gisele's opinion they didn't get enough credit for how long and hard they had to work.

Taking the week off after the incident on the street had given Gisele a lot of free time she wasn't used to and the best way to make use of it seemed to be by sleeping. She wasn't sure whether this was working off the sleep debt of many late nights and early mornings or because of the stress of the incident. Now getting up early for work seemed like a luxury she might never experience again. She didn't need to get up but sleeping in had lost its appeal. She was anxious and too awake to be able to snooze.

She padded on the balls of her feet to reduce the exposure to the cold floor and grimaced at the sight that greeted her in the mirror above the fireplace.

Gisele heard the sound of running water and for a horrible moment thought the worst, before realizing it only meant her companion was in the downstairs bathroom. She tensed. She didn't like the idea of the man being awake and nearby while she lay asleep and vulnerable.

• • •

Gisele let out a cry from the other side of the house.

Victor was out of the bathroom, through the hallway and into the front room within four seconds, gun in hand, safety off, slide jacked and ready to fire.

She was grimacing and standing on one leg while rubbing the sole of her left foot. "Splinter," she hissed, not looking up. "People who don't have carpets should be beaten, I swear. I can't get it out. My nails are too short."

He lowered the weapon and eased the safety back on with his thumb.

"Shit," she said, her eyes widening as she glanced up at him. "Did you fall into a wood chipper or something?"

He didn't comment. She was referring to the numerous scars that marked his torso and arms. Some were from minor injuries that he'd had to suture himself and appeared worse than they might otherwise. Others though looked as good as it was possible for a scar to look after being stabbed or shot. Most had occurred when he was much younger, when he knew less about how to avoid being injured and when his body could more easily repair itself. He was more careful these days. He had to be. Scar tissue had only eighty percent of the strength of healthy skin. Some wounds still caused him pain in the quiet moments when his mind had nothing else to focus on.

"I have to say," Gisele continued. "It doesn't make me feel very protected when you're a walking manual of how not to stay safe."

"Very funny."

"Yes, well. I'm finding a little humor helps me forget about being hunted and all the dead people."

He tucked the gun back into his waistband. "Try not to make any noise unless it's unavoidable."

"I impaled my foot on a monster splinter. What else was I supposed to do? Pain is what I'd call a cause of *unavoidable* noise." She tried to pry the splinter from her foot, hissing in pain and failing to get hold of it between her nails.

"I'll be back in a minute to pull that splinter free. I know a good trick for getting them out."

"It's okay," she said, grimacing. "I've got it. I can do some things by myself."

• • •

When he returned he was fully dressed. He carried two disposable cups of water. He handed her one. She sat cross-legged on the floor in the lounge, back to the wall and the coat draped across her knees.

"Drink this. You have to stay hydrated."

She took the cup and sipped from it. He stood nearby, drinking from his own, reacting to every sound of cars or people passing in the street outside.

"I've been thinking . . ." Gisele said.

"Go on."

"Whoever this woman is, I've never met her. So I can't have done anything to her to warrant all this."

"Directly, at least."

She nodded to accept the point. "Therefore it has to

be something I know or can do. Information I have that's a threat, perhaps."

"Could be. But what?"

"That I don't know. If it's information that I have, I don't know what it is. I don't know what I know."

"We need to figure it out, though."

"Now, that I *do* know." She sipped her water. "It can't be anything to do with Alek's business because I've never had anything to do with it. I've been in the UK for years. They must know that. So it has to be because of my job. I don't have enough of a life outside of work to have done anything to make me a target."

"You said you're not even qualified."

"I'm not. That's why this doesn't make sense. I haven't even taken my first case yet. I can't have crossed the wrong people, because I haven't dealt with any."

"They must know that too."

"Then this is all a big mistake. This woman thinks I have some knowledge I don't and wants to kill me for it. That can't be right, can it?"

She looked at him for an answer—an explanation—and with it a way out of a situation that would have seemed ludicrous a day ago. People wanting Victor dead was a common enough occurrence that the why wasn't always essential. But to the twenty-two-year-old woman before him, the why was everything. She needed to comprehend this for her sanity.

He said, "Maybe you read a document you weren't meant to or saw something you shouldn't have."

"But what? When?"

He shook his head. "We need to work it out," he said again.

"Then it must be a detail that out of context is completely insignificant to me."

"But everything to her."

Her shoulders sagged and she looked down at her hands. "I just don't know what it could be."

He studied her and realized that the lack of understanding created hopelessness and that what she required at this moment was simple assurance. "You'll work it out," he said. "I believe in you."

She looked up and her eyes met with his. She gave a half smile and he knew he had held off her despair, if only for a short time.

He said, "I'm going to fetch some supplies. I won't be long."

Her face dropped. "On your own? I don't want to be by myself."

"I won't be long," he said for a second time.

"Can't I come with you?"

He shook his head. "On my own I can avoid them."

She frowned. "And I'll give us away—is that what you're saying?"

She'd replaced the fear with anger. That was good. It was a coping mechanism.

"Yes," he said. "I can't trust you to stay hidden so you'll have to stay here."

"Thanks for that. You're such a bastard sometimes."

He turned from her, content that she would spend the time while he was away cursing him instead of crying and jumping at every noise outside.

Chapter 61

He found shops nearby that were open. There was a row of cafés next to a corner pub and a small convenience store. He bought a sandwich and croissant in the first café and a filled bagel and piece of carrot cake in another. In the convenience store he purchased some drinks and toiletries, including hair dye and scissors. After a short walk he found a phone shop and bought two prepaid mobile phones. He was back at the house within eighteen minutes. She was sleeping in the lounge, huddled in a corner with her coat over her like a blanket. He watched her for a minute to determine if she was really asleep or just pretending to be. When he decided she was sleeping he placed all of the food down nearby because he didn't know what she would prefer, and took a bottle of water upstairs.

He gave her half an hour to sleep and returned to the room. She was awake.

He handed her a pair of scissors and a box of hair dye. She studied them in her hands, as if she had never seen such things before.

"I thought you were joking before. I didn't realize you were being serious. You honestly want me to cut my hair?"

"And color it too. It's too attention-grabbing as it is."

"Is that a compliment?"

"If you like."

She took the box from him and eyed the smiling brunette on the cover. "Can't I go blond instead? It'll suit my skin tone better."

"The store didn't have a lot of choice, I'm afraid. The main thing is for you to blend in as much as possible. We don't want you attracting attention."

"Half the women in this town dye their hair blond."

"Please just do it."

Gisele sighed and looked at the scissors again. "Do you know how to cut hair?"

He shook his head.

She fed her fingers into the scissors and snipped the air a few times. "Okay. Fine. I'll dye and I'll cut it so it's just below my ears."

"Thank you."

"You don't have to thank me," she said, sighing. "I should be thanking you, shouldn't I? You want me to cut my hair in an effort to help me. I wouldn't have even thought about doing it."

He considered this, and nodded.

• • •

When she had finished he stood examining the results for a long time. Gisele didn't like such scrutiny from anyone, least of all him. The dye had colored her hair to a mid-brown and she had managed to cut a few inches from the length so the ends brushed against her jaw.

"Looks good," he said.

"Thanks." She wasn't sure she believed him. "I was right, though; it doesn't suit my skin tone."

"That helps us. The less you look like you, the better."

"I'll have to take your word for that." She paused, then added, "What about clothes? We should get some different ones, don't you think? Maybe some new glasses too."

"That's smart. That's a good idea."

She smiled for a second, buoyed by the praise. She studied him. "You were already planning that, weren't you?"

"Yes."

She hesitated, then said, "You're not a bodyguard, are you?"

"I said at the start I'm not."

"You're not a gangster either."

"I never claimed to be."

"So," she said, "what are you?"

"If I told you, you wouldn't believe me."

"Why don't you try me?"

His black eyes locked onto hers, studying her gaze, reading her thoughts. He gave a little nod of understanding and said, "Why are you asking when you already know?"

"I should have known I wouldn't be able to hide it from you."

"You should have," he said, eyes unblinking. "That kind of knowledge is very dangerous."

"Not to me," Gisele was quick to reply. "Not when you swore to protect me."

"From the people hunting you. I never said anything about myself."

"You can't fool me any more than I can fool you. If I had a gun to your head and my finger on the trigger you still wouldn't harm me. I don't understand why that is. It makes no sense at all to me. You say it's because you knew my mother, but that's not enough. It doesn't matter if it makes sense to me, though, does it? All that matters is it makes sense to you."

He stood still for a moment and doubt crept up Gisele's spine as she feared she had misjudged how deep his loyalty ran. But he blinked and turned away.

"How did you know?" he asked.

"When I was younger I overheard Alek on the phone, threatening someone with a *ubiytsa* who would do anything for him. I didn't know what it meant at the time as my Russian wasn't that good then. I haven't thought about it since. I've remembered it only now. It means 'assassin,' doesn't it?"

He didn't try to pretend otherwise. "What he said was untrue. I wouldn't do anything for him."

"I know. I can tell. But he wanted whoever was on the phone to think that."

He turned back. "Don't be under any false impressions about who I am, Gisele. I said before that I deserve your sympathy even less than your father's men. I meant it."

She didn't respond for a moment. When she spoke, there was a bitterness in her voice. "Don't worry, I know exactly what kind of a man you are. You're helping me now, but you could just as easily be one of the men hunting me, couldn't you?"

He didn't answer.

"Only you're not. You're protecting me, and for that reason I can fool myself enough to believe that you're not entirely awful, even if you don't believe it yourself."

He didn't respond to that either.

"Have you been through this before?"

"Through what?"

"Protecting someone. You seem to know a lot about it."

"I told you that I know about personal security. It comes with the job."

"That's not answering my question."

He looked at her with his standard stone-faced expression, but she thought she detected something in his eyes—like he was fighting to maintain the facade.

Gisele said, "She . . . she didn't make it, did she?"

He swallowed and exhaled and she saw that for the briefest moment he considered lying. But he told her the truth. "No, she didn't."

"What happened?"

"It's complicated. We were helping each other. We were under threat. People wanted us both dead. It was my fault. I left her alone when it wasn't safe. I shouldn't have." He paused and rested a hand on her shoulder. "But I'm not going to let the same happen to you, Gisele. I promise."

She looked away and nodded. "I believe you."

· Chapter 62 ·

The head of the department worked from a corner office of HQ's fifth floor. It was a spacious, modern room that he had personally decorated with cricket and golf memorabilia. He'd been a rower in his university days, but that was more than forty years ago and the sagging shoulders and protruding belly told of an indulgent, sedentary lifestyle. Anderton had met him perhaps thirty times and he seemed like an affable chap. He never tried to flirt with her and she knew better than to initiate such activities, even if she needed to. Which she didn't. She had the sharpest mind in the building. It was the reason everyone hated her, though they did everything in their power to hide that fact.

"What can I do you for, Nieve?" the director asked.

"I have a problem only you are in a position to help me with."

He looked at her over the rim of his reading glasses. "That sounds decidedly troublesome."

"Quite. I'm sure you're busy with all the drama here in the city last night."

"I am," he agreed, looking at her closely. "Downing Street is kicking my arse over this. Gunfights in the middle of London. Incredible."

"Yes, sir."

"You're not working on it?" the director asked, a certain tone to his voice. "It's not a narcotics situation?"

"It's not narcotics, but I do have some insight into the matter. Thought you might be interested in a few details about the chap running around shooting up half the city."

"Go on," he said. The director smiled at her, as though she were a child withholding a truth already known. "Don't keep me waiting; there's a good girl."

"He's a professional killer. A freelancer, as far as I'm aware. To begin with he worked primarily in Russia and Eastern Europe. His handler was a former FSB officer who's since switched to organized crime. The CIA believes this assassin killed some of their people in the aftermath of a hit gone wrong in Paris two years ago. The SVR wants him for kills in Russia and East Africa. And that's without all the rumor swimming around the water cooler about incidents in Minsk and Rome. Shall I go on?"

The director shook his head. "Then how is it he's still walking around?"

"Because the various parties haven't worked out that he's the same man."

"But you did?"

"I'm the best at what I do."

"Are you telling me you know why he's in London?"

Anderton nodded. "That would be my fault."

"Excuse me?"

"The shooters who've been engaging with him are a private security team consisting primarily of former members of our armed forces. They're following my orders."

The director sat as far back as the chair would let him. He stared.

Anderton continued. "They're hunting the stepdaughter of this assassin's former handler: Aleksandr Norimov. I don't want to bore you with the specifics but she's in a position to make my life very difficult. Alas, she's being protected by this assassin. He's making things . . . *awkward*."

"You can't be serious. Is this some kind of sick joke?"

"I assure you, it's no joke. I have a list of things you can help me with. Some are perfectly legal. Others are a little grayer, to put it politely. But the sooner we put our heads together to get this sorted, the sooner you can pop back to Downing Street to get some well-deserved pats on the back. And then, naturally, I'm going to require that you forget all about this conversation. Clear enough so far?"

"I suggest you listen to me very carefully, Ms. Anderton. You need to turn around and walk out of this office and start penning a suitably humble resignation letter. Obviously I don't yet understand all the details—and, by God, I don't want to—but I can confidently say there is nothing I can do to help you. You are, as they say, fucked."

She smiled at him. "I'm going to tell you a story, Jim. You don't mind if I call you Jim, do you, Jim?"

The director's eyes narrowed. He pushed an intercom button with a little finger. "Have security come to my office immediately."

"Back in 1948, a seven-pound baby boy was born in a sleepy village in rural Shropshire. He was—"

"I have no idea what you think you're doing, Ms. Anderton, but I suggest you keep your trap firmly shut and don't give security any trouble when they get here."

"The boy was a bright student from average means

but he went on to win a scholarship at Trinity College. Not only was he intelligent and a hard worker, but he was also gay. He kept it a secret as far as he could, but entered into a relationship with a fellow student. Things turned sour when this student decided he didn't want to be gay and ended the relationship. There was an argument. The boy was later found dead."

The director's face had gone white.

Anderton perched on the director's side of the desk and looked down at him. "The coroner ruled it a suicide but there was some doubt, wasn't there?"

"How do—?"

"Because I do my homework. I know all your dirty little secrets, just like I know the secrets of every man and woman in this place. Don't look so surprised. We're in the secrets business."

"What do you want?"

"I've told you. I want your assistance—phone-trace authorizations, restricted database access, that sort of thing. And, more important, I need a backdated authorization letter to absolve me of my actions up until now and for what will follow."

"What does that mean, *what will follow*?"

"It means things are going to get very dirty, Jim. But I want to come out of this clean. And now you want me to come out clean, don't you?" She smiled reassuringly.

"You know that is beyond even my power. Whatever happens next, what's already happened has to be explained. We can't just pretend it never happened."

She brushed some lint from the shoulder pad of his suit jacket. "You can have everyone else involved, how does that sound? The mercenaries work for Marcus Lambert's private security firm. He's a big old fish to catch, isn't he?

Been involved in all sorts of questionable activities over the past few years, hasn't he? When this is over I can give you the name of every shooter involved and evidence that Marcus had them brought to London. It'll all be wrapped up nice and fast and tidy. And the right people will hang for it. Well, except me."

"You're a monster."

"Oh, Jim." Anderton held his face in her palms. "I do find it amusing you say that as if it's a bad thing, when we both know that's precisely why you hired me in the first place."

· Chapter 63 ·

The winter sun was bright in a cloudless sky. Victor drove like the other city drivers—slow, within the speed limit, acting like everyone else and not someone hunted by enemies and on the run from the authorities. The car was stolen, but only recently. No one would be looking for it yet and it would be abandoned long before it became a risk.

He parked the car and left the engine running to encourage someone to steal it. He led Gisele on foot down a busy street. Iron posts lined the pavement, designed to look like the deactivated cannons from the Crimean War that had once been used in their place. Permanent reminders of an imperial past, ignored by those who walked by them.

Around him, people who had never jogged a day in their lives wore sportswear and trainers. Market traders shouted to advertise their wares and counted out change, fingertips red in the cold air while the rest of their hands stayed warm under the protection of fingerless gloves. He stopped at a street stall selling souvenir clothing. There were lots of football shirts and T-shirts printed with I ♥

LONDON and faces of Royal Family members. He picked out a hooded sweatshirt that read OXFORD on the front and a cap with an image of the city skyline. He paid the vendor.

"Very you," Gisele said.

He took her out of the flow of pedestrians and pushed the sweatshirt into her hands. "Put this on."

"You're joking, surely? It's about four sizes too big."

"It's only one size too big. It'll change your body shape."

"Why would I want to do that?"

"So the people looking to kill you will have a harder time picking you out of a crowd. Hurry up."

She did as instructed, pulling a face the whole time. He adjusted the strap at the back of the cap and fitted it to her head.

Gisele said, "I look ridiculous, don't I?"

"You look like a tourist."

"Like I said, ridiculous."

"We need to be as forgettable as possible. We have to be anonymous. If you look and act like everyone else, it will make it more difficult for them to spot us."

"What about you? You look the same as you did yesterday."

"I know how to make sure people don't see me."

"Yeah . . ." she said. "Must be useful in your line of work. Maybe after this is over I'll switch careers. Mine is dangerous enough as it is."

He didn't respond to that.

She stopped, thinking. "We agree that whoever this woman is, she's after me because of my job."

"It appears that way. We can't know for sure yet."

"Okay, Mr. Pedantic. We think that's it. But as I said before, I'm not a barrister. Any work I do is for the qualified barristers. Maybe this woman is really after someone else. Maybe it really is a mistake, her wanting me dead."

Victor thought back to his visit to Gisele's firm. He cycled through his conversation with the receptionist. *It's probably the office bug.* An innocuous statement at the time, but no longer.

He said, "While you were still going into work, was anyone off sick? Did anyone not show up that day or during the days beforehand?"

"I . . . I don't know."

"Please think, Gisele. Take your time. Were any of the other lawyers not in the office that day?"

The tip of her tongue was visible between her lips while she tried to remember. Then her eyes widened and she said, "Lester Daniels. He hadn't been in for a couple of days. I've no idea why."

"What kind of law did he practice?"

"That's a good question. He's kind of this old jack-of-all-trades at the firm. Bit of a renegade. I love the guy. Such a character. But what does this have to do with Lester?"

"Did you work with him at all?"

"Of course. All the time. I'm the firm's general drudge. Oh, shit. What are you saying? Is Lester involved in this?"

"Perhaps. Do you know where he lives?"

• • •

The Danielses' home was a three-story town house in the center of a parade of identical flawless residences with brilliant cream facades fronted by black wrought-iron fencing. One million pounds bought a mansion in most parts of the world. In a pleasant area of London, it bought a three-bedroom house with on-street parking.

"How well do you know Lester?" Victor asked as they approached.

"As well as anyone knows their boss, I guess. Perhaps better. There have been a lot of firm social evenings. Drinks in swanky bars when someone wins a case—that sort of thing."

"Do you know what car he drives?"

She thought for a moment. "One of those classic sports cars with a soft top. Racing green, he told me."

Victor didn't inquire further because there was no such car parked on the street. Vehicles lined each curb, nose to tail. There were no empty spaces and only enough road left between either flank for a single car to drive along slowly. Victor liked that. A Range Rover would have difficulty giving chase and there was nowhere for watchers to loiter.

Gisele drew a breath and pushed the doorbell. It rang with a cheery electronic jingle. Victor noted the speed with which it was answered, but not by Lester Daniels. He took the woman before him to be Mrs. Daniels, based on her age, the ring on her finger, and her expression. It was one of anxiousness and pain. He wasn't as surprised as Gisele, who hesitated and stammered when the woman asked, "What do you want?"

The lack of politeness and the tone matched his evaluation of her. She was stressed and worried and had better things to do than answer the doorbell to strangers.

"I . . . uh . . . I'm Gisele Maynard. I . . . I work with Mr. Daniels. I was wondering if I—we—could speak with him."

The woman looked at Gisele with wide, disbelieving eyes that shone with anger. "Is this some kind of fucking joke?"

Gisele was too shocked to respond.

Victor said, "Has something happened to Lester?"

The angry eyes snapped in his direction. "I wouldn't know, would I? He's missing."

"Oh, my God," Gisele breathed, putting a hand to her mouth.

"Who are you people? What do you want?"

Victor said, "May we come in, Mrs. Daniels?"

"It's Rose, and you haven't answered my question. Who are you and why are you here? This really isn't a good time. My husband is missing."

"As I was saying," Gisele began, "I work with Lester. But I've been off . . . sick for the last week. This here"—she put a hand on Victor's arm—"is my brother, Jonathan. I didn't know Lester was missing. I'm so sorry. Is there anything we can do to help?"

The offer seemed to soothe the anger from Rose Daniels's face. But pain replaced it. Her eyes moistened. "Thank you, that's kind of you." She stepped aside and held open her door. "Come inside, please."

"Thank you," Gisele said, and entered through the doorway.

Victor checked the street for any new vehicles or people, but there were none. He followed.

Rose Daniels was a small woman who seemed smaller still in the tall hallway. She led them through to the kitchen, where a mug of tea sat brewing and steaming on a wooden worktop. She took a teaspoon from its resting place near the mug and fished for the tea bag. Her hand was trembling as she carried it to a bin and she dropped it. She started to cry.

"Allow me," Victor said as he used his nails to retrieve the tea bag from the slate floor and took a square of kitchen towel from a roll to wipe up the mess.

Rose nodded her thanks as she dabbed her eyes and gestured for them to sit at a breakfast bar. Gisele complied, but Victor remained standing where he could see the hallway and the kitchen window without having to turn his head.

She began talking without any prompts.

"The police are useless. They say he's not missing. They say he's been using his credit card and his car has been recorded on CCTV. They haven't said as much, but I can tell they think he's run off with another woman. But Lester would never do that. He wouldn't. He really wouldn't."

"I don't believe it either," Gisele said. "Lester's a lovely man."

Rose cried again at that, but controlled herself after a moment.

"When did you last see him?" Victor said, trying to sound like a concerned acquaintance and not an investigator.

"Over a week ago," she said. "He left for work as normal on Wednesday and never came home. He wouldn't simply disappear on me without saying anything. Something's happened. I know it."

Gisele looked at Victor, who made sure not to look back in case Rose saw the exchange.

"I think," Gisele began, "that what happened to—"

Victor interrupted before she could continue: "Are any of his clothes missing?"

Rose looked away. "Yes. I checked, of course, after what the police told me about his card. But I don't believe it. There must be another explanation."

He saw from Gisele's eyes that she understood the

reason for his interruption. She said, "Was he stressed because of work? I know he had a big caseload."

"Lester loved his job. Even when he was overworked. If you're trying to imply he couldn't cope and disappeared, then—"

"No, I'm sorry," Gisele was quick to assure. "That's not what I meant. I don't know what I meant. This is all so shocking."

They sat in silence for a while. Rose sipped tea, then said, "Forgive me. I didn't ask if you wanted any. How rude of me."

She went to stand but Victor held out a hand to motion for her not to. "That's okay. We're going to have to go, I'm afraid. My sister is giving me a lift to the airport."

"Yes, yes. Don't let me hold you up."

Gisele said, "I'm sorry to have disturbed you at this difficult time. Is there anyone I can call for you?"

Rose exhaled sharply. "The damned police. You can tell them to do their job."

They said their good-byes and left Rose to her tears.

· Chapter 64 ·

Outside, as they walked away, Gisele said, "He's dead, isn't he?"

Victor nodded.

"But why? I don't understand. What did he do? Something he was working on? Someone he was representing?"

"That's what we need to find out. Whoever this woman is, she's connected to one of Lester's cases—and that case must have the potential to destroy her. If she thought killing the lawyer working the case would prevent it from going ahead, that suggests no other lawyer could step in. So either Lester is the only barrister on the planet who was able to take the case, or there won't be enough time for another to continue it now that he's out of the way. So, which case did you work on with Lester that has a built-in deadline? Possibly a case that he picked up only recently."

"I don't know." She saw the skepticism in his eyes. "I don't. I said I worked for him sometimes. I didn't say I knew the details of everything he did. I filed, I researched, I photocopied, and made him cups of Earl Grey. It's not as if I even met the clients. He would work on dozens of different cases at any one time. Like I said, he was a maverick. He did things his own way. He didn't even like to share with the other seniors. He would never tell me anything important. To have any idea what this might be about I'd have to go to the firm and check through his case files."

Victor shook his head. "You can't do that. They'll be watching."

"Then we'll never know what this is about. We'll never know why Lester was killed. We'll never know why I'm . . . Hold on." She stopped and turned to face him, forcing him to stop too. "If Lester is the barrister on a case that could, as you say, destroy her, why does she want me dead?"

He said, "Because you worked on the case too, even if you don't know you did. Lester must have told her that. He must have given them your name."

"Why? That makes no sense."

"I'm afraid it does make sense. They must have tortured him or threatened to kill him or his family. Before he was killed, he gave them your name. They asked him who else knew what he did and he said you."

"No. He wouldn't do that. Not Lester. There's no reason to. It was a lie. I don't know anything."

"Everyone talks in that situation. And you do know. There's a piece of information you have that she can't risk getting out. Lester was the original target, but you're a loose end."

"What the hell does that mean? That I have to be killed *just in case*?" She put her face in her hands. "So, all this is a *mistake*? Oh, my God, people are trying to kill me for *no fucking reason*."

"You scared them," Victor explained. "When they tried to kidnap you and you escaped, they panicked. They couldn't question you. They couldn't find out what you did or didn't know. They assumed the worst, which was that you indeed knew everything and could destroy them. It doesn't matter what the truth is. Lester gave her your name, and the fear of exposure is enough for her to send a team of mercenaries after us. Whether you are a genuine threat to her is irrelevant. Now it's gone too far. They can't let you live."

"What information could be so important to go through this, but so insignificant that I don't have any idea what it might be?"

"Her name," Victor said. "That's the only thing that makes sense. It's there in a file, innocuous and unimportant, but it connects her to something. And you've seen it: filing, photocopying, whatever."

"How could she have gotten away with it? Lester and me both being murdered? It would be too much of a coincidence, wouldn't it?"

"People like this don't get caught for crimes against civilians. They would have spun a story to hide the truth: maybe you and Lester ran off together before tragically dying in a car accident."

"That couldn't work, could it?"

"These things happen all the time. The reason you don't know about it is because it works."

"Then fuck her. We can't let her get away with this." Her hands were tight fists at her sides. "I want to bring her down. What else can we do? Keep running and hiding until they catch up with us again?"

"No," Victor said. "That's no plan. You're right: we have to go after her."

"Please tell me you know how."

He nodded. "Go through Lester's files. You have to figure out who she is and what she's scared of."

"But you said they'd be watching the firm. How can I?"

"We'll find a way. But first I need to speak to your stepfather."

• • •

The address Victor gave Norimov corresponded to a brownfield site on the south side of the river, between a long-disused power station and a development of new apartment blocks. There was a single route into the stretch of wasteland: a narrow path topped by loose gravel, just wide enough for a car to traverse. The land was uneven but flat. Signs near the path advertised the future homes that were to be built on the site.

Victor had been waiting with Gisele since eleven a.m.

A rented Subaru pulled off the road at five minutes past twelve. Late, despite Victor's warning. The car navigated the wasteland in a slow circle before coming to a stop in the approximate center.

A moment later the phone in Victor's pocket vibrated. He answered.

Yigor said, "I here. Where you?"

"Nearby," Victor answered. "Step out of the car, open all the doors."

"Why?"

"Because I'm telling you to."

"You crazy."

"Do it. Stay on the line."

Victor watched as the Russian climbed out of the driver's seat and proceeded to walk around the car, opening the passenger's door and both rear doors. No one else was inside.

"Happy now?"

"Deliriously so. Stay on the line. I'm coming over."

He stood up from where he lay on a shoulder between the old power station and the wasteland, some five hundred meters from where Yigor was parked. He returned to his own stolen Fiat and climbed inside. Gisele sat in the passenger's seat. Victor said nothing, and she obeyed his earlier request to stay silent. He activated the phone's speaker and set it in his lap so he could listen to Yigor while he drove the short distance to meet him. He parked ten meters away from the Subaru, climbed out of the car. He hung up and slipped the phone back in his pocket.

Seeing this, Yigor did the same. "What was that for?"

"To make sure you couldn't contact anyone."

"Why would I?"

Victor didn't answer.

"You hurt my feelings, Mr. Bad Man. I never—"

"Save it," Victor said, drawing his pistol. "Give me your gun."

Yigor looked shocked, then offended. "Why? You see I bring no one. You can trust me."

"I don't trust anyone. Give me your gun and I won't distrust you as much."

"You paranoid, man."

"The gun," Victor said. "Now."

The Russian screwed up his face and with big, exaggerated movements drew out his weapon. He threw it at Victor's feet.

Victor tucked his own gun away and retrieved Yigor's from the ground. He passed it to Gisele through the open passenger's-door window.

She said, "I told you that you could trust him."

"What now?" Yigor asked, hands in pockets.

Victor said. "You're going to answer some questions." He aimed his gun at the Russian's left knee. "You need to tell me everything you know if you enjoy the ability to walk."

The mobile phone vibrated against his hip. He fished it out and checked the screen, thinking Norimov was calling. He wasn't. A different number was displayed. For an instant he didn't understand. Then he did. The sender was Yigor, who was edging closer, then charging, the scrape of his shoes and the blur of movement in Victor's peripheral vision providing a split second of warning— enough time for Victor to drop the phone to free his hands and bring them up in defense.

The big Russian slammed into him. Even properly braced, Victor would have no chance to resist the momentum. Being only half-ready, the impact jolted him backward, ruining his balance, giving Yigor the opportunity to grab his jacket and fling him at the stolen car, where Gisele sat. Victor collided with the hood, toppling back onto it, then rolling laterally to avoid the elbow driven down at his skull. The sheet metal buckled and dented from the monstrous force.

Yigor's muscle was gym built and steroid fueled, but he had the speed of a lighter man. He grabbed Victor as he rolled off the hood, lifting him up and slamming him onto the ground, going down on top of him to crush and smother. Victor took the impact of their combined weight, losing the air from his lungs, but scooped up a rock into his left hand and drove it into Yigor's face, which tore a gash across his forehead.

Victor twisted and pushed out from under him as Yigor recoiled from the blow, creating some distance and releasing the rock as he came to his feet. He reached for the gun but it had fallen from his waistband in the struggle and lay unseen near his enemy's feet.

He attacked to distract him from noticing the weapon. The Russian blocked the punch and grabbed Victor's jacket as he followed through with another punch, pulling him closer and launching a head butt that Victor slipped and turned from, taking hold of the hand attached to his jacket, twisting it clockwise, forcing the Russian to release him or have his wrist locked. He chose the former. Victor backed off to create space, but circled so his enemy turned away from the gun on the ground.

Yigor used the pause to pull a folding knife from a coat pocket. Blood from the forehead wound seeped down the left side of his face.

Victor ducked low to avoid a slash at his neck, darting to Yigor's left to keep out of the knife's arc, and slipped around his exposed flank. A hook to the ribs caused the Russian to cry out and attempt a wild backhand attack. Victor batted the weapon from Yigor's grip. It whistled through the air, clattering on the hard ground too far away to risk going for.

Yigor ducked low and threw himself at Victor, pushing him into the car's driver's side and pinning him there with his superior weight.

Hands went for Victor's throat, palms wrapped around the neck, fingertips pushing against his spine, thumbs pressing down on his windpipe, cutting off his air supply. He punched up in return, striking Yigor's face, adding to the blood from his forehead and cheek wounds, but they were arm punches with no power generated from planted feet and twisting hips. Yigor smiled through them, asking for more, happy to take them. They both knew Victor would be dead long before Yigor's face broke apart.

Victor's chest burned for oxygen as he grabbed the man's hair in his right fist to lock it in place and drove his other thumb into Yigor's left eye socket. The Russian tried to pull away from the pressure on his eyeball but Victor could stretch his arm farther than Yigor's two could extend while maintaining the choke.

The Russian grimaced, then roared, lifting him off the ground by his neck and slamming him into the car's bodywork, but Victor didn't release Yigor's hair or lessen the pressure on his eye. Yigor slammed Victor down again harder, then, having no other option to avoid losing his eye, snapped his hands free to tear away Victor's own.

An anticipated move and Victor was already acting, kicking Yigor in the sternum and propelling him backward a few steps. It exhausted Victor to do so. He gasped and coughed, weakened by the strangulation.

He was still fast enough to block the first punch, but not the second. Victor's vision darkened. His head swam. He almost didn't see the next one. He jerked his head to the side, slipping it—just—with Yigor's thumb scraping across his ear before the fist smashed into the edge of the car's roof where it met the driver's door.

He howled and jumped back, letting Victor slide along the bodywork and out of range, sagging from the effects of the punch and oxygen deprivation.

The Russian clutched at his broken fist and snarled in pain and rage because he knew he was beaten with his dominant hand now useless, no matter how temporarily weakened Victor was. He came forward anyway, turning sideways, ready to fight to the end with only his left hand.

"Stop," Gisele shouted.

She was out of the car and looking at Yigor, holding the pistol Victor had given to her in shaking hands. The

Russian faced her, good hand rising, passive. Victor
blinked, trying to put the world back in focus.

"No . . ." he managed, because he saw what was going to happen.

Yigor shuffled toward Gisele, hand still raised. By the
time she realized he wasn't surrendering it was too late.
He tore the gun from her hand and aimed it at Victor.

The Russian said, "I win."

· Chapter 65 ·

Yigor held the gun in his left hand because the right had to be broken in more than a dozen places. It hung uselessly at his side, bloody and swollen. He used the gun to usher Gisele and Victor together and then over to his car.

"Why are you doing this?" Gisele asked.

Yigor said, "I want money. I sell you both and make all the money."

He walked a couple of meters behind Victor and Gisele. It was the textbook distance in such circumstances— too far for the captives to turn and take their captor by surprise, but close enough for the captor to respond should his captives try to escape. At that range, no one missed, even someone shooting with his nondominant hand. Only amateurs pushed a muzzle into someone's back, and even an amateur could turn around fast enough to disarm someone who did. Yigor was no professional in Victor's sense of the word, but he wasn't stupid, and, more than that, he was afraid of Victor. That was unusual. Victor's manner was carefully constructed to appear nonthreatening. Such a disguise of normalcy meant enemies were apt to underestimate him. That wouldn't happen here. Yigor's battered face and broken hand were painful reminders not to drop his guard.

Gravel crunched underfoot. Victor stopped when he reached the Fiat. He saw Yigor's reflection in the window glass and Gisele next to him.

"Open the door and get behind the wheel," Yigor said.

Victor stood still.

"No stalling. Just do it. Or I kill you both now."

"Then you won't get paid," Victor said.

"You want to find out? No, you don't. You want to keep alive long as you can. So open door."

There was no option but to obey. If there had been, Victor would already be acting. Driving the car was something he did not want to do. In the back he had a number of workable plans of action he could implement. But Yigor wasn't stupid.

Yigor waited two meters away with a clean line of sight. Even if Victor had a key he couldn't get the engine started and accelerate fast enough to avoid Yigor's shot from such a short distance. A guaranteed hit for anyone even remotely competent with a sidearm. A guaranteed kill shot for someone like Yigor, even left-handed. Victor couldn't risk it. He couldn't allow Gisele to be alone.

He opened the driver's door and climbed in.

"Seat belt?" he asked as he pulled up the lever to edge the seat forward a couple of notches.

Yigor hesitated because he hadn't thought that far ahead. There were pros and cons. Seat belt on meant Victor was bound to his seat, preventing sudden move-ment, but gave him a far better chance of surviving a deliberate crash. Off meant he couldn't risk any reckless driving but provided freedom of movement to try something else. It was a difficult choice. Which was why Victor had asked Yigor to make the decision for him, because the answer would reveal more about Yigor's thought processes than was smart to let an enemy like Victor know.

"No belts."

Victor nodded.

Yigor pointed the pistol at Gisele. "Get in the passenger's seat or I shoot your boyfriend."

"He's not my boyfriend."

"And he never will be."

She did. Then Yigor climbed into the back, sitting directly behind the driver's seat. It was the best place for a captor to sit in these circumstances. The Russian pulled the door shut behind him.

"Don't forget I have gun," he said. "Try anything and you will be shot. Maybe I don't get paid all the money, but that's life. But not for you. You'll be dead. Don't forget."

"I won't forget."

"That's good. You fight pretty well for a little man. I cannot lie. You hurt me. But I hurt you more, yes?"

"Tell that to your hand."

Yigor frowned. "I only need one to pull trigger."

"Don't do this," Gisele pleaded. "Alek will pay you."

Yigor laughed. "Norimov has no money. He's the poor man. Why you think I work against him all this time? She pay me plenty money to tell her about warehouse. She will pay even more for you two. I sorry, Gisele. You nice girl, but money is money." He gestured at Victor with the gun. "Now, you in front: drive car. Remember this gun. Do anything I don't first tell you to do, or try acting the crazy, and *bang-bang* in your back. Maybe I get lucky and you don't die. Maybe you become the cripple. Then you can watch me hurt the girl before I hand her over. You wouldn't want to miss that, would you? I'm pretty good at making people hurt. And you know what? I like doing it."

"A shocking revelation," Victor said. "You'll be telling me next you have trouble forming meaningful relationships."

"Relationships are for the pussies. Now start engine." He dropped the keys over Victor's left shoulder. "Keep thinking of the gun at your back, okay, Mr. Smart Mouth?"

Victor inserted the key and started the engine. "Where are we going?"

"To the warehouse."

"What for?"

"To wait. Nice and quiet there, yes?"

"I don't know the way from here."

"You stupid. I'll be the guide."

"Thank you."

Yigor laughed. "Nice try, my friend. I see what you want to do. You think if you are Mr. Polite, then I will be nice to you. You think maybe I will let you both go? You are the funny man. You a coward. I don't know why Norimov thought you could help. Look how you ended up."

"Manners cost nothing."

"Drive, Mr. Dead Man."

Victor did. Gisele kept her gaze on the road ahead. Her eyes were wide and full of fear. He wanted to say something to reassure her, but kind words were not his forte and he respected her too much to placate her now.

Yigor said, "And so you are knowing, if you try crashing car, then you will be the one who hurts. I'm not wearing the belt back here. So you stop fast and I use you as my air bag. *Crunch.* You'll be flat like a worm. And me? I'll laugh. Maybe do it anyway. I want to see what you look like after I crush you."

"I'll pass, if it's all the same to you," Victor said.

Yigor laughed. "I like that you are the Mr. Funny Man even when you are in the biggest trouble. You won't be so Mr. Funny Man soon, yes?"

Victor remained silent.

"Please, Yigor," Gisele said. "Let us go. Please."

He growled and raised the gun as if to pistol-whip her. "Keep silent or I hurt you."

She recoiled.

"Do as he says," Victor said.

"Yes, listen to your boyfriend the hero. But not a very good hero, yes? When I was little long time ago I wanted to be the hero like in the movies. What about you?"

Victor said, "Me too."

"But now I am the bad man. Same as you. Sometimes I wonder why that happened. Do you?"

"All the time," Victor said.

"Makes me sad, tell the truth," Yigor said. "Messes with my head. But too late now to be good. You know what I tell myself, make myself feel better?"

"What do you tell yourself?"

"Fuck it," Yigor said with a laugh. "That's what I say. Kids, they know shit. I knew shit. If I known you make the money being bad I would have wanted to be bad. But you, you've been bad, but it's good you helped Norimov. So you been bad but die as good. Nice shit, yes?"

"Beautifully put."

"Maybe I write poem about it."

Victor continued driving. Yigor called out directions,

guiding Victor through the urban streets. Gisele didn't speak. The hands of the analog dashboard clock ticked around. Five minutes passed, then ten.

"Next right," Yigor said.

Victor slowed and indicated. "You realize they'll kill you when you hand us over, don't you?"

"Tell me: why do you bother? I know they won't. They want the girl and now they want you. They don't want me. I make the money because I help them. You should have helped them too."

"Dmitri's dead. So are the others. Gisele and I will be next. Do you really think you'll be the only one who walks away from this?"

Yigor stayed quiet.

"You're a dead man, Yigor," Victor said. "And you're too stupid to see it."

The Russian's lips were pressed together and his nostrils flared with each angry breath.

Victor laughed and laughed.

"Hey," Yigor said, "you missed the damn turn."

Victor glanced back. "I'll take the next one."

"No, you fucked up. Turn the car around."

"The road is too narrow."

"Then back up."

Victor slowed to a stop and put the gear into reverse. "Watch the road for me."

Yigor laughed. "You keep trying, don't you, Mr. Funny Man? I keep my eyes on you all the time. Use your mirrors."

Victor pushed his foot down on the accelerator. Five miles per hour. Then ten.

"What's with the hurry?" Yigor asked.

"I'm bored of waiting," Victor answered.

Fifteen miles per hour. Gisele looked at him. At first in surprise, which quickly began to warp into understanding. Twenty miles per hour.

Yigor frowned. "What the fuck are you talking about?"

"Do you remember what you said before, Yigor? About the air bag?"

The Russians eyes widened in confusion, then fear when he realized how fast they were going. "Stop the car. *Now.*"

Victor did. He released his foot from the accelerator and slammed the brake pedal and wrenched up the hand brake. But before he did that, he pulled up the lever to adjust his seat, and kept hold.

The car came to a stop within two seconds. But the unlocked driver's seat was still moving backward, only stopping when it slammed its weight and Victor's directly into Yigor's shins.

· Chapter 66 ·

The car rocked back and forth on its suspension for a moment. Victor grimaced from the whiplash. His chest felt a little sore. Gisele hadn't been wearing her belt and was now unconscious and slumped in her seat. Yigor had come off worse. Far worse. Both shins had snapped. His knees were broken. Even his ankles were broken.

He groaned instead of screamed because the adrenaline in his system was negating the pain. Otherwise he would be unconscious like Gisele. It was one of the benefits of shock, but the disadvantages were going to be as costly for a man in Yigor's position. He didn't try to retrieve the gun that had flown from his hand in the sudden stop.

"What the fuck?" he managed to grunt, looking down at the wreckage of his legs.

Victor unclasped the seat belt and examined Gisele. She'd hit her head and was out cold but breathing well. He climbed out of the car. They were on a quiet road that cut between factories. No other vehicles. No people. No witnesses.

He circled the car and opened the far rear door. Yigor

stared at him. White showed all around his pupils. Sweat shone on his paling face. Victor ignored him and fished in the foot well until he found Yigor's gun under the passenger's seat. There was nowhere else it could have gone.

"Wait," Yigor said.

Victor closed the door. He circled back around the vehicle. Yigor's gun was a .45-caliber Colt 1911.

He opened the door next to Yigor.

"Wait," the Russian said again, this time through gritted teeth because he was shaking off the shock and now the agony of multiple fractures was intensifying with every passing second.

"Please," Yigor begged. Rivulets of sweat ran down from his temples. "No shoot me. Please."

"Give me your knife," Victor said. "Grip first."

Yigor's trembling fingers took it from his pocket. He struggled to turn it around in his hand and presented the grip to Victor by holding the blade. Victor took it in his left hand and tossed it away.

"Phone."

Yigor tried to pull it from his hip pocket, but screamed as he increased the pressure of his trousers against his injured legs in the process. He tugged his hand away and took a series of breaths as he fought to control the pain. Tears joined the sweat on his face.

Victor said, "Either you get it or I do."

Yigor hesitated, then tried a second time. He screamed again, but this time he didn't stop. He kept screaming until the phone was free. He didn't have the strength to hold it up, so Victor reached inside the car to take it out of his hand; he was too weak to try anything.

"Who is the woman?"

"I not know her name. We speak on phone only."

Victor looked through the call log. Between the most recent calls to Victor's phone and a call to Norimov, was another number.

"Is this her?" Victor asked.

Yigor nodded. "I sorry," he said, sobbing. "For everything. I got greedy. I should have said no to taking photo."

"You took the photograph of Norimov coming out of the restaurant?"

"Yes. I make threat. But not easy turning on Norimov. I had to think about it first. Not easy saying yes. I so sorry."

"Apology accepted," Victor said. "But I'm still going to kill you."

"No," Yigor spat. "You need me. I can call and help fix things, yes? You need me."

"I only need you to die."

"Then shoot. I care not."

"Unfortunately for you, your gun doesn't have many bullets."

Yigor frowned in confusion, then his eyes widened when Victor turned the pistol around so he held it by the barrel, steel grip protruding beyond his knuckles like the head of a hammer.

• • •

Gisele had woken up by the time Victor had driven the Fiat back to the wasteland, gently lifted her from the passenger's seat, and placed her in Yigor's rented Subaru.

"Holy shit," Gisele breathed, groggy and disorientated. "My head is killing me."

Victor squatted down so he was at her level. He took her head in his palms and peered into her eyes.

"Do you know where you are?"

"Yeah," she said. "Hell."

"Follow my finger with your eyes." He moved his index finger laterally and then in circular motions. "Do you feel sick or does anything else hurt apart from your head?"

"No."

"Then you'll be fine," Victor assured her. "You don't have a concussion."

"What happened?"

"Yigor's dead. You don't want to know any more than that."

She inhaled deeply and nodded. "Okay, what happens now?"

Victor said, "This is what we're going to do . . ."

· Chapter 67 ·

They took the Docklands Light Railway into the city, disembarking the train and making their way out of the station and into the heart of the city's financial district, the Square Mile. The streets were alive with men and women in business wear and heavy winter coats, sipping from take-out coffee cups or on the move, eager to get home after a day's trading, borrowing, stealing.

With Gisele at his side and a limited time frame, Victor couldn't perform the kind of thorough countersurveillance run he would have liked, but he circled his destination at a circumference of four blocks, spiraling inward as he analyzed the environs. It was an area of historic office buildings, ornate and beautiful. Bars, cafés, and eateries flanked the streets at ground level to sustain and entertain the workers.

The sun had retreated behind the horizon but the numerous lights from streetlights, headlights, and shining through windows and from signs meant he had no trouble checking every face and vehicle he saw. Victor bought a black coffee from a street vendor and sipped it as he walked slowly against the flow of pedestrians. Gisele declined one.

The air smelled as dirty as the sky appeared. Here, Victor looked like everyone else and Gisele stood out in the sweatshirt and hat, but she didn't look like the employee of a law firm and that was the important factor. As they approached their destination, Victor slowed their pace and took his time, searching for danger spots and anyone who could be a threat. He saw no one, but they couldn't yet risk getting too close to the building housing Gisele's workplace. If they were watching, they would be near the building, ready to act. Her disguise wouldn't fool them there.

"Is this the one?" Victor asked Gisele when they came to a tube station.

She nodded. "This is the closest, yeah. What do we do now?"

"Wait."

They did, loitering inside the main entrance so they were not exposed to any threats passing on the street outside. Victor was good at waiting. He could remain relaxed and alert for endless hours without becoming distracted or bored. He had killed many hard targets simply by waiting long enough for the perfect opportunity to strike. Similarly, he had survived many threats by outwaiting an enemy who was encouraged to make a mistake through boredom or distraction. Gisele did not have the same experience nor the same hunter's mentality, but she kept any nervousness or frustration in check.

After nine minutes, she said, "Him. In the gray overcoat. I think he works at the accountancy firm on the floor above. I see him in the café every lunchtime. Decaf skinny latte."

Victor didn't acknowledge the comment. He turned to follow Gisele's gaze. A small crowd of people was crossing the road, hurrying to beat the flashing traffic light and get out of the rain. They were heading toward the station, the density of the crowd increasing as they were funneled through the entrance. Victor set off in their direction, looking down as he fiddled with his jacket buttons.

A man bumped into him and apologized. Another did not. A third, wearing a gray overcoat, told him to watch where he was going.

Victor stopped and turned, watching as the man walked away muttering to himself. Gisele was looking at Victor and he nodded. She made her way over to him.

"Was that it?" she asked.

He nodded again and led her away from the entrance.

"I didn't see a thing."

"That's the idea. Here." He opened the man's wallet and Gisele spotted a white pass card and slid it out.

"That's it. Wasn't sure if theirs would be the same as ours, but I guess everyone would have to use the same ones to get through the lobby, wouldn't they?" She dropped it into a pocket. "What are you going to do with the wallet?"

"Dispose of it."

"Do we have to? Seems a little harsh. On him, I mean."

She gestured to where the man in the gray overcoat was standing before the station's electronic turnstiles, patting down the pockets of his coat and trousers and shaking his head. A station employee watched him with an unsympathetic look.

"How's he going to get home?" Gisele asked.

The man in the gray overcoat was becoming increasingly frustrated at his inability to locate his wallet. The station employee motioned for him to move out of other people's way.

Gisele said, "What if it's his kid's birthday party and he's going to miss it? Maybe the kid doesn't get to see her dad much. Maybe this is going to break her heart."

Victor saw the compassion in Gisele's eyes. He didn't know what it felt like, but he saw its importance. "Would you prefer that I return the wallet?"

"Yes, please."

He did, tapping the man on the shoulder and saying, "I think you dropped this."

He wasn't thanked.

They found a quiet area outside the flow of people. He made sure no one was in earshot and said, "There's no accessible entrance to the building aside from the main one, so when you're inside, walk quickly, like you're in a hurry, but not so fast as to draw undue attention. Keep your head angled down to give cameras a harder time seeing your face, but be aware of who is around you. Make sure you breathe. Holding your breath because you're tense will just make you more stressed. Take long, slow breaths. Don't forget what we discussed. Don't draw attention to yourself. If you're forced to engage with someone, keep it brief. Only provide the cover story if you're asked. Don't offer it. When we lie we provide too many details in an attempt to be believed. So do the opposite. Get to Lester's office and retrieve only what you need and then leave. If something feels wrong, it probably is. Trust your instincts. Just walk away. Remember to—"

She interrupted him: "I remember. We've been through it a hundred times already. If I don't know what to do by now, I'm never going to. But I do know it."

He saw that she was putting on a brave face for his benefit. In a way, she was trying to protect him, so he wouldn't worry.

She said, "Whatever happens, I hope you believe me when I say I'm sorry all of this has happened. You couldn't have known what a pile of shit it would be when you said you'd protect me. You've done so much. More than I can ever repay. I'm so sorry. I really am."

"There's no need to apologize, Gisele. None of this is your fault. And even if it were, I would still protect you."

She was shaking her head. "Knowing my mother is not enough of a reason for you to go through this for me. It's not. It's not enough."

"That's how it began, Gisele," he said. "But now I'm doing this because I know you as well."

"I . . . I don't know what to say to that."

"You don't have to. Just remember to—"

"I've got it, okay? Trust me."

He looked down at her. She was untrained and vulnerable yet spoke with impressive confidence. He realized he was more concerned for her life than he was for his own.

Victor placed a hand on her shoulder. "I do trust you."

· Chapter 68 ·

The building's exterior was a typical example of early eighteenth-century Edwardian architecture, but the interior had been completely modernized. The lobby was vast and formed the ground floor of a large atrium. Two rows of three lifts provided access to the five floors of offices that ringed the atrium behind glass walls. Two bright-faced receptionists sat behind a long, curved counter. A security guard stood before an electronic turnstile and failed to stifle a yawn.

Gisele kept her head angled down to protect her face from security cameras, as her companion had instructed her, but kept her eyes moving in an attempt to identify any threats. She exhaled through pursed lips, mouth already dry. What was she supposed to do if she did identify any? Knowing a few self-defense techniques and having a can of pepper spray was not going to do her much good if she came face-to-face with an armed mercenary.

But if her companion was right, that scenario wouldn't arise.

The lobby seemed even more massive than usual—vast

and scary. She avoided eye contact with the two people sitting behind the reception desk and touched the white plastic identity card to the turnstile reader.

"How are you today, miss?" the security guard standing nearby asked.

Damn, she'd hoped he wouldn't be paying attention. She glanced up at big, kind Alan and said, "No rest for the wicked."

He smiled and she wondered if he really cared as he seemed to or whether it was all part of the job. A blinking light switched from red to green and a double-glass divide parted to let her through the barrier. She looked over her shoulder. Alan the security guard was watching her. She told herself to relax. She knew him. She saw him every day. He wasn't one of them.

There were six elevators in two banks of three, opposite each other. She pressed the closest button and rubbed her palms together while she waited for a set of doors to open. She exhaled when they parted and no gunman was standing inside waiting for her.

She walked in backward to make sure no one was about to follow her. The wait for the doors to close after she hit the button for the law firm's floor was an eternity.

The ascent was thankfully swift and no one was waiting as she stepped out. She dared to hope that maybe this was going to work out after all. *Stay focused,* she reminded herself. *Mind on the present.*

Near the elevators was a fire-evacuation plan fixed to a wall. It showed the layout of the entire floor. She'd never noticed it before. She'd never paid that much attention to her surroundings.

One corner turned and she was in the firm's reception area. It was a tastefully decorated space that did a good job of making the firm appear friendly and welcoming. And it was, for paying clients.

Caroline, the receptionist, greeted her. "Miss Maynard, welcome back. I . . . I almost didn't recognize you."

"Oh yeah," Gisele said, nervously touching her hair. What with the stress of thinking about everything else, she had forgotten about the disguise. Thinking fast, she said, "Bit of a new look, right? Not sure I like it, but I had one of those crazy I-feel-like-a-change moments. You know?"

"Tell me about it. I think one of those moments is around the corner. But I'm talking about my boyfriend, not my hair."

Gisele laughed along with her, happy that she seemed to have gotten away with it.

The receptionist said, "Little late to be coming to the office, isn't it, hon? Nearly everyone has gone off to celebrate Bella's victory. Cocktails on the firm's tab. Nice work if you can get it, yeah?"

"She won? That's great news. Good for her. Tell her I said well done when you see her next. As for the free cocktails, why do you think I want to have a proper job here? Cosmos, girl. It's all about the cosmos. Anyway, I'm just nipping in to pick up a few things. I'm still under the weather but I don't want to fall any farther behind or I'll never catch up again." She felt her face growing warmer and feared a blush might give her away. She cleared her throat. Her mind raced for something else to say. She was going into the cover story needlessly. Like he said, giving too many details in trying to be believable. All she could think of was: "Has Lester come back to work yet?"

"No." Caroline's face was somber. "In fact, I'm getting a bit worried about him. Something is going on, I reckon. Not that anyone's telling me anything. Have you heard how he is?"

Gisele shook her head. She didn't believe she could lie with enough conviction.

"I hope he's okay," Caroline said.

"Me too." She began to walk past the desk. "I'd better get a move on. Doctor says I shouldn't even be out of bed."

"Let me know if there's anything I can do to help. Oh, I almost forgot. A guy came here looking for you."

Gisele's felt her pulse spike. "A guy? Who was he?"

Caroline shrugged. "Said he had a meeting with you. There was no record of one. I thought he was full of shit, personally. Weird, huh?"

She swallowed. "Yeah. What did he look like?"

"Dark hair. Real serious-looking." She gave a light-hearted impression of such a look, eyes narrowed and brow furrowed. Then she smiled coyly. "I wouldn't kick him out of bed, though. He looked like the kind of man who knows things, if you get me."

Gisele relaxed. "Don't stress about him. We know each other now. He's cool."

The receptionist grinned. "Good for you, girl. What's his name?"

Gisele hesitated, mouth open and unable to respond.

"Oh," the receptionist said, "like that, is it? Bit of a mystery man, is he?"

"Understatement of the year," Gisele said, smiling back.

The smile slipped from her face the instant she turned away. Her heart was racing. She was amazed she'd got this far on nothing but her wits. It was starting to feel natural. Maybe he was right: maybe she would make a good barrister someday.

The receptionist hadn't been exaggerating when she'd said most people had left already. The open-plan area where Gisele had her desk was empty. That would cut down on the conversations and lies she would have to engage in, and gave her a better chance of finding what she came here for. She didn't know how many of the senior lawyers were in their individual offices, but the general rule was if the bigwigs were working late, then so was everyone else. If they were partying, everyone partied with them. Still, a few workaholics might be about.

What would she say to them if she was challenged? They were all confident, intimidating people. She could hardly pretend to be ill with fake coughs and sniffles. She crossed the open-plan area and headed to Lester's office. No one was about. She licked her dry lips and turned the door handle.

Locked.

"Shit," Gisele said.

She fantasized kicking it open and striding in, but she knew she'd break her foot long before the door gave way, and be dragged out by security long before that. Then she would find out if Alan really was as nice as he acted.

What would her companion do in her place?

Gisele knew. He would kick it open. Easily, no doubt. Or he would pick the lock in seconds. She didn't even know what a picklock looked like.

Her left arm was hurting and she rubbed it as she thought through her options. The main problem seemed to be that she had no options.

If she couldn't come up with something fast, it was all over.

• • •

On a wide boulevard nearby luxury vehicles wet with rain gleamed in the glow of streetlights. While Gisele performed her role at the firm, Victor attempted his own, walking fast along the curb, his jacket sleeve brushing the side mirrors of parked vehicles. They were tightly parked, nose to tail. The car roofs were about armpit height; the big four-by-fours rose to his chin. Staying close to the cars gave him excellent concealment from any gunmen across the street, at whatever elevation, from whatever distance. A high-velocity round wouldn't be stopped by the bodywork, but the more bodywork between Victor and the shooter, the more chance of a ricochet or deflection if the shooter was good, or an outright miss if he was not.

The pavement was busy with pedestrians in business attire and winter clothing. Most chatted on their phones or toyed with them. He walked a little faster than those around him. Moving with pace would make it harder for anyone tracking him to take a shot. A continuous stream of people passed him on both sides, providing a good deal of cover and concealment. The movements of the crowd were unpredictable and would interrupt lines of sight from any position. He weaved through the pedestrian traffic, never walking in a straight line because he couldn't know where such a shot would come from. If he'd miscalculated this action it would prove fatal.

He identified the watchers within a minute. There were two: one at the intersection at the end of the street and another opposite the building. Both men, competent but nowhere near elite, because they were mercenaries, not pavement artists—soldiers, not spies. One sat on a bench reading a newspaper. A reasonable cover, except he held it too close to his waist to read comfortably, so he could watch the building entrance. The second man smoked. On first impression he was doing nothing more. He might have popped out of a nearby building to enjoy his cigarette in the sunshine, or perhaps he smoked while waiting for someone. His mistake was the three crushed stubs near where he stood.

Victor entered the building. He didn't look to see whether either man noticed him. If they knew who to watch for, then they would have, without question. If they didn't, then there was nothing to gain by looking in their direction except an increased chance of recognition.

Inside it was predictably grand, but unnecessarily so with huge chandeliers, frescoes, and bronze statues. Plenty of money had been spent but little class had been applied. The city had numerous private clubs more than a century old and had survived until this day through a steadfast adherence to excellence and tradition. This club was one of the many that tried too hard to emulate the originals. Victor was no snob, but he appreciated the difference.

"Mr. Ivanov," Victor said to a statuesque maître d' in a cocktail dress. "Table for two."

A brief check of the log. "Your date is waiting for you, Mr. Ivanov."

"Tremendous."

She led him through the tables, busy with the early-evening crowd. He walked directly behind her, scanning the interior for threats, but saw none. Every table was busy. There were no lone men or women trying not to look observant.

Good. This might work.

The maître d' motioned. "Here you go, sir."

Sitting at the table was a blond woman with green eyes.

Chapter 69

She didn't see him until it was impossible not to because the maître d' had helped hide Victor until the last moment, and she had been expecting someone else. When her gaze met his there was an instant of confusion that became surprise, then disbelief, but did not reach fear. Which surprised him in turn. She waited.

Victor held out his palms to show he was no threat. She sat so casually and unconcerned that he almost felt like none.

He gestured to the free chair. "May I?"

There was hesitation while she decided on the best course of action.

She said, "Be my guest."

He knew it would be a mistake to think she was acting out of passivity. He sat, never breaking eye contact. "No corner table available," he began as he nudged the chair forward. "But thank you for leaving me the seat facing the door. How thoughtful of you."

Her expression stayed neutral, her own eyes unblinking. He saw the surprise had already gone. Now her gaze was searching, evaluating; calculating.

"Why don't we keep our hands on the table?" Victor offered. "To avoid any misunderstandings."

He placed his palms flat on the tablecloth. It was cool and smooth—four-hundred-thread-count Egyptian cotton. She did the same. Her fingers were long and slender. The nails were unpolished but manicured.

"If you feel that's necessary. But we're both professionals. I'm sure we can behave with some civility." She paused. "Unless you're scared of little old me."

He smiled because it was a good taunt. To insist their hands remained on the table was to admit fear, but to remove them let her win this first contest of wills.

"Thank you for meeting me," Victor said, taking his hands from the tablecloth.

She said, "I did wonder why Yigor insisted on a face-to-face. I should have trusted my instincts."

"I'm glad you didn't."

"You do a flawless impersonation of the man."

"That sounded like a genuine compliment."

"It was. You can thank me by explaining why we're here."

He didn't answer because a waiter approached to take their order.

"Can you give us another five minutes?"

They sat without speaking for a moment until the waiter had gone. Victor used the time to separate out and analyze the conversations taking place all around him—a young couple eager to finish their meal and find somewhere private; a business dinner more about egos and posturing than commerce; a group of workmates discussing their day and how they were unappreciated and underpaid.

"What do you want?" she asked again.

"I'm here to talk. To see if we can resolve this with some, as you put it, civility."

"Well, I wasn't exactly expecting you to ask me to accompany you to Paris for the weekend."

"Perish the thought."

She said, "And how exactly do you propose we resolve this?"

"Simple. We go our separate ways."

"Just like that?"

He nodded.

"You're right, that does sound simple. But I'm afraid it isn't going to be possible. You have nothing to offer me."

"I don't? I've been in London just over forty-eight hours and I'm already sitting across from you. Where do you think I'll be in a week's time?"

Her expression remained neutral, but a little too neutral. She had to be concerned, but he couldn't shake her resolve.

She nodded by way of response, then said, "And I've known about you for half that time. Would you like to know what I've discovered already?"

"First rule of intelligence: it never tells the whole story."

"A sentiment I've spent my career living by. I'm sure you've done the same. And quite a career you've had too. Professional assassin. Freelance. Aleksandr Norimov used to be your broker, first for the Russian intelligence services, then when he went into business for himself. I've read all sorts of unverified reports about incidents in Paris, Minsk, even as far afield as Tanzania. Quite the well-traveled curriculum vitae you have."

Victor waited.

"Don't worry," she continued. "I don't expect you to

confirm anything. You don't need to. What I find particularly interesting is that you haven't worked for Norimov for at least half a decade. I know he sold you out to an SVR colonel a couple of years ago. Funnily enough, I've met this particular officer at a cocktail party in the Russian embassy here in London. This was before you two crossed paths and I only spoke to him for a few minutes, but I remember he was the most arrogant man I've ever met. Men who are that arrogant are usually sociopathic."

"Not only men," Victor said.

She cocked her head slightly and continued. "So, if Norimov sold you out to a man like that—and I admit I don't know why—I can't believe you found it in your heart to forgive him. Let alone put your life at risk for his daughter. A stepdaughter, at that."

"You want to know why—is that it?"

"Partly," she said. "Though in truth it doesn't matter why you're doing what you're doing. But whatever it is, it must be a fucking good reason." Victor's jaw tightened at the obscenity. She saw it. "Too unladylike for you?"

"There's enough ugliness in the world without adding to it, regardless of gender."

"I didn't take you for a hippie."

"Do you want to see my Greenpeace card?"

She smiled a little. She struck him as the kind of person who never allowed herself to laugh. To laugh meant to lose control. He could relate.

She said, "We've strayed off point. But I rather like that we can. Even though we're enemies it doesn't mean we can't be friends."

"I might go ahead and disagree with you on that."

The smile lingered. " 'You shall judge a man by his foes as well as by his friends.' "

Joseph Conrad, Victor thought, lips closed.

"Shall we cut to the chase?" she asked.

"Be my guest."

"I'm an officer of the British SIS and I'm fucking good. I have close ties with Russian and American intelligence. I have contacts in every police force in Europe. Interpol practically falls over itself to help me out when I make a call. What do you think will happen if I put all my efforts into finding out exactly who you are?"

"You'll find nothing."

She sat back and stared at his face. He knew she was searching for any of the various visual tells that would reveal he was lying. He also knew that she found none. "Okay," she said. "You've got a good poker face, I'll give you that. But we both know that the thing you hold dearest is your anonymity. Without it you're nothing."

"Do you have a point?"

She began to sit forward but stopped, knowing it showed her eagerness. Victor pretended not to notice. "My point, as you well know, is that whatever happens in this city is not the last of it. You've managed to stay alive and out of prison so far, so all credit to you, but I'm no arrogant SVR colonel or technology-reliant CIA officer. I've been doing this a long time, and the Office has been in the game longer than anyone else."

"Perhaps not something to brag about, given the state of the British Empire."

"Are you referring to an empire carved out by a tiny island barely visible from space that achieved what continents could not before or since? A little over a century ago that empire controlled a quarter of the world's land mass and a quarter of its population. Not a bad effort for the last empire the world will ever know."

"The Soviets might have something to say about that."

"An empire that falls apart within a lifetime is no empire."

"Alexander the Great begs to differ."

She smiled. "Look at us, discussing history and politics like we've known each other forever."

"I thought you were threatening me."

"Poppycock. I was merely helping you to understand the nature of your predicament."

"A while ago," Victor said, "you talked about cutting to the chase."

"It's good that you can maintain your sense of humor, considering the severity of your situation. I'm not sure I could in your place. Or maybe you're delusional. Perhaps that's why you're not as terrified as you should be."

"I'm not scared."

She raised an eyebrow. "Yet you felt the compulsion to state that fact?"

Her eyes were green fire that burned with the intensity of the sun. He fought not to look away.

"But I'm offering you an out," she said. "I'm offering you a deal. Call it mercy. Call it pity."

"I hand over Gisele and you let me walk away?"

"Nothing so unchivalrous, I assure you. You don't need to give Gisele to me. You don't have to give her to anyone. All you have to do is walk away."

"You make it sound so easy."

"Isn't it? What's so difficult? Don't tell me you're in love with her already."

Victor smiled to acknowledge the taunt. "No deal."

"I'm disappointed. For you."

Victor shook his head. "No, you're not. You're scared."

"Don't flatter yourself."

"You're terrified of being exposed. That's why you're risking everything to tear up London in the hope of killing Gisele. Hardly the actions of someone calm and relaxed."

"And why are you meeting me? You're here to negotiate a cease-fire. A side only does that when they are uncertain of victory."

"No," he said. "I'm not here to negotiate."

Her eyebrows rose. She sat forward sharply, eager to know, no longer concerned about showing emotion or maybe too intrigued to think to hide it. "No?" she echoed. "Then pray explain."

"I'm here for two things. The first is to tell you to leave Gisele alone. I'm not asking; I'm telling. I'm offering nothing in return. And if you're as clever as I think you are then you'll realize that whatever else you fear, you should fear me more."

She did well to hold his gaze without blinking because she had to recognize there was no bluff, no exaggeration. He meant every word.

"The second?"

He stood. Her eyes remained locked to his as he circled the table. "For this."

She said, "We're being watched. Right now."

"No, we're not."

"I'll fight," she said.

"It wouldn't make a difference."

The green eyes blazed. "Only one way to find out."

He stopped when he stood next to where she sat. She stared up at him. He was pleased to see fear at last in her gaze.

She said, "And if you do kill me, you're in a crowded London restaurant and you'll never—"

"Shh," he said. "I'm not that stupid. I'm not going to kill you here like this with all these witnesses. Not my style. Besides . . ." He lifted up her bag and drew out a wallet. He looked at the credit cards inside, her laminated ID, and then at her. "There's no rush, is there, Ms. Nieve J. Anderton?"

"You're making a very big mistake."

"I've heard that one before."

"You're a dead man."

"I've heard that one before too. Several times, in fact. Can you guess what all those who've said that to me have in common?" he whispered over her shoulder.

She stared at him, eyes narrowing in undisguised anger. "You think it makes a difference that you know my name? Do you think that scares me? A name is the easiest thing to find out about a person and the least important."

He dropped the wallet back into the bag and passed it to her.

He said, "What's mine again?"

They held each other's gaze for a long time until he was aware of a waiter at his side, who said, "Can I get you anything, sir?"

Victor would have said no but the waiter was not the one who had come over before. This one spoke with a South African accent.

The man added, "Don't even think about it, sport," before Victor could make a move. He heard the soft click of a hammer cocking. "Unless you want me to shoot you in front of all these nice people."

Anderton was shaking her head, the faux fear and anger replaced by genuine mirth. "You really thought you could trick me, didn't you? For shame."

· Chapter 70 ·

As Gisele stood outside Lester's office, frantically thinking about how to get through the locked door, the door of a nearby office swung open, startling her. A man exited, carrying a basket of cleaning products—sprays, brushes, cloths, and such. He was short and thin, wearing the uniform of the cleaning company that serviced the offices.

Gisele controlled her initial surprise and fear and smiled at him. He smiled back.

"Hey," she said, "don't suppose you have a key to this office?" She pointed at Lester's door.

The man continued to smile and nodded, clearly not understanding English, then went on his way.

Another door opened farther along the corridor and she heard the voice of one of the senior barristers talking on a mobile phone. Desperate to make herself scarce before he appeared, she hurried to the end of the corridor, where there were two doors, one marked HOMMES in gold paint, the other FEMMES.

There were five cubicles opposite a row of sinks. It was kept spotlessly clean and had all kinds of environmentally friendly hand soaps, sanitizers, and moisturizers lined up on the shelf behind the sinks. She went into a cubicle, dropped down the lid, locked the door, and sat down. *What now?*

She had failed at the first sign of difficulty. She needed his help, but wanted to do this on her own. She wanted to succeed. She had to do her part while he did his.

He hadn't told her exactly what he was doing, offering only vague assurances. He had been trying to spare her the uncomfortable details, she knew. She would never approve of his methods, but she had survived this far when by all rights she should have died several times over. She had known him for little more than a day but he was the best friend she could ever hope to have because he was sacrificing everything for her. He judged her for nothing. Her faults mattered not to him. He didn't care that she was self-centered and moody, and, yes, somewhat spoiled.

He was fearless and indomitable. She wanted to be like that. She couldn't imagine him weak or hurt or not knowing exactly what to do in any situation. He wouldn't feel defeated now. He would get the job done. He would act. When they had been trapped in the hotel room he had known straightaway what to do.

Her eyes widened. The idea came to her in a sudden, wonderful instant. Remembering what had happened at the hotel was the catalyst, but she thought of the fire-escape plan near the elevators and knew it would work.

She left the toilets. She didn't know where to find what she was looking for, which embarrassed her a little—she vowed to be more responsible in the future—but she found one soon enough. She paused for a moment. The alarm switch was fixed to the wall of a long corridor lined with doors leading to the offices of the senior personnel. What if one of them was working?

Gisele backtracked and found another switch in the open-plan area. Perfect.

She took a deep breath, fed her fingers into the gap, gripped the lever, and pulled.

The blaring wail startled her. It was louder than she had imagined.

Knowing she couldn't afford to hang around, she hurried over to her desk, lowered herself to her knees and crawled beneath it. She counted off the seconds in her head, having calculated that she needed to hide for at least a minute.

On sixty, she crawled out and rose to her knees first, so she could peer out over the top of her desk. No sign of anyone. The alarm made it impossible to hear even her own footsteps.

Walking fast, she made her way to the reception area. No receptionist. Caroline had followed procedure and headed down to the lobby. She would be waiting outside in the cold now. Gisele hoped she wasn't too cold.

She had no idea where it would be, so began with the bottom drawers of the reception desk, knowing that was how burglars opened drawers—bottom to top. Frustratingly, she found it in the top drawer: a ring of spare keys.

There had to be twenty of them. It was impossible to know which would open Lester's office, so she took the entire set. The weight surprised her. She rushed back the way she had come, the alarm blaring in her ears the whole time.

The thirteenth key Gisele tried turned out to be the right one.

He would be proud of her.

• • •

The Range Rover came to a stop. Victor heard the engine turn off and doors open and footsteps. The drive had been a short one and he had spent each and every second working through his options—planning and strategizing. So far, there was no workable course of action because Anderton had had one of the mercenaries handcuff him before bundling him into the trunk.

He'd traced every inch of the space around him for something to use as a pick or shim, but they were too thorough to have left anything he might be able to make use of.

The trunk opened and light spilled inside, making him wince. Anderton came into view a moment later, her green eyes regarding him with something between curiosity and contempt. Hands grabbed him and hauled him out.

His eyes moved, taking in the positions of the mercenaries—numbering five—Anderton, the two Range Rovers, and the vast empty space of the aircraft hangar around them. The fluorescent lights were bright and the air was cold.

"Where is she?" Anderton asked as she turned to face him.

The South African mercenary remained out of Victor's line of sight, but he kept track of his position by listening to his footsteps. He was standing a couple of meters to his seven o'clock.

Victor didn't answer the question. His gaze swept over the four mercenaries who stood before him. None had weapons drawn but he knew they were armed. Behind them, the second Range Rover was parked. Then, at the far side of forty meters of empty space, the exit. He pictured breaking Anderton's neck, but with a gun drawn behind him he would be dead in seconds if he tried.

"I'm waiting," she said.

"Get used to it."

She smiled and her eyes diverted for a moment and she nodded.

Pain exploded through Victor's brain as the South African struck him on the back of the skull with a handgun. His vision blackened and he dropped to his hands and knees, feeling the world beneath his palms rocking and shaking. He vomited.

"Careful," Anderton said. "I don't want him killed so soon."

"Apologies," the South African replied. "He's weaker than I expected."

The blackness slowly retreated from before Victor's eyes and the ground came into focus. He gasped and used the back of his hand to wipe the ropes of vomit hanging from his mouth. He didn't have the strength to stand.

Anderton stepped closer and her snakeskin boots entered his line of sight. "You know how this works, don't you?" Her voice was soft, almost sympathetic. "You know you'll tell me eventually, so why go through the pain first?"

Victor spat to clear his mouth. "There's nothing you can do to me that will make me talk."

"We both know that's untrue. You're just too stubborn to accept it. Don't be that man. You've done so well up until now. You're a professional. Don't end up bloody and begging. Let's end this in a civilized manner. Remember when we made that wager?" She squatted to her haunches so he could raise his head enough to look her in the green eyes. "I'd say I've won, wouldn't you?"

"Not yet," Victor said.

"Where?" Anderton said.

He spat on a snakeskin boot.

She sighed. "Your choice." She stood and stepped back. He heard her say, "Gentlemen, over to you."

Soles scraped on the ground and shadows fell over him. Then it began.

He tucked himself into a ball and covered his face and head as best as he could as the blows came from all angles. Kicks landed against his ribs and hips and arms. Punches rained down on every exposed part of his body. A heel stamped down on his left ankle. An elbow caught him above the right eye. A fist pushed through his guard and his vision blackened again and his body slackened, and he didn't have the senses left to continue protecting himself.

It became impossible to feel the individual hits as the pain became one horrific mass and his brain struggled to cope and his consciousness began to slip away.

"That's enough," Anderton said. "He's no use to me as a vegetable."

Victor wheezed and coughed, struggling to breathe, bruised ribs resisting expanding. He tasted blood and saw little more than smudged colors and blurred shapes. Sounds were quiet and distorted, but he recognized Anderton's voice:

"Not so clever now, are you?"

He couldn't respond even had he wanted to.

She said, "Where?"

Victor groaned by way of an answer. His mind still worked even if his body did not. While she was questioning him they weren't beating him. He didn't yet know how much damage had been done, but he knew his body couldn't take another assault. He had to stall. He had to recover. More important, Gisele needed time.

"Let me ask him," the South African said, and Victor saw a glint of brightness among the colors and shapes and knew a knife had been drawn.

"Is that what it's going to take to make you talk?" Anderton asked Victor.

Her face became clear through the fogginess. He met her eyes. "I'll . . . never . . . talk."

"You know what? I think I believe you."

The South African said, "I promise he'll change his mind within two minutes. Won't you, sport?"

Anderton stroked her bottom lip. "Maybe we don't have to go there."

Victor held her gaze.

"Maybe he's already told me everything I want him to."

Victor didn't blink.

"Let me cut him," the South African said.

"No," she replied, and he shrugged and backed off. "I have this under control." She looked down at Victor. "I have to say I wasn't confident that you were really coming to meet me. I wasn't convinced you would take the bait and come in Yigor's place. Not because I doubted my own abilities to manipulate you, but because I didn't believe you would leave Gisele on her own. After all you've been through in the past twenty-four hours I thought you would never leave her defenseless."

Despite the agony that wracked his body, Anderton's words hurt more.

She said, "Even if you believed you were tricking me, not the other way around, you must have known it was a dangerous course of action. Without you, Gisele has no one. Yet you risked that to meet me? Flattering, I suppose. You put both your lives in danger just to chat with little old me." She placed a hand on her chest, as if overwhelmed by a compliment.

Victor kept his expression even. If ever he had to hide his thoughts, now was the time.

"For what possible gain?" she continued. "To learn my name? *Really*? That was important enough to risk everything for?" She shook her head. "I don't think so. You haven't survived until now by being so foolhardy. So, why this sudden turnaround? Why take such a considerable chance? Why did you want to meet me here?" Her eyes widened. "Ah," she said, "because you didn't want me elsewhere. That's it, isn't it?"

She waited for an answer she didn't receive. He knew she would see through any lie.

But his silence seemed to say as much. "Oh, now I understand. You knew the meeting was a setup. You *knew*. But you came anyway. You walked straight into the trap because it guaranteed my presence and the presence of my men. Obviously, you didn't expect to get captured, but you wanted us all here to deal with you so they wouldn't be available to deal with Gisele. This is nothing more than a distraction." She tapped her lip. "But why is that necessary when we don't know—sorry, *yet* know—where she is? Or do we? She must be somewhere we've been watching, hence the necessity to draw us here away from it. You wouldn't go through all this for her to sneak back home and pick up her favorite blouse, would you? No. You'd only do this if it was really worth it. You'd only do this if you were working toward an endgame. *Bingo*. She's going after the case files, isn't she?"

"It never had to come this far," Victor said. "Gisele didn't know anything. She didn't know your name, despite what Lester Daniels told you. If you'd have left her alone, then you would have been safe." He smiled at her. "Instead, trying to protect yourself is the very thing that will bring you down."

Anderton's jaw tightened. She rose and turned to face the South African. "Get to the law firm. She's there right now."

"Let me kill this one first," the man said back.

"When you have the girl. If you don't get there in time, we'll need him to call her."

"Trust me," the South African said, "you don't want to keep him alive."

Anderton said, "I know what I'm doing. He's done. You three, go with him. Now."

Victor heard the four men hurry away, leaving one remaining mercenary with Anderton.

He looked up at her. "I'll never make that call."

She used the heel of a snakeskin boot to roll him onto his back. He was able to focus enough now to clearly see the smugness on her face. "Again, I believe you. I could have Sinclair slice you up to within an inch of your life and you still wouldn't give her up, would you? It's really quite sweet. If my life and liberty were not at stake, I could cry. I never knew hired killers could be so honorable."

Victor remained silent.

"But I don't need to do anything to you, do I? A moment ago you told me your every move without uttering a single word." She smiled her serpent's smile. "You've played a good game so far, I'll give you that. But I'm afraid you're simply not in my league."

• Chapter 71 •

Victor heard one of the Range Rovers driving away, tires squealing under the hard acceleration. The law firm was maybe fifteen minutes' drive through London's busy streets at this time of day. Gisele would be nowhere near finished by then, let alone out of the building.

"Rogan, don't take your eyes off him until I get back," Anderton said to the remaining mercenary. "I mean it. Not for a second." Then, to Victor: "Just in case you're not as hurt as you seem. I have no intention of underestimating you as you did me."

Victor looked away.

The mercenary called Rogan said, "It'll be a pleasure, ma'am."

Anderton winked at Victor and then approached the second Range Rover, the footsteps of her snakeskin boots echoing around the vast, almost empty space. Victor watched the vehicle drive out of the hangar and disappear into the night. He didn't know if she was going to join Sinclair and the other mercs, or heading somewhere else. Victor lay on the floor and thought about Gisele in the law firm, alone and vulnerable, with no idea people were on the way to kill her. He'd failed her. He'd failed her mother.

He refused to give up. While he breathed, it wasn't over.

Every inch of his body seemed to throb or ache or sting. He twisted his head until he could look at Rogan as he paced about nearby. The man had short graying brown hair. He wore black jeans and a denim jacket lined with wool. About six feet tall, solidly built, late thirties. His heavy workman's boots glistened with Victor's blood. He noticed the mercenary was clean shaven.

They made eye contact. When Victor didn't look away, the man's face creased in anger and aggression.

"What the fuck are you looking at?"

Victor didn't respond.

Rogan said, "You killed some of my best mates."

Victor spat out more blood.

"You hear me down there, you prick?"

The mercenary came closer. He put a light kick into Victor's flank.

"Forrester. Taff. McNeil. Cole," he said, punctuating each name with a kick. "They were my friends and you killed them. You rammed a fucking handgun barrel through Cole's eye socket, you sick fuck."

Victor said nothing. One corner of his mouth upturned.

White showed all round Rogan's irises. "You think that's funny, do ya?"

Hands grabbed him under the armpits and hauled him to his feet. He winced as he tried to support himself, shifting his weight onto his right foot to spare his injured left ankle. He didn't need to. The mercenary kept him upright. He was strong and had no trouble supporting Victor's weight. Rogan stared into Victor's black eyes.

"They were good lads."

"But not so good at their jobs," Victor said.

Jaw muscles bunched beneath the mercenary's skin. His grip on Victor tightened and he half scowled, half smiled.

"When that little bitch is dead, I'm going to really enjoy sending you to join her. That psycho Sinclair is going to have to fight me for the privilege of cutting you up."

Victor grinned.

Rogan shook his head, disbelieving. "Who in the name of fuck do you think you are?"

"I'm the man who's going to kill you."

He burst out laughing. Spit and sour smoker's breath struck Victor's face. If Rogan had any fatigue from holding Victor up for so long, he didn't show. Victor was glad the man was so strong.

When he stopped laughing, he said, "And, please, just for my own personal fucking amusement, tell me how you're planning on pulling that off when you're beaten to a pulp and cuffed?"

Victor stared back hard as he said, "Do you mean the handcuffs I've already picked?"

Rogan hesitated, surprised, then took a half step away—in part in the involuntary reaction to danger; in part to create a better viewing angle. His gaze dropped to see:

The handcuffs still locked around Victor's wrists.

Rogan glanced up in time to see a blur of movement before Victor's forehead collided with his nose.

The rest of his body was weak, but no punch or kick could damage the strongest bone in the human body.

The mercenary's nose was paper-delicate in comparison and he'd created the perfect amount of space between them for Victor's to generate the force to crush it flat.

Blood exploded across both Rogan's face and Victor's. The man's hands retreated from their hold on Victor to protect himself as he stumbled backward. Victor stumbled too, unable to properly support himself, but he grabbed the man's belt with both cuffed hands as he put his left leg behind Rogan's and they fell to the floor together.

His enemy was stunned from the head butt and blinded by the tears and blood in his eyes. Rogan didn't know what Victor was doing until palms pressed down over his mouth and teeth sank into the thin layer of skin and tissue to the right of his trachea.

The palms muffled the man's scream as Victor ripped a chunk out of his neck.

He turned his face away to spare it from the arcs of pressurized blood from the severed carotid artery.

Rogan was too overwhelmed by pain and terror to fight back but thrashed in panic as blood escaped his neck in machine-gun blasts.

Victor's weight pinned him down for the few seconds it took until Rogan lost consciousness. Victor rolled and lay for a moment, recovering from the exertion while the mercenary bled out next to him.

His hands were slick with blood and he wiped them on the man's clothes. He then searched through Rogan's jacket pockets, then through the pockets of his jeans. He found keys for the Audi, a Zippo lighter and cigarettes, but no handcuff key. He found the man's knife, but it was no good against his restraints. He spread his palms across the ground through the pool of bright arterial blood, but still no key.

He cleaned his hands again and forced himself onto his knees and tried to stand. A buzz of pain rushed through his head and his balance faltered. He managed to stay standing, weight balanced on his right foot. It was an improvement to be able to remain upright. Every part of his body seemed to be sending pain signals to his brain but the damaged ankle and bruised ribs appeared to be the worst of his injuries. Anderton had spared him before any irrecoverable damage had been done.

He glanced around the hangar. No sign of any handcuff keys or where they might be. He would have dislocated his thumbs, but the cuffs were on too tight and his hands too big to make such a means of escape possible. He staggered to where the Audi was parked. He opened a door and checked the glove compartment and door pockets, but still no key.

He used the vehicle to support himself and shuffled until he could rest his elbows on the front. He reached out and with both hands twisted and pulled until he detached a windshield wiper. With the aid of his teeth he tore away the rubber wiper to reveal the long, slender wiper blade.

He turned around and leaned against the hood to prop himself up while he fed one end of the wiper blade into the narrow gap where the handcuff bow fed, until it could go no farther. Despite the pain, he forced the cuff tighter so the teeth drew the end of the wiper blade farther into the mechanism, covering the next tooth and stopping it from locking. The bow could then be pulled back out of the mechanism and Victor had one hand free.

In seconds his other hand was released and the cuffs clattered against the hard floor.

Chapter 72

Lester's computer was password protected. Gisele had expected as much, but was still hoping for a minor miracle. She tried a few guesses: his date of birth, his wife's name—the usual kind of thing people had. She gave up after a couple of minutes. There was no telling how much time she had before someone would catch her. The alarm still sounded, but inside Lester's office it was a little more bearable, muted by the walls and door.

Having given up with the computer, she turned her attention to hard copies of case files. He had a filing cabinet full of them, but she limited the search to the priority cases—those with upcoming deadlines—and ones she had assisted with by scanning or copying documents or filing. She found herself reading about a man named Adeib Aziz, an Afghan policeman currently imprisoned at Bagram Airfield for killing a British intelligence officer named Maxwell Durant. She read the case against Aziz, or the lack thereof. He had been convicted based on the testimony of a single witness who had not been contactable since the conviction. Lester had taken on Aziz's appeal, working pro bono on behalf of an international human-rights charity. Lester was as ruthless and driven a barrister as Gisele knew, but he'd had a good heart too. If Aziz's case was not heard in a week's time, his appeal would be turned down by default and he would spend the rest of his life in an Afghani prison.

Could this be why the blond woman had killed Lester, and was mistakenly after Gisele—to stop Aziz from being released?

She searched further into the file, reading between the lines.

The blonde didn't want Aziz released. She'd had Lester killed to stop it happening. But why? What was so important about keeping him in prison? Unless he was innocent. If she knew he was innocent, then maybe it was she who was guilty instead. Were Aziz's conviction to be overturned, the investigation into Maxwell Durant's murder would be reopened.

Assuming Aziz had taken the fall for killing Durant, for the intervening years the woman must have thought she'd gotten away with it, that she was safe. But then Lester took on the case no one wanted. Now she was trying to protect the truth.

Gisele read on, because she couldn't believe anyone would go through so much purely to prevent Aziz's being released, regardless of the questions that might follow. There had to be something more concrete.

The file contained an afteraction report pertaining to the arrest of Aziz. The investigation and arrest had been carried out by a three-person team consisting of a private military contractor, William Sinclair, and two officers of the Intelligence Corps, Marcus Lambert and Nieve Anderton.

Gisele smiled to herself. The plan was working.

The fire alarm ceased blaring. The sudden silence star-tled her, snapping her attention from the file in hand. She dropped it. Pages scattered across the floor.

"Shit."

She tried gathering them up, but paused when she saw a line of shadow under the door to Lester's office. She held her breath as the handle turned and it opened.

"Christ, Alan," she breathed, palm moving to her chest. "You scared the hell out of me."

Big, kind Alan the security guard stood in the door-way. "I'm sorry, Miss Maynard. I didn't mean to startle you. Just checking out the . . . hey, why didn't you head to the lobby when the alarm went off?"

"Yeah, sorry about that. I assumed it was another false alarm. I've got so much work to catch up on."

He looked at her and she saw the suspicion in his gaze. "As it happens, it was the switch around the corner that was set off. You wouldn't know anything about that, would you?"

"I . . ." She shook her head. "I thought it was a drill. I'm sorry, I know I should have gone downstairs."

His searching eyes took in her hair and nonoffice at-tire, and the file pages scattered across the floor. "Perhaps you should come downstairs with me, miss."

She stood, gesturing to the door and saying, "Sure, okay. Let's go," so Alan looked away for a second, giving her time to pocket the afteraction report without his knowledge.

He ushered Gisele ahead of him into the corridor. She turned in the direction of the exit and saw a man walking through the open-plan area.

She knew he was one of them as soon as their eyes

met. He had tanned skin. He was stocky and wore khaki trousers and a leather jacket. An image flashed in her mind. This was the man who had shot at them in the hotel corridor.

Alan emerged from the office and saw the approaching man. "Who's this?"

"Never seen him before," Gisele said, making no attempt to disguise the fear she felt.

Alan picked up on it and stepped toward the man in the leather jacket.

"Be careful," Gisele said.

"Don't worry about me."

For a moment she was comforted by Alan's presence. He was so big he seemed indestructible. But then she remembered Dmitri and the others: bigger and tougher than Alan, and now all dead.

"Run along, and try not to set off the alarm again, eh?" He winked at her.

She did. As she turned the corner she heard Alan's commanding voice: "Who are you?"

"I'm the computer guy," the man replied in a South African accent.

• • •

Gisele pushed open the heavy swing door into the lady's room. She heard a muted thump from somewhere behind her as she stepped inside.

The man who wasn't a real computer guy was in the corridor outside. Gisele didn't have to look to know that he was following her. She hoped he hadn't hurt poor Alan too much. She pictured him waiting a moment to ensure Gisele was preoccupied when he entered in maybe twenty or thirty seconds. She breathed fast and hard, trying to think what to do. She was trapped. What would her companion do?

He wouldn't waste time, so neither did Gisele. She entered the farthest stall, closed and locked the door, shut the toilet lid and stood on it, then climbed up onto the cistern and over the partition wall.

She landed awkwardly on the other side, grimacing as she banged her knee against the toilet bowl. She hurried out, leaving the door wide open, and rushed into the first cubicle, put the toilet seat down, took off her shoes and then stood on top of it. She nudged the door far enough so it hid her from view but not so far that it might appear closed or locked.

The heavy swing door opened and a man's shoes clicked on the tiled floor.

Gisele's teeth clenched and her nostrils rapidly flared and contracted as she fought to control her fear and stay balanced on the toilet seat. She rested her shoes on the lid and slowly took the can of pepper spray from her handbag. The footsteps paused and she heard the door clunk shut.

For a terrible moment she thought the man would simply shoot her through the thin stall wall, but the shoes clicked again. A different sound this time, softer—the man taking a side step to view the cubicle doors. She willed him to see that the far door was the only one closed and locked and not see her deception.

Gisele listened to the sound of slow footsteps growing louder. As they came closer she could make out his shadow. She had to stop herself from crying out with relief when the shadow moved past the first cubicle without slowing. She waited. Her hands were so damp with sweat that the can of pepper spray began slipping from her grasp. The harder she squeezed it, the faster it slid.

If she dropped it and it hit the hard floor tiles . . .

She lowered her hands and caught the bottom of the can between her thighs; for the first time ever she was glad she carried plenty of weight there. While her thighs kept the can steady, she wiped the sweat from her palms.

The sound of shoes clicking on tiles ceased. Gisele pictured the man standing before the last cubicle door, maybe raising his pistol, ready to shoot.

This was it. *I trust you,* he'd said.

A loud crash indicated the man had kicked open the cubicle door.

Gisele was dropping off the toilet seat while the sound of the door banging still echoed around the room. She dashed out of her stall as the man was backing out, realizing he had been tricked.

She pushed the can up toward his turning face and pressed the button.

He roared as the vapor found his eyes.

His hands rose to protect them, and Gisele ran for her life.

Chapter 73

Sinclair followed a moment later, eyes burning and full of water, but he could still see well enough to shoot and hit. She was a canny fox, this one. He liked that. He liked that his eyes stung from the pepper spray. But there was no target to hit. She could not have run the full length of the law firm in the few seconds it took for him to give chase, so must instead be hiding. Multiple doors lined the corridor. He tried the handles as he moved, opening the unlocked doors and checking the rooms beyond without success until he reached the open-plan area.

He hoped to find her under a desk, huddled in a trembling ball. If she was hiding so, he could save the bullet and strangle her. She had a small neck and he had large hands. Perhaps one hand would be enough. He imagined her panicked gasps as he crushed her trachea between his fingers.

He decided against keeping his weapon drawn. Doing so would only be an admission of his inability to control the situation. He was in control. This was his moment.

Sinclair remembered a cold night in Helmand, terror-

izing a car of Afghans at a checkpoint, pretending he
didn't understand them as they begged and pleaded for
him not to shoot. He hadn't, but a man in the back of the
vehicle had beat his wife around the head, until she spat
out teeth, in an attempt to stop her screaming. When
Sinclair told the story, he never made it to the end without cracking up.

Sinclair stepped toward the door to a stationery cup-
board.

He opened it. Nothing.

A noise behind him. He turned to see Gisele running
across the far side of the open-plan area.

He followed. No need to run. It was too much fun to
have a premature end.

• • •

Gisele ran, rounding desks and chairs, passing the water
cooler and the color laser printer. She knew he was behind
her, but dared not look to see him chasing. She made it
down a corridor and around the corner into the reception
area. No Caroline behind the desk, as Alan hadn't given
the all-clear for people to return after the alarm.

For a second, she considered hiding behind the desk,
hoping the man in the leather jacket wouldn't think to
look there, but decided against it. She had to get out. Fast.

She pushed every elevator button.

"Come on, come on."

She heard the man's approaching footsteps. She hurriedly pushed the buttons again.

The man appeared. He smiled at her. "You've caused
us a lot of bother, missy. But this is the end of the road."
He reached under his jacket.

The elevator doors opened next to Gisele.

Her nameless companion stepped out and shot the approaching mercenary three times in the chest.

• • •

Victor led Gisele down to the ground floor and kept his palm on the small of her back as they crossed the vast lobby.

"My God," she breathed. "What the hell happened to you?"

He didn't answer. Even though he'd cleaned off much of the blood, his injuries were obvious.

When they neared the exit, he said, "There are more of them outside. They didn't see me come in, but they'll see us when we leave." He gestured toward a security guard near the revolving doors. "Stay next to him until I return."

"Hurry back," Gisele said.

Victor heaved open the door and left the office building, leaving the warm and still interior air behind and stepping into the freezing night wind that toyed with his hair and brought moisture to his swollen right eye. A page of discarded newspaper tumbled and swooshed along the pavement. On the far side of the road a young woman climbed into a taxi.

He looked both ways, surveying the locale, ready to move and shoot and fight and die if necessary. He seemed relaxed because he was relaxed. If there was any place in which he truly belonged it was in the heart of violence. He had no fear of it because he knew it was who he was.

They were waiting in case Gisele appeared. They couldn't know what had happened inside. They would make their move only when she did. For now they would leave him be, although they would not let him out of their sight. But that was exactly what he wanted.

He descended the stone steps. The wind hid the sound of his footfalls. The Range Rover was parked against the curb some thirty meters away. The lights, exterior and interior, had been extinguished, but Victor could see the shapes of three men. No features were visible, but they didn't need to be. The men who sat there were mortal enemies who would be dead before the night's end or would be Victor's killers. Victor had had many enemies. Many were still alive. But almost without exception they were a threat to him as he was to them because of his work. Hazards of the profession. Now was different. Victor would kill these men or be killed by them because of someone else.

In the Audi, Victor took the handgun from his waistband and set it between his thighs, grip up for quick access. He let the engine idle. He wanted the men in the Range Rover and anyone else watching to see the exhaust gases clouding in the cold air. He had the interior light on. He wanted his hands to be seen gripping the wheel. They would assume he was waiting. They would assume he was waiting for Gisele. They would shift physically and mentally from standby into readiness—from warm-up to poised in the starting blocks. He could feel their elevated heart rates and the buzz of adrenaline and other hormones flooding their bloodstream. He could feel theirs because he had no such sensations. His pulse thumped slow and steady.

He continued the act by glancing at the building's entrance, knowing they would see it, knowing it would only intensify their readiness. He felt their body temperatures rising, sweat beading, pupils dilating, vision focusing, hearing becoming selective. Almost.

One last misdirection: he took out his phone and held it briefly to his ear.

He mouthed, *Okay*.

Now or never.

He dropped the phone into his lap, released the hand brake, put the car in gear, stamped the accelerator, and yanked the steering wheel.

The tires squealed for traction, releasing a puff of burned rubber, then found their grip and the car launched out from the curb.

In the rearview he saw the driver of the Range Rover spring into action after a split-second delay, surprised by the sudden change in proceedings but reacting to it with impressive speed.

As Victor shot across the intersecting road, cutting through the flow of traffic, and hearing thumped horns and braking tires, he pictured frantic messages and hasty improvisations. They were chasing him because they thought they had been fooled. They had, but not as they thought. They would work it out soon, but he needed only to buy Gisele and himself a moment.

He braked hard and turned left, back end sliding out but turning into the skid to control it, then accelerated again as he drove along the north side of the office building, knowing they would think him heading to a rear exit, hoping to pick up Gisele before they could catch up.

Victor grabbed the phone as he worked the wheel in one hand, thumbed for her number, and when the line connected, shouted, "Be ready."

He didn't wait for a response. He dropped the phone and focused on the road ahead and the Range Rover he'd allowed to catch up behind.

Oncoming headlights brightened—two blurs of pale light enlarging and disappearing as they swerved through the traffic.

An orchestra of horns sounded. Brakes shrieked and tires squealed. Anticipating a collision, he fought the instinct to tense, instead allowing his body to stay relaxed and loose to lessen the chances of injury and death in event of a crash. He worked the wheel and the brake pedal, avoiding a head-on as he cut into the opposite lane to disrupt the narrative of the attacker, to make him have to think about his own survival and not just that of his target.

It worked because the oncoming Range Rover slowed—only for a second, but that hesitation told Victor his attackers, however reckless, cared more about living than winning.

Victor kept his foot on the accelerator, closing the distance to the Range Rover fast—forty meters, thirty, twenty, ten.

At five his enemy blinked in their game of death and heaved the wheel as Victor had known with certainty he would. They passed within inches, tearing off each other's side mirror, making both cars rock with the change of air pressure.

Victor stamped the brake and pulled up on the hand brake as he sped toward a coming intersection. Smoke was released with a scream from the tires and the car's back end swung around. Victor didn't try to fight it and let the vehicle go into a spin until it had performed a one-eighty, then accelerated hard and controlled the wheel until he was racing back to the law firm.

• • •

Sinclair groaned as he climbed to his feet. His Dragon Skin vest had caught the three rounds meant for his heart, but he'd still blacked out. He didn't know what had happened with Norimov's hired killer and Rogan, but the specifics mattered little.

The assassin was trouble and he was good. The presence of the killer necessitated the drawing of Sinclair's pistol. He could not afford to run into him unarmed and defenseless. He knew Gisele's protector would not offer him the kind of sportsmanship he would offer in return. Sinclair would not hunt a tiger from the elevated safety of an elephant's back. He would meet him on the ground, in undergrowth, man to beast. Shame on the hunter who hung his trophy without earning it.

He moved, content to hurry now that he was pursuing an equivalent and not a child. Properly employed haste, like the unflinching application of violence, was necessary here.

Another man might find rage in the continued interference of the assassin, and indeed Sinclair knew well his own capacity for emotion. Getting shot, even armored, was no fun, but the dull ache of the blunt-force trauma to his chest energized him instead.

He savored the pain and the thrill of base savagery; it fermented in his soul.

Sinclair rushed through the offices. Wade's voice barked through his earpiece:

"We've lost him. We've lost him."

Sinclair said, "What about the girl?"

"He left alone. He—"

"You idiots," Sinclair spat. "It was a trick. He's doubled back."

• • •

Victor braked hard outside and dashed up the steps as fast as his injured ankle let him. Gisele saw him before he reached the doors and came out, still scared but glad to see him.

"Where are they?"

"Close. We don't have much time."

She headed to the car, knowing it was the one he'd driven because of the open driver's door and running engine.

"No," Victor said, stopping her. "They'll be looking for it."

He went to hail a taxi but saw a minicab against the opposite curb. He grabbed Gisele's wrist and they hurried across the road. He pulled open the rear door and bundled Gisele inside. He climbed in after her.

"Oi," the driver said. "Bookings only, fella. You'll have to sling your hook."

"Drive us a mile south and I'll pay you for a day."

The driver thought about it for a moment. "No bull-shit?"

Victor put his hand on the door handle. "If we don't get going this instant then the deal's off."

"All right, all right," he said as he released the hand brake. "Just don't tell the guv'nor."

The car pulled away from the curb. Victor scanned the area. In the rearview mirror he saw a black Range Rover turn onto the street.

Chapter 74

Gisele sat behind the driver. Victor sat close to her so he could use the rearview mirror with an unobstructed view. He grimaced against the pain of many wounds while he watched the reflection of the Range Rover. It accelerated until it reached the law firm, then came to an abrupt halt outside, near the abandoned Audi. They thought he was inside.

He noticed the driver looking at him in the rearview—looking at his battered face and the blood on his clothes.

"What's going on?" Gisele asked, breathing hard. "How did they know?"

"The plan didn't work. It's my fault. I underestimated her. I'm sorry, I should never have left you alone."

"It was my choice as much as yours."

He kept his gaze on the mirror, seeing doors open on the Range Rover and two men rush out and up the steps to the building. He must have looked for a second too long because Gisele saw him and her head began turning.

"Don't," he told. "Keep looking forward."

She did, her face tense and her lips locked. He saw her palms rest on her thighs.

"It's okay," he said to her, even though it was not.

She nodded. She didn't believe him. She trusted her own instincts more than his words, even if no one had ever wanted her dead until a week ago. Victor couldn't remember such a time.

The driver noticed the tension. "Is everything okay back there?"

Victor said, "We're fine."

He saw in the mirror as the driver's gaze flicked to Gisele and lingered a moment.

"Are you all right, love?"

Victor reached out a hand to rest on hers, to tell her what to do, but she'd already said, "I get travel sickness."

The driver said, "Don't worry, darlin.' I'll take it nice and smooth."

• • •

Sinclair listened to Wade's sputtering excuses as he strode outside the law firm. The black Audi had been abandoned on the street, driver's door open and engine left running. No other door was open. Wade was still providing useless updates as Sinclair stepped forward to the edge of the steps, looking left and right along the street, seeing vehicles and pedestrians.

At the east end of the street, a cab had its turn signal on. Two human shapes sat in the back. At this range, no details were discernible.

I see you.

Sinclair shoved Wade aside and drew his pistol. He adopted a shooting position, one eye closed while the other peered along the weapon's iron sights, focusing on the smaller of the two shapes, ignoring the blur of colors and shapes that surrounded it. His brow was creased in concentration. His lips were closed and his jaw set, nostrils expanding and contracting with each deep, regular breath. Beads of sweat formed along his hairline. He slowed his breathing and with it his heart rate. He timed the beats, index finger compressing on the trigger—two pounds of pressure, then four, six, and holding the tension there, ready to squeeze a little harder; just another half-pound of force to trip the trigger and activate the firing mechanism.

The world around him ceased to exist.

I was born to do this, Sinclair said to himself. *Never miss. Never fail.*

The recoil kicked and he felt the reverberations flow all the way to his shoulder. He loved that feeling. The mechanical caress, dull and strong. As a child, it had hurt. Now he missed the pain.

Life is pain.

The pistol's suppressor caught the escaping super-heated gases as they exploded from the muzzle, deadening the sound but not killing it. The rumble of city life did that, wrapping up and smothering the weapon's bark in a blanket of car exhausts, voices, and footsteps.

Chapter 75

In the mirror, Victor saw the South African on the steps outside the law firm's building, lit by streetlights, haloing the rain around him. He had a handgun drawn. They were out of conceivable range—an impossible shot, almost—but the man adopted a shooting stance. For a second, Victor didn't believe he would take it.

He grabbed the back of Gisele's head and forced it down.

The rear windshield cracked around a small hole.

The minicab driver contorted in his seat, dead the instant the round punctured his skull and penetrated his brain. The mess was absolute. The deformed and tumbling bullet blew out the front of his forehead, the pressure wave following it exploding the skull, spraying bone, brain, and blood in a wide arc that splattered over the windshield and the car's interior.

The bullet continued its trajectory, leaving a fist-sized hole in the cab's front windscreen. Another followed it, tearing through the passenger's seat and dashboard and burying itself somewhere in the engine block.

Victor, keeping low, forced himself between the front seats and grabbed hold of the steering wheel. He heard horns and saw flashes of headlights and swerving cars. He felt the reverberations of more rounds striking the rear of the car. The side mirror shattered.

Metal screeched against metal as the right-side wheel well scraped along the door of a parked BMW. Shocked passersby stared as Victor fought to control the cab. The low whine of the engine and the wail of the BMW's intruder alarm filled his ears. Next to him, Gisele made herself small in the seat. She was scared but she didn't scream or panic or distract him with questions.

No more bullets hit the car as he pulled himself between the seats. They were now out of reach of even the gunman's exceptional skills. Victor reached down to activate the driver's seat adjuster to slide it back the full distance before climbing on top of the dead driver. He forced himself into a driving position and accelerated.

He kept as low as he could, which wasn't much, but the driver's body would provide some protection from further shots.

He took the first turn he saw, swerving left and onto a side street, clipping the bumper of a parked car, the roar of the revving engine echoed by the narrow distance between tall buildings. A guy in a suit went to cross the street ahead, but darted back when he saw the speeding cab.

Something was wrong with the vehicle's handling—bullet damage to a tire, maybe—and Victor struggled to keep it straight.

"Seat belt," he said to Gisele.

The wheel shed the peeling tire and it flipped and cartwheeled into the air. The bare wheel struck asphalt and sparked. Victor lost control on the slick surface, fought

the erratic swerves, jolting in his seat as the car sideswiped
a bus. He caught a flash of panicked faces through the
glass before rebounding away, smelling the acrid stench
of burned steel from the grinding wheel.

He fought to keep control as the nose of the cab exited the side street. He couldn't stop it from careering
into the lane of oncoming traffic. A horn sounded and
the vehicle spun as another bus collided with a rear-wheel
well. Tires screeched and left burned rubber on the tarmac. Glass pebbles from a broken window scattered
across the road.

Stunned pedestrians stopped and watched as the car
spun into a row of parked vehicles, denting bodywork
and breaking more windows. Alarms sounded.

The bumper clipped the rear of a taxi, knocking that
vehicle forward and further distorting the erratic path
Victor was taking. The tire-free wheel collided with a
curb at an angle and jumped it. He worked the wheel and
punched the horn when he saw he couldn't prevent the
cab from crashing into a bus stop. The two men waiting
for the next bus ran clear.

Headlights glowed and flared through the raindrops,
leaving smears of red and light as the wipers, still working, swept them away. The front crumple zone had done
its job and absorbed the majority of the impact, turning
the cab into an unrecognizable misshapen heap of metal,
but one that kept Victor alive, if not unscathed.

He heaved open the warped driver's door and stumbled out of the wreckage, bloody and disorientated. Gisele
climbed out too and he ushered her forward, shielding her
with his body as he staggered away, heading for the cover
of parked cars and storefronts. He reached for the gun in
his waistband but grasped only air, realizing too late that

he'd had it in his lap while driving and in the crash it must have ended up in the foot well or under a seat. He couldn't go back for it.

They had to keep moving. Their pursuers were close but their line of sight was impeded by the bus that had hit the cab and now blocked the intersection. The other people on the street didn't realize what had caused the crash but backed away from him anyway because he was covered in the cabdriver's blood and walking with determination instead of staggering like someone scared or in pain and in need of help. The blood dispelled any chance of slipping away unnoticed, but the dispersing effect it had on other people meant he could walk faster through the crowd.

• • •

Wade managed to maneuver the Range Rover around the bus by going up onto the pavement. Ahead the crashed minicab sat, damaged and dented vehicles near it, glass glittering on the road. A crowd had gathered, watching from a short distance away as a few compassionate or ghoulish individuals edged closer, peering into the cab.

Beautiful chaos, Sinclair thought, savoring the scene before him, reveling in the panic and aroused by the sight of destruction.

He breathed in air both sweet and terrible.

"Ease up," Sinclair said, gun clutched in both hands but held out of sight, ready to be snapped up and put into action.

Wade lessened the pressure on the accelerator pedal, slowing the vehicle as they passed the wreckage. No one inside.

"There," Sinclair said, pointing to a crowd of people

in the distance, a man and woman pushing their way through. He gestured to the two mercenaries in the back. "Pursue on foot. We'll head them off."

• • •

Gisele hurried. Her legs weren't moving as fast as she compelled them—shock was taking hold. Victor took her by the arm and pulled her along, limping on his injured ankle.

A man in front of them stumbled and fell. The echo of the shot arrived a split second later. Victor just about made it out over the background noise. The man on the ground wasn't dead, but the round had gone through a shoulder blade and exited through his arm. Blood quickly pooled under him. Another man screamed in shock and horror. Someone shouted for an ambulance.

Victor kept moving, accelerating into a jog and pushing through the crowd with one hand while the other held Gisele close to him. More shots sounded but no one was hit in front of him. Behind, he couldn't be sure, with the screaming and panic.

He exited the street at the first available opportunity, heading right into an alleyway.

Gisele said, "I'm hit. I'm bleeding."

He stopped and looked at her, pushing her back up against the wall of the alley so he could examine her. She touched her head. There was blood on her fingers and in her hair. He turned her head and separated her hair.

"You're okay," he assured her. "It's a scratch. From before."

At the end of the alleyway, Victor slowed to a walk and took Gisele's right hand in his left. He relaxed his face and they stepped out together, side by side.

"Try to smile," he said.

He didn't look to see if she was. He kept his eyes moving—gaze sweeping the street, the cars, the pedestrians, the buildings—looking for threats. Traffic was heavy and slow, as were the crowds of walkers. London at any time of the year, overcrowded and congested. He liked that. Gisele slowed him down, and the packed street offered good cover. The shootings one block away were irrelevant here. No one knew what had taken place.

Victor led Gisele across the road, dodging through the traffic, and down a covered precinct. The street beyond was quiet—few passing cars; few scattered pedestrians. He looked both ways along it, looking for the Range Rover or any other vehicle that could be a threat. Nothing. He listened for the sound of pursuers. No rushing footsteps echoing. Yet.

The farther they walked, the denser the crowds became. Tourists were everywhere, identifiable by their casual pace at odds with and offensive to the harried Londoners.

Sirens wailed. Victor caught a glimpse of a police car passing across an intersection up ahead, heading to the site of the crash and shooting. More would be coming. Good. The more cops in the area, the fewer opportunities their pursuers would have and the fewer risks they would be willing to take.

He took her into an adjoining side street. He wasn't sure where it would lead. He knew London well—as he knew any city where he had ever operated—but not every route.

The street exited onto a road lined with boutiques and coffee shops. Brave men and women sat at outside tables under retractable awnings and heat lamps, sipping steaming drinks and smiling and chatting. Victor led Gisele to the other side of the street, walking fast to slip through the traffic, ignoring the scorn of motorists who never got used to Londoners darting in front of them. A cyclist rang a bell in annoyance after swerving to miss them.

A woman in a woolen hat spotted the blood on Victor's clothes and trickling down Gisele's face. The woman nudged her partner and Victor read *Look at those two* on her lips. Her partner tilted up his reading glasses to get a better view. Victor reversed direction, heading north, away from the couple.

He saw a tall man some twenty meters away, a shadow of stubble around a mouth set with determination. Another mercenary followed a little way behind.

"In here," Victor said.

He shoved open the door to a restaurant and pulled Gisele inside behind him.

· Chapter 76 ·

The restaurant had a high ceiling and ornate metal tables and chairs. Similarly ornate mirrors covered the walls. Victor waved a hand to dismiss a waiter's "Table for two?" and hurried through the room, eyes picking out the ways in and therefore out, seeking an exit instead of a way deeper into the building. His instincts told him to head for the kitchen and an inevitable back door, but he felt a breeze on his face from an entranceway below a sign for the toilets.

A waitress overloaded with bowls and plates stepped out in front of him and was thrown out of his path, sending soup and salad across the floor. Gisele apologized on his behalf.

Through the entranceway, he turned to follow the corridor, saw doors leading off to the men's and lady's toilets and the fire exit at the far end propped ajar to let an air funnel inside.

From behind him, he heard the crash of the restaurant door being flung open.

"Run," Victor said.

• • •

The two pursuing mercenaries charged through the restaurant, knocking diners and staff aside, jumping over the spilled food and puddles of soup, knowing exactly where their targets had gone, thanks to a waitress yelling in the direction of the toilets.

They entered the corridor, moving fast, the first leading with longer strides, heading for the open fire exit, the second following a meter behind, view blocked by the taller man.

He drew a pistol from beneath his jacket.

• • •

Which Victor batted out of his hand as he charged out of the adjacent men's room, slamming the man into the wall with his momentum, elbowing him in the face, sinking him to his knees.

The lead man turned and snapped his pistol up, but not fast enough to stop Victor from stepping inside and striking him in the chest with a short left punch. He staggered backward, gasping, dropping his weapon to reach out with both hands, searching for purchase on the walls to his left and right.

The scrape of metal alerted Victor to the man behind him going for the gun while still on his knees. He scooped it up, twisted around one hundred eighty degrees, arms straightening and aiming.

A side kick sent the gun out of the mercenary's hands for a second time. He rolled out of the way of Victor's next attack, but Victor didn't try for a third because he knew the taller man would be recovered behind him. Victor spun around, blocked the knife thrust meant for his back, dodged a second, grabbed an outstretched arm when the third came and swung his attacker face-first into the men's-room door.

Victor disarmed the man of his knife, slipped the second man's counter, then dropped him to the floor with a kick to the back of the knee, creating the space for him to strike the taller mercenary, catching him in the mouth with a right elbow. Then Victor sent him sprawling by hitting him in the jaw with the heel of his palm.

He went for the closest gun, but the prone man recovered fast and charged him from behind, powering him into a wall, making him toe the pistol away as he stumbled. He caught his attacker with a backward head butt, then twisted around to follow up with another head butt, with his forehead impacting the bridge of the mercenary's nose—not shattering it, because he was already stumbling back, but sending blood streaming from the nostrils.

He ran because the tall man was rushing for the second gun and he was going to reach it before Victor got to him.

The gun clacked and a bullet took a chunk from the fire exit as Victor dashed through it. He veered out of the line of fire an instant before a second round buried itself in the brickwork opposite.

The fire exit led out into a narrow alleyway just wide enough for a car to squeeze down. Victor headed right, as he had instructed Gisele to do, and found her staring at him, tense from the gunfire.

• • •

Sinclair heard the gunshots too. They were muted by a suppressor and subsonic ammunition, but he heard them all the same. He stood outside the Range Rover, holding an MP5 out of sight behind the open rear door.

A voice through his earpiece: "We've lost him in the restaurant . . . In pursuit. He's heading west."

"Stay back until I say otherwise," Sinclair replied. "I have him."

The mouth of the alleyway was fifteen meters away on the far side of the street. The gunshots had come from that direction. He waited. The target and her protector appeared. Sinclair stepped out of cover, began bringing up the submachine gun, when Wade said, "Careful. Cops."

Sinclair glanced to where a police car had stopped at the end of the street, no doubt looking for the culprits responsible for the recent crash and shooting.

"Get in the motor," Wade screamed. "We gotta move out."

The siren grew rapidly louder as the police car sped closer. Sinclair didn't look. He didn't need to.

"Fuck 'em," Sinclair said, raising his weapon.

• • •

Victor saw a man on the far side of the street, partially shielded by the open rear door of the Range Rover. The man wore khaki trousers and a leather jacket. The South African. The man called Sinclair, who had made the near-impossible shot that killed the cabdriver. Though mostly out of sight, Victor could see the fat, integrated suppressor of an MP5SD held in cover.

Sinclair wasn't looking his way. He was glancing to his right, at the cop car pulled over at the mouth of the street. The MP5 started to rise.

"Gun!" Victor yelled, and pointed in the hope the police officers would see.

Instead of hanging around to find out, he darted to

his right, away from the gunman, dragging Gisele down into the cover of a parked vehicle.

• • •

The cop car skidded to a halt near Sinclair before he'd found the shot. All he needed was an instant, a heartbeat, but it didn't come. In his peripheral vision he saw the armed-response officers exiting their car, weapons up.

"Don't fucking move." They came forward. "Hands in the air. Drop the gun."

"As you wish."

He released the MP5 and it clattered on the road surface. The first cop approached Sinclair while the other stayed back, covering.

"Turn around. Keep your hands up."

Sinclair did as instructed.

The cop came closer, putting his gun away to take out handcuffs. He stood behind Sinclair. The cop reached up and took hold of Sinclair's right wrist, but didn't complete the maneuver.

Sinclair wrenched his arm down and spun to the right before the cop had a chance to act. Now facing him, Sinclair slammed his knee into the cop's groin and with his left hand pulled the pistol from the holster in one fluid move.

Even if the other cop had reacted fast enough he couldn't have taken the shot. Sinclair was using his partner as cover.

He pushed the Glock's muzzle against the closest cop's ribs and fired three times. Before the corpse had hit the ground the gun was raised and the second officer was flailing backward, taken out with a double tap to the sternum. A third between the eyes followed.

Sinclair turned back toward his prey, but they were gone. At the end of the street, the two guys who had pursued on foot were boarding Wade's Range Rover. Sinclair approached.

"You lunatic," Wade yelled at him. "You've fucked us all. I'm done with this shit."

Sinclair executed him with a single shot to the face.

He looked at the remaining two mercenaries. "Anything to add?"

They shook their heads. Sinclair pulled Wade's corpse from the driver's seat and onto the road. He climbed in.

"This is Unit Two," Anderton's voice said through the radio. "I see them."

· Chapter 77 ·

The second Range Rover turned onto the street ahead of Victor and Gisele. They couldn't turn back—that would mean heading in the direction of their pursuers. There were no alleys or side streets leading off. To the right lay an impassable wall of brick with barred windows. To the left plywood rose two and a half meters, securing a construction site beyond.

"This way," Victor said.

He stood before the plywood with his hands cupped as the Range Rover accelerated toward them. Gisele didn't hesitate. She used her left foot to push off and he heaved her up. She cried out as she landed on the other side. He followed, leaping up and hauling himself over. He dropped down and pulled Gisele to her feet.

He grimaced, his injured ankle worsening from the drop, but they pressed on, scrambling down a slope onto an expanse of cracked asphalt stained with red building sand. There were huge piles of sand and gravel at one end of the area, a portable office cabin at the other. Directly ahead was the steel frame of a ten-story building.

Behind them, a section of plywood collapsed as one of the Range Rovers crashed through it, blasting chunks of wood into the air. The vehicle tipped forward and dropped a meter before its front tires hit the slope and its suspension absorbed the impact.

The only way to go was onward into the shelter of the partially constructed building. The Range Rover roared down the slope behind them. Victor and Gisele passed between steel columns, stepping up onto the poured concrete floor. The ceiling above was concrete too. Construction materials and cables lay everywhere. Some walls had been erected. In places, plastic sheeting formed temporary barriers. He glanced over his shoulders to see their pursuers gaining with every second.

"Keep going through until you reach the other side," Victor said to Gisele. "Then find somewhere to hide. Don't come out until you hear my voice." He gave her the mercenary's knife. "Take this."

She tried to push the weapon back into his hand. "No. You take it. You need it."

"Do as I say, Gisele. Or we're both dead."

She looked at it, then at him. "What are you going to do?"

He didn't answer because she already knew. *"Go."*

Victor watched her hurry away. In seconds she was lost in the darkness. He turned around, eased himself into position, side-on behind a support column, and waited. Their enemies were near, frantically chasing for them, high on the thrill of the hunt—there was nothing quite like it—and intensified by the fear of failure. Victor would use that against them.

He rocked his head from side to side to crack his neck. His hands tingled.

Death was close.

• • •

The Range Rover had blown a tire and collided with a horizontal stack of girders. Steam billowed from under the hood and it struggled to reverse, wheels throwing out great sprays of wet red building sand that painted its black bodywork and coated windows. The mercenaries inside abandoned it.

There was no denying it: the vehicle was a wreck. The noises emanating from the engine were of a beast wounded and succumbing to the cruel hand of mortality. They drew their weapons and waited for Sinclair to join them.

Using hand gestures, he told them what to do.

He moved noiselessly through the construction site, silenced MP5 out before him, gaze focused along the iron sights. Where he looked, the muzzle pointed. He was eager to kill, to finish this. Not for fear of police intervention, but for his own personal satisfaction. He lived only to see death. He breathed slow, regular breaths. He was excited but calm in battle. The sweat tasted like honey on his lips.

He had heard the sound of plastic sheeting flapping in the wind. Somewhere in the darkness was a killer with a gun. Sinclair moved slowly. He had all the time in the world. He knew this was it. His enemy was lying in wait, ready to ambush.

Not that Sinclair felt at risk. He was the predator. He sat at the very top of the food chain, every other living thing below him. His prey.

He pictured the killer, gambling that they would be rash or stupid. Hoping they were going to walk into his trap.

Praying, more like.

Sinclair had set a trap of his own.

He'd signaled for the two mercs to move forward while he circled around the flank. However good Norimov's assassin was, he didn't have eyes in the back of his head.

The two men would die, serving as bait to bring Sinclair's prey out into the open.

He would feast on them all.

· Chapter 78 ·

Victor waited in the shadows. He crouched low, where it was darkest, listening to the quiet scrape of shoes on concrete or the crunch of heel on gravel, noting when they broke apart and formed to separate sounds, one growing increasingly quieter while the other grew louder. The sounds were close, but they overlapped and echoed around the space. Victor waited. The two men were moving too fast. They were attempting caution but too anxious to make it work. Adrenaline and limited visibility were not conducive to accurate special awareness.

If he could take the first out without the second's knowledge, the second wouldn't be a problem. He changed positions, closing the distance between himself and the first man. He stood side-on to another column, watching the man's shadow approach.

Victor sprang out of cover, but his ankle slowed him. He took the man by surprise, but was not fast enough to take him down noiselessly.

The mercenary managed to squeeze the trigger, but the weapon was already twisted away from Victor. Muted muzzle flashes brightened the darkness before Victor knocked the gun out of his hand an instant later. It clanged off a steel column.

Victor dropped his forehead into his enemy's face, darting back at the same time as the man recoiled, then turning to intercept the second gunman, who was responding to the noise, hurrying through the darkness, gun up. The second gunman failed to get his sights lined up on Victor, who was moving laterally, disappearing behind columns and partially constructed walls. He reappeared a moment later, coming at the gunman from his flank.

Victor caught the second man in the face with the edge of his right palm, then across the top of the gun-holding hand with his left forearm. Shock and pain overloaded his nervous system, jolting the weapon from the man's grip. The mercenary fought back, fast and strong, trying to hit Victor with hooks and elbows.

He slipped aside, waiting for his opponent's overeagerness to create an opening, too slow and weak to exploit the man's lack of skill until he left himself exposed. Victor slammed him with an elbow. The man lost his footing and collapsed to the floor, down but still conscious, cheekbone broken.

Victor grabbed the pistol, not hearing the first mercenary until he was already on him, grappling, trying to get the gun out of his grip. He was not the best fighter but was bigger and stronger and uninjured.

The weapon was pushed upward, forcing Victor's arms above his head, using his extra reach and strength in an attempt to free the weapon. A kick to the side of the man's knee took four inches from his height as he sank downward. Victor exploited the momentary weakness to pull their arms down and slam his enemy's fist against a steel column.

A smear of blood was left on the metal, but the man didn't let go, so Victor did, letting the gun fall from his fingers. It struck the ground and the toe of his shoe sent it skidding away.

His enemy released him as he knew he would and went for his throat, but Victor was already moving, using his greater agility to slip from the grapple and land a solid punch to the man's chest.

The impact knocked the mercenary back a step, but he was as tough as he was strong and within a second he'd recovered. He rushed Victor, who timed the inevitable takedown attempt and stepped aside, letting the man stumble into space, losing his balance and recovering too slowly to stop Victor from leaping onto his back and snaking an arm around his neck until the pit of his elbow was at the front of the mercenary's throat.

The second man was on his feet already and going for his gun, so Victor released the choke and went after him, grabbing the outstretched pistol and fist as they turned his way, then wrenching them down and pulling toward him, muzzle harmlessly pointed at the floor, tipping his enemy off-balance. The man yelled in surprise and then in pain as Victor ripped the gun from his grip and smashed it into his face. The first impact dropped him to his knees. The next opened up his skull.

Victor turned, seeing the surviving mercenary going for his own disarmed pistol and scooping it up into his hands, but immediately letting it fly from his grasp as he contorted from the four bullets Victor put into him.

He glimpsed Gisele in the darkness and motioned for her to come to him. She did, keeping low and moving fast. He led her back the way they had entered.

A noise. He pushed her into the cover provided by the crashed Range Rover as an MP5SD opened fire.

"Keep down. Get behind a wheel."

Gisele did, cowering as bullets slammed into the vehicle shielding them, puckering the bodywork with holes, cracking glass, making the car reverberate with multiple impacts.

The subsonic nine-millimeter rounds fired from the MP5 had too little power to pass all the way through the car, but it wouldn't protect them for much longer. Victor didn't need to put his head into the line of fire to know the gunman was stalking closer. There was nowhere to run to.

He returned fire, shooting blindly to keep the mercenary at bay, before the pistol jammed, the slide not locked forward. Blood on the weapon had dirtied the chamber and the next round failed to seat. Victor abandoned it and shuffled to where the car's fuel inlet was located. He gestured for Gisele to give him back the knife, reversed his grip, and drove the blade through the car's bodywork approximately twenty centimeters below the inlet. Metal squawked as he tugged it free. He waited a second. Nothing.

Gisele whispered, "What are you doing?"

Victor stabbed with the knife again, five centimeters lower to account for the fuel tank being approximately a quarter full. Which was more useful to him than a fuller tank. This time when he pulled the blade free, petrol trickled out of the hole.

He stabbed twice more to widen the hole and soaked a handkerchief in the petrol. He stuffed it into the hole and looked at Gisele.

"When I say go, run like you've never run before. Okay?"

"Where to?"

"Anywhere that's not here. Find somewhere to hide and don't come out until the police arrive."

She nodded. He lit the handkerchief with Rogan's lighter.

• • •

Sinclair kept his index finger depressed on the trigger until the magazine emptied. Brass clinked on the ground and crunched underfoot as he moved to get a better angle, releasing the spent magazine and slamming in a second.

He stalked closer to the road. He had the MP5 up, stock comfortable against his shoulder, eyes peering along the iron sights.

Without losing focus on his prey he continued to move in a semicircle, seeking a line of sight. He released a quick burst to keep them in place, to make them hesitant to leave the protection of the vehicle. Then the killer yelled, *"Move!"* and he rose from cover, sprinting away from the bullet-riddled car as the woman did the same. They set off in opposite directions and it made Sinclair hesitate for an instant, unsure who to aim at first.

He swung the MP5 to track the girl, putting the iron sights in front of her to account for the speed of her movement. Hitting a moving target was not about aiming at the target, but knowing where the target would be by the time the bullets reached their mark.

But he hesitated because orange light glowed in the darkness, casting flickering shadows. Fire. Near the vehicle's fuel inlet.

That's not good.

He turned and ran.

The burning handkerchief ignited the petrol vapor, which ignited the liquid petrol and oxygen inside the enclosed fuel tank.

The resulting explosion sent a huge gout of flame flowing from the car. The overpressure wave picked Sinclair from his feet and tossed him to the ground. Searing heat washed over him.

He coughed as black smoke and fumes flowed over him. He didn't know he'd been knocked down until he tried to move, but his body wasn't responding as it should. With difficulty, he managed to sit up. He then stood, a little wobbly but strength and coordination coming back to him as the sounds reaching his ears grew louder.

He retrieved his submachine gun and headed after the girl. However much he wanted to kill Norimov's assassin, that guy was a pet project. It was the girl who truly mattered.

Another time, sport.

Through the swirling black smoke, a figure leaped at him.

· Chapter 79 ·

Sinclair used the MP5 to parry Victor's thrust, knocking the knife from his grip but leaving himself exposed to the punch Victor connected with. The South African grunted and flailed forward, twisting around as he stumbled, bringing his submachine gun up, aiming at Victor—

Who was fast enough to grab the weapon before Sinclair could aim it, one hand on the barrel, the other on the stock, directing it upward, muzzle pointed at the ceiling, but also twisting it against the rotation of Sinclair's wrists. He had no option to release it or suffer a break.

Victor tossed the weapon. The gun was too long and therefore too impractical to employ at such close range. If he tried, he would only be disarmed as his enemy had been.

It sailed through the air, hitting a wall, crunching broken glass as it hit the floor somewhere in the darkness.

"You should have taken the bullet," Sinclair said. "It would have saved you a lot of pain."

Victor had his guard up in time to ward off the subsequent attack, and they traded blows, some scoring hits, others parried, neither landing anything meaningful until Victor was hit with an open-palm blow to the chest, knocking him off his unstable balance. He slipped and blocked another. A third hit him in the side of the ribs. He sagged, and risked a sweep at Sinclair's load-bearing leg.

The lingering effects of his injuries slowed him and the sweep was checked with a kick, jolting him off-balance, restricting his movement enough for Sinclair to grab him by the jacket and swing him ninety degrees and into the wall. Victor responded with a head butt now that they were close, but again he was too slow or his enemy expected it, and the attack missed, only glancing the South African's skull, causing no real damage.

Sinclair backed off to create space and responded with a forward kick. His heel missed Victor's pelvis by an inch as he sidestepped and grabbed the outstretched leg before Sinclair could withdraw it, pulling him closer, feinting another head butt that made Sinclair twist away, putting himself farther off-balance. A short sweep put him on the ground, hard.

Victor stamped down but Sinclair caught the foot before it could crack ribs and twisted to break Victor's one good ankle, but Victor turned with the movement to save the joint.

The South African released him, rolling away from his vulnerable position on the ground and was fast on his feet, attacking even faster, going for the takedown.

Victor had been expecting it, but couldn't react in time to avoid it altogether. He broke the fall by rolling with the impact, going for where lay a section of pipe. Sinclair's grip was not secure enough to stop him, but he was on top of Victor before he could employ the weapon. Sinclair batted it out of Victor's hand, who then blocked the first punches aimed at his head, twisting and rocking to lessen the damage of those that got through his guard.

Sinclair pushed his forearm against Victor's throat, leaning forward to apply extra pressure but leaning too far. Victor grabbed him by his jacket and wrenched him off-balance. He gave up the choke to stop himself from falling, but Victor bridged with his hips and pushed the South African clear. As he rolled onto his back, Sinclair tugged a knife free from a belt sheath and stabbed the point down at Victor's chest.

It caught his triceps as he scrambled away, grabbing a woven rubble sack as he rose to his feet, more slowly than his enemy. He took another slash to his arm before he had the sack stretched between both hands. He used it as a shield to turn away attacks as he backed up, creating distance, waiting and timing. He knew he was too slow and too weak to match his opponent otherwise.

His timing was good, but his reflexes were dulled. He caught the incoming thrust with the sack, stopping the blade from puncturing his ribs and the heart beneath, but he couldn't prevent it from slicing through his shirt and skin. He gritted his teeth and his arms shook with the strain of keeping the knife point from puncturing farther. Sinclair was slightly shorter but far stronger than Victor in his injured state. He had the advantage of leverage, though—better braced, while Sinclair was coming forward, head not in line with his hips.

Victor wrapped the sack around Sinclair's arm and stepped away. Not fast enough to stop the knife cutting him again, but fast enough so that Sinclair stumbled forward under his own exertion. Before he could recover his balance, Victor used the sack wrapped around the arm to swing Sinclair around and into a pile of cement bricks. He tumbled over them but regained control, landing on his feet, charging Victor.

The torn sack struck Sinclair in the face, blinding him long enough for Victor to land a front kick into his chest, propelling him into a temporary wall and knocking a safety sign away from its mounting. Sinclair lashed out with the knife, catching Victor as he followed up with a punch, drawing blood from a shallow cut to his shoulder.

Victor grabbed the knife-holding wrist in one hand and used the other to drive Sinclair back into the wall, trying to impale his skull on metal rods exposed by the dismounted sign, but only gouging the scalp. Blood seeped through his hair and down his neck.

The South African ignored the wound and slammed his knee into Victor's abdomen, doubling him over, but he whipped his head up as Sinclair tried to wrap an arm around his neck, catching him under the chin with the top of his skull, cracking teeth and stunning him long enough to twist the knife from his fingers and into his own grip.

He attacked, thrusting with the knife, but far too slow to score a hit on the South African. Sinclair spat out blood. "You'll have to do better than that, sport."

Victor ignored him, attacking again as Sinclair circled, moving to the left—away from the knife—arms outstretched, hands ready to parry and try to catch hold of Victor, palms turned inward to keep the vulnerable arteries on the insides of his forearms protected.

Sinclair stayed light on his feet, always moving, careful not to present a static target for when his opponent struck. The injured ankle restricted Victor's movements too much to exploit the weapon in his hand. He couldn't cover distance fast enough. Sinclair easily outmaneuvered him, scoring with kicks and punches when Victor missed thrusts and slashes. And each blow further weakened and slowed him. He spotted the MP5 in the shadows, but not close enough to risk going for.

"There's no dishonor in giving up," Sinclair said as Victor reeled from an elbow to the face. "We both know this is only going to end one way."

Sinclair was too patient to try anything risky. He didn't need to. Victor kept attacking because he had no other option, trying feints even though he realized he had neither the speed to trap his enemy nor the strength to overpower him.

A kick to the thigh sent agony detonating through Victor's leg and he dropped to one knee, slashing with the knife to keep Sinclair from closing the distance.

The South African laughed at him. "Now, this is just cruel. Have some dignity, sport. I promise I'll make it quick."

Victor maintained eye contact as he stood.

Sinclair nodded in understanding. "Okay. Have it your way."

He glanced around, saw where the section of metal pipe rested on the floor a couple of meters away, and scooped it up into his hand. Victor had no choice but to let him. He wasn't fast enough to intercept.

Sinclair said, "Time to put you out of your misery."

He approached. The pipe was almost a meter in length, far outranging the knife in Victor's hand. He knew Sinclair would be every bit as focused as he had been before, picking his moment to exploit his weapon's better range. One decent strike would be all it took to shatter bone.

So Victor reversed his grip, grasped the point between finger and thumb, and threw the knife.

Sinclair hadn't been expecting that. He was too focused on his own strategy, not Victor's; too patient to make the kill.

The blade struck Sinclair in the neck, a little to the left of center, five centimeters above the clavicle. His eyes widened and he stumbled back a step. He didn't reach for it straightaway. He maintained his defenses. Until the blood pushed out from either side of the blade and rained down his chest.

He knew he was finished but he wasn't dead yet.

He dropped to one knee and Victor was running, pain fierce in his ankle, because he knew Sinclair was going for a backup pistol in an ankle holster.

Victor dived to the ground and slid, scooping up Sinclair's MP5 and twisting onto his back. He depressed the trigger. Fire flashed from the muzzle.

Sinclair, pistol out of the holster and rising to aim, took the burst across the torso and shoulders, contorting and flailing and then dropping. The body armor wouldn't save him this time.

For the briefest of moments Victor felt relief as he lay in the darkness, but then he stood and heard Anderton's voice behind him say, "Drop the gun."

Victor didn't. He pointed it at Anderton. She had stepped out from behind a wall of plastic sheeting. She moved with slow, awkward steps because she had a gun to Gisele's head.

"I'm sorry," Gisele said. "She found me."

He rose to his feet. "There's nothing to be sorry for."

Anderton kept one elbow close to Gisele's torso so her arm didn't protrude too far beyond her hostage. Her other hand held Gisele in place as a human shield. Gisele was breathing rapidly but shallowly. Scared, but in control. She was wasted as a lawyer, Victor thought. She had the talent to be an exceptional assassin. Not that he would wish that life on anyone.

"Drop the gun," Anderton said, still calm and composed.

Victor shook his head. "No."

Anderton's eyes were wide in disbelief. "No? This isn't the time to start kidding around. I'll kill her."

"No, you won't," Victor said.

"Why not? She's my hostage. If you don't do as I say, she's dead."

"She's not your hostage," Victor said, stepping closer, sights drawing a bead on Anderton's head. "She's *my* hostage."

Anderton didn't respond. For a moment, she didn't know how to, then she said, "I don't think you appreciate your situation. You're going to do exactly as I ask, or—"

"You won't kill her," Victor said.

"I *won't*? You clearly haven't a clue what I'll do. You think because I'm a woman I'm not capable of—"

"I know what you're capable of, Ms. Anderton. But I know exactly what you'll do. Gisele is my hostage, not yours. Do you know why? Because she's the only thing that is keeping you alive. If you squeeze that trigger, you will die a second later. So kill her. But make sure you enjoy that last moment of life first."

Anderton shook her head.

"She's my hostage," Victor said. "While she lives, you live. You need to protect her. In fact, you're the best protector she could ever wish for. You're a better guardian than me because you'll do absolutely anything to keep her alive. Because her breaths are the only thing keeping you breathing."

Anderton shook her head again, but slower, weaker. "I'll kill her."

"No, you won't. You're not the suicidal type. You're a survivor. Everything that's happened has happened because you'll do anything to survive."

"Don't fuck with me."

"I assure you, that's the last thing on my mind. We both want the same thing."

"That's right," Anderton said, hissing the words, eyes wide and bright in realization and optimism.

"That's right," Victor agreed. "Neither of us wants you to die. Put the gun down. If you keep it pointed at Gisele, then eventually you'll have no choice but to squeeze that trigger. Do you know how long it takes to do that?" He didn't wait for an answer. "Point-three seconds to apply enough pressure and activate the firing pin. My gun has a slightly heavier draw, so it'll take me point-four seconds to shoot. Unfortunately for you, it'll take point-nine seconds for you to change your aim. Put your gun down and I won't shoot. There's nothing personal between us. All I want is to keep Gisele safe. You want to live. Lower your weapon. That's the only way you can survive this. You're a survivor, so live another day. Drop it, or find yourself in a closed-lid casket."

Anderton swallowed. Her face was wet with rain but also sweat—panic and fear oozing out of every pore as she realized that she was no longer in control. "I'm going to count to ten."

"No," Victor said. "I'm going to count to ten."

"I was right before. You are insane."

"That's a distinct possibility. But it doesn't change the fact I'm going to give you ten seconds to put the gun down or shoot her. Two choices. First choice: you live. Second: you die. Ready?"

"Wait."

Victor didn't wait. "Ten," he said. "Nine."

"Stop."

"Eight."

"Hold on—"

"Seven."

"—a fucking second. Let—"

"Six."

"—me think. You're—"

"Five."

"—fucking crazy. I—"

"Four."

"—will kill this—"

"Three."

"—bitch."

"Two."

Victor could see the white all around Anderton's irises. She roared in frustration and anger and fear.

"One."

"*Okay*. You win. You're insane enough to actually do this, aren't you?" She threw the pistol to the ground. "I've survived this far. You're right; I'm not dying for this girl. Not today. Not ever."

"Good choice," Victor said, the MP5 still aimed at her skull.

"You promised not to shoot me," Anderton reminded him.

"I did." Victor dropped the submachine gun. "And I'm a man of my word. Now let her go."

Anderton nodded, then released Gisele. She let out a

massive breath and staggered toward Victor, legs weak from the overload of adrenaline. She was crying.

Anderton backed away. "I hope you understand that this isn't over."

"It is," Victor said. "You just don't realize it yet."

She disappeared back where she'd come from and Victor heard her sprinting away and sirens somewhere on the street above them. He held Gisele's head to his chest and gave her a moment to let her emotions out. The sirens grew louder and the rain heavier. She stared up at him. He saw her brow furrow in the way it always did when she was working up the courage to ask him something.

"Why . . . why didn't you shoot her?"

Victor retrieved the MP5 from the floor and held it in one hand to push the muzzle against his temple. Gisele's eyes widened in panic and she reached out to stop him.

He squeezed the trigger.

Click.

"What with?" he asked.

Aftermath

London, United Kingdom

Chapter 80

Frost and mist covered the common. The short grass was frozen into a crystalline white carpet that cracked and crunched with each footstep. Victor disliked the sound. Too much like nails on a blackboard. Nearby, Canada geese didn't seem to care. A flock was gathered on and around a duck pond, making their distinctive honking noises at the swans and ducks that also used it. His breath clouded. Despite the cold, he wore sunglasses to filter out the glare of a bright sun. Joggers and dog walkers passed on a path that cut across the heath. Victor stood far enough away that he could not make out either Norimov's face or Gisele's.

They sat together on one of the benches overlooking the pond. From this distance he couldn't read their lips, but he wouldn't have even if he'd been standing closer. He respected their privacy. He didn't know much about family relationships, but he knew enough to understand they had a lot to work out.

He stayed on stag until finally Gisele stood and began walking away. Victor caught up with her.

"You can give that a rest, you know," she said.

"Not until it's over."

She rolled her eyes. "It will be. I've got her by the balls over this business in Afghanistan. If she has any sense she'll make a run for it. The rest of my firm knows all about the case now. Lester, bless him, was doing it pro bono without their knowledge. Aziz is going to have his conviction quashed, and then she's screwed. It's only a matter of time before she goes down."

"When she does, I'll give it a rest."

They walked some more. She said, "How's the ankle?"

"Getting better. Slowly."

"I'm glad. What are you going to do when Anderton is out of the picture?"

"What I always do: disappear."

"What . . . for good?"

He nodded.

"But you don't have to. The police aren't after you. They're after her."

"It's not as simple as that. It's better for everyone that I go."

"But you saved my life. Several times. And I still don't know you. I want to rectify that. I figure you're a little more personable when we're not being chased."

"No good will come of it, Gisele."

She said, "Why don't you let me decide if that's true? My mother liked you, after all."

"Because she didn't know me. You know more about the real me than she ever did."

"And I want to know more. You've done so much for me. At least let me buy you a coffee, or something."

"No," Victor said. "If you're in my life then you'll never be safe. I won't do that to you."

"So, that's it? Once Anderton is behind bars, I'm never going to see you again?"

"That's the way it has to be."

"I don't believe that's true. I think what you're really trying to say is that you don't want to see me."

He didn't respond.

"That's it, isn't it? You've never given a shit about me, have you? You did this for my mother, not for me. And now you're going to go because you've done your job and that's it for you. All done and dusted. Over. The End. Yes?"

He nodded. "That's right."

She exhaled through her nostrils, lips locked, jaw flexed. "Fine," she said. "Fuck off, then." When he didn't immediately move, she said, "What the fuck are you waiting for? Go. *Go.*"

He turned around and walked away.

Anger instead of pain. The better way.

· Chapter 81 ·

Marcus Lambert sat in one of the luxurious leather seats in the passenger compartment of his Gulfstream jet. Opposite him sat Anderton. He regarded her with an even expression while she said her piece.

"In a way I admire him," she was saying. "Whatever his name is. He found the girl under our noses and kept her alive despite our best efforts. That kind of guile is rare. God, I wish we'd had him on our team back in Helmand. Can you imagine it?"

"Admire," he repeated.

"Yes, admire. But he still needs to be taken care of. As does the girl. Marcus, I need another team. I need a larger team this time. I need more resources. Boots on the ground and guns aren't enough. It's not too late to fix this."

Marcus poured himself a neat Belvedere on the rocks.

"Well?" Anderton said.

He sipped the vodka. It tasted no different from any other kind of vodka, but appearances mattered more to him than enjoyment. He'd worked too hard not to sample the best. He'd worked too hard to throw it all away.

"No," he answered. "The answer is no. No more men. No resources. It's time to abort and bow out."

"I beg your pardon?"

"It's over, Nieve. Even if you kill them both, that's yet another crime to keep buried. You can't have shootouts in the middle of London and expect to stay hidden. That's tantamount to lunacy. You said you would take care of this. Instead you've quadrupled our exposure."

"I'm taking care of it."

"Like we took care of it in Helmand? And now look where we are. We couldn't keep the murder of one British intelligence officer suitably quiet. It still came back to haunt us. I think your unnamed assassin has proved he will not go down without a fight. That's even more exposure. It's time to cut our losses and take a trip to a non-extradition country."

Anderton laughed. She actually laughed. That's how delusional she had become, Marcus thought. She said, "Don't be so cowardly, Marcus. This is far from a lost cause. It's out in the open, yes, I admit that. But proof is such an abstract concept and I refuse to accept defeat until I'm in chains. By the time this is over I'll have them branded as terrorists. And when terrorists are shot, there will of course be media attention and so on, but ultimately it will come out that Gisele is the daughter of a Russian mobster and the mystery man . . . well, we can create whatever narrative we like for him. Throw in a bit of the Official Secrets Act, and there'll be no loose threads to pick. Trust me."

"I do trust you," Marcus said, thinking *I don't*. "But there comes a time when the cost of victory is too great. This is a battle that cannot be won cleanly. Better to fight it another day. In court, if necessary. But not on the street. Not with bullets. We must be reasonable. We must not let our emotions rule us."

Anderton was shaking when she said, "No, Marcus. It's far too late to keep this clean. But we have to finish it. There's no other option."

Marcus sighed, then nodded. There was no arguing with the woman. All he could do now was go along with Anderton and cover his own ass as much as possible. There were few things he'd like better than to put a bullet in the stupid girl who had created this shit storm, but he wasn't going to do anything that might get himself killed in the process. The job was compromised. The truth would come out. It was only a matter of time.

He wasn't about to give up all he had achieved. He refused to spend the rest of his life behind bars. Not for a spoiled woman overcome by ego.

He looked at his watch. "Last chance, Nieve. Come with me to South America and leave all this behind. What do you say? We can be in the air in twenty minutes."

Her green eyes blazed. "I don't run away. I fight until the end. You know me. But send me a postcard."

"I had a feeling that would be your response."

He pushed a button on the chair's console. A man entered from the cockpit. He had a silenced pistol in one hand and a hypodermic syringe in the other.

"What is this?" Anderton said, rising from her seat.

"It's for the best," Marcus replied, as the man stepped closer.

· Chapter 82 ·

Andrei Linnekin sat in the uncomfortable office chair of his spartanly furnished office. The chair was deliberately uncomfortable. It was an ugly hunk of plastic and thin padding that made his back sore and his ass numb. The Russian crime boss had personally fished it out of a junkyard. He couldn't sit still on the chair. He couldn't relax in it. It reminded him he had to stay sharp. He couldn't become comfortable. When he did, his reign at the top would be over.

He said, "Before we continue, there is something you must understand. This is a matter of principle. I'm a man of honor before I'm a man of power. I keep my word, first and foremost. That is important to me. If I say I'll do something, I'll do it or die trying. I have no ego. I know I've been lucky to get where I am today. I have no more intelligence than any man. I have no more strength or courage. But I am where I am nevertheless. I have been attacked, although I am unharmed. All my men know this. They are upset because they failed me and are scared of the repercussions that may follow. There will be none. It is I who failed them.

"I believe in integrity and I believe in justice. I believe a man is only as good as his word and I believe that we are only treated as we allow ourselves to be treated. Forgiveness is against human nature. To forgive a wrong is to invite another. I believe in justice. No wrong should go unpunished."

"I understand," the visitor said.

"You do? Good. Because I cannot continue with this unless you do. Because you are to deliver justice. I appreciate your involvement. You come highly recommended. Is it true you killed Yuri Ibramovich?"

The oligarch, once a member of the Moscow mafia, had formed a breakaway outfit and used his criminal organization to force his way into legitimate businesses. He had been found dead in his fortified dacha, his throat slit from ear to ear, his murder having gone unnoticed by the army of mercenaries who patrolled his home.

"I never discuss my previous work."

"I'll take that as a yes. But I have lots of killers working for me. If it were merely a matter of having a man killed, I would have had no need to ask the bosses back home for help. Before this nameless f—" Linnekin stopped himself, cursing, then punched his desk because the man who terrorized him still held power over his actions. He took a composing breath and began again. "Before this nameless *fuck* can be killed, he must be found. He could be anywhere by now. My men wouldn't know where to start. I don't know who he is. I want you to hunt him down."

"I assure you that my associates and I are well versed in locating the invisible. You'll hear from me again only when it's done."

"The money will wait for you in escrow. I don't want to give that man another thought until his blood runs cold. Make sure he knows who sent you before he dies."

The visitor nodded and stood and left without a word.

Linnekin watched the woman walk away. She was slim with good bone structure. Reputedly an expert shot. A redhead.

To himself, Linnekin said, "Let's see if the price of crossing me was worth it."

This team had never failed. They were efficient and ruthless.

Four Scandinavians: a Finn, a Swede, and two Danes.

ACKNOWLEDGMENTS

As always, thank you to those who work the magic behind the scenes and help this wordsmith along the many highs and lows.

At my publishers: Hollie Smyth, Jo Wickham, Tom Webster, the sales team, Sean Garrehy, Anne O'Brien, and Thalia Proctor. Special thanks to my editors: Danielle Perez and Ed Wood.

My agents: Scott Miller and Philip Patterson. Thanks also to Isabella Floris and Luke Speed.

And, finally, a big thank-you to my friends and family.

Don't miss Tom Wood's

The Game

Available now from Signet

Algiers, Algeria

The killer was good. He moved with a fluidity and an economy of motion that made him seem relaxed, almost carefree, yet he was ever aware of his surroundings and always alert. He had a lean, forgettable face that looked a little older than his thirty-five years. He was tall, but of average height for a native of the tallest nation on the planet. A resident of Amsterdam, Felix Kooi worked as a freelance assassin with no allegiances. He sold his services to the highest bidder, whatever the job, in a career that had endured at least ten years. That career was about to come to an end.

Kooi had a room at the El Aurassi Hotel but spent little of his time there, always leaving shortly after dawn and returning only during the evening, never using the same route or the same entrance twice in a row. Each day he ventured around the city like a tourist, always walking, never visiting the same location more than once, but exploring every medieval mosque, museum, and sightseer destination Algiers had to offer. He ate in restaurants and cafés, but only those serving Algerian and North African food. He walked on the seafront but never lazed on the beach.

Today Kooi was in the old town—the casbah—and had spent an hour wandering around the market near the El Jidid Mosque. The market was a huge, sprawling arrangement of tented stalls selling everything from wicker baskets to live chickens. It was centered on an irregular square and seeped along the numerous adjoining alleys and side streets. He seemed to do nothing beyond browsing, enjoying the sights, sounds, and smells of such a vibrant gathering of people and merchandise.

Victor had followed Kooi for three days. In that time he had learned that Kooi was good, but he wasn't exceptional. Because he had made a mistake. A mistake that was going to kill him.

Victor's CIA employer didn't know the reason for Kooi's cover as a tourist in Algiers. Procter didn't know whether the Dutch assassin was preparing for a contract, meeting a broker or client, obtaining supplies, or lying low from one of the many enemies he had no doubt made in a decadelong career as a hired killer. Victor had followed him for three days as much to determine that reason as to devise the best way to kill him, even though he didn't need to know it in order to fulfill the contract. Such knowledge was important because maybe someone was as keen for Kooi to live as Victor's employer was for him to die. Getting caught in the middle of such a tug-of-war was not something Victor was eager to repeat.

Three days shadowing Kooi around the city had been a necessary aspect of the precautionary measures Victor employed to stay alive in the world's most dangerous profession, but unnecessary because there was no secret to uncover. Kooi wasn't working. He wasn't meeting a contact. He wasn't on the run. He was on vacation. He was acting like a tourist because he was a tourist.

And that was his mistake. He was a tourist. He was in Algiers to relax and have a good time, to explore and see the sights, and too much of his focus was on being a tourist to effectively protect himself from someone like Victor.

A merchant selling carved wooden statuettes caught Kooi's attention and he listened and nodded and pointed and examined the man's wares. He said nothing in return, because he didn't speak French, or else didn't want the trader to know he did. Victor watched from a distance of twenty meters. Kooi was easy enough to see, being at least half a head taller than the locals occupying the space between him and Victor, and Victor's similar height ensured that his line of sight was rarely interrupted unless he chose for it to be.

Kooi was aware and alert, but he was a tourist and his countersurveillance techniques were basic, and basic had never been a problem for Victor. He was more cautious in return, and Kooi hadn't come close to identifying the threat. He had seen Victor, because Kooi was good, and like Kooi's, Victor's height and ethnicity made him stand out in Algiers, but because he was only good and not exceptional, he hadn't marked Victor as anything other than a tourist. Victor knew this because Kooi's behavior hadn't changed, and no one who learned an assassin was following them acted exactly the same as they had prior to the acquisition of that knowledge.

The Dutchman's lack of precautionary measures in his downtime told Victor he hadn't experienced the same kind of professional learning curve that Victor knew he had mastered by virtue of the fact he was still capable of drawing breath. He wasn't envious of Kooi's comparatively charmed existence, because that existence would soon be over.

"Mister," a voice said to Victor in heavily accented English, "you buy a watch."

A young local man stood to Victor's right, showing his lack of teeth with a wide smile. He wore brightly colored linens. His black hair jutted out from the top of his skull in unruly clumps. His sleeves were rolled up to reveal skinny forearms ringed by wristwatches, counterfeit unless the man had several hundred thousand dollars' worth of merchandise weighing him down while not having enough money for a toothbrush.

"No, thank you," Victor said, shaking his head in an exaggerated manner for the kind of emphasis necessary to persuade local traders to try their bartering skills elsewhere.

He didn't seem to notice. "I got for you Tag Hour, Rolax, all the nice ones. Look, look."

"No," Victor said again, his gaze on Kooi, who had a wooden statuette in each hand and seemed to be deciding on which to purchase. He chose one and handed over some cash for the winning selection. The Dutchman was smiling and nodding, pleased with his purchase or amused by the trader's rapid-fire overselling. He slipped the statuette into a thigh pocket of his khaki shorts.

"Look, look," the young watch guy said again, about ten decibels louder. He waved his arms in front of Victor's face.

He gestured with his hands to show he was interested in the watches when his only interest was in stopping the local from attracting attention. Kooi wouldn't hear over the din of the market, but he might notice the young man's waving arms and the shiny watches glinting in the sunlight.

"That one," Victor said, pointing to a Rolex with hands that didn't sweep.

A toothless grin stretched across the seller's face and he unclasped the watch while Victor counted out a fair price for it.

"No, no," the young local said, "not enough. More. More."

Victor obliged him with another note, having followed the bartering convention of underpaying. However much he offered, the local would want more.

He slipped on his knockoff Rolex and left to follow Kooi, who had extended his lead by another five meters in the interval.

"Bye, mister," the young local called behind him. "You have the good day."

Kooi took his time strolling through the market. He took a circuitous route, but only to make the most of the experience rather than for any tactical consideration. He continued to check his flanks on occasion, but Victor walked directly behind his mark. It would take a one-hundred-and-eighty-degree turn for Kooi even to see him—a move that would give Victor plenty of notice not to be there when he did.

Fabric stalls and small stores selling local fashions lined a twisting side street into which Kooi veered. He didn't stop to examine the wares, but he walked slowly, head rotating back and forth in case anything caught his interest. Victor let the distance between them increase, because now that they were out of the main market square, the crowd density had dropped by around thirty percent. Had

Kooi been more active in his countersurveillance, or had he simply walked faster, it would have made Victor's task more difficult, but even if he did lose him, he knew where the Dutchman was staying.

Kooi was in Algiers for another week based on his flight and accommodation bookings, so there was no time pressure, but Victor would take the first opportunity that presented itself. Regardless of Kooi's relaxed attitude to his own security, he was a competent professional and therefore a hard target, and there was no guarantee Victor would get more than one chance to see the contract through to completion.

He hadn't identified a weapon, and Kooi's khaki shorts and short-sleeved shirt were not conducive to hiding a firearm, but he could easily have a knife in a pocket or in a belt sheath or on the end of a neck cord. Plus, bare hands could be equally deadly if employed correctly.

There were no requirements to the successful completion of the contract beyond Kooi's death, but Victor preferred not to identify an assassination as one if it could be avoided. He planned to keep it simple—a mugging gone bad. Common enough the world over. He had a folding knife in the pocket of his linen trousers. It was a local weapon, bought from a street vendor not dissimilar to the toothless young watch seller. Not the kind of quality Victor would prefer to work with, but it was well made enough to do the task he'd purchased it for. As long as he could get within arm's length of Kooi, he could cut any one of several arteries that were protected only by the thin skin of the neck, underarm, or inner thigh. A seemingly superficial cut, luckily placed by an aggressive robber, inducing death in minutes before medical help could reach him.

All Victor had to do was get close to Kooi.

The Dutchman continued his exploration of the city, leaving the old town and wandering to the docks, where he gazed out at the Mediterranean and the many boats and yachts on its blue waters. He took a seat outside a restaurant with an ocean view, and used his teeth to pick grilled lamb from skewered brochettes and ate aromatic couscous with his fingers. He was slim and in shape but he had a big appetite.

Victor waited nearby for the hour Kooi spent over his meal and followed as his target headed back into the city. He didn't take the same route back—that would have been too reckless, even for a man as relaxed as Kooi—but he walked in the same direction, taking streets that ran close or parallel to those he had already walked.

Kooi surprised Victor by heading back to the casbah market. That didn't fit with his MO of never visiting the same locale twice. The market crowds enabled Victor to close the distance between them, and he pictured the rest of the route back to Kooi's hotel. There were numerous quiet alleys that would present all the opportunity Victor needed to complete the contract. He could get ahead of Kooi easily enough, knowing his ultimate destination, and come at him from the front—just another tourist exploring the wonders of Algiers—maybe sharing a nod of recognition as a couple of guys with similar interests, strangers in a strange land, the kind who could end up friends over a few beers. By the time Kooi realized the man heading in his direction was a killer like himself, he would already be bleeding.

A simple enough job. Dangerous given the target, but uncomplicated.

Victor was surprised again when Kooi led him to the

same part of the market square they had been in earlier. He wasn't exploring anymore. He had a purpose. The Dutchman removed the wooden statuette from his shorts and set about swapping it for the one he had rejected previously. The merchant was happy to oblige, especially when Kooi gave him some more money.

"Hey, mister," a familiar voice called.

Victor ignored him, but the toothless young man sidestepped into his path, his arms glinting with watches. Kooi headed off.

"You buy another watch, mister? For your wife or lady. She like nice watch too, yes?"

Victor shook his head and moved to step around him, losing a couple of meters on Kooi in the process. The local didn't let him pass.

"I give you good price. Buy the two, get the one cheap. Good deal. Look, look."

"No," Victor said. "No wife. No lady. No watch. Move."

But the young guy, buoyed by his earlier success and Victor's reappearance, didn't want to understand. He blocked Victor's path, waving and pointing in turn to the women's watches that circled his lower wrists and mispronouncing the brands.

"Please," Victor said, trying to get around the guy before he lost Kooi, but not wanting to hurl the seller away and risk the attention such a commotion would create.

Kooi turned around. He caught something in his peripheral vision, or maybe he decided to examine some novelty after all. He eased himself through the crowd, not looking Victor's way—yet—as he made for a stall.

"Good price," the watch seller said, holding out both arms to block Victor's attempts to get by. "Your lady like you a lot." He smiled. "You know what I say?" He puckered his lips and made kissing noises.

"Okay, okay," Victor said. "I'll take that one."

He reached for his wallet to end the standoff before Kooi noticed, but the Dutchman glanced over when the young trader clapped his hands in celebration at securing a second sale.

Kooi saw Victor.

There was no immediate reaction. He stared for a second, because he realized he had seen Victor before. He stared for another second, because he didn't know where. He stared for a third second, because he was assessing the chances that a lone Caucasian male he had seen before and who had just been directly behind him was simply a tourist too.

And he ran.

ALSO AVAILABLE FROM
NATIONAL BESTSELLING AUTHOR

TOM WOOD

THE GAME

After executing a hit on a fellow assassin in Algiers,
Victor—the world's deadliest hit man—is contracted
by the CIA for an assignment that will take him
across Europe to the bloodstained streets of Rome...
and straight into hell.

**"A strongly plotted story, exciting and thrilling from
beginning to end."**
—Mysterious Reviews

Available wherever books are sold or at
penguin.com